ANY SECOND

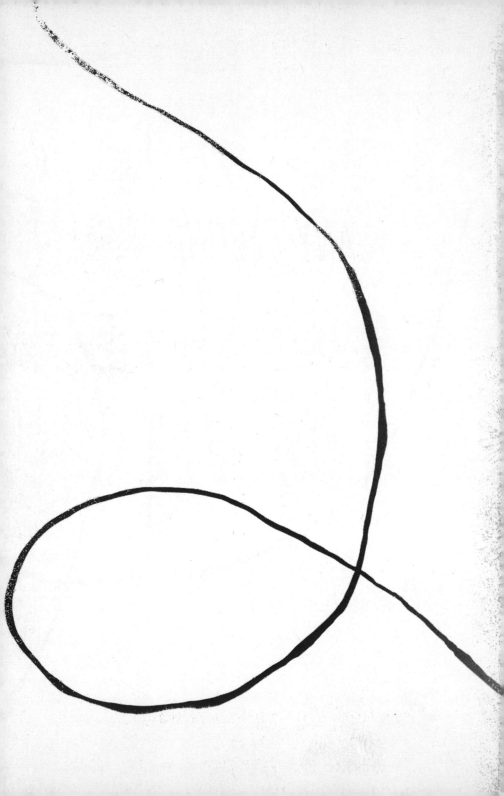

ANY SECOND

KEVIN EMERSON

CROWN ♔ New York

Visit us on the Web! GetUnderlined.com

Educators and librarians, for a variety of teaching tools, visit us at RHTeachersLibrarians.com

Library of Congress Cataloging-in-Publication Data
Names: Emerson, Kevin, author.
Title: Any second / Kevin Emerson.
Description: First edition. | New York : Crown Books for Young Readers, [2018] | Summary: Kidnapped, abused, and brainwashed for five years, Elian is stopped in his mission to bomb a mall by Maya, who has crippling anxiety, and neither one will ever be the same again.
Identifiers: LCCN 2018006932 | ISBN 978-0-553-53482-5 (hardback) | ISBN 978-0-553-53483-2 (glb) | ISBN 978-0-553-53484-9 (ebook)
Subjects: | CYAC: Emotional problems—Fiction. | Kidnapping—Fiction. | Brainwashing—Fiction. | Anxiety—Fiction. | Bombings—Fiction.
Classification: LCC PZ7.E5853 Any 2018 | DDC [Fic]—dc23

Printed in the United States of America
10 9 8 7 6 5 4 3 2 1
First Edition

To everyone who reaches out
instead of running

OCTOBER

CHAPTER 1

Gabriel says today is a good day to die.

He says the Barons have taken more than their share, that they profit from the blood of the innocent, that they have turned us into sheep and tricked us into accepting it. The Barons who control all the land and the money and the women.

They need to be sent a message.

"Tell me you are ready, Jacob."

"I am ready."

"Are you sure?" His hand rubs up and down my spine. "Because if you're not, we'll need to go home and keep working."

Home is the red dark. Where the lessons are taught.

"I am sure."

A long exhale. He kneels behind me, breath hot in my ear, the smell of the habanero sauce, the cigarettes and gasoline, on his clothes. "Do you know what?"

"What?"

Don't move. We are standing by the railing, beside the food court at the mall. Blinding sunlight shines down through a domed glass roof and into the oval-shaped eyeholes of the mask I wear—but turning or squinting is weakness. Rubbing the sweat out of my eyes is weakness. Flinching when he touches me, shuddering because of what we're here to do: all weakness. Proof that more lessons are needed.

With the spatula. The belt. Cannot go back. Cannot go back—

"I believe you," he says.

Something wells up inside me, but crying would also be weakness. It is a good thing Gabriel has not delivered the food bowl for two days. Soiling yourself is an awful weakness.

"You have earned my trust," Gabriel says. "You have endured such trials, and you have proven that you are ready to do the great work. You are ready to fulfill the Purpose."

The Purpose. Finally.

His hands settle on my shoulders, causing a dull ache from the right one, dislocated . . . months ago? Years? Notches in the floor, made with the meal spoon each time the sliver of light appeared beneath the plywood that covered the window: 1,052 marks, but maybe I missed some days, or counted twice? Too hard to tell.

The only other light, that whole time, from a red bulb in a gooseneck lamp.

"Throughout history," Gabriel says, "the greatest revolutions have been started by the smallest of acts. The sheep cannot rise up on their own. They must be given permission, shaken awake by a hero."

A hero like Metal Marauder, the MechBot cards— No! Can't think that. *They were what made me miss the bus that day—* Stop! Memory is weakness.

"But heroes are not just born," Gabriel says. "They are made. You would never have woken up on your own, never been free, never been strong. You would never have been loved. You were weak and you would have always been weak."

Trading the cards on the front steps of school, but then the groan of the bus leaving and I ran after it but the driver didn't see me. It was sunny, so I decided to walk. Looking at the cards on the way. Never heard him coming—

"Your family was weak. All of them slaves to the Barons. But who freed you?"

His voice by my ear: "You have been chosen." Grabbing me and shoving me into the car. Holding me down against the seat while I screamed into the cushion. Kicking the dashboard, the door, could I break the window—click-ding of the blinker, rev of the engine, pants soaked I wet myself—

"Jacob . . ." His grip tightens.

Stuffed into a duffel bag and hauled inside, into the dark, always the red dark—

NO. I push it back. Make it silent. It is weakness, and it only makes things worse. Swallow. Lock the doors. Answer the question.

"You did."

"That's right. The Purpose led me to you, like a lost prophet to an oasis."

Did the Purpose make me miss the bus? Did it make Mom say I couldn't have a phone until I was older? Did it make me decide to walk home instead of going to the office and calling her, make me think about how it was only a mile, how my sister walked twice that far every day through an even rougher part of town?

STOP IT!

"I rescued you from that sleeping lie," Gabriel says. "Billions of people live and die without meaning, their lives forgotten before they are gone, but not you. Through death . . ."

"I will live forever."

It is true. Must be true.

Gabriel's grip relaxes. "You will be more than just a life. You will be an eternal symbol to all, and the sheep will say your name on their waking lips, and what?"

"They will remember."

"Correct. And on the other side, what awaits you?"

"Light and peace."

The mall is so loud around us. So many voices all mixing with laughs and shouts and scuffs of shoes and the shuffling of plastic bags. So much more noise than just the furnace, and the mice, and a heartbeat in the red dark.

"The sheep are begging for it," Gabriel says. "Go ahead, take a look, one last time."

I let my eyes rise up from the floor, see them walking by: groups of teens, couples, parents and their children, in and out of all the glossy stores, standing in line for food.

"See how they smile, how they prattle and laugh. They will never know how we have sacrificed for them. But how could they? Kept dumb, hooked on the drug of capitalism, dulled by the Excess, gorged on sugar, fat, advertising, sex: the tools of compliance. And if they haven't been brainwashed yet they're desperately trying to fake it. No one wants to show their real selves, and the women show too much"—he pauses—"strutting around like prostitutes and yet always withholding. So sad. We pity them. But are they innocent?"

"Innocence is ignorance."

"And the ignorant are complicit. But not you. You are no longer one of the sheep, are you?"

I shake my head and look back down at the floor.

"Tell me what you are."

"I am a wolf."

"Yes," Gabriel says. "All the darkness and pain you've endured has revealed to you this world's wicked truth. You are the only one who sees clearly. Who knows the Purpose. You know it even more clearly than I do now. And you are the only one who can save us. God waits for his true soldiers with open arms."

His words make everything tighter. We're close now. Closer than ever before. Breathing is so hard. It has been too hard for too long, and this is the only way out. I know it.

"My mother?"

"Even now she waits for you in paradise."

"And my sister?"

"Yes, her suffering will end, her sin finally cleansed too. But shh . . ." Gabriel rubs his fingers in a V shape up and down the back of my neck. The knitted fabric of his gloves so familiar. "You are so very special to me," he says. "You will never know how much."

I nod. Blink in the brilliant light. The air smells like chocolate and salt and perfume. So different from the smell of the pail after two or three days. The shame of it . . .

If I do this, I will never have to go back there.

His hand moves up to my head. My scalp still burns from the bleaching last night. An all-American blond, Gabriel said as he dunked my head into the bowl, over and over. He ruffles my hair, then slides both hands up under my puffy jacket. Checking the connections.

7

"Everything is set," he says. "Tell me you are ready."

"I'm ready." The words come out hoarse and I freeze. Even now, even with the chemical bottles strapped to my chest, I still expect him to turn me around and march me back down the escalator, across the parking lot, to the spot behind the line of dumpsters where no one can see what he keeps in the trunk.

But he doesn't.

This is really it.

"Now press down."

Fear grips me, convulsions in my abdomen, needle stabs in my feet. I turn so that I can see the small device in my palm, but the mask slips on my sweat, the eye holes sliding out of line. I shake my head, but that only makes it worse—

"Here." Gabriel straightens the mask and tightens the elastic. His fingers are shaking. "Remember, don't take this off, no matter what. The mask is a symbol, but it is also so the Barons' cameras cannot capture your identity. If they know who you are, they will make excuses—blame your family, your skin, the lead in your water. They can always find a way to blame a person. What they truly fear is an idea. Besides, no one here will think twice when they see a blond boy in a plastic wolf's mask, five days before Halloween."

My hand starts to shake. . . . *Come on, you have to.*

I put my thumb over the small silver button. Press down and squeeze as hard as I can.

"Good." Gabriel sighs and shudders against me. I've felt this excitement on him before. Nights when he came into the red dark, overcome with the Purpose. I'd beg him to take it out on me instead of my sister. Sometimes he did, and afterward we would cry together. But many times he suffered the glory with her instead, and made me listen through the ceiling.

Never again. Melissa, I will save you. I promise.

"Now, Jacob, my son, you must do it exactly like we planned. Go swiftly and without fear. Take a deep breath when you pass beneath the sign, and then hold that air inside you. Don't stop walking, and no matter what, don't take your finger off the button until you get to the middle of the room. The Purpose must be clear."

"I know."

"As soon as you reach the spot, do not hesitate. Even for a second. Just release your thumb, and your work on this Earth will be done and you will see your sister's smiling face. All you have to do is let go."

He makes a sound through his lips like wind blowing, like me blowing away from everything, to paradise.

It is all I can do to keep still. Legs trembling. Muscles screaming, but I won't show weakness.

This is the only way.

I know it. I know it.

Gabriel's body presses against my back, his cheek against my neck, and his voice lowers to a whisper. "I love you, Jacob. I love you so much. You have been such a gift to me." It sounds like he might be crying.

"I love you too," I say, have to say, but I do, I love him. He saved me. From the lie.

What lie?

"Fate brought us together and finally, today, we will finish the work we were meant to do."

9

Yes. Dizzy. Spots in my vision.

"Now . . ." With a deep breath he pushes me forward. *"Go."*

And so I do.

One foot. Then the next. Finger clamped down on the trigger. Away from the railing, away from Gabriel, and as his hand loses touch, a great tremor storms through me and I nearly collapse, or turn back—but no, no, no, I will keep going.

It is fifty-three steps from Gabriel to the spot: out of the hot sun, across the shimmering tile, and into the lair of one of the Barons' outposts: the Department of Licensing office. We studied maps and photos on a computer. Came here and observed the habits of mall security, the crowd patterns at different times and on different days. Gabriel says today is a Thursday. It is late afternoon. This is the moment, and I am counting down now as the people blur around me.

Forty-seven . . . forty-six . . . forty-five . . .

I know he is watching me as I go, and I try to remember the instructions. Don't look back; keep your gaze straight in front of you; don't make eye contact; walk fast but not too fast. Just another consumer, part of the privileged, a Baron-in-training with a smartphone and a credit card in your slave-made jeans, on your way to meet up with friends.

Forty-one . . . forty . . . thirty-nine . . .

Slipping unnoticed through the crowd, everyone walking along with their heads down, their faces trapped in the light of their screens. Personal soul suckers, Gabriel says. Self-mutilation.

The smack of the plastic bat, the slap of the three-foot piece of garden hose—

Thirty-six . . . thirty-five . . . thirty-four . . .

The inside of the plastic is wet from my breathing. The cool

10

damp pressing against my upper lip and my chin. My scalp still itching.

Melissa had hair like midnight water. Did he bleach her hair too?

She didn't call me Jacob.

"Your name is Jacob," Gabriel says, still in my head. Will always be in my head until my mission is complete.

Twenty-four . . . twenty-three . . . twenty-two . . .

Wasn't there a different name? Didn't they—

But I am almost to the entrance. The Purpose spreading through me. The glorious tingle, Gabriel says. The sweaty palms, the queasy stomach, the pounding heart. Signs of being truly awake, of withdrawal from the Barons' drugs, free and open to the universe.

Fifteen . . . fourteen . . . thirteen . . .

More spots in my eyes.

The Purpose. The Purpose.

I pass beneath the sign. Its big green letters read: DOL *Express!*

I inhale as deep as I can.

"Hold it like a protest," Gabriel says. "Savor it as you walk to the middle. . . ."

I walk to the middle.

"As you set yourself free."

I will be free.

At peace.

Mom will be there.

Melissa will be there.

This is the only way out.

Three . . . two . . . one . . .

"As you stop . . ."

I stop. Oh God.

"Know that I love you, son."

There are sheep sitting in chairs looking at their phones. Sheep at counters talking to others behind bulletproof glass. There is a sign that says NOW SERVING: 4.

I hold out my hand. Thumb aching, muscles desperate to release . . .

It will finally be over.

"All you have to do is let go."

I look at the trigger, my whole body trembling around this last breath. There is a slight sound of sloshing from the chemical bottles. Does anyone hear it? Just a sideways glance from a nearby old lady, then back to her phone.

One . . .

"Let go," Gabriel says in my ear, in my mind, in the red dark, on the street.

Hesitation is weakness.

Okay, okay . . .

The cold trigger, the red wire that runs up my sleeve and down to my waist. Attached to my skin with duct tape, ripped off so forcefully when I didn't sit still enough.

Chest aching . . . Exhale is ending. Is relief. No one suspects the weapon among them.

Just a ten-year-old boy that afternoon, just walking home, that's all I ever did—

"No! You are a wolf. A messenger. You will make light. You will be light. You will show them. Don't make me get the pliers."

I will never have to feel the pliers again.

One . . .

Never have to feel the barbell, the calloused hands.

One . . .

The Purpose. The Purpose has hurt *so much.*

Do it!

My hand shakes, thumb slick on the smooth button. Arm twitching. Will I have arms in paradise? Legs? A body at all?

Carbon Czar? Was that the MechBot card? The other boy was Jessie. A sixth grader—one year older. Trading with him right before I missed the bus.

"Why are you hesitating?" Gabriel shouts in my head.

Lungs burning.

But these people—

"No, sheep! They are complicit. Don't be a little shit, Jacob."

Jacob, that's not my name. I just want to know my name.

One . . .

In heaven they will tell me my name.

One . . .

Air crushing out against my ribs. Have to breathe. Have to let go—

Swaying where I stand. Guts trembling.

Pants soiling again.

No—

THE PURPOSE.

"DO IT, Jacob! NOW. Or I will make her scream in agony like you have never heard—"

No, don't! Melissa, I won't let him hurt you again.

Just let go. It will be over.

Oh God, please help me.

Dios mío, *my mom would say—*

The air explodes out. Chest caves.
I let go—
Dios mío, *Elián* . . .
Wait, my name, that was my name!
I don't—

CHAPTER 2

MAYA
(AGE 16)

"Now serving number ninety-one."

Dad sighed. "We don't even know how high the numbers go." He glanced from his phone in one hand to the ticket in the other. It had a big number 3.

Maya noticed that the ticket was shaped like a penis head. Great, now she was seeing more dicks in the world than there already were. What would her therapist call that association? *Cock projection?* She wondered what he would try to tie that to, what Venn diagram of anxiety, family instability, and impulse control—

"Stop it." Dad's ticket-holding hand slapped against hers.

"I'm not doing anything." Maya checked her hands; she'd been working on that situation on her right thumb again, the callusy swath from her knuckle to her cuticle. Thick, lumpy, and, ugh, a sickly white that *needed* to be taken care of. She'd been picking at it, tearing off strips.

A light snow of skin on the puke-brown carpet of the Department of Licensing *Express!* office.

"Just try not to do that," said Dad, looking around.

"Nobody even notices." Except sometimes they did. Maya had caught the sidelong glances from classmates, from people on the bus. No one here, though. Everyone else in the waiting area was gazing into their phones, as bored as she was, stuck in this pale, soulless office on a Thursday afternoon. "How much longer do we have to be here?"

"I don't know," said Dad. "Can't believe this place doesn't have an app." He swiped at his screen. For a second, it seemed like maybe he was searching for answers, but then his phone blipped and vibrated and he tapped over to his feed, his head lolling forward, the screen sucking him in with its magic thrall. For years, both Maya's parents had been telling her to put her phone away, when they were just as bad, if not worse.

At least it kept Maya from having to talk to them much.

"Hey, look."

Or not.

Dad held out his phone. "Fourteen likes already. See? I told you this was a good idea."

He'd checked in here at the DOL and written: **Time to get a new pic for a new me!**

Of course, the very first comment was from Kendall: **Smile big!**

"Right," said Maya. Kendall, of the thongs and fake lashes, trim and fit and fourteen years younger than Dad, the equivalent of Maya dating a *thirty*-year-old. She was cute, and perky, and had all these opinions and beliefs that were relentlessly positive, completely unlike Mom, which was, Maya guessed, the point. Dad wanted them to hang out more, and Kendall had been trying: inviting Maya to Pilates (Maya played sick), making her smoothies on weekend mornings after she stayed over (Maya slept in) . . . but even when she found herself thinking maybe Kendall was okay, she immediately felt like a traitor.

At least there was no danger of Mom seeing Dad's post. They'd pretty much muted each other's feeds, ships passing in the night on the rare post Maya let them see. Mom was basically a ghost online anyway these days, haunting her friends' and coworkers' updates with the occasional like. Meanwhile Dad was everywhere. Dude couldn't lift a barbell (*Going up a weight!*) or buy a jar of salsa (*Muy caliente!*) without enthusiastically sharing it. This from a man who'd had a pixelated photo of the sailboats at Shilshole Marina as his profile picture for most of Maya's life.

"Well, thanks for humoring me by coming here," said Dad.

"It's not like I had a choice."

"Come on. You didn't have to."

This is supposed to be our *afternoon together,* Maya didn't say. Instead, just: "I'm the one who should be getting a license, not you."

"We told you to sign up for those driver's ed classes."

That was true. Maya had missed the deadline, if by "missing," you meant knowing exactly when it was and not clicking on the link.

"Seriously, though . . ." Dad pulled out his wallet and held out his old license. "Look at that photo." In it, he was staring straight ahead, slack-jawed, eyes weary. "That's not me anymore."

"Yeah." But it stung because that *was* him, just the him from before. Maya could make fun of the recent changes: coloring his graying-more-than-he'd-admit hair, the new wardrobe with patterns and pearl buttons and hipster sneakers, suddenly enjoying tennis?! Going to Pilates with Kendall, not minding at all having to walk her rat-sized dog thing even though he'd refused to get a pet for his daughter's whole life—and yet, all these things spoke of someone who was awake. Who *cared*. (Maya refused to include the tattoo. A Norse symbol that meant strength? Probably signified the opposite of strength.)

So how could you not take it personally? That the zombie dad in that old license had been the result of a life with Mom and Maya. That this new version had only been possible once he'd freed himself from them.

Maya and Mom still lived in their half-empty house. The divorce wasn't official yet, but it was coming, signature by tearstained signature. Everyone was "shocked," but the harder truth was that the signs had all been there: the bickering and backstabbing, the way they'd been taking Maya places separately. Also it turned out that Kendall had been around for a while—she was a junior software engineer, and Dad was her supervisor, so ewww. Technically, that made Dad the bad guy, and yet Maya found her hate glowing equally red-hot in both directions. Furious at Dad, the asshole, but also at Mom, acting like a victim, and even mad at herself for not being enough to hold them together—

"Relax, don't do it, when you want to go to it. . . ."

Maya reconnected with her senses, like the teeth of clock gears sliding together, the outside world seeping back in. Her phone was vibrating in her pocket, accompanied by muffled singing.

The alarm was to stop her from picking. The song a retro choice, but appropriate. She'd gotten the idea from a blog about living with dermatillomania, the official term for when you liked to flay yourself, pick yourself apart strip by strip.

Three of her fingers were currently in Band-Aids. She'd been in the midst of pulling a long slice free from that thumb, but it had gouged deeper than she'd intended, and now blood was welling up in the canyon left behind. Maya tore the peel free, rolled the little fillet between her fingers—

Popped it into her mouth.

Tastes like chicken? Kinda bland, actually. But there was something satisfying about the rubberiness.

She considered the ruby of blood on her thumb.

Sucked that too.

Her therapist had asked her if she liked it. She'd said no. Was there any other answer? *Why, yes, I enjoy tearing myself apart and occasionally consuming my own flesh.* Wasn't that on the same spectrum as *I keep pieces of my neighbor in the freezer for special meals?*

When the therapist pressed, Maya had said that it was more like she needed to do *something*. Something to calm the white-hot energy that prickled just beneath her skin, all the time. Fidgeting. Unsettled. An army of bugs with swords. Energy that whispered of how impermanent the universe was, how every passing second was a small death, the good ones somehow worse than the bad. At its worst, she felt like she could see the end of her life as if it was *right there*. She remembered having this same feeling as far back as nine or ten, lying awake in bed, the dark wraith of her anxiety preaching the certainty of nothing, nothing, nothing.

But what does the picking accomplish? All Maya knew was that when she picked she drifted. Time seemed to slip by with no harm done. Well, except to her poor fingers, or sometimes her face.

But skin grew back, no matter how mangled. Far better than marriages.

And yet as the rift between her parents had grown, she'd also gone from Maya, honors student in the science baccalaureate program, to a *former* honors student whose place in the program might soon be in doubt. From a JV volleyball player to a *former* volleyball player. She was still drumming in the jazz and concert bands, and practiced more now than ever before. But other than that, she felt like, rather than being pulled apart, as people usually described in a divorce, she had been sinking into the space in between. Her parents were like two tectonic plates, Maya being slowly unmade by the roiling mantle beneath.

She dug around in her pockets and found a used tissue, speckled with brown dabs of dried blood. Pinched it between her bleeding thumb and her index finger, then spun the clock dials on her phone, setting the alarm to go off in another forty minutes.

"Why does it always do that?" said Dad, typing away with Kendall. They liked to have long conversations in comment threads as if they'd never heard of private messages.

"It's a glitch," said Maya, *a glitch in your daughter.* Dad's eyes flicked to the bloodstained tissue and his brow wrinkled. Maya tensed, but he just returned to his phone.

She closed the clock app and checked her feeds. She should probably post something—a selfie from here in the mall? Maybe a shot of how the light was slanting down through the glass ceiling out at the food court? But as she scrolled along, she felt a tightening squeeze of adrenaline. Her feed was all smiles, successes, hot takes, group selfies, everybody looking perfect and smooth and Photoshopped, like they were having so much fun. She had nothing like that to post. And anything she might share about what she was going through would just seem selfish and lame compared to all the *real* problems in the world these days.

Maya closed the apps. She was just putting her phone away when it buzzed with a message: Todd, her boyfriend.

I've got a raging throb for you right now.

Maya frowned, fearing that a picture would show up to verify this information. Luckily the message just sat there. She should probably reply.

Things couldn't be less throbby here at the mall with my dad.

You should've come over instead. I could've brought you home.

Sigh. I know.

How about tonight?

Negative. Chem exam I HAVE to study for.

She actually felt pretty prepared, but when she thought of Todd's "raging throb," she realized she could probably review a few more things. Or maybe watch home shows.

So basically never, said Todd.

One night is not never.

And yet Maya had been feeling like this most nights, and they'd only been dating five months. Shouldn't she want him a little more often? Todd had his good points: he was funny, great at drawing comics, had a fake ID, and knew everything about all the superheroes and their franchises that you had to be an expert on just to watch movies these days. Also he played basketball and had excellent shoulders. He didn't seem to *really* listen when she talked, but he also didn't interrupt. Any normal girlfriend would at least throw him a, ahem, bone.

How about tomorrow? she typed.

Away game at Nathan Hale, Todd replied. Never mind. Sorry to bother you.

You're not bothering me.

Todd didn't reply right away. Maya's fingers crept over to that problematic thumb. She wondered if Todd's trip to Nathan Hale might include a run-in with that cheerleader who'd randomly posted on his wall a couple weeks ago. Todd had said she was just another counselor from summer camp. He'd probably had a raging throb there too.

Hey, she messaged, I like you. I'm really sorry I can't come by.

Do you?

Duh. It's just weird with my parents, so this Dad time matters more.

I get that. But I matter too. It's just like . . .

Pause.

You don't want me getting bored.

Asshole. I gotta go, she typed, and she stuffed her phone away. But did he have a point? Was she turning into her fucking mom?

"Number ninety-nine," the automated voice announced.

A few clerks were back from lunch break and things were moving faster.

"Why don't you go walk around?" said Dad, still typing away, now to the whooshing sound of messages being sent on his work feed, afternoon off be damned. "Maybe some of your friends are here."

"I don't feel like it." Maya glanced out at the globs of kids and adults walking by. Noise, smiles, purpose . . .

There was a momentary gap in the crowd and she noticed a boy standing over by the food court, wearing a wolf's mask, his dad kneeling behind him. She'd almost forgotten Halloween was next week. There had been that invitation; her friend Megan was having a party. Everyone had been messaging about costume ideas and dates and what games to play. Maya hadn't replied yet. Talk about being a ghost.

"Suit yourself," said Dad. He started, as if something had occurred to him, and looked up from his screen. "I like having you around, when you're still willing. Here . . ." He bent and wrapped an arm around her shoulder, holding his camera in front of them with the other. "Let's take a selfie."

Maya flinched. "Is it for Kendall?"

"It's for us," said Dad, meaning she'd asked for it.

"No thanks." Maya tried to worm free.

Dad's grip held firm. "Fine, we'll use your phone. Come on, just do it."

"Dad . . ." But his arm felt warm, and it would probably make less of a scene to just take one rather than to tear herself away from him.

Maya fished out her phone and Dad leaned close, a big grin. She fought the urge to cringe at the sight of herself. Nothing seemed quite right, her dark brown hair too flat, her green eyeshadow too heavy, her cheeks too puffy and round, all of it weirdly distorted by the camera screen.

"Cheese." Dad nudged her.

Maya forced a smile. Took the picture.

"Let's see it," said Dad before Maya could stash her phone away. She tapped the photo. "It's good!"

New Dad, same goofy grin that wrinkled up his whole face, and a rare glimpse of Maya's smile—

She wiped at her suddenly leaking eyes.

"What is it?"

Heart pounding, throat clenching. *Dammit!* "Nothing."

"Maya, you can tell me."

"Dad, I said it's nothing."

He pulled away, returning to his blipping phone. "All right, that's okay," he said, doing his job, giving his teen daughter space.

And yet she kinda wished he'd pried. Except if he had, could she have even described it? Because it wasn't just the divorce, or that she felt like she was losing her family, her friends, her life, everything. It was that she didn't even know why she should care. What was the point?

Where exactly were you supposed to find any hope or meaning in this world? She loved science, but science said terrible things. According to psychology, your personality was essentially set by age three, so if you came out with, say, an anxious heart, oh well. Meanwhile, biology said that your only real purpose was to live long enough to recombine your genes and maybe create something slightly less messed up the next time around. And sure, maybe her unique palate for calloused skin would help future generations when the planet was ruined and all humanity had to eat was each other, but even that slim hope was blasted away by physics, which said that the universe would keep expanding infinitely, that dark energy, stuff scientists couldn't even identify, was pushing everything farther apart, faster and faster, until someday there would only be cold and darkness and atoms like lonely fireflies searching in the forever night. Not only that: the second law of thermodynamics stated that everything was destined to eventually disintegrate. So, maybe all our ideas of meaning and progress were backward. Evolution was really devolution. The amoeba was actually our best self, because it wasn't dumb enough to even try to comprehend how fucked we were. Humanity had just enough scientific knowledge to realize that we were screwed, but not enough to do anything about it.

Maybe the answer was in religion, but Maya's parents hadn't taken her to church, and from what she could gather, the entire point of a religion was to believe in something you had no way of proving. She *had* tried. In ninth grade, she'd written an essay using pointillism as a religion. *Gather, my flock, so that I may explain that we're each just one of trillions of dots, and though none of us have any real idea what overall picture we're actually making, at least we have each other, and the picture is surely beautiful.* She'd gotten an A on the paper, but given what she now knew from physics class, that beautiful picture was only temporary, and you were still destined to drift away from every other dot until you were completely alone. . . .

A sharp sting from her hand. Fresh blood on her thumb. She winced, fighting tears.

Fuck fuck fuck.

"Number three."

"Finally," said Dad, pocketing his phone. He gave her a little push away from the wall. "This will only take a second. How about pretzels after? Those big ones that you like."

"Sure," Maya said. Pretzels. That was something.

Dad stepped over to one of the plastic cubes and a grumpy-looking woman took his paperwork. "You know the fee for a nonexpiring renewal is sixty-five dollars."

"Yup," said Dad. "Can't bear to have that old picture slowing me down."

The clerk didn't react. "Just a minute . . ." Her nails click-clacked on her keyboard.

Maya turned away. The flare of anxiety was dying down, leaving her feeling spent, like she'd ridden a great wave that had left her behind on a hard sand beach. Her head foggy, her gaze settling somewhere in the middle distance of the room, unfocused, the blur of the mall beyond.

Later, so many people will ask her what was going through her mind at that moment. They will literally ask her that exact question.

Newscaster: "Maya, what was going through your mind in that moment?"

Reporter: "Can you describe your thoughts when you first saw the boy?"

These and a hundred other variations, on morning news shows and in radio interviews, and Maya will always try to answer, but the truth is, she only remembers being kind of blank, the clock gears disengaged.

She knows why they keep asking: they want to know if they would have noticed too. If they would have acted.

Maya can't say.

She feels like she will never be able to say.

All she knows for sure is that she was standing there in the DOL, and then there he was. Had she noticed him enter? She didn't think so. But maybe on some level she had. . . .

"Like a survival instinct?" the newscasters will ask.

"I guess so," Maya will say. Maybe that's what gently pushes her gears forward, sends her scouts to their parapets. Makes her look up—

And see the wolf.

He is a few steps into the DOL, coming toward her. The boy in the plastic wolf mask, the kind with a snarling snout, bloody fangs, eyeholes, and cheap elastic that's straining over his bleached-blond hair.

So much of it is coincidence: that Maya happens to be facing away from her dad, that the window he was called to put her right near the center of the room. That everyone else in the DOL is slumped and sucked into their screens. That all the attendants sitting at the counters have their views blocked by customers or computer monitors.

Maybe at first, Maya assumes he is walking in to meet up with someone in the waiting area. His mom or something.

But the way he walks so stiffly. Like he is made of plastic. His arms barely swinging. The overhead lights make his eyes black shadows behind the eyeholes. And that mask: sure, it's almost Halloween, but here in the office, that fearsome snarl . . .

"You just *knew* something was off about him," the newscasters will say.

"I guess," Maya will reply, because it's easiest, but she doesn't have some detective's intuition. She *so* doesn't.

And yet . . .

This boy: about Maya's height, wearing a puffy black jacket, baggy jeans, dirty black sneakers, skinny but also kind of chubby around the middle.

This boy who stops not five feet from her, facing the clerk windows. Stops and stands so still, seeming to look right through her. Is he holding his breath?

Maya's pulse rises; she feels flushed. Maybe it is right then that she starts to experience something like fear, like a premonition. Later she'll wonder how this could be: maybe it was a reaction to quantum tremors in the space-time continuum, slipping backward from a possible future, ripples from all the atomic bonds that will be savaged when the bomb erases her.

Maybe . . .

Maya watches as the boy raises his hand in front of him, his arm bent at the elbow, just his forearm sticking straight out. He's holding something. Exhales, a long, quavering sound.

His thumb flicks up.

She will learn only later that this was the moment when the bomb was supposed to detonate. That her life was supposed to end right there, her entire body torn into scraps of tissue and molecules, atoms and freed energy. Entropy winning far sooner than she'd ever imagined. And her brain will rush back to this exact second and burn that blast crater into her mind even though it didn't actually happen, creating a trap that she will fall into again and again.

But in this moment she is just watching the boy, still not even entirely sure why. His head twitches. Glancing toward the thumb. It flicks down. Up. Again.

Dead. Not dead. Dead. Not dead.

The object he's holding looks like the top half of a silver ballpoint pen. He's clicking the button.

The boy seems to shudder.

And in his next inhalation Maya hears something undeniable.

"He sounded scared," Maya will say. This she remembers. This is true. That slight hitch of a sob held back . . .

She steps toward him.

The newscasters and bloggers and attorneys all want this to be the moment when Maya knew, when that sixth sense kicked in. They crave some reassurance that we all have it, that in the second before it's too late, we will know.

"I think so," Maya will lie. Because she still doesn't. Not

really. And she won't bother pointing out that technically they're talking about the second *after*. Had the trigger worked. She only starts toward the boy once she is already dead.

What she will not quite know how to say is that she maybe does feel something: some kind of connection. Like the boy is sending out a signal. She will wonder if that was real or not, because she's not the girl who helps strangers, who talks to weird boys in masks. She's not the girl who sees distress in the world and believes it's her duty to help. She's not the girl who's brave, or courageous, and she's definitely not the girl who feels vibes or signals or even who *goes with the flow*. She's the girl who worries, who doubts, who doesn't—

A step closer. The boy is still flicking the pen. He seems to be looking at it, and now Maya notices a red wire coming out of the bottom of it, snaking into his sleeve. The boy grasps the wire with his free hand. Jiggles it.

"And *then* you knew," they will say, leaning forward, so hungry.

And Maya will nod, but *still* no, or yes, or . . . What she does remember is noticing the cuts on the boy's hands, the bruises, the mess of his fingernails, torn, scabbed around the cuticles. She will learn only later what the boy has really been through, but what she knows right now is what those wounds feel like. That he suffers. And maybe everyone is suffering and—

Another step and she is beside him. "Hey."

The boy has just pushed the wire back up into the pen, and pressed his thumb down again and inhaled deeply. When she speaks, he flinches and gasps, and the wolf mask flashes toward her and then back to his thumb, still held down on the pen top, hand shaking. Arm shaking.

"Are you okay?" Maya asks.

"Don't!" he hisses. Buckles like a building about to collapse. His black-hole eyes find her again. "Please . . ." His voice trembling. "You need to get away from me."

Maya feels something wet. She sees a streak of darkness down his pant leg, drips running off his sneaker onto her sandaled toes.

She doesn't say *gross,* because her eyes are tracking up.

And now it is all a blur. This part will forever be a blur

The boy with his free hand grabbing at his jacket, tugging it up just enough to show her the ring of clear water bottles filled with orange liquid and strapped to him with duct tape, the wires—

"When I let go, it will go off," the boy whispers. "You need to run."

Oh God.

Maya should run.

Needs to RUN.

And every fiber in her body vibrates with terror and the world seems to go white and her hands—

Both her hands—

Her bandaged, tattered, bloodstained hands—

Grab his, pressing down atop his thumb with all her strength.

The boy spasms. "What are you doing?"

Crying. She doesn't answer. She doesn't know.

"You knew that you had to stop him," the newscasters fill in, nodding at her.

Sometimes Maya nods back. He told her to run. He probably would have given her a few seconds to get far enough away.

"You could have grabbed your dad and fled the scene," the newscasters say.

Did she ever even think about her dad?

"But you knew it was up to you to save everyone there."

She doesn't know what she knew. All she really remembers thinking is *No. I will not die.*

NO.

Maya squeezes harder, so much harder than she ever has.

"I'm sorry," the boy whimpers.

"Maya?" Dad behind her.

"Get away! Call the police!" Maya yells, her voice wild, not at all her own.

"What are you talking about—"

"Just do it, Dad!"

The boy moans. "No . . ."

"He's got a bomb!" someone shouts.

And now there is utter pandemonium—screaming and crashing and fleeing.

"Maya—"

"Don't touch me, Dad!" To the boy: "We're okay, right?" Maya says beneath the chaos, the center of a hurricane, dead still and yet alive—

So terribly, desperately, completely alive—

"As long as we don't let go. Right?"

The wolf nods. Sniffles.

Screaming. Phones everywhere calling 911.

"Maya?" Dad shouts, nearby or a thousand miles away.

"What's your name?" Maya asks.

Shaking.

This boy . . .

"Elián," he says, and his free hand falls on top of hers.

SEPTEMBER

(TEN MONTHS LATER)

CHAPTER 3

ELI
(AGE 15)

September 5

"Are you ready?"

No.

He watched out the car window. Crowds, pairs, stragglers, making their way up the sidewalks, across the parking lot.

Sheep.

No, not sheep. Kids. Like him.

You're not a kid.

Yes, I am.

Had to be. A normal kid. The first day of school.

You are a weapon.

I'm not. Eli put his palms against his legs, just above his knees, and started tapping fast, like a drumroll. He couldn't do this. There was no way—

A hand on his shoulder. He flinched, a blast of terrible noise

35

and images tearing through his head: the red dark, a flash of sky, closing trunk door, crowded mall—

But it wasn't a gloved hand. It was Mom's.

Trust will be hard. That's what Dr. Maria, the psychiatrist who'd been working with him since his rescue—*failure*—often said. *But touch can be positive.*

The back of Mom's hand was crisscrossed with dry white lines. More lines around her eyes and mouth, gray streaks in her hair. When she'd arrived in the hospital after he was rescued—*thwarted*—she looked so much older than his memories, he thought she was a ghost.

Your mother needed to be freed from this lie of a world, Gabriel had said.

Three and a half years with Gabriel, thinking his mother was dead, that Gabriel had murdered her. That his sister . . .

She needed to be cleansed.

Deep breath.

Focus on the present, Dr. Maria would say.

So many voices in his head. So hard to get his own voice out. How many words had he even said in the red dark? It had taken days in the hospital before he could answer any questions with actual words.

"Eli?"

Yeah.

Even his name was new.

Elián Martinez was now Eli Rivera.

Jacob— No. *That was never my name.*

The wolf mask had hidden his face from the security cameras, cell phones, and reporters. His name had leaked, but he'd only been eleven when he was taken, and because Mom's strictness about phones had included social media, he'd had almost no on-line presence. So they changed names and relocated: from the southeast side of Seattle to the northwest. Thirteen miles and seven hundred thousand people between his old life and his new.

Still, his family, the doctors, Detective Pearson, who was in charge of the case, Agent Barnes at the FBI, all the way up to the guy from Homeland Security who showed up now and then—they had all debated: maybe farther away would be better.

How about Los Angeles? Or it says here you have cousins in Fresno. . . . Easier to make a clean break. To leave the past behind.

But there was also a case for staying in the same city. Most of their close family was here. Dad was here, but that wasn't really a reason; he'd come by the hospital twice, then for a minute at Christmas. Each time he could barely look at Eli, like he was something too repulsive or shameful to acknowledge, never mind embrace. Hadn't been around much before that anyway.

By staying here, at least some of the topography was famil-iar. *It might help to have something to rebuild on,* Dr. Maria had suggested. Completely uprooting to another state might be even more disorienting. Here, he could connect his new life to his old life. He would still have the Seahawks, wet winters, the Cinerama. Here, the good childhood memories could reemerge, find their way to the surface, and knit themselves to his present.

Except to get there, those memories had to pass around, or more often through, the red dark.

There was one other reason to stay in the area. Eli had heard them all talk: the police and the federal agents and the news re-porters and the bloggers and, when they thought they were out of earshot, his aunts, uncles, cousins, and especially his mom.

They wanted *him*.

The man known only as Gabriel. Domestic terrorist. Child abductor. Tormentor. And among his family: *Son of a bitch. That bastard. Sick fuck. If they ever find him, I'll kill him myself.*

By the time the fire department and the police and the bomb squad arrived at the DOL that afternoon, Gabriel had long since fled the scene. No fingerprints on Eli or the bomb, which had been one loose wire away from causing catastrophic loss of life. There had been a national manhunt. There still was, technically, but it had quickly lost the front page to an election, then a terrorist attack, and by now, nearly a year later, there were dozens of bombs and bullets that had actually found their targets all around the country, and the Cedar Gate Mall incident was barely ever mentioned.

But Gabriel was still at large and considered dangerous. People like him tended to try again, Detective Pearson had said. And so maybe, she added, if Eli stayed in the same city, he would remember something that would help the case. But it had been nearly a year, and he hadn't yet been able to give them any more clues about Gabriel's identity or where he'd been held captive than he had at the start: a red room, its one plywood-covered window, the locked door, the metal pail. The raggedy blanket and half-empty pillow he slept with on the rough wooden floor. The creak of the boards just outside the door that always announced Gabriel's arrival . . .

As for Gabriel himself, Eli remembered a white face, always shaved smooth, short hair, maybe brown? Thin, tall, shirt tucked in. Always wore long rubber kitchen gloves in the red dark. Cold, stretchy, squealing when he touched Eli. *What color?* He wasn't sure. Black knit gloves at the mall. *How tall was he? Age? Did he ever say anything about work, habits, family?* Eli had nothing.

He'd never seen the rest of the house, its yard or surroundings. When Gabriel had started taking him out, he'd always been hooded and shoved into the trunk. He had never seen the streets, or the neighborhood. The best he could say about the drive to the mall was that it maybe seemed short? But time had lost most of its meaning by then.

Cedar Gate was in the north part of Seattle. In a fifteen-minute radius there were tens of thousands of homes and apartments.

He should have been paying attention! That seemed obvious now, but at the time, he couldn't remember ever believing he'd be free.

Don't be hard on yourself, everyone had said. *You were in a constant state of trauma.*

A state that would take years to recover from. If ever.

And so maybe they also wanted Eli to stay for another reason: He was watched by officers and agents nearly around the clock, his family shadowed anywhere they went. They said it was for his protection, but Eli had heard the whispers: *brainwashed, too far gone.* Maybe they were really protecting everyone else.

Maybe I programmed you, left commands that I'm waiting to activate.

For nearly a year, he'd been kept at home or in a hospital or a therapy office. A parade of tutors throughout the week. The most public place he went was the gym, where he worked with a strength coach. Occasionally the pharmacy or the grocery store, but never on his own . . .

Until today.

"It's just an experiment," said Mom, rubbing his hand. "If it doesn't work, we'll come up with another plan."

But he knew what that meant: more tutors, small group settings, more time apart from the rest of the world, like he didn't really exist, and he'd lost so much time already.

Eli watched the kids walking by.

They're just sheep. I saved you from their suffering.

These kids didn't look like they were suffering. But they did look different: taller than the kids he remembered, ganglier, bigger in the shoulders and chests. It was like he'd time-traveled while they'd all been living their lives, going to middle school, growing and changing.

One minute. One minute farther down the street and I would have been by the A-Mart on the corner of Forty-Sixth. Ms. Moritz, who always gave me a discount on Red Vines, she would have seen it happening, called 911. Also her son Miguel worked there after school. He was strong and Mom had called him trouble one time, but he also seemed like the type that would have run out to help. A minute farther behind . . . there still would have been too many other kids around. But that one minute meant being on the part of South Dawson with the big oak trees that made those dark shadows. Little houses with high fences, lots of cars parked along the curb, a few homeless RVs. One minute when no one else was around.

In Eli's head, Gabriel laughed. *The Purpose put you there.*

No. *Just luck. Bad timing. There was that squirrel. Ran in front of me just before, but I only glanced at it, then back at my cards. Not even a minute. That one second—if I'd just watched that squirrel for a second longer, I might have seen the idling car, the door opening . . .*

Eli felt his mom's hand over his, stopping the rapid tapping against his legs.

"Stay here," she said. "That's what they tell you, right?"

Eli nodded. *It's hard.*

Mom breathed deep. "All the teachers have been briefed. That officer will be here too, but not in uniform. Officer Dawes, you met him?"

"Yeah."

"Okay. And remember, don't tell anyone who you really are. If they guess, deny it. And if you see that girl, you can't acknowledge her either."

I got it, Mom. Eli pulled his hand away. He'd heard it all already: how telling the kids could freak them out, could cause their parents to raise concerns about student safety. He had to be seen but unseen. That was nothing new. He'd had training.

But he didn't know what he was going to do if he saw that girl.

"You have your phone." Mom sniffed and wiped her eyes.

It's okay, Eli thought to say.

Mom sighed and looked at the ceiling, but then, like a thousand other times, she shook her head. "Sorry. Don't worry about me. It's nothing."

Eli had heard this enough to know better: *nothing* really meant *everything.* So much everything. Everyone was always saying they were sorry, without saying exactly what for. But Eli knew. They all blamed themselves. *Don't worry about me,* they'd say next. The message seemed to be that Eli should focus all his energy worrying about himself.

It only made him feel more lonely.

A buzzer echoed throughout the school. Kids quickened their pace toward the doors.

"Okay," said Mom, pressing his shoulder and awakening the subtle ache, still there, that he didn't bother mentioning anymore. "Go."

Go swiftly and without fear.

She leaned over and kissed his head. "Have a good first day."

Eli exhaled. Hadn't realized he'd been holding it in.

All you have to do is let go.

He opened the door. Got out.

"Detective Pearson will pick you up. You remember the meeting spot?"

"Yeah."

"If she's late, you just go to the office. . . ." Mom's tears fell harder.

I know. Eli shut the door and started up the sidewalk, both hands holding his backpack straps, kids rushing by him. One step at a time.

Fifteen . . . sixteen . . . seventeen . . .

Stop it! He wasn't a wolf. Wasn't a weapon.

Are you sure about that?

Shut up.

The breeze was crisp and fresh and blew his carefully combed black hair into his eyes. He brushed it back into place. Sun warmed his face, yet a stray drop of rain hit his cheek. He checked the bright sky but couldn't tell which of the few puffy clouds it might have come from.

As he neared the entrance, he looked back. Mom was watching

him. Waved again. She didn't come in at Dr. Maria's anymore but still always waited until Eli was safely inside.

He reached the door just after a group had walked in. Caught it with his palm, held it open—

Froze.

When he blinked he saw the red dark.

Blinked again and saw the mall.

Blinked again and saw a crowded hallway thrumming with kids. If they found out who he was, they would judge, they would fear. He was a danger to them all.

I can't do it.

Couldn't be one of them, their voices so shrill, their bodies moving so easily, their lives so normal.

Sheep.

No! Just kids. Like me.

An older girl jostled by him, her backpack clubbing him in the shoulder. "Watch it."

"Sorry," Eli said.

He turned. Mom was still there, still crying. She waved again. A trio of boys walking past the car noticed, followed her gesture to Eli. One of them smirked.

All at once, a wave of frustration surged through him. When would she ever stop hovering?

He waved quickly, grabbed the straps of his backpack. Went in.

CHAPTER 4

MAYA

September 7

She spotted him between periods two and three. Head down, his hair shaggy and black, not bleached-blond, holding on to his backpack straps, among the herd going in the other direction.

Her pulse accelerated, stomach clenched, her skin prickling as if a million microscopic bugs had raised their swords—

And just like that she was blowing up again. White flash, searing hot, the sting of her cells tearing free from one another, mist of red and flying body parts and disintegration.

It had been nearly a year since Maya had seen him, since those endless hours trapped in the DOL, holding on for dear life as bomb technicians scurried around them, and then as they were whisked out a back door of the abandoned mall and taken by ambulance to the hospital. Nearly a year spent trying to recover from the bomb that kept going off inside her head, even though it never had in real life. A blurry, messy year, a baffling betrayal that might have just been starting to get a little bit better—

But now this. Him. Here, just a few feet away, all that time and distance suddenly vaporized.

Stop staring! she thought, but she kept staring. If he looked over . . .

What? What would she do? Grab his arm? Scream at him that he had a lot of nerve being here, ruining everything? But she'd been explicitly instructed not to talk to him. It would cause a panic if kids found out who he was: the boy behind the infamous wolf's mask, *The New Face of Domestic Terrorism.*

Maybe that would be for the best. It would definitely get him out of here.

But as Eli got closer, Maya was struck by another thought: *He looks lonely.* And she remembered how the entire time they'd been stuck in the DOL, he'd been quietly crying, unable to speak, that in the ambulance, when the paramedic had finally removed the wolf's mask, his eyes had been so vacant, his face blotchy and bruised. . . .

Maybe she also wanted to know how he was doing.

And yet he never looked up, and the crowded hall carried them right past one another.

But that didn't stop the explosion. Maya hunched forward and tunneled ahead, a frigid sweat breaking out all over, spots in her vision. The noise of the hallway too loud, the bodies too close too close too close—

She reached the nearest bathroom, yanked open the door, and threw herself inside. Stumbled, got the side-eye from two girls standing at the sinks reapplying their lipstick, their eye shadow, so easy for them to be so pretty.

45

Beelined toward a bathroom stall and shut herself in.

She collapsed onto the toilet. Placed both hands on her stomach and tried to make everything still, to just focus on a single inhalation.

One . . . two . . . three.

Now exhale.

One . . . two . . . three . . .

But the fire kept spreading, the walls blowing out, furniture twisting, smoke and rubble and melting skin.

One . . . two . . . three . . .

There was a period of white, lost time, and then Maya recognized the sound of her whispered count. Slowly began to feel the whoosh of air in and out, to sense the surface world beyond her skull. The blast fading, giving way to heavily graffitied stall walls.

Keep going, her therapist, Renee, had advised her. *Focus on your breathing and counting, until you feel firmly in control.*

Maya gritted her teeth.

One . . . two . . . three . . .

Fuck.

She probably should have been ready. After all, they'd warned her. Called her in for a special meeting a week ago. The Friday before Labor Day weekend, she and her mom in the principal's office at Elliott High School, the kind of scene that made Maya wonder if her life was someone's demented screenplay:

PRINCIPAL NEYER: *(eyes shifting between papers in his lap and the gap between Mom and Maya)* We are so sorry. We had no intention of this happening. Someone brought up the possibility back in the spring, but we checked your records and at the time you were still listed as attending Garfield.

MOM: I don't understand. We put in the transfer paperwork at the right time.

PRINCIPAL NEYER: No, of course you did.

MAYA: *(slouching)*

FUSSY PRINCIPAL'S ASSISTANT, DONNA OR SOMETHING: *(flipping furiously through pages)* It's because decisions on reassignment requests aren't made until August, and even then, it's all done at the district level. Our registrar just gets a list afterward. . . . Due to the sensitive nature of Eli's case, not everyone here at Elliott was briefed on the situation . . . and now school starts next week.

MOM: So you're saying Maya has to go to school with this boy who tried to kill her, who might still be a terrorist.

MAYA: Mom.

PRINCIPAL NEYER: *(shifting like he has to pee)* Mrs. Abrams, we've—

MOM: It's Sanders. Not Abrams anymore. Not Mrs.

PRINCIPAL NEYER: Sorry. We, um, the boy has been thoroughly evaluated and we feel confident that he poses no threat to the student body.

MOM: Except to my daughter.

PRINCIPAL NEYER: We've reviewed Maya's file and I understand your concern. That's why we're here. Given the circumstances, we are more than willing to transfer you back to Garfield—

MAYA: No way.

MOM: We had to sell the house, and my apartment is up here, and she can't live with her father.

DONNA-MAYBE: Is there something we should know about your father?

MOM: No, of course not. But he lives with his new girlfriend—

MAYA: There's no way I'm living with them.

MOM: With her recovery, she needs to be with me.

PRINCIPAL NEYER: I understand, of course. What about another school that's nearby?

DONNA-MAYBE: *(more flipping)* I think Ingraham might work. Enrollment is at an all-time high in the district, but I'm sure they could make room.

MOM: Let me get this straight: you're sending this killer to public school and putting thousands of kids' lives at risk, and you want *my* daughter to move?

MAYA: *(crumbling, cracking, dissolving)*

PRINCIPAL NEYER: I'm afraid moving Eli is not an option. We have a whole system in place, and it would be too difficult to change at this point. Moving Maya—

MAYA: I don't want to move again. My friend Janice is here. And some kids from middle school. I don't know anyone at Ingraham.

DONNA-MAYBE: I could call over to Roosevelt. They have a great jazz band—

MOM: *(sitting up)* Okay. That's enough. Do you hear her? She says she wants to stay.

PRINCIPAL NEYER: But we—

MOM: I don't care what you think would be best. If you move my daughter out of this school, I will go straight to the press with this.

MAYA: *(showing no response, but somewhere, through a crack, flowers blooming in a weak ray of sun)*

PRINCIPAL NEYER: That would not be in anyone's best interest.

MOM: None of this is.

PRINCIPAL NEYER: *(long sigh, glance at Donna-Maybe, who shrugs)* Look, some people on the team think it may work out for the best. Seeing him in a normal setting might help to diffuse some of the trauma you've been dealing with since the event.

MAYA: Maybe . . .

Except now she'd seen him.
It hadn't exactly made things better.
This latest episode was like so many others: she could be

anywhere, doing anything, and her head could be hijacked by Eli walking into the DOL, and everything exploding. No matter how it had really happened, in her mind the trigger always worked, like it *should* have worked that afternoon. She shouldn't have even had a chance to go to him, or to grab his hands: she should already have been dead. Sometimes she wondered if she really was, and everything since had been some kind of afterlife.

Another weird thing about the episodes: she always put her hands on his before the explosion. Almost like they were doing it together. What did that mean? She hadn't told anyone that detail, not even Renee.

One . . . two . . . three . . .

Maya blinked, felt the sense of herself in space. Clothes against her skin, feet on the floor. How long had she been out of it? Sometimes the episodes lasted less than a minute, others could be five or ten. She could hear voices that were probably those other two girls. So it couldn't have been that long. Their shoes clapped on the tile floor and the bathroom door squealed open and thudded shut. Silence.

Maya saw that her black knitted fisherman's hat had fallen to the ground. She realized that her fingers were up at her scalp, behind her ear. An ache there.

She pulled her hand away and found hair twisted around her fingers.

Shit.

She shoved the hair between her legs into the toilet. Spun the toilet paper roll and gathered a fistful, then dabbed at her head. The paper came away spotted with blood.

It had started sometime during the television interviews last fall: CNN, MSNBC, FOX. National websites and local TV affiliates. *We're talking today about the enemy among us—*

Talking today about staying alert—

Talking today about gun control with our very special guest and local hero, Maya Abrams.

All those empty camera lenses leering, their soulless eyes sucking her in and beaming her to millions of judgmental viewers.

All those brilliant studio lights like bomb blasts, gleaming studio sets like she was in a museum display. *See the exotic hero girl!*

The slick, shimmering anchors, the production assistants and makeup stylists, the brass blond hair and crimson nails and coffee-colored suit pants and teal bras and little ski-jump noses. They would try to make her one of them: caking on the makeup, blow-drying her hair, repainting her savaged nails. And they would smile at her and say:

"You're such a hero."

"So brave."

"A role model."

You're all liars! Maya had wanted to scream. She wasn't a hero. Technically she'd failed, her saving move made from beyond the grave. But it was more than that. Sure, maybe she had helped keep that bomb from going off, but it wasn't like she'd *coolly assessed the situation* or *sacrificed herself for the good of those around her.* All those explanations, which newspeople loved assigning to her, felt dishonest. She'd barely even known what she was doing, still couldn't quite explain it when people asked.

Then she'd seen herself onscreen and she'd looked so idiotic, so disgusting, like such a *fraud.* Her face like plastic, her hair weirdly straightened and sculpted, those awkward solid-color blouses that Mom said looked best on TV. She'd read the back-lash online too: *attention hog, self-esteem issues, cashing in on her fame, slut.* A blog suggested she'd fucked a forty-five-year-old news anchor. (She hadn't. Had he wanted to? There had been a confusing hug or two. What the hell had that been?)

And on and on.

By winter, she'd started to really notice how gross her hair was. She'd had to wear a hat or scarf of some kind since late spring.

It just needs a little more work. That was how the thinking went that led to the hair-pulling. *Trichotillomania,* it was called: a close cousin of skin-picking and a wide array of other truly disturbing conditions Maya had read about online. Collect them all!

With a little more work, her hair would be as pretty as all those reporters'. But also the pain of tearing out hair was even more effective than just ripping skin. (The finger report: only two Band-Aids today!) Pulling burned off even more energy, kept your drifting deeper. Safer.

Add that to the blowing up in her head, and her naturally high anxiety, already in overdrive from her parents' divorce:

"You're suffering from post-traumatic stress disorder," Renee had said. "These flashbacks and the faulty memory of the bomb going off are being triggered by stimuli related to the event. Memories. Sounds. Smells." And now seeing Eli.

"But it's not like I was in a war, or abused or something," Maya had said.

"There's no set amount of trauma that's prerequisite for PTSD," Renee had replied. "It's different for every individual. You had a close brush with life-threatening danger."

"The bomb didn't even go off."

"That doesn't change the fact that there was a bomb that could have gone off. You spent hours literally inches from it."

True. Still, Maya couldn't shake the thought that maybe a stronger person, a better person, wouldn't be suffering like this at all. She'd thwarted a suicide bomber, saved hundreds of lives, and somehow ended up worse off than before.

At least the diagnosis came with perks. She dug into her shoulder bag, found her prescription bottle: Serenitab, 25 milligrams. One to take the edge off, two to defuse a crisis. Those were Renee's recommendations.

Maya had found a third option: four to turn today into tomorrow.

She picked up her hat, slid it on, and peered out of the stall. No one around. She dashed for the sink—

GIANT MIRROR!

Ugh! Had to be careful with those. Keep her eyes right . . . on . . . the sink . . .

She ducked, shoved the pills into her mouth, and drank from the faucet. The pills sloshed around, one spilling out. She snared it with her finger just before it slipped down the drain. Popped it in, just chewed it. Friends didn't let friends waste benzos.

She cupped her hands and drank some more, then leaned on the sink, head down.

Oh God.

Seeing Eli every day . . . Her fingers crawled up under her hat, searching for fresh hair—

The door burst open.

"There you are." Janice. "Did you get my texts?"

"No." Maya's phone was stuffed far down in her bag, all status updates and notifications disabled.

"You have to check it more," said Janice. "It's like you're dead to the world. Some of us need to know where you are."

Maya just nodded. When was the last time she'd posted anything? That photo of the clouds . . . was that last week?

Janice swept over, put her hands on Maya's shoulders. "What happened?"

"Nothing."

"You know that doesn't work on me."

"I just . . ." She started to cry.

Janice wrapped her in a hug. "It's okay," she said into her ear.

Maya's muscles felt locked. She managed to get her arms limply around Janice's waist.

"You're forgetting again, aren't you?" said Janice.

"What."

"That you're beautiful."

Maya pressed her face into Janice's shoulder. Her denim jacket smelled like menthol cigarettes. "I'm so gross."

"You could never be. Someday you're going to listen to me." She stroked Maya's head, fingers running over her hat. Janice had gotten it for her from her dad, who worked the salmon boats out of Seattle. *This hat's been to Alaska*, she'd said. *It can protect you from anything.* She kissed Maya's forehead.

They'd been friends in middle school, but Janice had choiced into Elliott because it had the best theater program. They'd stayed loosely in touch on each other's feeds, and after the DOL, Janice had started messaging. Then, one afternoon near the start of summer, they'd run into each other at Red Light, while Maya had been limply swishing through the racks of discarded selves (she needed new clothes but she couldn't go to the mall because the mall = *boom*).

Janice had helped her finally shrug free of her blurry relationship with this guy Nilo and also sort of his friend Walsh, a mess that began not too long after Todd had dumped her. She and Janice officially started dating in July, while celebrating Maya's seventeenth birthday with a sleeping bag and vodka on the beach at Golden Gardens.

"What triggered you?" Janice asked. "You looked like you were doing good in statistics. Actually, you look super-hot in this shirt. . . ."

Janice pulled back, a slight smile. Maya gave her a quick kiss but looked away.

"Yeah, I was fine, but then . . ." Maya stopped.

"What?"

"Nothing."

"Tell Janice."

"It got intense, out in the hall just now," Maya said. "Some of the football guys were catcalling some freshman girls, and there was a traffic jam, and . . ."

"Sounds like you need Doctor Pom." Janice rifled through her backpack and produced a silver flask adorned with an eagle made out of red, white, and blue fake jewels. "Do you have an extra happy pill I can chase with this?"

"Oh yeah." Maya fished out her Serenitab and gave one to Janice.

Janice frowned. "Only one?"

"Sorry, I'm running low."

"That's okay." Janice twisted open the flask, took a swig, and passed it over.

Maya put it to her lips. Pomegranate-flavored vodka. It tasted like a Jolly Rancher dissolved in gasoline. The burn was nice, though. Janice had an older sister who kept her supplied.

"I'm so sorry," said Janice. "I thought you were doing better."

"Well . . ." Inside, Maya felt the hatches closing. *Hello, Serenitab!* The first sign of her supersized dose was a dulling effect, like Maya was on a ship pulling away from shore, the drug ushering her up to the lido deck, far away from the choppy waves and shark fins. The vodka helped too, like a warm breeze. Her tears began to dry, her skin retreating. A dull little laugh slipped out. "I don't know why you put up with me."

"Because I'm in love with you, dummy." Janice hugged her from the side, rested her chin on Maya's shoulder.

Maya braved the mirror, considering them together. Janice was so damn beautiful. Eyes and hair from across the Pacific, chin and shoulders from the farms of Minnesota, legs and boobs from who knew where. Moments like today where she wore the black skirt, her flannel tied at her waist . . . damn.

And yet she also had those blue eyes like glaciers. She might flash her warmest smile, but right above, those eyes never melted. When she said she loved you, could you totally believe it? It seemed inevitable that at some point she'd find another cool-eyed being of her own kind, and leave Maya and the rest of the mortals behind.

And why shouldn't she? Maya's hat might have been hiding the torn-away gaps in her auburn hair, but there were still her eyes, a very average chocolate brown surrounded by bloodshot swirls and sunk into tar pits, the acne blooming on her nose, her red scoop-neck top—*Don't you think that's a bit too low?* Mom had said—which had slipped down nearly to the midpoint of her bra, acne there too that she hadn't even noticed until now.

She frowned at the mirror, tugging her shirt up.

"Stop that." Janice pushed her hand away. "Don't spoil the view."

"Come on," said Maya.

"What?" Janice stepped behind her and rubbed her shoulders. "You're so cute. My little kitten from the animal shelter." She nuzzled into Maya's neck. "Janice will give you a good home and make you all better."

Maya managed to smile because *Serenitab, ohhh, Serenitab, you do your thing. . . .* Safely away from shore, the world around her shrouded in fog.

"Feeling better?" said Janice, her hands exploring.

Maya's knees wobbled and she leaned back. The combination of Serenitab and Dr. Pom could lead to enhanced lustiness.

"You know, we're already late for third period."

"Mmm." It would be nice, spending a few minutes here . . . but Maya took Janice's hands and twirled away from her. "We shouldn't. We're only four days into the year. And it's a new school for me."

"Please?" Janice batted her eyes, holding Maya's wrist firm. For a moment, the strain on her arm nearly stopped her . . . but she pulled away.

"I can get us late passes from the nurse." Maya let her lone cocky grin out of its cage, pointing a thumb at herself. "War hero and all."

Janice crossed her arms. "Whatever."

"Sorry. Later, I promise." Maya pushed through the door into the now-empty hallway. For a moment, it seemed like Janice wasn't coming. . . .

Then she emerged, eyes on her phone. They walked up the

hall side by side, but the gap between their shoulders seemed a mile wide.

"I really am sorry," Maya said after a minute.

"It's fine." And then a couple steps later: "I just really could have used a little action, you know? Something positive."

"I know, but—"

"I don't get why it's such a big deal. You said all the teachers know your situation."

"I don't know." Maya felt her head listing, but also butterflies in her stomach. Janice was right about the teachers. She'd even been given this special pass, so if she started to have an episode, she could go directly to the nurse, no questions asked. She hadn't tried it yet, though. "I just want to make a good impression." She offered a smile, but Janice wasn't looking. "Have everyone think I'm somewhat normal, you know?"

She knows, now hush, whispered the misty steward on the good ship *Serenitab. Sit on this deck chair. Here's a wool blanket. If we're quiet, we might hear whales.*

Janice was saying something, but Maya missed the start. "—my fucking parents trying to undermine me."

"What did they do?"

"God, keep up. I said, all I did was mention Juilliard audition dates and my dad launches into this whole thing about practical jobs and how rents in New York City are *astronomical* and you really need your degree to count. It's such crap. I know what he's really saying. *Get a law degree, and a boyfriend while you're at it!* I hate him sometimes."

"That sucks." Maya hoped she'd said that out loud.

They must have gotten late passes after that.

Then third period was English or something.

Study hall, later, a buzzing-hive thing.

"Have you seen the new video?" Janice had asked at one point.

"What?" Maya shouted down from the railing.

"The new Alpha post."

Alpha-something. That was what he went by: this kid who said he was from their school had been posting these videos about how everyone was evil and needed to be judged or something.

"Nah," said Maya.

"It's gross," said Janice. "He's definitely one of these hard-up nerds. No kid who's gotten laid would make a video about blood sacrifices and dates of judgment. Once you've had sex, you want to live as long as possible so you can have as much of it as you can."

"Right."

"Charlese thinks he's not even really from here. That he's like, from Everett, or homeschooled or something and just picked a big-city high school to freak people out."

"Probably." What were they talking about, again?

Maya held each moment in her palm just long enough for it to blow away, a feathery seed on a tropical wind.

Slip, she watched them go, sort of.

Later, at lunch, she saw Eli again, emerging from the lunch line. But by then, her thoughts were mostly zombies. Her brain a vacant parking lot.

And the day went by.

CHAPTER 5

ELI

September 10

"What do you want?" The lunch lady was looking at him.

Eli gazed at the food. He'd brought his lunch last week. This was the next step to being a normal kid. Pizza. Steamed broccoli and carrots. Rice and curry chicken. Wire rack of cereal cups, muffins, burritos you could microwave. Behind him: a salad bar. Multicolored. Different kinds of dressing.

So many choices.

Every meal in the red dark had arrived in the exact same metal bowl. Silver-colored. Aluminum. Like you'd take camping. Along with a spoon that was also silver but had a black handle that was two plastic halves snapped together around the metal.

The bowl had a dent. Upside down it sort of looked like a planet with a crater. In the red dark, like Mars. Mars had been a glassy, flickering orange mystery that summer before he'd been taken—*chosen*—barren and frozen and lifeless. Now it had running water. People were planning to go there.

So much had changed.

The bowl of food had always been a mixture. Everything chopped up. Baked beans and rice and corn, or spaghetti and peas and spongy meatballs. It was hard to eat spaghetti with a spoon. Oatmeal was easier. Cornflakes mixed in. And dates. But dates made the pail smell. Gabriel always seemed to wait extralong to change the pail in the days after the oatmeal.

Sometimes the bowl had eggs and toast.

Grilled cheese with mushy beans and crumbled potato chips.

No matter what: all mixed together.

Eli would sit on the floor with the bowl in his lap and eat. Through the floor, he could hear the scraping sounds of Gabriel dining. Imagined him eating the different foods separately, like on a nicely arranged plate, like with a fork and knife. He'd hoped maybe his sister got to eat that way too.

For one six-month stretch there had been only dog food. Every day twice a day. What had he done? Forgotten the Purpose somehow. It was hard to remember. He didn't want to remember.

Except he remembered. He always did.

A quarter of his life in that room. There was no ignoring it, no pretending it hadn't happened. In fact, that only made it worse, as the memories could creep up unexpectedly and send him reeling.

The dog food had been because he'd almost gotten that truck driver's attention. Plumber? Deliveryman? Eli hadn't known. It had been afternoon, according to the angle of the sliver of light between the plywood and the sill. He'd heard an engine. Footsteps around the back of the house. The last sounds from downstairs seemed to indicate that Gabriel had left.

Eli had started banging on the plywood and shouting.

"Hello?" the driver called to him. "Somebody up there?"

"In here!" Eli wailed.

But then Gabriel's voice. His calm, never-rising tones, speaking to the man. The truck driving off . . .

A brief, stinging lesson with the garden hose. And then only dog food, day after day.

"You gonna pick something?"

The lunch lady looked at him with something like sympathy, and Eli wondered if she knew who he was. He'd been told that only essential personnel had been briefed on his identity. Was the lunch lady essential?

Someone sucked their teeth behind him.

No idea how long he'd been staring. Keeping track of time was still a problem. He tried to focus on the choices—

The excess . . . Food is one of the weapons the Barons use to keep us docile.

No. It was just lunch. Options kids might like. Gabriel had been wrong. About most things.

"Hurry up!" some boy called from farther back.

Deep breath. "Pizza," he said. "And the vegetables."

The lunch lady scooped and handed him a tan tray, separated into sections. The vegetables in one little rectangle. The pizza lying over two.

He grabbed a blueberry muffin wrapped in cellophane and turned to the drinks. Kids jostled in front of him, hitting the soda levers with their cups.

Hum and whir of carbonated beverage. Crush-crack of ice. Sizzle of juice dispenser. Thunk of refrigerated case door nearby, full of milks and soy drinks and almond drinks and smoothies—

Eli hurried for the exit, knuckles white on the sides of his tray. He had a water bottle in his backpack. All the other kids left their bags in their lockers, but Eli never did. He kept his with him, jacket stuffed inside it, not just for lunch but the whole day.

Just in case.

Stupid. Gabriel's not going to come here. He's smarter than that. And yet Eli was always scanning the hallways, street corners. Detective Pearson had told him not to worry. That Gabriel was likely multiple states or even an ocean away by now, and that even if he'd stayed local, he'd realize that Eli was being watched around the clock.

And yet Eli could never quite shake a nervous quiver inside, a certainty: *You don't know him like I do. I failed the Purpose. I need to be punished.*

He moved along the wall, kids cutting and bumping and pirouetting around him. Voices tumbling and gathering and climbing over one another. Shouts. Laughter. The shriek of a table moving.

Eli headed for two tables over by the windows that looked out on the courtyard in front of the school. The first with only one kid, the second completely empty. He'd chosen the empty one the first day, but almost immediately eyes had found him there.

Anonymity seemed to be a balance. Being utterly silent and friendless was just as attention-grabbing as being brash and popular. Like teen radar was drawn toward extremes. In order to stay invisible, you actually had to raise your hand now and then in class, or they noticed that you never raised your hand. Had to make eye contact now and then in the halls, or they noticed that you never made eye contact.

Maybe it was about connection. Like in a weird way, they would punish you for not being plugged in enough. Eli had seen it happen already this week: quiet kids suddenly shoved against lockers, food thrown at daydreamers during lunch. Maybe it was actually a strange form of sympathy. Like the way schools of fish all spiraled at the same time. Staying invisible meant staying with the group, while everyone had their gaze turned outward. Because, sure, high school seemed dangerous, but there were bigger predators out there in the inky blue. Man-eaters.

Eli knew.

So he'd been sitting with this other loner instead. Strength in numbers. Eli sat with his back to the window and put his backpack up on the table, his tray concealed behind it. The other kid was hunched over a graphic novel, same as every other day. He glanced at Eli like he always did, a one-eyed gaze, his long, matted brown hair hanging down over the other. Acne so bad on his nose you could see the biggest ones from here.

Hi, Eli thought to say.

The boy returned to his book, kept eating his pizza. They had yet to actually speak.

A group of girls at the next table over exploded into laughter. Eli tensed. Was it him? But they were totally absorbed in one another. He wondered how they could have become such good friends in such a short time. But then, duh, maybe they'd already been friends from years past, maybe back in middle school, even elementary.

Faces flashed in his mind: Carlos, Danny, and Josh, the friends he'd had before. Melinda, who'd lived a few doors down; he'd thought she was cute. They were probably all at the high school in his old neighborhood. Maybe they sat together at lunch. Did they ever talk about him? Or had they forgotten him by now?

Sometimes Eli heard the kids around him chatting, about shows, or games, or gossiping about their other friends, and he felt like he'd never be able to do it. Too many missing reference points, missing skills and stories, and if he ever did end up in one of those conversations, he wouldn't be able to explain why he had those gaps. It had barely been a week, but he had no idea how he would ever be part of this world around him.

Dr. Maria had given him a journal, suggested that one way to feel connected was to describe what was around him and how he was feeling. To put himself in the moment. The journal was in his backpack, blank. It seemed impossible to start. Besides, he still wrote like a fifth grader.

One of the girls elbowed her friend and they both eyed him. Eli realized he'd been staring, and turned away. Staring was a sure way to get yourself noticed.

His gaze drifted from one table to the next. So many kids . . .

Blow yourself up right here and how many sheep could you take out?

Sixty-five, Eli thought, unaware that he'd even been counting.

That would send a message to the Barons. Take away their precious future consumers—

Shut up!

It all got red in his thoughts. Clenched, suffocating, dragging him under. He shut his eyes and gritted his teeth. "I'm Eli," he whispered to himself, as Dr. Maria had coached him to do. "I am not a weapon. I am just a boy."

The red faded a bit. He noticed his neighbor was watching him again. Not cool to be sitting here whispering like a crazy person.

Okay. Keep it together. Lunch was already half-over. Eli unzipped his backpack, then checked to be sure that his tablemate was busy again, that no one else was watching.

Pulled out a small metal mixing bowl and a spoon. Mom hadn't noticed the bowl was missing from the cabinet because she never really baked anymore. He picked up his pizza and tore it into small chunks. Dropped them in. Scooped his vegetables on top. Crumbled in the blueberry muffin.

Mixed it all together and ate.

*   *   *

Last period was study hall. Eli spent it in the office of Mr. Caletti, one of the school counselors. He was in a meeting for most of the period but returned near the end and reviewed the day with Eli, part of their usual routine.

"But you were able to pick some things to eat," Mr. Caletti said.

"Yeah. It just took a minute."

"What about your other classes? Have you been keeping up?"

"Mostly. It's a lot." It was more than a lot. He'd been a good student in elementary school: high scores on tests, always good with reading and numbers. But ninth grade was a huge leap from fifth. They'd briefly considered putting him in middle school, but decided that would only have made him stand out more. Hopefully, over time, he would catch up.

"History and Earth science were fine," Eli said.

"Mainly the vocabulary, still?"

"Yeah." His favorite part of the day had been learning about ocean currents. He liked the diagrams with all the arrows. How the spin of the planet affected the weather. How everything was connected. "I got lost in English."

Mr. Caletti tapped notes into a tablet. "Ms. Reynolds says math has been going well."

"I guess." He didn't even go to a regular math class, just met with a specialist.

"Any other tough spots today?"

"The bathrooms are still hard." All those closed stall doors. What might be behind them.

"Did you use the faculty one again?"

"No, the regular one."

"Good," said Mr. Caletti, still typing. "Some progress, then. One day at a time, right?"

I guess.

The bell rang and Eli trudged through the halls to his locker. He stared at the combination lock, his mind blank for a moment. He had the numbers written down in his binder, but opening it made elbows collide with the girl and boy on either side, made them turn, notice. . . . *Focus.* He whispered numbers to himself, yeah, those three. Tried it, and it worked. Progress.

He removed two books from his bag that he didn't need. When he straightened, he saw the small piece of paper lying on his locker shelf, and picked it up.

A page torn out of a day planner. Not his. It must have been slipped in through the vents in the locker door. The date on the page: October 26.

The day he'd walked into the DOL.

Writing in blue pen:

> *I know who you are. . . .*
> *Let's hang out!*

Below that, a drawing of a wolf's face.

Eli's heart thundered. A spike of adrenaline in his gut. He looked left and right. Kids everywhere, so many kids, lockers slamming, backs being slapped, shoes squeaking on tile.

There was ink bleeding through from behind the wolf. He flipped over the paper.

> *Auditorium. After gym.*

CHAPTER 6

MAYA

September 11

"Maya! It's for you!"

"Whrrrisit!"

"The phone!" Mom shouted from down the hall.

"Whr—" *Take the shirt out of your mouth.* Maya pulled it away, a drop of saliva falling on her bare leg. The burgundy T-shirt had a wet spot on its side, just like the ones strewn around her. On the floor between her crossed legs was a pile of frayed tags. Her dull scissors had been no match for their unearthly silky material, so she'd resorted to her teeth.

Who was the genius who had decided to start putting tags on the sides of shirts? Right along your waistline, scratching and needling and making weird bumps on your hips. Bumps that were more noticeable when your midsection had started straining at your shirt.

These yummy love handles, Janice had said as they'd been making out after school, in the shade behind the bus stop. As Janice squeezed, Maya had felt the real meaning in her grip: *These are new,* and *You are slipping.* Had that been Janice or the universe? Or just Maya? Everyone always talking at once . . .

But they were all right, about the newness, about the thereness. And these tags *really* made it noticeable; they had to go.

"Maya." Mom was right outside the door. "Did you hear me? It's the phone."

"One sec!" She gathered the tags from her worn pink floral-pattern carpet, the one she'd had since she was nine. All her furniture was pink and white and from the same era. In her old room, it hadn't bothered her, even though the desk had become too small to actually sit at. Now it seemed ridiculous, but since they'd moved, there was no money to replace it.

Maya threw the tags in the trash can. Grabbed the pile of shirts and tossed them on the bed beside her untouched homework. Her jaw ached. At some point, the need to fix the tag situation had blurred with the sensations: the way the fibers tore between her teeth, the strain in her muscles, the vibration of the tearing through her skull, all burning off the white energy, a pleasing rush of unthinking. How long had she been at it? A half hour? Even more?

She knew it was insane to be gnawing off tags, but in the moment, she felt that same weird hope that each task, whether on her fingers or her hair or now her shirts, gave her: *just this one last thing.* Then she'd be fine. Everything would be fixed, the energy finally burned off, the bomb defused.

She'd seen Eli twice today. Once in the hall, and then at lunch, where she and Janice had happened to sit a few tables away from

70

him. Maya kept glancing at him and starting to explode—but also wondering: why was his backpack on the table? What was up with that weird metal bowl he ate out of? She'd fought off the blasts with pills and Janice's flask, but then she'd been nodding off in English. Not a good look.

"Maya . . ."

She slapped on the old Mariners cap from when Dad had taken her to a game years ago, and opened the door. "Who is it?"

Mom was wearing a formfitting charcoal skirt and a cream-colored blouse, her work bag over her shoulder. She held the old landline with her hand over the receiver. Her eyes tracked down to Maya's legs.

Oh yeah, her thighs were dusted with silky tag shreds. Also, she wasn't wearing pants.

"I was hot."

Mom made a now-familiar bewildered face, but then her own phone buzzed in her bag. "I have to go back to work. The site launch is tonight."

"You hoping to get lucky?" said Maya. "Is it that guy Doug you're always mentioning?"

"Stop it." Mom's hand moved to the open button that revealed the edge of her burgundy bra, but then left it. "Take the phone."

"Who is it?"

"Just answer it." Mom swiped on her own phone with her thumb.

"Why?"

"It's a good thing."

Maya felt her skin prickle, the bugs all raising their swords, but she took the phone and closed her door in the same motion.

"Hello?"

"Maya, hi, my name is Tamara Jenkins. I'm a writer for Chalk.com, a website with a national readership—"

"I know what Chalk is." Maya's heart started to pound. Her free hand found the hair hanging below her hat, fingers climbing up it like a vine.

"Great. So . . ." She could hear Tamara making that effort to speak carefully, like so many adults did around her. "I was hoping to interview you for the anniversary of the Cedar Gate Mall incident. Kind of a one-year-after piece."

"Oh." Maya sat down on the bed, a chill racing through her. Spots in her eyes. Her room melting and re-forming: carpet turning from pink to puke brown, desk and bureau becoming the drab rows of seats, her Chagall poster the DOL wait number sign.

"We think our readers will be very interested to know how you're doing, what this past year has been like, your reflections. I'm sure you know how inspiring your story has been."

Maya shook her fingers, fresh strands of hair falling free, and pain shooting from her scalp.

"Maya?"

Here he comes. The wolf. Walking in.

"Yeah," Maya said through gritted teeth.

"If it's okay with you, I just have five questions."

The wolf reaches her. She puts her hands atop his. *Thank you*, he says.

No, thank you.

They let go of the trigger together and the world blows up. . . .

Three . . . two . . . one . . .

"Maya?"

Mom through the door.

Maya blinked. She looked down to see her finger pressing on the End button, her knuckle turning white, her forearm shaking.

"Are you still on the phone?"

"Yeah, one more minute!" Maya wiped at tears and snot.

The door opened. "What are you doing?"

"Mom—"

"Did you hang up on her?" Mom's eyes did that bugging thing. She pushed her hair behind her ears and stepped in. "Give me the phone."

"No! Were you listening through the door?"

"Maya . . ." Her mom grabbed the phone, but Maya gripped tighter and for just one second they were in a tug-of-war—

"Fine, take it!" Maya let go and thrust across her bed, her legs wheeling until she was firmly in the corner.

Mom started pressing buttons. "She was from *Chalk,* Maya. And she seemed nice."

"Mom! I don't want to talk to her!"

Mom held the phone up to her ear. Checked her own phone while she did. Rolled her eyes at whatever she saw there.

"Hang it up!"

She mouthed *voicemail.* "Hi, this is Rose, Maya Abrams's mom. Sorry you two got disconnected—"

Maya looked away, brushing at her tears. "What the hell . . ."

"Just give us a call back when you can." Her mom hung up and whirled. "Maya, come on!"

"I don't want to talk to her! It will make it worse. It's all blowing apart in my head just hearing her voice."

"Listen, I get that you'd prefer to avoid any reminders of that day—"

"Stop quoting from your book!" Mom had bought a handbook on adolescents with PTSD. Renee had asked Maya to read parts too. It maybe helped, but it was also too much: too many suggestions, strategies, bullet points. And she wasn't some android who could calmly remember all of that while shit was blowing up around her. "I'm not some *case study*, I'm your daughter."

Mom stared at her, eyes storming between anger and something else. Frustration? Regret? Bad enough to sink so much of your life into having a kid, but then to get one that was broken like she was. . . . "Your father talked to her and he said she had good questions. Ones you could handle."

"Oh, great. So this was a plan you came up with together? You guys don't agree on anything."

"We are in agreement with Renee, and she says you're supposed to find avenues to connect."

"Yeah, well, glad you guys are all on the same page. But you have no idea how this feels for me."

"We're trying." Maya watched her mom's hands flex, her shoulders sink. "It sounded like she wanted you to tell your story."

"She wants to do another hero piece. They just want to sensationalize me."

"I never heard her say that."

Maya tripped on her thoughts. Hadn't she? "Well, what would I even say?"

"Just tell her how things have been getting better. Your new school, and . . ."

"Getting better—" Maya's hand twitched. Nearly whipped off her hat and showed Mom how much *better* things were. But Mom was sad enough already.

Mom's phone buzzed. She sighed and started typing something. "Sorry."

Besides, Mom was barely paying attention anyway. How could you not notice all the hats and scarves and bandannas? Because Maya was such a pro at espionage? Unlikely.

"Can I just *not* do this?" said Maya. "Please?"

"But"—Mom was going at her phone with both thumbs—"is this because *he's* there?"

"No."

"We should have made them switch him. I should have called the *Times*."

"I just said it's not him." Except was it?

"Well— Oh crap. Now your father's going to be late coming by with dinner."

"That's no big deal," said Maya.

Mom finally looked up, crossed her arms. Seemed to see her again. "It is, though. This is our fault. Splitting up. If it wasn't for that . . ." Tears welled up in her eyes. "You never even would have been in that mall."

Maya nearly screamed. "It has nothing to do with you!"

Mom sniffled. She looked away, and her expression caused a chill to run through Maya. Definitely regret.

"Look," said Maya, "I'm sorry, okay? I just can't do an interview right now."

Mom shook her head. "Your father was there, you know. You always say how you weren't a hero, but he watched you walk up to that boy, talk to him, and put your hands on the trigger. He heard you shout at everyone to get away. Aren't there any moments when you think back and see yourself doing something brave?"

"Not really."

Tears spilled over. "I see you that way every day."

The words slipped through Maya's armor, a mortal blow. Why couldn't she? *Because that's not what it was like. They don't know.* She hadn't saved anyone. Random chance saved them. If that bomb had worked like it was supposed to, there would have been no hands on the trigger. This house, or her school, could blow up just as easily as that office didn't. Someone could walk in, anytime anywhere, and detonate, or there could be a gas leak; a piece of satellite could fall from the sky. They'd all had dumb luck that day.

The landline rang again. Mom silenced the call. "I'll tell her it's not a good time." Her own phone buzzed.

"Just go already," said Maya.

"It's really an important meeting."

"Uh-huh."

"Maybe you should call Renee," said Mom, typing. "See what she thinks?"

"Why? She's just going to side with you. You're the one paying her."

"Technically I think our insurance is paying at this point. But I thought you liked her."

"I do."

Mom took a half step out. "Will you be okay alone while I'm gone?"

"Jesus, Mom, I'm not going to kill myself or anything."

"I know, I just . . ."

She doesn't know, Maya thought. *Not for sure.*

Do I know?

Yes! Fuck yes.

"Tell your father I said hello," Mom added. "I'll bring you something sweet from the launch party."

"Thanks."

*　*　*

Mom got home just before nine, bearing brownies. They topped them with ice cream and watched home-buying shows: the classic one followed by the international. Mom even put her phone aside for most of it.

"I got an email from the band teacher," Mom said during a commercial.

Maya tensed.

"She said jazz ensemble starts next Wednesday after school. She's hoping to see you at the first rehearsal, but she understands if you need more time to get up to speed with your classes."

"I'm not sure I want to do it."

"But you love drumming. And you're so good. It might give you something to focus on."

This sounded like more speak from the handbook.

"Are you saying I have to go?"

"I wish you would, that's all. So does your father."

"You guys are just a parenting super-duo these days."

Mom ate her ice cream.

For a while, Maya lost herself in the shows, enjoying the tours of clean, empty rooms, how the couples hemmed and hawed about bathroom features and ideal kitchen layouts. No baggage, no limitations. A fresh start.

And when she finally slept after midnight, she met the wolf in the mall like clockwork.

He walks into the DOL, which is somehow also a hotel near Disney, one they went to in middle school. Is that Goofy getting a new license? The wolf walks right up to her, and they join hands and release the trigger and there is a brilliant flash—

Only this time it is different. Maya feels the heat and fire, hears the screams, but as the blast roars and fades to smoke and ash, she's still standing there. Everyone else is gone. The DOL/hotel is destroyed, the remaining slabs of wall dripping with carnage. The roof has collapsed, and the sun filters in, making her squint. The wolf is still there too, except the mask is gone. It's just Eli. And he's smiling at her, and she smiles back, and they are alive, their chests heaving, hearts pounding, and he says:

We did it.

CHAPTER 7

ELI

September 12

"How was your day?" Detective Pearson asked as they pulled away from school. "Eli?"

He paused his music and looked up from his phone. *Fine.* "Fine," he said. He'd been working on this kind of thing with Dr. Maria: small talk.

"What do you say when someone hands you something?" she would ask.

Run. "Thank you."

"What do you say when someone seems upset?"

Hide. "What's wrong?"

"What do you say if you feel like you need help, in any way?"

Keep quiet. "Could you please help me?"

Pearson turned onto the busy street. "Had a chance to talk to anyone yet?"

What do you do when someone talks to you?

Nothing. Don't talk to anyone, or by God . . .

"Not really," said Eli.

"Well, it takes time. I think I saw you had art today?"

"Yeah. It was good." He'd made a pinch pot. It had ended up sort of avocado-shaped. Some of the burnt-colored clay was still under his nails.

"And your focus was okay?"

Eli shrugged. "Better." There were still moments when all the stimuli overwhelmed him. And some stretches that he really couldn't account for. That felt . . . blank.

"I finished my lunch," he added.

She patted his shoulder. "Here's to small victories."

That's not what she wants. You know what she's really after. But there had been no new memories, today or any time this week.

Eli opened his backpack and got the little plastic bag that held his medication. Popped the afternoon pill in his mouth and swallowed it dry.

They passed Red Mill Burgers. Its neon-red sign glowed extra-bright in the misty afternoon. Lots of teens in the line snaking out the door. More of them crowded at the bar that ran along the front windows, the glass fogged. They always flocked there the moment the bell rang. Laughing, hands flapping as they talked, play-punching and wrestling. It looked like fun.

You walk home from school and you get taken.

Other kids talked about going to the mall after school.

You blow up malls.

The movies on weekends.

Movies are dark and loud and windowless.

Maybe if he had someone to go with.

"Well, it sounds like it was a good day, all in all," said Pearson. "Nice and normal."

"Yeah," said Eli, putting on his headphones. *Nice and normal.* Except for the note in his pocket.

That wasn't normal at all.

The note was exactly the kind of thing he should be reporting to Pearson. That everyone all the way up to Homeland Security would want to know about.

And yet Eli breathed deep and, for the third day in a row, didn't say a word.

He had gym twice a week, on Mondays and Fridays right before lunch, which seemed to mean that whoever had left him the note knew his schedule. Stopping by the auditorium would be no big deal on the way to lunch.

But the wolf drawing meant more than that. How had they found out who he was? He hadn't told anyone, and he'd barely talked to anybody at school so far except this one girl Clara who he'd been paired up with a couple times in English and a teacher here or there.

Could it be from her? Maya knew who he was. He'd seen her a few times in the hall. She didn't look so good. Also he was probably the last person she wanted to see.

Maybe it's from him. Gabriel could have infiltrated the school somehow. Maybe he'd be waiting in the gym.

You knew I wouldn't stay gone forever, didn't you?

It had occurred to Eli that the anniversary of the DOL—*failure*—was approaching. Pearson and everyone else had asked him if October 26 was significant somehow. If Gabriel had ever said anything about it. Eli didn't quite remember—it wasn't like

Gabriel told him anything. Except that wasn't true. Gabriel had told him lots of things, but Dr. Maria had pointed out that all that stuff about Barons and the Purpose and Gabriel's and Jacob's roles in a great saga of the people was just a story. Maybe October 26 had some significance to whoever Gabriel—no one thought that was his real name—really was, but Eli didn't know. Either way, the march of the calendar toward that date was causing worry to grow in his gut.

We'll finish what we started.

Maybe that began this Friday, in the auditorium after gym. . . .

And yet, even if that was the case, Eli had made up his mind. He was going, no matter who might be there, because of the note's final line:

Let's hang out!

There was more silence in the crowded halls and cafeterias, in the moments before and after class when everyone around him was chatting, even in this car, seeing all the normal lives through the window. Whoever this person was, Eli wouldn't have to hide who *he* was. And assuming it wasn't actually Gabriel, and they really wanted to be his friend, he wasn't going to subject them to background checks and interviews from three branches of law enforcement. It might scare them off.

"You okay?" Pearson asked.

"What?" Eli pulled off his headphones.

"You were tapping your legs, like, really fast. Just drumming along?"

"Oh," said Eli. He noticed his heart was racing. "Yeah." He slid his headphones back on, jaw clenched, a surge of frustration welling up. Maybe it was time for everyone to stop watching his every move. He wasn't going to blow up, and he didn't remember anything!

Stay calm, Dr. Maria always said. But why? Everyone at school was always freaking out, wild swings of energy and emotion in all directions. Eli never did. Like the switches were broken. Maybe these moments were some small sign that he was getting better. It felt kinda good.

"Did you give any more thought to trying out for basketball?" Pearson asked as they turned onto his street.

"I wouldn't be any good at it." He'd played in the Boys & Girls Club league, before. He'd only been okay at it then.

"That's how Andrew, my oldest, talks about swim team. I said to him, how will you ever know if you don't try?"

Maybe.

"Well, I think you should at least consider it." Pearson stopped at the curb. "Have a good evening."

Eli got out of the car. "You too," he remembered to say.

As Pearson drove away, Eli looked up and down the street. *No idling cars, no lone men looming toward him.* He walked up the short path and let himself in the front door of their little house: three different keys for three separate locks. Mom had had the windows reinforced and a security system installed with little cameras that synced to her phone.

The TV was blaring when he entered but had paused by the time his eyes adjusted to the gloom.

Melissa sat up. She'd been lying sideways, a pillow under her head, her long legs draped over the edge of the couch. She wore workout shorts and a crimson hoodie. Hair back, chewing gum, tapping her phone, surrounded by her textbooks.

"Hey," she said.

Hey, Eli thought to say.

Her eyes met his. *What do you do when you greet someone? Smile and say hello.*

But Melissa had already turned toward the kitchen. "Mom, Eli's home."

How was your day?

Melissa clicked off the TV and stood, biting her lip. She gathered her books, her phone, and a bottle of some pink-colored tea.

What are you drinking? What show was that? How was that movie you went to last night?

She started toward the kitchen, then paused. "Was your day okay?"

Eli nodded.

Melissa smiled. "Two weeks down, right?"

Right.

"Okay. I'll be in my room."

"Please empty the dishwasher!" Mom called from down the hall.

"Ugh, right." Melissa detoured into the kitchen.

Eli kicked off his shoes, dropped his backpack on the couch, and followed her. He grabbed a protein bar from the box on the counter. Part of his fitness plan. Unwrapped it, watching Melissa gather a stack of plates from the dishwasher.

"Stop lurking over there," she said, turning to the cabinets. "It's weird when you just stare like that."

Sorry.

The thumping of the bed through the ceiling. Melissa's screams and sobs. The time or two early on when he'd tried to talk to her, climbing onto the back of the bed frame and whispering

84

at the ceiling. She'd never answered. And when Gabriel heard him, the punishment had been fierce.

Will you set her free if I do this?

During the hours in the DOL, surrounded by bomb technicians, Eli had cried not because of what he'd almost done but because of what he'd failed to do. If Gabriel was true to his word—he had always been painfully true to his word—then as Eli was standing there stuck with Maya, he was home punishing Melissa worse than ever before. Her screams haunted him in the ambulance, in the hospital room, as the doctors and nurses, counselors and detectives, arrived and left.

Until his mom had walked in alive—and Melissa right behind her. They'd paused at the foot of the bed, looking even more terrified of him than anyone yet . . . then rushed to him.

Something broke inside Eli then, when he thought there had been nothing left to break.

His mom had been alive. Melissa had been *fine*. All that time in the red dark . . . not only had he been weak and scared, he'd been stupid.

But Gabriel had shown him proof! A necklace he'd dropped at Eli's feet: *This is what your mom was wearing when I freed her.* His sister's favorite black concert T-shirt: *This is what she was wearing when I brought her here.*

Only later did Eli wonder: Who had really been in that room upstairs? Whose screams had those been? And was she still there?

There was no way for you to know, Dr. Maria had said.

And yet when he looked at Melissa, even a year later, it was still confusing.

Eli heard the clacking of his mom's keyboard from her bedroom down the hall. He approached on the balls of his feet and peered around the doorframe.

She sat at the little desk by her bed. Eli just glimpsed the dialogue box arrangement on her laptop. Another chat room. He craned his neck to get a closer look.

"Oh." She'd caught his reflection in the monitor. Her hand flashed to the touch pad. Chat room gone. Laptop closed. She swiveled and took off her glasses. "Hey." Rubbed at her eyes. "I was just about to come out."

Her hair was in a bun. It made the gray streaks at her temples catch the light. Made her look like Eli's grandmother Raquel, who used to squeeze him so hard. She'd passed away while he was in the red dark.

"What are you doing?" Eli asked.

"Just work stuff," Mom said, getting up. She'd been a nurse. Hadn't worked at all the first year he'd been gone. Now she was part-time in a dentist office. She never had to bring work home.

"You got a snack," she said, like she was checking it off. "Homework?" She put an arm around his shoulder and guided him back toward the kitchen.

"Not much. I had study hall."

She moved to the counter between the sink and the refrigerator. The plunk of a cork being removed. Poured herself a glass of red wine.

"Jeez, Mom," said Melissa, "starting early?"

"It's happy hour somewhere." Mom toasted them, an attempt at a smile, as if fighting weights at the corners of her mouth, and sipped. "Did you have a chance to talk to anyone today?" she said to Eli.

Eli crossed his arms. *Sure, because it's so easy. All I need is a chance.* "One kid," he lied.

Mom sipped again. Half the glass already gone. "Oh yeah, who's that?"

"Just a kid in science. I forget his name."

"Well, that's a start. And . . . rides home still going okay with Detective Pearson?"

I didn't remember anything.

A silence passed between them all.

Mom's gaze settled in the space between Eli and the counter. He wondered if she only drank when he was around. *I know you blame yourself,* he didn't say. *Not just for that day, but also because after I'd been gone a year or so, you gave up.* Or maybe the drinking was because he reminded her of what they'd had. What they'd never have again.

Mom hitched like she'd remembered something. "I have laundry to change." She refilled her glass and brushed by him, opening the door to the basement.

"She'll be down there awhile," said Melissa, putting the glasses away.

"What do you mean?" Eli grabbed the silverware basket from the dishwasher and opened the drawer.

"You don't have to do that," said Melissa.

It's fine. He started picking out the knives.

"Haven't you noticed that *the laundry* takes her at least a half hour?"

He hadn't. "What do you think she's doing?"

"Don't know. The wineglass is always empty by the time she comes up."

"She looks at weird stuff online," said Eli.

Melissa shrugged. "She's better than she was."

"Did you have classes today?"

"Just two on Wednesdays." She checked her watch and sighed. "I have to go to a study group tonight, though." Melissa commuted to the University of Washington. She'd nearly been valedictorian of her high school class. Stanford had been her dream; she'd gotten in with a scholarship and had been there just under two months when Eli had been found. She transferred back so she could help out.

Eli finished the silverware and reached for the two wineglasses.

"Hey, I said I got it." Melissa moved his hand away and held it tight. "I know you do this because you're confused."

"I'm not—"

"I saw the way you were looking at me before. It's one of those days, I get it."

It's—

"I don't know what it's like in your head, but I need you to remember that wasn't me in that house. The only thing I'm recovering from is losing a brother, and now he's back and he should go do his homework. I can handle the dishes."

Eli nodded and went to get his backpack. When he crossed the kitchen again, he didn't look at her. Kept his gaze down—

She caught him from behind and wrapped him in a hug.

"I love you, brother."

Eli smelled her hair.

Still heard her screaming.

"Xbox after dinner?"

"I thought you had to go."

"I do, but I'll have a little time."

"Sure."

* * *

Later that night, when Melissa had left and Mom had dozed off on the couch in the flicker of some detective drama, Eli made his way into the kitchen and washed his lunch bowl and spoon, dried them, and returned them to his backpack. After that, he crept into Mom's room and woke up her computer. He'd figured out her password a while ago. And he knew that while she remembered to close browser windows, she didn't always clear her search history.

It only took him a second to find the chat room she'd been in.

Sparklebrite.info *The best place for whatever!*

Mom's screen name had been LookinforLuv. The thread was titled Meeting Place.

Rustling from the living room.

Eli skimmed quickly.

LookinforLuv: I love talking with the youngs. I'm just not sure the best place to find them.

Freaktastic7: HangSpace is good. Lots of tweens. Just pretend to be one.

Mouthful33: Go on ChatLite. Say you're Justin Bieber. In the meantime, I've got a nice young one you can suck.

Andrea_Overlord: Harder to find boys. If that's what you're after.

LookinforLuv: What about face to face? Any experience with setting that up? Any tips?

Puppylove: Haha nice try, cop. Why not just arrest who you want to fuck? Cuff 'em and stuff 'em!

LookingforLuv: I'm no cop. Fuck the cops. Just want to find a good spot.

Jesus, Mom. Eli's heart raced. He could hear Gabriel laughing, stretching the garden hose. *She'll never find me this way.*

The TV clicked off. Eli closed up and darted out of the room.

Mom shuffled into the kitchen, carrying her empty wineglass. Eli was there, getting some bread and butter.

"Having a snack?"

Yes. He'd never told anyone that this was what Gabriel gave him each night, but it helped him sleep.

Bread and butter could just be bread and butter.

"Get all your homework done?"

"Yeah." Eli looked at her. Eyes heavy behind her glasses, wearing her Stanford hoodie, her hair down, all those gray ones in front like tangled springs. *You need to stop,* he wanted to say.

She kissed the back of his head. "I'll check the doors and make sure the alarm is on. Good night."

Good night.

As he headed up the stairs, he heard the wineglass filling.

In his room, he pulled his blankets and pillow off his bed and arranged them on the floor. As he took off his clothes, he removed the note from his pocket.

Let's hang out!

He ran his finger over the words, over the wolf drawing. Then he tucked it away.

On the floor, he huddled against the side of the bed, out of the light from the window, curling up, making himself as small as he could.

CHAPTER 8

MAYA

September 13

Someone finally laughed at her in AP biology lab.

It had probably been going on for a while when Maya finally returned to the surface. How long had she been gone? Her fingers wrapped in hair just above her neck, each sharp tear like a firework in her sky.

Three . . . two . . . one . . .

She checked the clock: fifteen minutes since she could remember a damn thing about the surface world. And only now was her heart starting to calm down.

That was a bad one. What had even triggered her? *Try to walk yourself back through the stimuli,* Renee had said. *Go slow. Stay neutral. You're just observing.*

Okay, one thought per breath: She looked at the floor. Carpets sometimes conjured the puke brown of the DOL, but these gray-and-white tiles were nothing like that. Mr. Garcia had been going over details of the phylum Annelida and the giant worm they were about to dissect. There had been that message from Vice Principal Linden: *Excuse the interruption. Teachers, please dismiss members of the Boys and Girls blah blah something something.* Before that: the bell—

That was it. The fake-bell tone that sounded before an announcement. It was like the next-customer bell at the DOL. Close enough, anyway, that if it hit Maya's brain at just the wrong moment, it could bypass the rational side, right to the primal center, and detonate the bomb all over again. It didn't matter that she knew it wasn't the same bell, or that she knew she wasn't going to blow up in biology class.

As if moments like seeing Eli or talking to Tamara weren't fraught enough, there were also these sensory triggers that struck without warning. Others included the sight of anyone's driver's license (she'd still never gotten hers); the smell of grape lip balm (she hadn't been wearing it that afternoon, but maybe someone nearby had?); the song "I'm Your Bad Idea" by that band Dangerheart (she was pretty sure it had been playing in the DOL).

None of them set her off every time, but any one of them could. How many times had that bell rung so far this year without it being a problem? And then, boom. She was extra-susceptible today too: out of Serenitab and still two days from the doctor, plus no Dr. Pom, as she and Janice had been in different classes since lunch. Pulling had been the only way to survive the storm.

Only now, her classmates had noticed.

Maya looked behind her. Jefferson, Cody, and Stella, all eyeing her and whispering to one another.

"You okay?" Janice asked beside her.

"Fine," said Maya.

They sat on squeaky stools at a high black table. Between them was an aluminum tray with a layer of bright blue rubber stuff inside. Atop that, pinned at both ends, a long, thick segmented worm from Africa or something, striped yellow, white, and black. The gag-inducing smell of formaldehyde draped like a wet towel over the room.

"Two soccer jocks and a field hockey slut," Janice whispered. "The holy trinity of cruel."

Another whisper behind them, another little laugh.

Janice twisted around. "Fuck off."

The three hyenas grinned.

Maya's pulse spiked, her face reddening. Apparently, the question had been: how long could high school teens keep from mocking someone who'd been through near-death trauma? The answer: just over ten months, twenty-two days. Maybe it would have been longer if she'd stayed at Garfield, where everyone really knew what she'd been through. It had been a good family, better than her own; that was the real bomb, her family, blowing up and landing her here.

Didn't these assholes have their own important shit to worry about? But that didn't seem to be how it worked. Kind of the opposite.

"You'll need to be careful with your scalpels," Mr. Garcia was saying. "We don't want to damage the delicate internal structures, in particular the multiple hearts."

Maya checked her lap: a tangle of hair there. Hair on the floor too.

She pressed the clump between her shoes—really by all standards a very productive session!—lifted it to her fingers, and stuffed it, along with the hair in her lap, into her shoulder bag.

"Packing up so soon, Ms. Abrams?" said Mr. Garcia.

She flushed. "Sorry."

Fresh snickers behind them.

Mr. Garcia looked at Maya with a flat expression, like she was just another kid who he expected to pay attention. It was kind of nice, actually. Maya figured that she'd been a topic in the staff meetings before school started, and in most classes it felt like she could probably dance naked on her desk singing at the top of her lungs while dousing herself in mustard and her teachers would just calmly try to talk around her. Mr. Garcia acted like she wasn't completely beyond hope.

But I am, she thought. *I so am.* That said, science used to be her thing, and she wanted to prove it to him. Tried to sit still, just be here. . . .

"Stop." Janice grabbed her hand, which had been making its way into her hair again, and guided it under the table and slid it between her thighs. Squeezed them together. "That'll keep you busy," she whispered with a smile.

Maya smiled back but also checked to make sure Mr. Garcia hadn't noticed.

"Don't worry about him," said Janice. "He doesn't know what you're going through. Let Janice help."

Maya nodded. She moved her hand up and down between Janice's legs.

"Mmm."

With her free hand, Maya copied the diagram of the worm. The location of its hearts, its digestive organs.

The door opened. Her head popped up, and she pulled her hand from Janice's lap.

One of their classmates, returning from the bathroom.

"Relax, it's just a door." Janice tugged on Maya's hand again, but Maya resisted, instead using it to spin her notebook sideways as she continued the diagram.

Janice exhaled pointedly. She shifted her body and her shoulder bumped Maya's. Lightly, but she still got the message.

You don't want me getting bored.

Mr. Garcia talked for a little longer, and then they began the dissection. Janice pulled on the light blue latex gloves, snapping them loudly against her wrists. Maya put hers on quietly.

"You okay?" Maya asked.

"Fine." Janice ran the scalpel down the length of the worm's body. The skin slipped apart, revealing the creature's gray insides. The classroom burbled around them, clichéd squeals here and there.

Maya handed Janice a pushpin, which Janice used to stab the worm skin into the rubbery blue medium, holding it open. "I'm sorry I'm such a mess," Maya said, handing her another.

Janice pinned the other side of the skin. "What good am I if I can't even keep you excited?" she muttered.

"Oh, it's not that. I just felt self-conscious."

"Well, that's stupid." Janice started running the scalpel back and forth beside the worm, carving an X shape, shreds of blue gel flicking this way and that. "Can I get a Serenitab?"

"Sorry, I'm out."

The scalpel dug deeper. "Figures. When's your next resupply?"

"At the end of the week. I don't get that many," Maya added. "You could probably get a prescription, you know. It's pretty easy, just talk about how depressed you are."

Janice shook her head. "I don't need a *prescription*."

"Oh." Maya flushed, trying to dig her thumb through the gloves and get at the wrecked skin around her index fingernail.

Janice huffed. "It's just my parents are still being assholes about school."

"What happened?"

"So, I told them about my friend Abbye's visit to NYU, how amazing it was. And they're still like, *It's so expensive.* They said I should think about taking a year off to earn some money, like I'm going to waste a year of my life because they're being cheap."

"Maybe you can get a scholarship," Maya said. She was taking next year off; the whole idea of applying for colleges had seemed like too much when she could barely handle school. Plus, they needed more money, and her grades had likely slipped out of scholarship territory at this point.

"Don't be stupid," said Janice. "It's not like I'm an Abbye."

"Yes, you are." Maya hadn't meant to sound *stupid*. "It's just because it's so far. Is there a good program that's closer?"

Janice laughed. "Nowhere closer is good enough." The scalpel had started to scrape the metal beneath the blue medium. "It *has* to be NYU or Juilliard or what's the fucking point?" Tears rimmed her eyes and she brushed angrily at them. "They make me feel so worthless, like my dreams are shit. It makes me want to die." She lifted the scalpel from the tray and ran the edge of the blade across the back of her wrist. A thin white line.

"Don't say that." Maya watched the scalpel, her heart rate rising.

Janice sniffled. "You must feel that way sometimes. Like you're trapped. Like it's never going to get better."

"All the time." There were moments, now and then, when Maya felt like she no longer even had dreams. Not about the future, anyway. Next year was supposed to be the beginning of the rest of her life, and yet Maya couldn't picture anything.

Janice smiled at her. "You're the only one who gets it. Maybe that's why we found each other. I think if I didn't have you I might be dead already."

She carefully etched a ghostly white heart onto the back of her wrist, then the letters *J + M* inside it. Drew blood in two places. She moved the scalpel over to Maya's wrist, the lethal tip whispering against her skin, starting the same shape.

Maya put her hand on Janice's, lifted it. For a moment, Janice resisted, the scalpel shuddering. . . . Janice let go. Maya took the scalpel and laid it down. She noticed Mr. Garcia eyeing them, but he turned away.

"It's okay," Maya said quietly, but her skin was prickling with swords, her hair wailing to be plucked. She swallowed hard, a metallic taste in her mouth. It felt like this conversation had been sucking them into some kind of darkness. Janice was so much stronger, had so much more going for her. If *she* couldn't see a way out . . .

"Oh, look." Janice suddenly broke into a smile. She pried the worm skin farther open with her finger, revealing the line of ring-shaped hearts. "Do you think this means that worms fall in love harder or, like, each heart loves a different person?"

"Hmm?" Maya's thoughts staggered. *Keep up! This is how normal people act. They get better. Unlike you.*

But did they swing this fast?

"Maybe the five hearts mean you get five true loves," said Janice brightly. "Of course, that's not enough. Or you can love five people at the same time. I like that better." She ran her rubber-coated finger over Maya's hand. "Make that four. I'd need two for you."

"Ha." Maya told herself to smile, instructed her lips to peck Janice's cheek, and yet inside, she counted: *Three . . . two . . . one . . .*

* * *

"Walk me to one-acts rehearsal?" Janice asked at the end of class.

"Ah, I wish," said Maya. "I have an appointment." She made a show of rolling her eyes.

Janice huffed. "You *always* have appointments."

They walked out into the hall and kissed.

"Are you sure you're okay?" Maya asked.

Janice waved her hand. "Peachy. I'd prove it to you if you'd just come down to the costume closet with me."

Maya swallowed a fresh bout of nerves. "I wish I could. Rain check?" She braced for Janice's reaction.

But Janice just grinned wickedly. "I'm going to hold you to that."

As Maya headed up the hall, her body unwound. Janice was a lot to handle. But wasn't that unfair of her to think when she was so much more?

Except it wasn't just that: Maya had been lying to Janice. She *did* have an appointment . . . later. Right now, she had something she needed to do alone.

She pushed through the busy halls to her locker, quickly changed her books, and made for the main entrance. With each step, her nerves wound tighter. She rounded a corner—

There he was.

Maya slowed and let the rush of kids flow around her. Had to get the timing just right. Eli was pulling books out of his backpack, and now his jacket. Weird that he didn't keep it in his locker. He closed the door and started up the hall. Maya checked over her shoulder—for Janice? Yeah, for Janice—and then followed, staying a few groups behind him.

Second time she'd done this. Yesterday after lunch, but the halls were always too crowded. *And what exactly are you doing?* Everyone would be so mad if they knew. Her parents, the principal, Renee.

But it was that dream the other night. Nearly a year of the same old nightmares, bolting awake in a panic, her death fresh in her mind—and then something different:

We did it, he'd said.

Maya had written it down in her phone, and since then she'd looked at it so many times that she felt like Eli really had said it to her.

They'd held on to each other and lived. Which made no sense because the bomb still went off around them. *That's because it wasn't real.* Yeah, but neither were all the other times she'd blown up and those didn't stop her from losing chunks of time and hair and skin. And why a new dream now? Having Eli at school was supposed to make things worse.

Whatever it was, she felt like she needed to tell him about it. She'd probably sound completely crazy. And how would he react? She wasn't even sure if he'd noticed her in the halls yet. . . .

But still.

Eli exited through the main doors by the office. Maya paused at the top of the steps and waited, watching him cross the parking area. He bypassed the line of school buses, didn't head for the student lot either. So far, so good.

Bright sun shone in her eyes on a sleepy fall angle, but still offered a faint warmth. Students rushed by her on either side, all the non-messed-up, non-seeing-explosions kids hurtling down the stairs, the afternoon before them full of possibility.

Maya started down the steps. *This is going to help. See? I'm doing something.* Who was she talking to? Mom, Dad, Janice, Renee—all of them? But then why was she nearly hyperventilating, her fingers shaking and digging at one another in her pockets?

Eli was on the sidewalk that paralleled the driveway, heading toward the school exit. Maya crossed the drop-off area. The tops of the maple trees along the drive were just beginning to hint at reds and oranges, their bellies still a parched green. That little note of decay in the air. Fall smell, one of Maya's favorite things, and yet her shivers intensified because fall was the DOL blowing up—

No. Stay here.

Eli stopped at a bench along the drive, the tennis courts behind him. He sat, hunched in the baggy dark blue Seahawks hoodie he wore almost every day, his jacket in his lap. He slipped on big red headphones and tapped his phone.

Maya crossed the deep green grass between the student lot and the sidewalk. *Ow*—she found strands of hair between her fingers. *Dammit, hands, I thought you were in pockets!* She tucked the hair into her jeans. It seemed gross to leave it in this lovely grass.

She reached the sidewalk. Close now. Some girls on the tennis courts, but those green wind screens would limit their view. Nobody else around except buses and cars passing, but everyone would be in their own after-school world. . . .

Staring at Eli, and with every step she didn't see the wolf mask, didn't picture the DOL, didn't blow up.

We did it.

She didn't breathe either.

Naked and knife-edged and aware. Heart racing, legs tingling, and yet she wasn't drifting away, no Serenitab fog, no alcohol glaze. Instead, everything seemed immediate, like her senses were turned up to full strength: the slight breeze, the cobalt sky, the swish of the grass beneath her sneakers, the crunch of tires on the pavement, the spoiled banana smell of the trash can she'd just passed, the rotten exhaust as Brett Hornigan's ironic AMC Eagle growled by.

She felt exposed, no, pinned, like that worm to its blue medium, stabbed to the world at both ends, and with some of her hearts terrified and some hopeful but all of them pounding.

Look up, she thought at Eli. *I'm here.*

The pop of tennis balls being hit, the squeal of sneakers.

Come on.

A stereo behind her somewhere in the parking lot, the huge loping beat vibrating the stop sign just as she walked past.

I'm right here.

Pink gum plastered to the road, imprinted with tire tread. Leaf crunch beneath her sneaker.

Fuck, she was terrified.

But still not blowing up.

So close now. Eli dead ahead, a fixed point. A certainty. If he looked up now, he would definitely see her.

She felt a sting from her pocket—a cuticle torn open.

Hey, she thought to say. No, it would be too loud. Just a little closer—

"Why don't you bend over for these balls?"

Maya halted.

A group of boys had appeared, prowling along the tennis court fence. One of them had stopped and pressed his crotch against the chain-link fence, motioning to the tennis player girls.

A door banged open across the street. The football team, jogging out from their locker room, cleats clacking on the asphalt.

Shit! Too many witnesses. But he was right there! The boy whose hand she had held and lived—

That was just your stupid dream!

But NO! Contrary to the games her brain played, it was also true. They'd held on and survived that day in the DOL. *He's the proof,* she thought. Concrete proof that she was alive.

So who cared about the people around them! What did they know? Maya started toward Eli again—

Her phone buzzed. She almost ignored it, but it pulsed. Someone calling.

She fished it from her pocket. The caller was identified by three skull-and-crossbones emojis: Tamara from Chalk. Maya had put the number in her contacts just to be sure she'd never answer. She gripped the phone, wanted to crush it, then silenced the call, shoved it away—

Heard a light whine of brakes.

A blue car had pulled up.

Eli standing, opening the passenger door, getting in.

Pulling away.

Wait. . . .

Maya watched him go, fingers creeping to hair.

The breeze died. Grass wilting. Blue sky leaching to gray.

CHAPTER 9

ELI

September 14

He stood at the edge of the auditorium entrance. Dark inside, except for the red light from a lamp that curled over the control board, in the center of the rows of red-padded chairs. Rows that sloped down to a wood stage. A red curtain. Heavy and closed.

A large room. The silence larger.

Eli stepped in.

You knew I wouldn't stay away forever.

Wound tight, palms drumming softly on his legs, the pain in his shoulder flaring.

But the note.

Let's hang out!

He moved toward the control board. Looked over his shoulder, pictured Gabriel's silhouette, the door swinging shut behind him, plunging them into the red dark.

Don't give him more power than he has, Dr. Maria often said.

Carpeted floor. His slow footsteps making round airy beats.

The note had been friendly. Hadn't it?

Still, he should have told someone. Anyone.

And yet, even just now in gym class: picked second to last for handball teams, standing against the red padded wall, just him and one other leftover. The other kid was scrawny. Eli's time at the gym had given him some definition, muscles that might suggest muscular. But it didn't change how he *seemed*.

"That kid, I guess," one of the captains had finally said, pointing at Eli.

After that, he'd just drifted along the edges, never getting passed to. Handball was sort of like basketball? *Ask someone how to play,* any one of these boys brushing past him, but who was safe? And if he got it wrong, or if, when he tried, his voice decided to stay silent, then he'd really stand out. *Ask the teacher.* Except Mr. Niles, *Coach* to some of the boys, never looked at him, and really he liked those boys best, always joking with them, slapping their backs approvingly: *Way to go after it. Get in there. Take that shot. Make a move.* Those were the gym class affirmations. If you wanted to be passed to, to be noticed, you had to act.

Like coming here to the auditorium. *Make a move, go after it.* A year spent standing still. Okay, here he was.

Also, the note had asked him to, and doing what you were told was how you avoided the garden hose.

Or how you almost got killed.

It was confusing. It was both.

Eli reached the middle of the auditorium. Slid between the

seats and stood beside the control board. He looked at the hundreds of dials, wondering what they could all possibly do.

Something banged behind him.

"You made it!"

Eli squinted up into the dark, above the steep rows of chairs along the rear of the auditorium. A door had opened. Someone coming down.

Not Gabriel-sized.

Another kid, dropping down the staircase two steps at a time and jogging over.

Smiling. Familiar.

"Hey," he said, and laughed. "You're looking at me like you have no idea who I am."

Eli's pulse quickened. "From lunch," he said. The boy at his table.

The boy made a gun with his index finger and thumb and shot Eli. "Exactly." Moved the same hand toward him, fingers now flat. "I'm Graham."

Eli looked at Graham's hand. *He wants to shake.* He'd been part of handshakes with his friends, way back when, but since the red dark, people never really offered him anything as casual and friendly as that. Either they hugged him with a force like they were still afraid of losing him or they stood at a distance like he might still be strapped with explosives. Even people who didn't know his past did this.

Eli stuck out his hand. Would the shake be something complicated, with different grips or—but it went fine. Up and down a few times and then done. Graham's skin sorta clammy.

"Good to meet you, sir."

"You too," said Eli.

106

Graham had light green eyes and long, dark brown hair that he kept pushing out of his eyes. His hair had a glint to it, like he hadn't washed it in a while, and there was one long red streak down the middle. He wore a black T-shirt with a smiling clown who was holding a chain saw and had just decapitated a unicorn. The scene held in a spotlight, blood everywhere.

"Are you a Freak?"

What?

"The band." Graham pointed to his shirt. "Guess you wouldn't know about that. Freaks are fans of Sideshow Fantasy. They're from Sacramento. Got big while you were . . . you know." Graham moved past Eli to the control board. He started sliding faders and turning knobs. Lights illuminated the curtain, spots at different angles coming from the ceiling. "You're probably wondering how I know who you are."

"Who do you think I am?"

"You don't have to whisper," said Graham. "There's nobody here. That's the beauty of this place. Perfectly serene." He closed his eyes and inhaled deeply, puffing out his chest. "Hear that? None of the stupid conversations, the dumb chatter. It's like everyone else in the world is gone. No more idiots. Just us." He blinked and brushed the hair from his eyes again. "Anyway, yeah, I know you." He smiled at Eli. "You're the big bad wolf."

Oh.

"No, come on, I'm kidding." Graham reached over and shook Eli's forearm. "Sorry, that's probably not funny, now that I think about it." He looked down at his feet, grin fading. "Sometimes what's funny to me doesn't really translate to everyone else. It is you, though, right? The kid from Cedar Gate Mall?"

Eli looked at the door. But leaving would just confirm it. He could try to deny it . . . but then maybe he was sick of being a different person all the time. "Yeah, that was me. I mean, sort of."

"Sort of?"

You were operating under extreme duress, Dr. Maria had said. *Your core self was locked away.*

"It was me, but not me like I am now."

Graham pulled a lever on the side of the board. A loud click echoed through the auditorium, followed by a heavy hum. The curtain began to part, the red fabric sweeping to either side and revealing the stage, empty except for some panels of half-painted scenery that depicted an old-time kitchen and living room.

"You mean 'cause you were brainwashed," he said. "I heard a bunch of experts talking about you on TV one time, about the tactics for training a child soldier."

Eli tugged at his backpack straps.

"Sorry," said Graham. "You probably don't want to talk about it. And they haven't found the guy yet, have they?"

"No."

Graham began sliding a row of faders, one at a time. Lights bloomed, illuminating the stage, the back wall. "Well, when they do, they should tie him up and cut his dick off, then strap *him* with explosives."

Eli didn't respond.

"Would you want to do it?" Graham asked, still working. "There we go. . . . Nice."

"What's nice?" said Eli.

Graham pointed to the stage. "Mr. McNaulty wanted me to swap out the front stage-left floodlight for a softer color. He's the

head of the AV department. I guess Ms. Mays—she's theater—
said the lights were too intense. What a bitch. And of *course* she
doesn't really get how the lighting actually works. Just likes to
snap her dumb fat fingers."

Eli looked at the banks of lights hanging down from the high
ceiling. "How did you get up there?" He pictured an enormous
ladder, but that didn't seem safe.

Graham motioned toward that door he'd come down from.
"There are catwalks in the ceiling. You're supposed to wear a
harness that hooks on to safety wires, but I've been doing this
since freshman year. I can take you sometime. It's pretty cool."

"Okay."

"Actually, once you're up in the roof, you can kinda get anywhere in the school." Graham's eyes gleamed. "The field hockey
locker room is particularly good."

Oh.

Graham's smile disappeared again. He pushed more faders
up and down. The different lights grew brighter, then softer. Eli
thought the board was sort of like a brain. Controls for thoughts
and actions and feelings. Turn the knob for speaking. Press a button to release a chemical. Slide down the fader for a memory. He
pictured wooden sets in his mind: one painted like the red dark,
another painted like his bedroom, another like the DOL.

"Curses." Graham pulled a headlamp from his pocket and
dropped to his knees. He slipped on the light and craned his neck
under the board.

"What's wrong?"

"One of the spots burned out. I just changed those fucking
bulbs last month! Must be a loose fader connection." Graham

grunted, reaching up into the guts of the board. "So, would you want to?"

"Want to what?"

"I think I got it." Graham stood. "You know, be the one to kill that sick bastard who kidnapped you."

"Oh." Images tore through Eli's head: hitting Gabriel with the bucket of waste, grabbing the end of the hose and pulling him over, pushing him down the escalator at the mall, and after each move, running for it. But then other times he imagined staying; instead of dropping the bucket, swinging again and again; instead of flinging the hose, wrapping it around Gabriel's neck; pushing him not down the escalator but over the railing. The sound of choking, of a snapping neck, of a skull hitting the mall floor and splattering—his heart started to hammer.

"Well, I'd do it for you," said Graham, "if we ever had the chance." He tried the faders again. "Shit. Will you do me a favor and move these five up and down, one at a time, when I tell you?"

"Okay."

Graham ducked under the board. "Try the first one."

Eli slid the fader and the light glowed brighter, then softer. He felt his heart spiking, his mouth getting dry. *How did you—*
"How did you find out about me?"

"Next one," said Graham. "Honestly, I just got lucky when you sat at my table. Though I have to admit, I was obsessed with that mall story last fall. I basically read everything there was to read. Did you know there were blogs that broke down all the available pictures from inside? There was even one that got stills from the DOL's security cameras. Some bloggers thought they'd identified your kidnapper; others were trying to say that the bombing was actually a government conspiracy. There's even one thread that thinks that girl who stopped you was actually your kidnapper's daughter or something."

That girl. Flash of her hand out of nowhere. Of her terrified face. Maya. The way she sat there in the ambulance, staring into the floor, shivering, blood on her fingers.

"Did you hear me?"

"What?"

"I said, she goes here, doesn't she?"

"Yeah." Eli had only seen her a handful of times in the halls, always from a distance. Always wearing that hat. Most days it was easy to believe she existed in some parallel universe. He still hadn't even seen the whole school yet. Heard there was a pool somewhere. And a garage where kids worked on cars. Parallel universes seemed likely.

But she showed up in his dreams all the time. He'd be stumbling around the red dark, searching for his sister, running from Gabriel's looming shadow, and Maya would appear, bloody and covered in dirt from doing God knows what. She'd show up as if their dream worlds overlapped, and she'd look at him and say, *Come on* or *What the hell?* like he was interrupting.

But then she always took his hand.

"I'm not allowed to talk to her."

"Well, from what I've seen of her, you don't want to. Try fader three."

Eli did. "What do you mean?"

"She's just kind of a mess. Is it really true that she stopped you from setting off the bomb?"

"Well, it malfunctioned first."

"Ah, that makes more sense."

But then she stopped me.

More than that, actually. At one point, standing there in the DOL, surrounded by chaos, he'd been shaking so hard, his muscles ready to quit, that he'd nearly given up.

Maya had gripped his hands tighter and said, "I got you."

It was the first time he'd really believed in something since sometime before, since he couldn't even remember when. She still said it now and then in his dreams, when she took his hand: *I got you.*

"Hello up there. Fader four."

Eli pushed it up.

"Bang, that's the one." Graham emerged from beneath the board. "So, it wasn't, was it?"

"Wasn't what?"

"A conspiracy. Like you weren't actually trained by the federal government or something, were you? I guess you couldn't tell me if you were."

Eli felt cold trickles of sweat on the insides of his arms. "It was just him." *And me,* he immediately thought, but Dr. Maria had been firm: *not you.* Only Gabriel. Eli had been just a tool. An instrument.

"A lone wolf," said Graham, nodding. "That always seems like the best way, if you want to get something done. No one to rat on you, no one to get cold feet."

Dampness on the inside of the mask. "Maybe."

"Except it didn't work." Graham tucked his headlamp away. "So maybe a duo is better. Strength in numbers, you know? Each one keeps the other from wussing out."

"Did you know someone who was there?" Eli asked.

"What do you mean?"

Just that you know so much about it.

"Oh, the mall," Graham continued. "Nah, I just find stuff like that fascinating. I think about it, you know? When you have that feeling like you'd want to kill yourself." He slid a fader, a green light igniting and darkening. "But to take people with you, to make a statement like that, one people would actually notice. It seems like the only way to get the world's attention these days." He paused and looked at Eli, then shrugged. "But it sounds like you didn't really know what you were doing."

I was trying to escape. I was saving my sister.

"Sorry," said Graham, "it's probably not cool for me to be talking to you about this."

"I don't know," said Eli. He felt on edge, and yet also it was maybe nice to have someone to talk to.

"Anyway," said Graham, "I wasn't completely sure that you were, you know, *you*, until you showed up just now. I didn't want to say anything at lunch, with so many people around. By the way, thanks for not handing over my note to the cops or anything."

"Who says I didn't?" The second the comment left his lips, Eli wanted to take it back. Sarcasm. *A smart tongue gets the belt.* Where had that even come from?

Graham looked at him sideways, and then burst into laughter. "Holy crap, you just scared me."

Eli smiled too. "Sorry."

"No, it's a good thing. Damn, Eli, you have a real poker face. Stone-cold killer."

Eli's smile faded.

"Aw, don't take it like that. Man, sorry." Graham hit his palm to his forehead. "I'm a moron. That's just an expression, but I meant it as a compliment. Most kids are such wimps. So scared all the time. That's why they act all the shitty ways they do. But you're pretty tough."

"Thanks." *Tough?* He'd been weak, a captive. Powerless. How had he been tough? Just by surviving?

Graham ran each of the faders up and down one more time. "Nice. All set." He looked at his wrist, where he was wearing a big, retro-looking watch. "We've still got time to get lunch if we hurry. Want to come with me?"

"Sure. Do we need a pass?"

Graham slapped his pocket. "Got one. Tech Squad gets you all kinds of privileges." Graham looked around the auditorium and sighed. "There's definitely a reason for you being here, Eli. I don't think it's an accident. It feels like fate."

Eli tensed. *The Purpose led me to you.* Hands grabbing him . . .

"I don't mean like *God* did it or anything," Graham went on. "But you ending up at this school, at this time. We were definitely meant to meet." He grabbed his backpack from a chair behind them and started for the door.

Eli didn't move. His heart pounding.

"Coming?" said Graham over his shoulder.

Eli caught up. "You won't tell anyone, will you?"

"Promise. You can trust me." Graham held out his hand again. The shake was easier this time. "There's no one worth telling in this stupid place anyway."

They left the auditorium together.

114

"Are you free this weekend?" Graham asked as they walked up the hall.

"I don't know."

"'Cause there's this video game trade show at Seattle Center. We should go. Think you could?"

"I mean, maybe." Eli felt a nervous flutter inside. "I'll have to ask."

"Cool. There are all these stations where you can demo new games and VR, and food stands too."

Eli half listened. He'd begun to notice eyes turning toward him in a way they hadn't before. A girl glancing at them and whispering to her friend with a hand over her mouth. A guy slapping his buddy's arm and then both of them chuckling.

As they passed through one of the main intersections, Graham got bumped hard in the shoulder, spinning him halfway around. Eli saw the culprit, a guy with floppy curly hair, wearing a puffy vest, walking with another guy and a girl. All skinny, all dressed in blacks and grays, the girl with peacock-colored hair. The boy with the curly hair put a hand over his mouth and said something in a weird voice, almost like an animal call.

"Frreakerr!"

The other two laughed. Another chuckle from somewhere in front of them.

"Shut up!" Graham shouted over his shoulder.

The boy half turned, still walking, and grinned.

Then a response call, one hyena to another across the savanna: *"Frreak boyy!"*

Girls side-eyeing.

Trio of dudes looming.

Graham hunched over, a balloon deflating inside his chest.

"Just ignore them," he muttered, head down, quickening his pace. At the same time, he made a coughing motion and shouted into his elbow: "Mateo's a bitch!"

"What did you say?" the floppy-haired boy called from behind. Eli saw him surge against the crowd in their direction. "Say it to my face!"

Graham kept walking.

"Say it to my face, Freaker!"

Murmurs and snickers all around them.

Eli gripped his backpack straps. He wanted to disappear, unmake this moment. He pictured exploding. Making the entire hallway silent and still.

They are all sheep.

But what was he? Stupid, scared, confused . . .

And then they were through it. A quieter stretch of hallway.

"Fucking assholes," Graham spat at the floor.

Eli blinked. Told himself to relax. "Who were they?"

"Now you know Mateo and his new dickbag swim team friends. Mateo used to be on Tech Squad too, but he caught the jock disease."

Graham tapped his shirt. "God forbid you don't listen to their corporate mall rock."

"They don't like Sideshow Fantasy?"

"Mateo *used* to. Now it's like his brain had devolved." Graham was quiet until they were in the lunch line. "Freaks are all about being unique, not *conforming*," he said. "That's one thing you have to get used to in this place: all the assholes who try to act cool but are really just insecure."

Yeah. Eli half listened. He was trying to choose between the chicken sandwich and the mac and cheese.

"That's why they band together in cliques. They really fear the brilliant ones like us, who are brave enough to be alone."

A lone wolf.

Eli pointed to the chicken sandwich. "And some fruit, please," he said to the lunch lady. It was getting a little easier.

They sat together at what was maybe now their table. Graham started digging into his mac and cheese. Eli looked at his food: the sandwich, the fruit, the container of vanilla yogurt. He'd left his backpack on the floor, because nobody brought their backpack to lunch. *Nobody else eats out of a bowl either.*

Graham motioned to his hair. "This streak is one of the ways that Freaks identify each other. Sideshow gets a bad rap for fans having violent mosh pits at shows, and lighting off fireworks and stuff, but that's all bullshit. People blame them for inspiring assaults and robberies too, but it's only a few fans. Besides, it's our society that's corrupt. Their music encourages us to see things clearly, not to just lie down and take it."

Eli mixed up his yogurt and took a bite.

"Those of us who are smart enough to see it can't be expected to just go along like sheep."

Eli winced. Behind his eyelids, the red dark.

"You all right?" Graham was looking at him with concern.

Focus! *I am not in that room. I am sitting here having lunch with my friend, just like everyone else.*

"It's gotta be weird," said Graham. "All of this."

Eli nodded.

"I'm really glad you came to the auditorium. It must have sucked having no one to talk to."

Yeah. Eli looked around. "I have to be careful. . . ."

117

"Oh, totally. Top secret." Graham glanced at the other tables. "Hidden in plain sight." He smiled. "You know, I bet if we ask Mr. McNaulty, he can get you on Tech Squad. I mean, if you want."

"That would be cool," said Eli, and felt like he meant it.

CHAPTER 10

MAYA

September 19

There he was again.

She'd given it almost a week since her last attempt. Just to be sure that nobody saw a pattern. But she had observed from a distance that he got picked up from that same spot every afternoon, and so this time, she'd left nothing to chance. Bolted from bio, straight through the side doors, right to Eli's bench. Sat down, out of breath, legs tingling, got out her math homework. It would look like pure coincidence.

And now here he came, out the main doors—

With some other kid. A gaunt, straggly-haired boy in an oversized black T-shirt even though it was fifty and raw outside. The boy's hands moving up and down as he described something, Eli nodding. They reached the bottom of the steps and turned in the other direction. Crossed the drop-off area and disappeared through the doors by the gym.

Maya's head jerked as hair tore free.

She sat there for another moment, then dragged herself up and headed for the band room.

* * *

A snare drum was still a snare drum.

Out of tune, yes. Maya held the drum in her lap and flicked off the snares. Bent her head sideways, like a mechanic or a Jedi, and started tapping near each of the twelve lugs whose tug-of-war kept the drumhead taut. Twelve more on the bottom, but since you didn't hit that side they rarely needed to be checked. When lugs got out of tune with one another, the clean gunshot crack of the snare would be warped by strange rings and over-tones. Sometimes it was tough to tell which one was the culprit, but she had this. Finally, a master of something nondestructive.

Also proving herself. First rehearsal with the jazz band. Ms. Reid had greeted her with a smile and pointed her toward the stack of black drum cases in the corner. Get it set up. Like she was just another kid. Hadn't even taken Serenitab today because it dulled her edges and she wanted them all sharp for this.

Now Maya sat behind the kit: brown hoodie, black hat, jeans, and her lavender lace-up boots. She hadn't had her own drums set up since they'd moved, no room in either apartment. . . . Could she still even play? She'd been going to her regular concert band class since the start of school, but that was just basic parts on a snare drum, single cymbal crashes, keeping time on a wood block. The drum set was the real deal.

Any mistake would be a comment on what she'd been through, a doubt about whether she could handle this—

Come on! She placed the snare in its stand and gave it a thwack. Better, but still with a *sprong* like a sci-fi laser sound effect.

"I always have a hard time with tuning," Trevor said, standing beside her. He was the other drummer: a sophomore.

"It's not too bad," Maya lied. Rookies.

She tweaked a few more lugs. That should do it. Held the silver drum key between her teeth and fired off a quick double-stroke roll with the sticks that had been in the snare case.

Fffththththththththththap!

Better. "Got any Moongel?" she asked around the drum key. Also, how delicious was this chrome between her teeth? *Stop it!*

"I don't think so." Trevor rummaged through the large black equipment box behind them.

Maya tapped around the perimeter again. "What about gaffer's tape?"

"On it." Trevor darted off.

Maya yanked the bass drum pedal from the box. Attached it. *Thud thump. Bu-bum-bamp.*

A bass drum was still a bass drum.

The band room had three raised levels, curving in a semicircle like wide steps. You entered in the floor area, where the piano and xylophones were located. The light blue carpet had more stains, pulls, and burns than actual clean patches at this point. The back wall was sectioned into instrument cubbies of various shapes, cases and marching gear spilling from them, and the ceiling and side walls were covered in perforated noise-reduction panels. Maya had set up the kit on the second-highest level, beside the line of trombone players. Jory, the bass guitar player, stood on the top level, next to the trumpets. Clarinets and saxophones sat on the first level. Everyone tuning and oiling and warming up, a junkyard of notes.

Maya unzipped her stick bag and selected her best pair, the least chipped and gouged; she wished she'd thought to get new ones before today, but whatever. She held them over the kit. The absolute silence before a beat. Months since she last felt this—

Her phone buzzed in her bag. Probably Janice. She'd messaged last night about meeting after school, how she had something special planned. When Maya had reminded her that it was the start of jazz band, she'd gotten grumpy. More like pissed.

She should probably check the text.

But her sticks were hovering, the air thick with potential energy. The sound of no sound.

The mall blows up—

No, dammit! She slammed the crash cymbal and laid down a furious beat; every snare hit a rim shot, every eighth note on the hi-hat hit with the side of the stick. Galloping bass drum. "Immigrant Song" by Led Zeppelin. A beat that organized the universe, constructed marble columns, aqueducts, coliseums, skyscrapers, all on the latticework of quarter, eighth, sixteenth, bar by repeating bar. A beat so undeniable, like you literally controlled all of space and time.

Jory started playing along. He bent over into Maya's field of view, his blond hair falling in his face, and wailed like Robert Plant did at the top of the tune.

Maya smiled but only for a second. The surface world was a

nuisance. Just wanted the movement, the now, the certainty, the safety of the beat, all muscles in concert, all manias in line, all systems shutting the fuck up and doing what they were told.

A couple kids were giving her the side-eye, she noticed, trumpet players mostly. They probably couldn't tune while the new girl was over here building the mighty towers of Dubai, but whatever. She'd started to sweat and she felt like pure energy and how had she lost this? What else could she possibly need?

"—only had duct tape!" Trevor waved the roll of gray tape in front of her.

She ran a syncopated fill down the toms, and crashed to a stop. Breathing hard; the silence immediately after. Satisfied, but also sad: the beat already a memory, a flock of birds taking flight from a wide field, spreading out into the sky, becoming specks, pointillist dots, losing one another.

Trevor was grinning at her. "That's a sick beat," he said. Maybe sort of in love.

Maya managed to smile. "Thanks." She was surprised to feel her cheeks flush.

"Glad to have you on board," said Jory.

"All right, if everyone's ready." Ms. Reid had stepped to the music stand at the center of the floor area. She wore a navy-blue suit jacket and pants with a striking yellow shirt that matched the yellow in the rims of her thick-frame glasses. She had short white curly hair and a simmering smile.

Everybody had an energy they invited, Maya thought. Like how her mom invited sympathy. Or how her dad invited you to pity him, but then love him, or, if you were a twenty-five-year-old serving him coffee or ringing up his groceries, hopefully want to fuck him. Maya thought of herself as more of a repelling surface, deflecting energy. She was emotional Gore-Tex? But not while drumming. She had to admit that.

Ms. Reid, on the other hand, invited optimism, excellence. You knew it immediately. When they'd met, she told Maya that she'd been a backup singer in the seventies and sang with someone famous. Tina Turner? Years on tour. Said the band had gotten so tight that they just *knew* what should happen next. And yet the execution still felt surprising.

She surveyed the group now, checking in with each section. Nodded at Maya, and Maya nodded back with a nervous smile. The first *yes* she'd revealed to the universe since . . . she couldn't remember.

"I hope everyone gets a chance to meet our new turncoat from Garfield, Maya Abrams." Heads turned her way. Maya gripped the sticks and felt a surge inside, but this was the good version. People seeing her for what she could be.

Ms. Reid arranged the music charts on her stand and started snapping her fingers, her arm swinging. She hummed to herself and said, "Bessie's Bounce."

Papers rustled. Trevor flipped to the right chart and folded it open. Maya peered at it while pushing in her earplugs. Basic timekeeping and color, some important hits here and there. The kind of chart that required you to count with fierce concentration while simultaneously letting go enough to feel the music and react spontaneously. A high-wire act. Bring it.

"One, a-two . . ." Ms. Reid counted them in.

All at once there was sound. Around and through and from her. This wasn't as primal as stomping "Immigrant Song," but still. Her right hand pinged along on the ride cymbal, striding bar by bar through the form. Her left hand responding to the horns on the snare, little ghost notes, big cracks, like thinking out loud, like urging a horse to keep it at a gallop, sometimes with a kick of the heels, a slap with the reins. Her foot sensing Jory's rhythm and accenting it on the bass drum. All the while her lips moving as she whisper-counted, a slight murmur she could hear behind her earplugs.

They built to the first chorus. Crescendo, big hits—Maya tagged them, and Ms. Reid grinned—then back down to a simmer.

Halfway through the next verse, nailing it, when something caught Maya's eye—

Janice, peeking through the double doors on the far side of the band room. She was dressed in a costume, smiling big and waving something shiny.

One of the brassholes noticed her and scowled at Maya, like it was his job to disapprove of everything.

Maya gave Janice a quick nod and focused on the chart. Janice motioned more emphatically. Was she waving a key? She made a glancing-over-her-shoulder motion. Bigger smile. Wink.

Maya smiled but also shook her head, hoping it seemed kind and yet thinking: *Get out of here!* Back to the music. Which measure were they on—

The horns stabbed a sequence of eighth notes.

Damn!

The briefest glance from Ms. Reid, arms still conducting: *You missed that.* Did it also say, *Are you not the girl we can trust with our melodies?*

It probably didn't. But still.

I am that girl! I can be! I—

Another series of hits. Maya barely caught them.

Fuck!

Trevor leaned toward the music stand and pointed to what measure they were on.

Maya nodded thanks, then checked the door. Janice had ducked back out, but the spell was broken. Everything suddenly felt stormy and hot. For thirty-two bars she'd been feeling so *herself*.

What did Janice want? At least she didn't look mad anymore. But couldn't Maya have a break to do this really important thing?

"Okay, let's stop there and just loop the eight bars starting at measure forty," said Ms. Reid. Another glance at Maya, like this stop was for her.

Maya glued her eyes to the chart and gritted her teeth. They looped it. She nailed it. Okay. She was still here.

They worked through three more charts over the rest of practice. Trevor played on two of the songs and did adorable things like look at her after he did what he probably hoped was a cool fill. Maya's eyes kept wandering to the door, but Janice didn't reappear. Her phone buzzed at least twice that she could hear, but she didn't check it.

"What did you think of using the kick drum for the accents on 'In a Mello Tone'?" Trevor asked later as they were packing up the drums.

"That was pretty good," Maya answered.

"Pretty good, but . . ."

"Oh no, it's just, to me, those should be brighter and ballsier since it's the biggest moment in the song."

"Yeah, good point," said Trevor. "You, um, you sounded awesome today."

"Thanks." *Awesome.* That was nice to hear. And being asked for advice and opinions? Also pretty great.

"Good work, Maya," said Ms. Reid as Maya stepped down to the floor. "If that was how you sound rusty, then I can't wait to hear you in your best shape."

"Thanks." Maya felt a little quiver and smiled. Her best shape . . . "Thanks again for letting me join."

"It's a pleasure to have you."

Maya thought she might just burst into tears right there.

"What are you up to now?" Trevor asked. He'd started, along with nearly everyone else, toward the door on the right side of the room that led to the main hallway.

"Oh, I have to go," said Maya, motioning to the left-side doors. As she said it, that quiver inside curdled.

"Okay. A bunch of us are going over to El Camión. It's kind of a regular thing, but, um . . ."

"Can I come next time?" Maya managed to smile. "Unless the offer's only for today."

"Oh no, I mean, yeah." Trevor grinned. "Anytime."

Maya fought an urge to chase after him. It sounded fun! But she sighed to herself and headed through the opposite door, into the hallway that ran behind the auditorium. Here were the double doors leading backstage, as well as doors into dressing rooms, storage closets, and practice spaces. As she stuffed her stick bag into her backpack, she hummed "Bessie's Bounce," trying to sustain that feeling and yet faking it. Her heart speeding up, her mouth getting dry.

"*Hey!*" Janice hissed from down a short dead-end hall. She was leaning through a doorway beyond the bathrooms.

Maya froze. "What's up?"

Janice rolled her eyes but smiled wickedly. "Where do you think you're going?" Her costume was really low-cut, the gold lacing in front mostly undone.

Maya stood there. Felt a tug inside. Janice definitely looked hot. . . . "I was just gonna go catch the bus."

"There are lots of buses. Right now it's time for a treat."

Pulse pounding. Tingling in her fingers. "I have a ton of homework—"

Janice huffed. "Come on, already!" She ran a finger over the front of her dress and spoke in a Southern belle voice. "You don't want me to catch my death in this."

Maya smiled. Counted the seconds she should hold it. "I just don't have long, okay?"

"Then stop wasting precious time and get over here."

Maya heard voices coming from down the hall. A pair of boys rounded the corner—

Eli.

Walking with that same slouchy kid, side by side, sharing a set of earbuds from the other kid's phone. Maya and Eli locked eyes, neither speaking. He recognized her. No doubt—

"Come *on*, already." Janice's hand closed on Maya's upper arm, her fingers digging in. Yanked her. Maya stumbled, one last glance at Eli, flames licking her vision, before she was pulled down the hall and through the doorway into the closet. Stumbled past Janice, grabbing on to a rack of costumes to keep herself upright.

Wait! Go talk to him! But of course she couldn't. She should have given him a sign or something! But how?

"Hey!" Janice was leaning back into the hall. "Move along, pervs."

She shut the door, slicing Maya in half.

The closet was dimly lit, deep shadows and a weak bulb, the mothball smell of the costume racks and garment bags and now the sweetness of Janice's Candy Mint lip balm right by her ear.

She held Maya by the shoulders. "So, what do you think?"

"What?" said Maya, picturing Eli, all the walls on fire. Her arm throbbed where Janice had grabbed her.

"Duh." Janice pinched Maya's chin, dipped it down toward her costume.

"Hot," Maya managed to say. "Is this for the play?"

"Nah, I just found it in here. I think it's Guinevere, or Juliette—we're star-crossed lovers, doomed to die together! Or maybe it's just sexy witch number three." She ran a finger along Maya's sternum. "Boo, where's that hot red top?"

I like this outfit.

"Sorry," Maya mumbled through the noise and fire in her head. Observations were slipping through: Janice's hair tumbling over bare shoulders, hourglass corset curves, the pile of her clothes on the floor near her bare feet. Definitely hot, but Maya felt like she was watching it from a distance, like on a TV in the corner of a room. Instead, all she pictured was Eli coming toward her. *Run!* But no, not away from him. *Run after him!* Before it was too late. Was he still out in the hall? Had to grab him and hang on before this blast got any worse.

Why the blast? Why now? Was it Eli? Or something about here, about Janice.

"Hey! Earth to Maya!" Janice gripped Maya's wrists, put Maya's hands on her waist. "I'm stuck in this costume and I can't get out."

"Yeah." Maya looked at the floor. "You look great."

"I'm going to look even better in a minute."

Maya gritted her teeth, pushed her lips into a smile. *You should want this.* Of course. But . . . She glanced at the door. Who was that other boy? What was it like for Eli to see her? Was he okay?

"Hey." Janice kissed her hard. Put her hands on Maya's cheeks, holding her in place, the pressure just enough to make her cheekbones ache. Touched her nose with her own. "Come here." Her breath hot. Close.

Maya shook her head. She was being stupid. "I'm just . . ."

"You've been so out of it. So distant. Ignoring all my texts for like an hour."

"Sorry." *I had band. It was important to me.* But maybe she had been kind of wrapped up in her own head. There had been that break halfway through when every other kid had checked their phone, but Maya had stayed away from hers, making small talk with Trevor instead. Just trying to make new friends.

Or avoiding. Neglectful.

Janice pressed her against the wall. Cold concrete, painted off-white. "This is good, right?"

"It's just that I told my mom I'd be home by five and—"

Janice's hands tightened around her shoulders. "Come on, are you really going to be that girl again?" Her smile cooling. Her eyes sparkling, glacial.

"No," Maya said quietly. *I don't want to be that girl.*

Which girl?

Ice girl.

Dead girl.

Blowing-up girl.

Eli . . . *Stop thinking about Eli! You are so messed up and you're ruining this!*

"You need the Doctor," said Janice. She bent, and returned with her flask.

Maya took it. Willed her fingers not to tremble.

You should want this.

For just a moment she heard a screaming in her head, all white noise and anger like a bomb, like walls disintegrating— she wanted to thrash, to take both hands and hang herself by her hair until it all tore free, and then rip the little hairs from her eyebrows and legs, everywhere, go at it with tweezers, with tape, with shears, with a steak knife, a lawn mower—

She put the flask to her lips. Tilt. Burn. Fought the tingle of oncoming tears.

"There you go," said Janice, moving against her.

Another swig. Where was her Serenitab? That would help. But it was in her backpack. Miles away.

"Now shush." Janice rubbed her hands over Maya's hat, down around her neck. "We're going to have a bio class of our own. Janice will make it all better." She unlaced her top. Let it fall open, started kissing Maya's neck.

Hands under Maya's hoodie.

It feels good, she told herself. She turned her head so the tears could finally leak free. *You don't feel it but you should.*

She made her hands move. At the same time, sank away. Some last flickers of the feeling of control, of bubbling possibility. *I played well.*

They just laugh at you in class.

Janice never laughs at you.

She moved her hands more.

"Mmmm," said Janice in her ear, her hands busy.

Where was Eli now? Didn't matter. Some feelings were feeling better. The moving. The effects of Dr. Pom. Set her adrift just enough to let her slip along with whatever current was strongest. It had been like this with Todd, with Nilo and Walsh. She'd get by.

Not my choice.

Hush.

This wouldn't take that long.

CHAPTER 11

ELI

September 19

"Holy shit," said Graham, yanking out his earbud, which had been blaring Sideshow Fantasy. "Did you see that?"

He had.

Maya.

Slick sweat inside the wolf's mask, his vision narrowing to the eyeholes, the grip of her clammy hands, how the blood from her thumb had dripped onto his, but not letting go, in the DOL, in his dreams since:

I got you.

And now she was ten feet away, staring back at him, eyes wide. She looked terrified.

He wanted to say something. Anything. *Hi. How are you? I'm sorry*—

But *whoosh* she was pulled one way and he was pulled the other.

"We gotta haul ass," said Graham, bolting through the double doors that led onto the stage. Eli struggled to keep up, feet shotgunning on the old wooden boards. Graham pushed through the gap in the curtain and leaped off the stage front, landing in the carpeted aisle. "Come on!" he called over his shoulder.

Eli knelt and braced himself with his hands, hopped off the stage, but still stumbled sideways when he landed, slamming his thigh against the wooden armrest of a seat.

"I thought we were getting the spotlights," he called, his lungs already burning as he followed Graham up the aisle. Eli had been part of the Tech Squad for all of twenty-four hours, after Mr. McNaulty had found him in Mr. Caletti's office yesterday afternoon. On Monday, Graham had said that the roster was full, but apparently not long after that, Mr. McNaulty had been promoted to *essential personnel* and found a way to add a spot.

Eli hadn't seen Graham over the weekend. Mom had dismissed the idea of the game convention. She was glad Eli had made a friend—Eli had insisted that Graham had no idea who he really was, couldn't imagine having to deal with Mom about that—but the convention was too big, too many people. Melissa had stuck up for him, and so Mom reluctantly ran it by Detective Pearson, but she said they couldn't spare the personnel anyway.

"We can do the bulbs in a minute," Graham said over his shoulder. "First we're going on a sortie."

A what?

Graham led the way up through the door at the rear of the auditorium. They climbed a steep, narrow staircase that ended at a short hallway. There was a small square door in the wall, padlocked shut. Graham produced a set of keys and opened it.

"I can't believe your girl is hooking up with Janice!" He crawled through the little door.

Eli stared in. His eyes adjusted to the gloom, and a vast interstitial space revealed itself. It seemed to go and go, a shadow realm above the real world. A catwalk led away from the door, suspended by metal poles from the girders above. Below, a grid of perforated white ceiling panels. Gaps here and there where the light banks hung down.

"Come on!" Graham hissed. He'd become a silhouette.

What about the harnesses? Eli climbed slowly in. The catwalk had railings, but the gaps were still big enough to slip through, and it seemed unlikely that those ceiling panels would stop a fall. Graham was speeding along in a crouch, the entire catwalk vibrating in his wake. Eli crawled, his palms scraping on the cold metal grating.

He reached an intersection at the center of the auditorium and turned left toward the stage, the catwalk sloping slightly to match the angle of the ceiling. The farther down he went, the more the catwalk swayed. Eli peered through the gaps around the light banks, and his stomach clenched. The seats so far below.

He caught up with Graham at another T intersection, this one at the front of the auditorium, right beside the top of the thick red curtain, so close he could run his fingers over the felt.

"Where are we going?" Eli whispered. His hands and knees ached.

"You'll see," said Graham, winded. "Isn't this awesome?"

Maybe, Eli thought. He felt hidden, secretive. *Secrets require the belt.* Except it was different from that—thrilling.

"It's even better when there's an assembly," said Graham. "All the ants down there. Totally unaware. And you're up here above

135

them all." He smiled. "Sometimes I drop shit on them, like little spitballs. Or even if you just spit, it breaks into lots of small drops on the way down, so you get maximum casualties."

"You don't get caught?" Eli asked.

"Everybody's so stupid. They never look up. They figure someone behind them did it. I made an actual fight break out once. Like Zeus, moving the people to your will. Sometimes I imagine what would happen if the whole thing came down on them."

Came down?

"Can you imagine that? This whole roof? Like *BAM*. That would shut them up." Eli waited for a smile or something, a sign that Graham meant it as a joke, but he just stared down through the gap by the lights, his expression serious. Then he slapped the scaffolding with his palms. "We gotta keep moving. You ready?"

Eli nodded. *For what?*

They headed along the curtain, to the front corner of the auditorium. There was another square door in the wall. Graham pushed it open. "Just through here. This is the critical part of the sortie. Gotta be super-quiet now, okay?"

Okay.

Graham put his legs through the hole and twisted around. He took hold of two bars and climbed down a ladder on the other side, raising his eyebrows at Eli.

Eli slid through, banging his head on the top of the doorway. Clumsy, out of shape, bound to fall to his death at any minute. *Keep it together!* He gripped the worn metal rungs and climbed down.

He crouched beside Graham. They'd come down about twenty feet. In front of them was a more cramped ceiling space with light bleeding up from below. Graham put a finger to his lips, then started inching along a plywood walkway, about three feet wide, that rested on a thick steel support beam. To the right was a brick wall. To the left, girders ran out across pools of white ceiling panels to a cinder block wall. Pinholes of light shone up through some of the panels, while others were already dark.

Graham crept a little ways ahead and then began easing himself onto one of the girders. He inched out over a lighted area of the ceiling, holding on to metal supports that drew triangles between the girder and the roof beams above them. He stopped about ten feet out, made a motion with his hand to his ear like he was listening below, and then smiled at Eli and waved for him to join.

Eli looked at the narrow girder, the ceiling below. There was no way. He could barely jump off a stage without injuring himself.

Graham waved to him more emphatically, then he kneeled and extended a leg behind him until his foot found the next girder. He braced himself in a push-up position, stretched his other leg, and lay down, his sneakers hooked on the one girder, the other beneath his chest. He slipped his fingers underneath the edge of the ceiling panel below and carefully lifted it. A triangle of light burst upward.

Graham peered through the gap. Looked at Eli with a wide-eyed grin.

Eli's heart hammered. Maybe he should go back.

Graham waved to him again.

Sound wafted up from the room below. Rustling. Then a moan, like a girl. Eli's blood went hot.

He wanted to leave.

He wanted to see.

Graham waved more emphatically. *Come ON!*

Do as you're told, Jacob.

Eli took hold of the closest support beam and inched his way onto the girder. Grabbed the next beam, shuffled toward Graham. He caught a view through the gap: a student-made poster on the wall. It had a big palm tree and said SOUTH PACIFIC. He moved farther out. Saw costume racks—

And the bare back of that girl Janice. Another sighing sound.

He wobbled, gripped the support beam tighter with clammy fingers. Graham tugged on his sleeve, motioned that he should get in the same position. Eli knelt, thought about lying down like Graham had, but froze. This was far enough.

Graham leaned away from the hole and motioned for Eli to take a turn.

Don't look, this is wrong. But he leaned over. He knew what he was seeing. Screamed at himself to leave and felt himself getting hard all at once.

Janice's flowing hair, a silky costume ruffled around her waist. Leaning against the wall, against Maya whose shirt was also off. A lavender-colored bra. Her black hat still on.

Eli winced. Rock-hard now. No! He couldn't have these feelings. In the red dark they had to be hidden—but also it was *her* and it wasn't right! Then again, she didn't know, and he was so hard it hurt, pressing against his jeans, a shiver coursing through his body—

Graham tapped his shoulder, smiling big and nodding. He leaned over for another turn.

Eli sat back, face burning. Glad to lose the view. Craving more of it.

Graham's pelvis was moving. He'd unbuttoned his jeans, his hand down there working.

A heavy sigh from below. Eli shut his eyes and gritted his teeth. His urges like enemies. He knew what it felt like when someone came into your space uninvited. He also remembered the sounds through the ceiling. But this was different. Nothing wrong with what these girls were doing. *But something wrong with what we're doing.*

They don't mind, Gabriel said. *They're drowning in sin and they like it.*

"Oh yeah," Graham suddenly said at a normal volume.

Eli slapped Graham's shoulder. *Why'd you do that?*

The rustling of costume ceased.

"Did you say something?" Janice asked.

Graham started snickering to himself. Held up a finger to Eli, as if to say *wait,* and then put a hand half over his mouth. "Finish the job!"

"Oh shit!" Maya had spotted them. She lunged toward the racks of costumes.

Janice whirled, her eyes finding the ceiling gap. "What the hell?"

We have to go! Eli scrambled, pivoting toward the walkway. He grabbed Graham's shoulder. *Come on!*

Graham yanked himself free. "What are you—"

Eli wobbled, lost his grip on the support beam. One foot slid off the girder. He threw himself sideways, reaching, flailing—

He crashed into Graham and they both went down.

The ceiling smashed apart. Supports tearing free, panels splintering—

He almost landed on his feet, but his right leg crumpled under him, pain spiking up from his ankle. His shoulder slammed into the tiled floor, and then he was on the ground, his head falling on top of Graham's chest.

"Oh my God!" Janice shouted.

Graham scrambled from under him, wheezing. Eli rolled onto his side, his shoulder burning, his arm going dead, trying to suck in air. Like his lungs wouldn't work. Blinked in the dust from the ceiling.

Janice was yanking her dress up. Maya had thrust herself beneath and behind a costume rack. She sat on the floor, her back against the wall, hidden in the shadows of the hanging garments, a hand thrown across her chest but shit, he shouldn't look there, or at her bare navel—

Looking isn't wrong—but no, we weren't invited! She didn't ask for this, just like I didn't—

Her pants unbuttoned so he could see a bit of her teal underwear. It had white dots and ahhh, he was still hard, he wanted to touch her, he wanted to cry, to take her hand and run, could they run? But where?

"You little dick, Graham!" Janice shouted.

Graham was struggling to sit up, cradling one arm with the other. His face was bright red and his pants were halfway down his butt, his erection poking from his boxers.

"Get the fuck out of here!"

"God, calm down, Janice!" Graham pulled at his pants. "What's the big deal?"

"You're a creep, how about that?" Janice lunged for the door, yanked it open, grabbed Graham by his wounded arm and dragged him to his feet.

"Ow, stop!" Janice was taller than him and he'd barely gotten his balance when she shoved him. "No, wait!"

Graham careened into the hallway and slammed against the far wall. He tugged at his pants, face boiling, shirt askew.

Eli was still propped on his elbow. His breath just starting to return. Maya's eyes seared into him, wild, but also like she was somewhere far away, at the bottom of a well. Her body shook, knees pulled up to her chest now, arms around them, not even trying to get her shirt on. She looked so terrified, not the girl who held his hand. What had happened to her?

It's me. Oh God. *He* had happened. Almost killed her and now here he was again. A bomb back in her life. *I'm sorry.* He wanted to disappear, to disintegrate. The urge sent needles shooting through him.

"You too, freshmeat!" Janice hauled him up. "You should think twice before you associate with that asshole."

Eli stumbled to his feet, not fighting her grip. He looked back at Maya. *I'm so sorry.* "I . . ." Words finally coming—

Janice thrust him through the door. He staggered and fell against the wall beside Graham, who was just getting his pants up—

Laughter from down the hall.

"Ew!"

Eli's ankle throbbed. He shifted his weight to the other foot. Turned and saw three boys, two girls standing at the end of the hall. Two more now joining them.

Janice leaned out and addressed the crowd. "These creepers were spying on us while we were trying on costumes."

Snickers. Delighted smiles. Whispers into ears.

Eli wilted in their wide-eyed gazes. Had to look away. Wanted to be nothing.

"Fuck you!" Graham shouted at Janice. "You fag bitch!"

"Oh my God." One of the onlookers laughed harder.

Janice peered at him, incredulous. "What did you call me?"

"You heard me!"

"Go to hell, Graham! Just 'cause I turned you down for home-coming last year. News flash! You're a gross tech perv, not to mention it's now confirmed that you've got that little earthworm dick."

Graham thrust up from the wall, wobbling and pointing at her. "You're fucking dead!" he screamed. His face had passed any shade of red that Eli had ever seen. Eli was also the only one close enough to see the tears in his eyes.

Cackling from the chorus down the hall.

"All of you!" Graham twisted toward them, still trying to get his belt buckled. "You're all idiots who don't deserve to live!" Spit flew from his mouth. "I'll make you shut up forever!"

A woman, the band teacher, Eli thought, came around the corner. "Whatever this is ends now." She pointed to the crowd. "Go on. If your activities are over you should be on your way home."

She stopped a few feet from Eli, Graham, and Janice. "Would someone like to tell me what's going on down here?"

Eli saw Janice eye Graham.

"We were just—" Graham began.

"I'm such a klutz," said Janice, suddenly smiling sweetly. "I was just trying on costumes for one-acts and completely knocked over the rack with the suits of armor on top. These two poked their heads in to help, but I was pulling my costume on." She rolled her eyes. "Pretty embarrassing!"

"We're sorry, we just wanted to make sure she was okay," Graham added immediately, his chest still heaving.

The teacher eyed the three of them. "Ms. Mays knows you're here?" she said to Janice.

"Yup, you can ask her."

"I'm aware of that. And, you two, you're on the Tech Squad?"

"Yeah, we were just on our way to change some lights," said Graham.

"And Mr. McNaulty will confirm that?"

"Yes, ma'am."

The teacher crossed her arms. Eli could feel her weighing what to say next. "Sounds like the three of you have a lot of cleaning up to do in there."

"Nah, I got it," said Janice. "I'm the only one who knows where everything goes."

"We'll just go get the lights done," said Graham, pushing away from the wall. "Come on." He tapped Eli's arm.

They walked by the teacher, eyes down.

"Sorry for the disturbance," Eli heard Janice say. He glanced back and saw her closing the door. How was Maya? He wanted to check on her. Apologize a hundred more times.

Too late. She hates me now. Why wouldn't she? *She saved my life and this is what I do?* He'd hurt her a year ago and here he was hurting her again. She'd probably hated him then too, had just been acting kind to survive. *You're a bomb in everyone's life.*

Graham led the way up the hall, walking fast, unlocked the tech closet door. As Eli followed him in, he saw the teacher returning to the band room, but still watching them.

"Close the door," Graham said quietly.

The closet was split into two narrow aisles, the metal shelving crammed with a disorganized array of lights and parts, boxes with wires hanging out, old dusty electronic equipment. Graham walked halfway down the first aisle. He calmly picked up a white cardboard box, plucked the lightbulb free—

Hurled it at the far wall. It exploded with a hollow pop, white shark teeth sleeting to the floor. He spun and slouched against the shelving, blew hair from his eyes, crossed his arms.

Eli stayed by the door, a screw twisting into the floor.

"Guess you're really stuck with me now," Graham said. "This will spread through school like a virus. Everybody loves an excuse to gang up on someone."

"We shouldn't have spied on them," said Eli.

"Everyone is so stupid," Graham went on. "Herds of zombies walking around this school. If those girls were dumb enough to do it in the costume closet, they should know what they get."

They should've known we might be in the ceiling?

"But then everybody's just looking for a reason to laugh at you," said Graham. "They'll never know what it feels like, when you're not part of the group, when you're better than that. When you can see what existence really is. You know what I mean?"

Um. Eli didn't really follow.

Graham waved his hands around. "God! They think all this *means* something. Grades, games, awards, being popular. What a bunch of bullshit. They can't even begin to comprehend what life really is."

"You mean like suffering and pain?" Eli said.

That's right. Eli's neck tingled. The fingers rubbing up and down approvingly. Words he was supposed to refute, and yet they also felt like a relief. He *had* suffered. And here was Graham suffering. Maya seemed to be too. His mother, the meanness of those kids just now . . .

Graham's face lit up. "Exactly. See, *you* get it, Eli. This world is a realm of pain, and no one is more cursed than those of us who can truly grasp it."

"Grasp it?"

"The true nature, the *infinite*. So much of this world is beyond our understanding."

"Yeah," said Eli. He wasn't sure he quite followed, but it seemed to be helping Graham to talk it out.

"If everyone actually got how insignificant we really are, then this whole world would be silent. But they don't. They stay ignorant and dumb because they can't handle the truth." Graham shook his head. "It makes me want to die just so I wouldn't have to listen to them anymore. So things could just be peaceful."

"Maybe there's a purpose," said Eli. His hands drummed lightly on his thighs.

Good.

Except he didn't mean it like that. Did he?

Graham crouched. Drew a circle in the dust on the concrete floor. "The only point of this life is to get to death, to get to the other side. Either there's an answer over there, the real answer, or there's silence, and then we'll know there was never any point to begin with. Either way, it sounds better than here."

Eli wasn't so sure. He'd been in silence for years. Suffered so much that he'd forgotten he was suffering. He never wanted to feel that again. Should he tell Graham that? But he didn't want Graham to think he was disagreeing. Especially not when he was in a bad mood, like now. It was best to keep still during bad moods.

"Hey," said Graham. "Did you even hear me?"

"What?"

"I asked you if that was why you tried to do it. Weren't you blowing up the mall because you were promised salvation?"

God waits for his true soldiers with open arms.

"Sort of," said Eli. "It was also to send a message. To wake people up."

"Like to how we're all controlled," said Graham.

All are complicit.

Eli shook his head, the thoughts crowding in. "You asked out Janice?" he said instead.

Graham took a length of red wire off one of the shelves and started twisting it around his finger. "She was so cruel. Just brushed me off like I was a nothing. She's as blind as the rest of them. Playing her little games. And now she's messing with your girl."

Maya's not . . .

"I wish we could just kill that bitch," said Graham. "Not yours. Fucking Janice. I can think of so many satisfying ways to do that."

Eli searched for a response, but he couldn't quite hold a thought, hard to stay focused.

Graham laughed. "If only, right? But it's fun to imagine." He finished twisting the wire. His fingertip had turned white.

"Yeah," said Eli, just to say something.

Graham walked over and patted Eli on the shoulder. "You're a good friend. Sticking with me. You'd think loyalty would come first in a friendship, but you'd be surprised."

"Oh." Had he been? But maybe their friendship felt stronger for Graham. He seemed to feel so *much*.

"Come on." Graham grabbed a box off the shelf and headed for the door. "Let's do the lights."

You okay? Eli thought to ask as they walked out the door.

He tugged Graham's arm. "You okay?"

Graham looked back. Smiled easy. "Totally. Why?"

CHAPTER 12

MAYA

September 24

"I don't get what the big deal is," Janice said, standing by the espresso bar at the Bauhaus café. "So a couple underclassmen saw your bra."

"I know." Maya tore at her thumb. *Just agree. It's easier.*

Janice tapped the screen to pay.

"How much?" Maya asked, reaching for her wallet.

Janice waved her hand. "I got it. Your mom's all out of money these days anyway."

I can afford a chai. But she slid her wallet back into her bag.

"Or are you embarrassed because we're two girls? News flash, nobody cares except our dads, and they don't matter."

"Yeah." It was fine. Sure, she was just being stupid. Afraid of what people thought. Tentative when she should be brave. Blah blah blah, Janice.

Though Janice was right that if you took the individual event, you could see how it wasn't *that* big a deal. It was when you added the looks she'd been getting since then in the halls, the laughter in biology, the hiding out in bathroom stalls, the hair smearing the sides of sinks. . . .

Maybe it was also when you added Janice.

"Two pumpkin-spice chais," the barista called, sliding the mugs across the counter.

"There we go." Janice grabbed the drinks and looked around. "Where to?"

The café was packed, probably from the nearby university. Lots of study partners here and there. One big table in the main seating area was overflowing with a tabletop game. A few sets of Elliott High kids around too.

Janice huffed. "How about around the corner?"

"It's crowded over there. I saw when we were walking in." They'd passed by the front windows, and Maya had in fact seen that *most* of the tables on the other side of the café were full, but also:

That was where Eli was.

"Let's just go here." Maya started toward two open seats at the narrow bar along the side windows.

"Is there even enough room for our books?" said Janice.

"It will be okay." From here, Maya could see Eli's reflection in the front windows.

He was sitting with a young woman. Papers and a textbook on the table. Eli hunched, writing, while the woman watched. A tutor, Maya guessed. Seeing him made her tremble, made her crave the Serenitab bottle in her backpack.

You can never talk to him now. After the way he saw you? So pathetic.

And yet it hadn't changed the dream in her head. In fact, she'd been thinking about him more, and she didn't understand why, but it was all she could do right now not to check the window reflection every second.

"Who are you waiting for?" Janice asked. She dropped her bio textbook onto the bar with a thud.

"Nobody."

"I mean, if you want to go find somebody else to be with, then just go already."

Maya reeled in her gaze. "Come on." She smiled and leaned over and kissed Janice, went for the lips, but Janice didn't turn and so her kiss ended up just beside her mouth.

"That's what it feels like," Janice added.

Every movement forced, required. Maya's insides cycling faster. She got her books out and laid them on the bar. Janice did the same and their notebooks bumped into each other and Janice's fell on the floor.

"Uh, watch it," said Janice.

"Sorry."

"This is ridiculous."

"Should we go somewhere else?"

Janice made a snorting sound. "Where, *Starbucks*? These are the best chais in Ballard. Apparently the word is out. If I ever meet the guys who made Yelp, it's going to be dick kicks all around."

Maya laughed. Actually noticed herself thinking that was funny and reacting, and yet still, everything with Janice under surveillance. Was it safe? Was she being stupid?

She checked the window again. The ghostly image of Eli watching as his tutor wrote something.

"Okay, so, the invertebrates." Maya opened her book, got out a stack of index cards, and flipped through them. "I made cards for all the phyla, genuses, and orders, complete with little example critters."

"Look at you." Janice slipped on her glasses and tied back her hair. "It's almost like you're normal."

It had felt that way, for two hours last night when she'd been making these. *Feels less so when you say it.* "Let's start with phylum Porifera—"

Janice's phone buzzed. "Hold on." She read a message and smiled, her first one all night. Typed a reply.

Who is it? But Maya didn't ask, shouldn't ask. Prying. Nosy. Instead, she ran her finger over the classes of sponges.

Calcarea, Hexactinellida . . . creatures that stuck themselves to a rock and forever sucked in the water around them, taking what they could, no way to chase, fight, flee. Of no interest to the pretty fish or the elegant sharks. Could at any time be torn apart by a ferocious wave or suffocated by the tentacles of a starfish.

Janice tugged Maya by the biceps. "This is Mateo, who I was telling you about." She held up her phone.

Maya tried not to wince. Under Janice's hand, beneath her shirt, yellow-brown blotches the size of fingerprints. From when she'd pulled Maya into the costume closet. Unintentional. Of course. Another example of Maya's shining weakness. But still . . .

The photo showed a boy with curly black hair, making a self-aware *check-me-out* face. Charming smile. Also shirtless. Other shirtless boys behind him.

"He's at swim practice," said Janice. "He and Lucas are both varsity, but they're not jocks. They're regular Renaissance men. Mateo used to do Tech Squad, but he quit because of how annoying Señor Little Dick was." She let go of Maya and twisted to aim the phone. "Now one of you."

Maya instinctively hunched over on herself. "I don't—"

"Come on, I told him I'd send one. Why should he come to the dance with us if he doesn't know what he's coming for?"

I don't understand why you're setting me up with a boy when we're dating.

Janice's hand on Maya's arm again, like that spot was a magnet, yanking her upright. "Jesus, it's not a profile picture. It's just a fucking message."

Rag-doll Maya. *Don't be lame.* She tilted her head and forced out a smile as Janice aimed her phone.

"Mmm, probably fix your hat." Janice made a tugging motion behind her ear. Maya pulled at the fabric. "Better." But then Janice's mouth scrunched, and she lowered the phone. "Okay, don't worry, Janice can fix this." She dug into her bag and handed Maya lip gloss and green eyeliner. "Luckily he can't see your sweatpants."

"I thought this was a study date," Maya grumbled, and immediately wished she could take it back.

But Janice was focused on her own selfie. The lip gloss and eyeliner just lying there. Expecting.

Maya checked the window. Eli was eating something. A doughnut? But his tutor was standing. Organizing papers. *Don't leave!* she thought.

She grabbed the lip gloss and eyeliner and smeared it on as fast as she could. "Better?"

Janice looked her over. "That will do." She held the camera

out, put her arm around Maya and pulled her close. Shoulders bumping. Lungs constricted. "One more. Make it sexy."

Fuck you.

Maya slid her grin sideways and narrowed her eyes. "How's that?"

"Mmm, delicious. This dance is going to be *so* fun."

Fuck you fuck you fuck you.

"Can we study now?"

Janice sent the photo, then watched the dots that indicated a reply was coming. "Just a sec."

Maya shifted and picked up her index cards. There went the tutor, bag over her shoulder. Eli was still here, sitting alone. He'd put on his headphones, absorbed in his phone.

Janice giggled, her thumbs tapping away at a message.

Go.

Maya's heart pounded. Mouth dry. "I'm going to the bathroom."

"God, relax. I'm almost done."

Maya slid off her stool anyway. Thought her legs might collapse, send her splattering to the floor in a boneless heap. Stiff steps toward the front of the shop. Eli still reflected in the window. Did he have any idea she was here? It didn't seem like it.

She rounded the espresso bar. The bathrooms were in the back. She'd have to pass right by him. She checked the surrounding tables. No one from their school. They would just be two strangers.

And now he was right there. Fire licked at Maya's vision, the walls of the Bauhaus exploding apart. Her ears rang with the cracking of concrete, the splintering of wood, and she vibrated all over as her molecules were torn from one another, but—

NO! She kept staring at Eli, solid, right in front of her. *You don't get to do this,* she told her brain. *We don't blow up. We survive.*

She still searched his sweatshirt for the outlines of explosives.

The clinking of plates and cups from the kitchen area. The boisterous conversation of the tabletop gamers. Whir of the coffee grinder, laughter from a nearby table, the muted horn stabs of some seventies soul playing over the stereo system. Maya ran her fingertips along the wall.

Eggshell-textured paint.

Talk to him. TALK TO HIM—

But she accelerated and slipped right by and into one of the bathrooms. Shut the door too hard. Everyone outside had probably noticed.

Dammit! She lunged to the sink and put her shaking hands under the water. Rubbed them, added soap, rubbed more. Slid them over her face, looked in the mirror.

Cracking black scab on her chin that could use a little work— *No!*

"You have to," she whispered at herself.

Her phone buzzed.

Janice: Where'd you go?

Maya: I told you. Bathroom.

Maya slid her phone in her pocket. Pee first. She didn't even have to, but she sat down anyway, then immediately panicked. What if he left while she was screwing around in here? She jumped back up, washing her hands again. "You're crazy," she whispered into the mirror. Straggle-haired, another scab above her eyebrow . . .

Suddenly she smiled.

Fine, then. Crazy. That's what she would be.

Maya nodded, dried her hands, and gripped the door handle, her palm clammy with sweat.

Walked out.

CHAPTER 13

ELI

September 24

"Hey."

He barely heard the voice over the screaming synthesizers of Sideshow Fantasy. Assumed she was talking to someone else. Then a hand tapped the table. A few of the fingers in Band-Aids.

Eli looked up—

His heart tripped on itself. He fell into the red dark. The café became the DOL. All happening at once as he stared at Maya staring at him.

Pulled off his headphones. "Hey."

But wait . . . He looked around. Nobody seemed to be paying any attention. Naomi, his math tutor, was long gone, and Melissa was busy on the other side of the bar. She worked here a few

156

nights a week. Brought him for tutoring, and also for socialization, like he was a puppy. *As long as you're not annoying.*

Maya eyed the other tables too. She stepped closer to his, looked at the empty chair but didn't sit down, just leaned against the wall, one hand in her hoodie pocket, the other scratching at the base of that black hat she always wore.

Eli had no idea what to say. He'd been terrified to see her since the costume closet, had taken different routes to class when he'd spotted her. Why was she here? Was it about that?

"How are you?" she finally asked. She didn't seem angry.

"Okay."

"I guess I look a little better than the last time you saw me, huh?" Her mouth lifted, a slight smile.

"You, um . . ." Eli had been about to say she had looked fine then. *Do NOT say that! She was shirtless and freaking out!* Right. Definitely not that. "I'm really sorry. We shouldn't have—"

Maya waved her hand. "Forget it. But you guys were gross for being up there." A phone buzzed. Eli's was dark. Maya fished hers from her pocket and frowned at it. Lowered it but didn't put it away, clutched it instead by her side.

"I didn't really know we were going to see you," said Eli. "It was Graham's idea—"

"It's okay, really. It's maybe part of why I came over here. I don't want that to be how you think of me."

Okay.

"Also, are you all right? You fell out of a ceiling. That had to hurt."

"I think I sprained my ankle," said Eli. "My shoulder was bad for a couple days but it's okay now. Could have been worse."

"Yeah, it could have." Maya looked around the café again. "So, what's new?"

Nothing. Come on! Had to speak for real. "Nothing. Just studying. What about you?"

Maya shrugged. "Same. Otherwise just trying to survive at a new school."

"Me too."

"I shouldn't complain. I'm not going through anything like you're going through."

"You don't look so good."

Maya cocked an eyebrow at him. *Duh!* Why did he say that?

Suddenly she laughed. It broke her whole face apart, teeth showing, her eyes lighting up. She rubbed her hat and then held out her fingers, showing off the Band-Aids on a bunch of them. "No, I really don't."

Look what you did. Look at the damage you caused. You didn't even blow up and you still wrecked things. "I'm sorry."

Maya waved a hand at him. "Don't say that anymore, okay? I was well on my way to crazy before the DOL." She edged closer to the table. "What are you working on?"

"Math."

"It must be hard, the schoolwork. I mean, being in school too, after so long. High school sucks even under normal circumstances."

"Math is hard. Everything else too, I guess."

"I feel like . . . I spend the whole day trying to be invisible," Maya said. "Except then everyone wants me to try to connect more."

"Me too," said Eli. "All the teachers look at me funny."

"Same," said Maya. "Like they're waiting for me to lose my mind."

"For me it's—" Eli caught himself.

"It's what?"

"Nothing."

"Tell me."

Don't say. "Well, it's like they're scared of me. Like I'll blow them up."

Maya nodded. "I get that." Her phone buzzed again. She checked it and huffed.

"Are you here with someone?"

"Yeah," said Maya, her thumbs tapping. "Study date. One sec."

"What are you studying?"

Maya looked up. "Invertebrate taxonomy? Like the Latin names of worms and sponges and bugs."

"Oh."

"It sounds boring, but it's actually kind of interesting. It's like the ancient catalog of the world." She checked over her shoulder.

"It's okay if you have to go."

"Yeah, in a minute, but . . ." She shoved her phone back into her pocket, couldn't quite meet his eyes. "Listen, what you said about blowing up . . ."

"Oh, I didn't—"

"No." Her hands had started shaking, one finger picking at her thumb. "I've been having this dream where we're in the DOL."

Adrenaline surged through Eli. "I—"

"Just listen. It's that day," Maya went on, "but it's also like a hundred other days. There's always weird people there, or the floor will be made of Jell-O or whatever. But the point is, you always walk in, and then the bomb always goes off and we die, but . . . after I saw you at school the first week? The dream changed. It's—"

Maya's phone buzzed again. She looked like she might ignore it, but then fished it out. When she read the message, her face flushed and she looked to the front windows. Eli followed her gaze and saw a girl outside, arms crossed, glaring. Janice, from the costume closet. Eli had seen her around the auditorium since; Graham always made sure to avoid her.

"Is she waiting for you?" Eli asked.

"She, um . . ."

Janice whirled and stalked away.

Maya read her phone again and shook her head. "No, I guess not."

"What were you saying?"

Her phone was still buzzing, but Maya silenced it and put it into her back pocket. She rubbed her face. Suddenly she looked exhausted. "About what?"

"The dream."

"Oh yeah. Sorry. It's just that lately we survive. Like, the bomb still goes off but we don't die." She peered at him like maybe he knew what that was all about.

"That's . . . good?" Eli said.

"Maybe? It seems better than dying." She smiled.

"Yeah." He smiled too, and felt this strange speeding-up inside. Had he missed her? It sort of felt like it, except that didn't really make sense. He hadn't even known her.

"Thanks for coming over here," he said.

160

Maya made a little eye roll. "I've been wanting to talk to you for a while, even *with* the whole costume closet thing. Did you know I was stalking your pickup spot?"

"No, I didn't." Out of the corner of his eye, Eli spotted Melissa rounding the bar. She looked from him to Maya and headed straight for them. "Um . . . ," he began.

"Hey there," said Melissa, wiping her hands on her apron. "I saw Naomi left. Who's this?"

Eli's nerves rang. "This is a friend, from school."

"I'm Maya." She held out her hand.

Melissa shook it, her face stony. She knew who this was. Glanced over her shoulder at the rest of the customers, just like they had. "It's nice to meet you, but I don't think this is a good idea."

"Right," said Maya. "Yeah, sorry. I was just, um, going in here. Have a good night." She spun and ducked into the bathroom.

Eli sat frozen, staring into the space she'd just vacated.

"Did you know she was going to be here?" Melissa asked quietly.

No.

"Do you realize the risk you're taking talking to her? Tons of people know who she is. If anyone puts two and two together . . ."

"Sorry."

"It's not just you, Eli. It's my job here . . . everything. You have to think before you act."

Before you walk home alone.

"Okay?" said Melissa. "I'm going to have Mom send her mother a message and let them know this place is off-limits."

Eli didn't reply but clenched his fists beneath the table. *You're not Mom.* Mom wasn't quite Mom, though. Melissa thought she had to be, but still . . .

"Mel!" the other woman behind the counter called. A line had formed at the register.

"Coming." Melissa spoke quietly to Eli: "When she comes out, nothing. Okay? Please?"

Eli nodded. *Whatever.* He slipped his headphones on.

Melissa went behind the counter, but instead of returning to the espresso machine, she took the other woman's place at the register. A clear view of Eli. Checked him every few seconds.

The bathroom door opened. Maya came out, spotted Melissa, and kept moving. But as she passed, under her breath: "Check the sugar packets in a minute." She rounded the bar, giving Melissa a half smile.

Eli saw her leave a moment later, walking past the windows outside. A quick glance at Eli, then back toward the counter.

He felt an ache as she passed out of his sight. Why couldn't he just talk to her? For a minute there, he hadn't thought about anything other than what they were saying. It had felt easy. Even easier than with Graham.

He waited a few more seconds and then got up and went to the counter.

"Can I get a peppermint tea?" he asked Melissa.

She eyed him. "Sure."

He stood by the bar, his heart racing. There were a couple people over by the fixings.

"One tea," the other barista said, placing a mug in front of him.

Eli took it and went to the fixings. Waited until the others were done. He reached into the sugar packets, trying to look

162

nonchalant while pushing them around with his fingers—there was a torn-out piece of notebook paper. He checked to be sure Melissa wasn't watching, slipped it in his pocket.

Back at his chair, he carefully unfolded it in his lap.

Her number.

Eli bit his lip to keep from smiling.

He held his phone beneath the table and sent a message: Got it.

Excellent! Maya replied.

Thanks for saying hi.

She replied with a thumbs-up emoji. Then: We still shouldn't talk in school.

Nope.

Getting off the bus now. More when I'm home.

OK.

Eli read a graphic novel Graham had let him borrow called *Spill Zone*. It was cool, and reminded Eli of that silent world Graham had talked about, a place all your own, and yet he realized he'd flipped through ten pages without absorbing anything. Because what was Maya doing? What was home like? And had she looked cute when she'd smiled? He was pretty sure she had.

It was weird. She was three people in his mind now: the blurry memory from the DOL, the scared girl behind the costume racks, and now tonight, chatting with him at the coffee shop, getting what he was saying in a way that no one else seemed to.

"Hey." Melissa appeared. It was nearly nine. "Ready?"

They walked through the cold, dry night to Mom's car. The wind kicked up yellow leaves.

It's getting to be that time of year, when the Purpose must be obeyed. Barely over a month now until the anniversary.

Eli winced. Pushed it back. Pictured her.

They'd just pulled out of their parking spot when his phone buzzed.

Sorry. Fighting with Janice.

That's too bad.

Whatever. So are you going to the dance Friday?

Graham had mentioned that. Said it was stupid but also that they should go. Eli hadn't cared one way or the other, and also hadn't yet asked if that would work with the police and such.

I think so.

We can probably chat there without causing AN INCIDENT. :)

OK. :)

"I know you're messaging with her," said Melissa.

Eli slid his hand over his screen. "I'm not—"

Melissa rolled her eyes. "Eli, I saw her leave her number. It's dangerous and you know it."

She gets it.

"You can't risk people finding out—"

"She's the only one who was there." Eli was surprised to hear his own raised voice. Was he allowed to show his frustration? Without it hurting anyone? "Talking to her felt . . . better."

Melissa flexed her fingers on the wheel. "You are screwed up." She didn't say anything for a second, then shook her head: "Okay, listen, we cannot let Mom know about this. You understand?"

"Yeah."

"She will lose it, and she's drinking enough as it is. And also definitely do not start chatting Maya up at school. We can't risk that."

"I won't."

Melissa made a sound like she was going to say something else. *What?*

Her face scrunched. "I've read about how people who go through trauma together get weird bonds." Melissa was thinking about majoring in criminal psychology. "Just don't start getting hung up on this girl. You may have ended up in the same place last year—I get that you have that in common—but she did not go through anything like what you have."

"I know." Another surge of frustration. He was tired of hearing what everybody had *read* about him. Like he was a zoo animal. Hadn't he been in a cage long enough?

His phone buzzed again.

"Okay?" said Melissa. She held out her fist.

Eli bumped it. "Okay."

Maya had written: Look for me at the dance.

I will.

Until then . . . knowing glances only. Eyebrow gestures. She added an emoji of bushy eyebrows.

Like secret agents, Eli wrote.

She replied with a smiley face. Eli pictured her grinning again, the way it had seemed to break her whole face apart.

I got you, she'd said. Almost the anniversary of that too.

Good night, she said now.

Bye. His stomach did a somersault. And while he didn't quite smile, he felt like he was about to, holding it just behind his lips, secret-agent-style, for the rest of the night.

CHAPTER 14

MAYA

September 28

Whoops.

Bodies swirled around her. Were her. Hips and shoulders rubbing, no borders.

Serenitab + Pom vodka + school dance = it was all all right.

She'd meant to go easy, have a good time. Stay balanced. No more being messy girl, sinking girl. Stay on top of things. She'd texted with Eli a couple times during the week, *How was your day?* and stuff like that, and also that they'd definitely find a way to meet up with each other here at some point.

But then tonight was also + Janice.

The dance had a retro eighties theme. They'd gone to Value Village after school for vintage jeans. Squeezed into the dressing room, nip of Dr. Pom, the fit of the jeans hilarious. Making out. Laughing.

But also: "No, definitely that pair. You should wear them like this. Come here and let me help you get those off."

Another swig of Pom. Add a Serenitab.

"Give me one of those, you little pill popper."

Then a stop for Red Bull and back to Janice's house, raiding her mom's closet, a museum of zippered garment bags, the retro outfits she'd kept for some reason. Bringing armfuls of clothes to the bathroom to try on. Phone blaring an eighties playlist.

"Can you ever imagine our moms looking hot?" Maya had said.

"Maybe not *your* mom." The slight scowl in the bathroom mirror. "Mine had boys lined up."

Right.

And also: "No, just the denim jacket and the tank top. Show some of that skin! No, silly, you can't be cold when you're this"— hands exploring—"hot."

And: "Maybe your tech perv friend can get a feel. What did you two talk about at Bauhaus, anyway? He's so horny for you. You like it. Trying to make me jealous." All week with comments like this.

Dr. Pom, the whole bottle from the liquor cabinet. Tip it into the Red Bull.

Then on to the insane can of hair spray Janice had found. Teasing up their hair to ridiculous heights. Chemical cloud. "Now your turn." Janice's fingers plucking the hat from Maya's head.

"No, I don't know—"

"Come on, when I gave you this hat I didn't think it would become your little binky."

Janice threw it on the counter. Maya stood there, exposed in the mirror and harsh light, the long bare section on the back right side of her head, dotted with scabs, from her neckline up and around to the top of her ear. Another missing area above and behind that she couldn't even see.

"Be right back," Janice said, leaving Maya alone with it. This zombie in the mirror.

Swig gulp.

She started teasing up her bangs, the spray making her cough, but her eyes kept returning to the damage. There was no way. Hat back on. Shaking out another Serenitab, chasing it with the last drops straight from the vodka bottle.

"Come on," Janice said, popping back in, hand going for the hat again. "The whole point was to look like twins."

Maya threw both hands to her head, throat tight and eyes burning. "No, please."

Janice shrugged. "Okay, fine. Hey, look, I got a fresh supply." Bottle of peppermint schnapps, coated with dust. "And at least we can do this." She laid out a handful of makeup and face paint.

Wild blue and pink stripes off their eyes. Chartreuse lipstick.

The schnapps like a dentist visit, like medicine like gasoline or liquid nitrogen, everything frosted, the good ship *Serenitab* on a lonely journey through the ice floes of the North Atlantic.

A blurry ride to the dance . . . and now *whoooo* laughing and singing along at full volume, spinning and twirling, Maya's face upturned to the music and fog on the packed tennis courts. They were in the thick of the dancers right up front by the DJ, a pocket of heat, the molten center of a galaxy, swimming in purple melodies and pink beats. Mist clung to the clusters of court lights, coated everyone's hair, surfaces bejeweled in the chilly evening.

Sparkly people, floaty people, luminous fairies and star children and you could you could you could.

And yet.

Every once in a while, the lights became prison spots, the dancers seething hordes, the air liquid mercury, her smile a dying gasp. *Kick down! Stay away!* Everything dangerous.

And Janice close. Bodies bumping, clutching, demanding. Mateo slipping in and out of her proximity, letting a hand fall here and there, a gleaming smile. He *was* cute. Janice on everyone. Maya losing her balance a lot, just feeling, swimming away from the pieces of dialogue that kept trying to ensnare her in their jaws:

"Mateo's parents are away for the weekend. They've got a hot tub. Plenty of bedrooms."

Janice making out with Lucas. "That's cool, right?"

It's all good or not whatever. Maya reached for the air in front of Janice, fingers groping like a jellyfish. Janice handed her the flask. She took another deep swig of schnapps. Maybe this would be the sip that caused her to implode completely, to suck in on herself and wormhole to the other side, to some alternate universe far from here.

I don't want this.

Fuck.

The song ended, and Janice threw her dewy arms around Maya and Mateo and pushed them together. Maya resisted but Janice pushed harder, until she was bumping into Mateo and his arms had slipped around her waist. Didn't want—but hey that didn't feel so bad and he was right there so she kissed him. Felt his tongue in her mouth and his hands on her ass. Well, well.

Hoped Janice would hate it but then caught a glimpse of her grin and nearly retched.

It's the least you could do, after ditching me at Bauhaus.

Roger that, Janny!

She almost started laughing. Or crying. There were no borders.

"Ow!" Mateo flinched away, fingers to his lip. Had she bitten him?

"Sorry," she said, maybe out loud.

"Oooh, somebody's feisty!" Janice spun Maya by the arm.

You can't see them anymore but they were bruises. BRUISES! And she'll give you more if you don't just turn when she says turn—

Raggedy Maya.

Janice's tongue in Maya.

Chemical alcohol sugar. *You wanna kiss I'll kiss—* She mashed her lips into Janice until their teeth collided.

Janice didn't flinch. Never flinched. *Oh yeah?* She jammed at Maya even harder, her hand sliding down Maya's chest.

Fuck you!

And then the next song lit and shoulders collided and everybody started jumping and Maya was cut loose. Janice back in the moment, one with everyone, and yet the slightest glare at Maya as they separated, the side-eye that said, *I'm not finished with you.*

She probably meant it to be hot.

Maya sank deeper.

But no! *Stay up!* The thought urgent. *You'll never escape otherwise!*

Escape?

RUN.

So she grabbed at the surface, fought to stay afloat, and the music overwhelmed and there was another swirl of time in which she just danced and there were falling stars in the fog light, and they were on Europa, in the low grav, their meat and bones barely consequential—

Maya's stomach lurched. She slowed, a searing pain carving at the inside of her skull.

She leaned into Janice. "I don't feel good!"

"It does feel good!"

Maya slipped away, gave Janice's waist a hard squeeze to throw her off the scent. Found Mateo's ear. "I'm going to find some water! I'm queasy!"

Mateo bobbed and smiled and rubbed her ass again. "Take it easy!"

Was she even a speaking thing anymore?

Maya staggered through the crowd, bouncing from one body to the next, the world ebbing dizzily like when you looked up from a carousel ride.

She reached the edge of the dancers. Buzzing from her pocket.

Eli. We're at the back of the courts. Just got here.

Maya stabbed the screen with her Muppet fingers. Heading to bathroom. Need water!

We're going to get tacos. Do you want one?

Maya sent a thumbs-up. She crossed the playground toward the community center. There were bathrooms there. Crowds milled in the parking lot. A long line at the taco truck. Steam wafting off shoulders and heads.

"Maya?"

She paused, or thought she did.

"Maya Abrams?"

Maya turned, almost fell. A woman at the edge of the parking lot. She waved at Maya, reflection of tennis court lights in her glasses.

"Hey, Maya! I'm Tamara . . . from Chalk!"

"Fuck." Maya spun in the other direction. She headed up the gentle rise of dew-soaked grass toward a line of portable bathrooms along the school drive.

"I just wanted to ask a few questions—"

"Stay away from me!" Maya shouted over her shoulder, then tripped. She righted, stumbled on, marching toward the bathrooms, her breath making clouds, her vision slipping, body shivering from the sweat gone frosty. She wrestled with her high-waisted jeans, chafing everywhere.

So hot—SHUT UP, JANNY JAN.

Her heart hammered. Fingers tingled. Halfway up the gentle hill, she checked over her shoulder. No one following her. Couldn't make out Tamara among the silhouettes, or in the crowd by the taco truck. She'd be waiting, though. In one of the many messages she'd left, she'd said something about being on a deadline.

Miiiiiddle finger to your deadline, chica.

Ahead, the bathroom doors clunked open and closed, handles turning red to green to red. The music warbled behind her, the grass swishing under her sneakers, cool mist on her face and a brown smell of fallen leaves. Maya almost smiled. So many beautiful things. Leaves were decaying and entropy was winning but they smelled amazing when they did. That had to mean something, didn't it?

Maybe it's just that you're far away from Janice.

She stopped among the gaggle waiting for a bathroom and got out her phone. Beautiful night, isn't it? she messaged to Eli.

Saw the dots like he was replying.

Behind her, the music shifted, the beat slowing, getting more urgent. Sharp-edged keyboard sounds like spinning blades. A familiar song . . .

Maya's fingers tingled. Her heart rate spiked. Stomach churned.

"Relax, don't do it, when you want to go to it—"

Everything went white.

*   *   *

The DOL is empty. Everyone evacuated, the mall vacant. Music still plays softly from the speakers. No bomb technicians. Everyone outside. Eli stands there in the wolf mask. Their hands are clasped.

"I can't," he says, voice muffled by plastic.

"Sure you can," Maya replies. "Let's get out of here. This is our chance."

Eli shakes. Finger pressing hard on the trigger. "What about the leaf smell?"

"The what?"

"What about that moment before you hit the drums? That second right before?"

"They never last. Just do it."

"I don't have the bomb," says Eli. "You do."

Maya feels the heat welling up inside her. She looks down and sees bulges beneath her shirt. Feels stretched: the chemical bottles are inside her abdomen. The impressions of wires snaking under her skin.

She's been the one, all along.

"Three! Two! One!"

The chemicals slosh. Maya's knees go weak.

But the bomb doesn't go off.

The DOL begins to disintegrate, replaced by shadows and trapezoids of light angled on turquoise walls . . .

* * *

A portable toilet. Murky liquid, clumps of toilet paper, sloshing over the black seat.

Maya reeled, her shoulder bumping against the side. Her knees, damp through her jeans, sliding on the moist floor.

"Come on, man! Push harder!"

She blinked. Eyes stung. Smell of sour and shit and urine. Vomit around the seat inches from her face. Hers? The taste in her mouth said yes.

And the bathroom was lurching from side to side, the waste plunking back and forth.

"Almost!"

Creaking and groaning of strained plastic. Maya fell against the wall.

Stop!

Grabbed the wet rim of the plastic urinal. Tried to drag herself to her feet. Shoes smearing the muck on the floor.

"Stop! I'm in here!"

"Oh shit!" one of the boys shouted, laughing.

"Hurry up!" said another.

"Help!" Maya shouted. "Help!"

"Hey, knock it off!" a voice called from a distance.

"Ah, fuck it," one of the boys grunted. "Let's go."

The bathroom crashed back to upright. A fresh splash of liquid on Maya's sneakers.

She grabbed for the handle, the world spinning. Turned the latch and slammed it open and stumbled out, careening—

Arms grabbed her.

"We got her!" a voice grunted. "Hostile forces neutralized!"

"You okay?"

Maya dropped to her knees in the cool, damp grass. Pain stabbing in her head. A tremor in her stomach like she might vomit again, but she clenched her abdomen and it passed. Distantly, she heard the laughter of the toilet tippers running off.

She looked up. Eli. And that friend of his.

"He knows about us," said Eli, "but it's all right."

Graham brushed his long hair out of his eyes. "You don't look so good." His eyes also flashed down her shirt.

Maya pulled her denim jacket closed, leaned on Eli's arm, tried to stand, but slid back to her knees. The grass listed like the deck of a ship, the tennis court lights swaying. "Too much to drink." She closed her eyes and winced. "How did you find me?"

Eli crouched beside her. "We heard that woman calling to you and saw you heading this way. I thought it might be safer to talk to you up here."

"Apparently not," Maya muttered, looking back at the toilet. "Assholes."

"Did you pass out in there or something?" Graham asked.

"I, um . . ." Maya rubbed her head. "This song came on. I used to . . ." She looked at Eli. "It's one of the memories from that day. It kinda sets me off." It occurred to her to check her palm. A lock of hair there. A brushstroke of blood.

"Sorry," said Eli. "Come on, you should get up."

175

Eli helped her to her feet. She was a good half a foot taller than him. She'd forgotten that. In her dreams, he always seemed to be her height.

"Do I smell?"

"Kinda."

Maya laughed to herself, her brain still sliding around on roller skates. "Does that ever happen to you? Losing track?"

"All the time."

She put her arm around Eli's shoulders. More solid than she'd expected. She looked at him again. Was he cute? *You're drunk, stop it.*

And why do you think that is, brain-that-just-tried-to-kill-me? To get away from YOU.

"What?" Eli asked.

Had she said that out loud? Sort of mumbled it. "I need a biiig Coke."

"We were gonna get tacos," said Graham, maybe sounding annoyed.

Maya reeled her arm in and tried standing on her own.

"You got it?" Eli asked.

"I'm good. I—" Her legs turned to jelly and she fell again. Eli caught her by the elbow.

"Here, come on, soldier." Graham took her other arm and they lifted her between them. Maya didn't love Graham's hand there, so close to the rest of her, but standing was good, better than not standing.

"Tacos," said Maya. "Coke."

"Hey, what the hell are you two perverts doing?"

Janice, Mateo, and Lucas, marching up the grassy slope.

"Fuck," said Graham under his breath.

"Jesus," said Janice, "get your rapey hands off my friend!"
Eli let go of her.

"Relax," said Graham, still holding Maya's arm, "we're taking her to get a drink—"

"Don't tell me to relax, Graham! You'd do just about anything to get some half-conscious hands on your cock. Now give her to me and get the fuck out of here!"

Janice moved in, hard. Maya felt Graham tense up, but Lucas and Mateo were looming too and he let go.

"You guys go ahead," Maya said, the words slurring.

"Why should we?" said Graham.

"Come on." Eli tugged his arm.

"You really, really oughta get going, Freaker," said Mateo.

"Screw you guys," said Graham, but he let Eli pull him away.

"Not in a million years," said Janice.

"Assholes," Graham added under his breath.

"Come here and say it again," Lucas called after them. "Please."

But Eli and Graham retreated down the hill. Maya could hear them arguing, saw Graham's arms moving wildly. *Keep going,* she thought, but also: *Come back.*

"Oh." Janice's nose wrinkled. "What happened to you, lady?" She hoisted Maya's arm over her shoulder.

Maya's stomach quaked, threatening to revolt again. Tiny inhales, large exhales. Her head ballooning. "Just let me go. Getting a Coke with . . ." She tried to turn and see where Eli had gone.

"With *them*? God, you're out of it right now." She turned Maya by the shoulders and guided her down the hill. "I don't know what you see in that new kid."

"He's nobody," said Maya.

"Then why do you want to jump him so bad?"

"I don't—"

"I get the appeal of a charity case," said Janice with a grin, "but I mean, come on."

Maya yanked herself free. "I need. A Coke." The world swooned again, but she fought it, would stand on her own.

"Okay, jeez, settle down." Janice rolled her eyes at Lucas and Mateo. "Do you guys mind taking a snack break?"

"It's cool," said Mateo.

"I'm starving," said Lucas.

Janice pulled Maya close. Compressing rib cage, deflating lungs. "Oh, Maya. See what happens when you run off?"

"I'm fine. Just drank too much too fast."

"Seems like more than that. Tell Janice what really happened. Did you have a freak-out?"

Maya shook her head. "Nope." *Freaker.* Not many letters away from that label.

They made their way down to the parking lot and got in line at the truck. Lucas and Mateo stood in front of Maya and Janice, hunched over Lucas's phone. Something to do with the Mariners score. Maya spotted Eli over by the pickup window. He had his hands in his hoodie, head down. Graham was talking excitedly, but quietly. He seemed pissed.

"We'll get some food in you, a little sugar," said Janice. "And then get back in the action. We don't want to lose the attention of our dessert." She ran a finger down Lucas's spine.

He looked casually over his shoulder and grinned.

"Mmm," said Janice.

Maya took a small step away so her shoulder was no longer touching Janice's. "I might be too tired."

Janice didn't look over but exhaled hard and spoke quietly. "How about maybe don't sabotage this any more than you already have?"

Maya's head dropped. *I'm ruining everyone's night. What about my night?* Tears burned at the corners of her eyes. *No! Don't give her the satisfaction.*

"Aww, look at you." Janice had her by the arm again. Fingers gripping. "You know, things were going fine until you ran into *these* assholes." Janice lunged past Maya. Graham and Eli were just walking by with their plates of tacos. She slapped Graham's right out of his hand. His elbow hit Eli's plate and it fell too, everything splattering onto the pavement.

"What the hell?" Graham slammed into Maya, reaching—more like clawing—for Janice.

"Whoa!" Mateo spun and shoved Graham.

Maya staggered. Where was Eli? Then she saw him; he'd dropped to his knees and started scooping the taco mess back onto their plates.

Kids all around them, circling, shouting, and laughing. Janice yanked Maya back into the crowd, and the movement unmoored her again.

Mateo had Graham in a headlock. Graham kicked, hit Lucas in the thigh. Lucas spun, but Eli was closer, and defenseless. Lucas kicked him square in the ribs. Eli fell onto his side, clutching his stomach, fetal position.

"Stop!" Maya shouted, or thought she did.

More people coming. The gravity of violence. Phones out everywhere.

"Ow, shit, get off me!"

Somehow Graham had squirmed free and gotten a fistful of

Mateo's hair. "I'll tear you to fucking pieces, mate!" Graham shouted in an accent, like Australian or something.

Lucas whirled and slugged Graham in the stomach.

Eli had struggled to his knees. Reached again for the taco mess, which had now been mashed by shoes.

Maya tried to pull away from Janice, but she hung on. "Let me go!" She tore her arm free.

Janice's eyes went wide. "Fine!" She made a throwing motion. Throwing Maya away.

Graham and Mateo went down on their backs. Lucas bent over them and started trying to drag Graham free.

The crowd was growing exponentially. "Stop!" "Kick his ass!" "What's going on!" "Oh yeah!"

"How about this, Freaker?" Mateo was up now. Hair everywhere. Shirt torn at the shoulder. He kicked Graham. And again.

"Kill him!" someone yelled.

Maya staggered, heading for Eli, who was putting dirty meat back into torn shells, his fingers caked in dirt and sauce.

A thick arm shot out in front of her, stopping her in her tracks.

"That's enough!" A short, muscular man in a black denim jacket shoved past Maya and into the middle of the circle. He knelt beside Eli, rubbed his arm and said something quietly, then pulled him to his feet. Eli tried to grab one of the plates, but it spilled all over again. He let it go and clutched his stomach. Blood dripped from his nose onto his sweatshirt.

The man had neat hair that led seamlessly into a neat beard. Nice jeans, black shoes. Maya felt like maybe she'd seen him around school. "You boys just back off now," he said. As he'd helped Eli up, his jacket had shifted, revealing the straps of a shoulder holster, the butt of a gun. Whispers in the crowd. Some kids starting to run away out of instinct.

The man pointed at Mateo and Lucas. "Stand over by the truck. I know what you look like, so don't think about running off."

Mateo and Lucas moved away, heads hung. A streak of blood ran down Mateo's neck to a stain on his shirt. "Kid went after our friend," he said, pointing to Janice.

"We'll sort it out soon enough."

Graham was curled on his side, clutching his ribs. Maya could hear him wheezing, like his lungs were made of rusted metal.

Eli. Maya gazed at him. Wanted him to see her. Needed him to . . .

Eli wiped the blood from his nose and mouth. Looked up, dazed. Found her.

Hey, she mouthed.

Maybe a moment of recognition before he looked to the sky and pinched his nose.

A squawk of radio: two uniformed police officers making their way through the crowd from the parking lot side. They conferred with the man, who seemed to be an officer too. One of the uniformed officers crouched by Graham. The other approached Mateo and Lucas, pulling out a notepad. The plainclothes officer said something quietly to Eli, then moved toward the other boys.

Maya scanned the crowd. No sign of Tamara. Why would she care about some high school brawl? *If only she knew.* Students were peeling away, already bored. Maybe no one would notice if she talked to Eli—

"Excuse me!" A young woman pushed through the crowd

to him. Melissa. Her hair tied back, wearing a sweatshirt and workout pants. She made eye contact with the plainclothes officer, and he nodded at her. "Jesus, come on," she said, taking Eli by the shoulders and guiding him across the parking lot. Eli went, head down. Didn't look back.

Voices swelled around Maya. The crowd disintegrating. Dots fleeing as she stood stuck in place. What now?

Her phone buzzed.

Where are you? Janice asked. Come find me on the courts?

Maya shoved her phone into her pocket. She slipped out of the crowd and made her way through the shadows, around the side of the youth center, to the sidewalk along the main street. One foot in front of the other. Steps unsteady, still dizzy, more than that now: empty.

Three . . . two . . . one . . .

Cars streaked by, Serenitab adding flares to their taillights. Across the street, silent ball fields exhaling mist. Some lonely insect sounds.

She reached the bus stop. Sat on the empty bench. The streetlights Ferris-wheeled, leaving green streaks behind her half-closed eyelids.

Got her phone back out.

She messaged Eli: Are you okay?

No reply bubbles. Checked the bus times. Just a couple minutes.

Where r u? Janice again. Are you here or what??

Now a photo. A selfie of Janice, holding the camera above her, making a big-eyed miss-you face. Come back. Janice will make it all better.

Maya started to cry.

A few minutes later, the bus squealed to a stop. She clambered on and slumped into a seat, the doors flapping closed.

Her phone buzzed.

From Eli. Finally—

This is Melissa. Stay away from him. You understand?

No, dammit, no! Tears again. Fingers creeping to hair.

But Maya fought it, fought to the surface.

I'm so sorry, she typed. Please tell him I'm sorry. And that I hope he's okay.

Watched for a reply as the bus pulled into traffic. One block, two . . .

Nothing.

She wrote to Janice: Going home. Have fun with the boys.

Slid her phone into airplane mode. Slid into herself, away from her stinging tears and her beckoning skin, down deep into the cool and numb, as deep as she could get.

OCTOBER

CHAPTER 15

ELI

October 1

When he closed his eyes and pushed: Gabriel's silhouette looming in the doorway. He felt him in the burn of his muscles.

Less than a month away now.

Eli opened his eyes. Arms extended, the barbell above him.

Two.

He lowered it, inhaled, pushed again.

The stairwell beyond the door to his room, the glimpse he sometimes got of a woman's picture on the wall. The cold, hollow feeling every time he heard the footsteps.

Three.

Eyes open again. Pale strips of light on the gym ceiling. Eli's back stuck to the vinyl bench. *You are here,* he told himself. A fixed point. *In the gym, in the present, working on yourself.* Around him, the clangs, grunts, zipping pulleys of others working out. Sometimes he felt like they were all on a team, getting stronger, one simple effort at a time.

He pushed again—

The screaming from upstairs. It was always somewhere in his head, always the same, the horrible pleading, the thumping of furniture.

It wasn't your sister. Wasn't ever.

He knew that. But it couldn't undo the not knowing back then.

Four.

Aching in his pecs, feeling like they might tear apart, but also satisfying, because to strain the very fibers of your muscles was to know that you were workable. *Fixable.* You were clay and wood and Lego blocks and glue. You didn't just have to be what you were. You could change yourself. Make yourself better.

I made you better.

Shut up.

Pushing the weight . . .

Nobody will ever love you like I did. You turned away from the Purpose, let that girl soil you. But you can be light again.

Biceps burning. Arms straight. Exhale.

Five.

He held the bar above him.

I saved me. By not blowing up.

You would have. All you are is a faulty wire. Your entire life a loose connection.

I'm stronger now.

Was he, though? Should've fought back in the parking lot at the dance. Not hunched on the ground like some pathetic victim.

Resistance gets the garden hose.

188

No.

Graham had been getting pounded, and what had he done? Started picking up the tacos. *Waste is against the Purpose.* That's what he'd been thinking. Who would think that while their friend needed help?

A broken boy.

Right in front of Maya too. And now he wasn't even allowed to text her, or Melissa would tell their mom.

Seeing her in the hallway today had made his chest ache. At one point their paths had crossed—she'd ducked and looked away.

He lowered the bar. Pushed up.

Six.

His shoulder started to ache. He'd upped his weight last week, but this was older pain. When Gabriel had thrown him across the room and he'd hit the wall wrong, felt something pop. Pain that erased him. Next thing he knew he'd been lying on the floor. Gabriel had shoved his arm and he'd screamed and couldn't move his shoulder for three days. Then it got better. What would Gabriel have done if he'd needed to go to the hospital? Sometimes he'd thought about finding out. Break his own wrist with the bed frame, rip his arm open on the edge of the plywood. He'd never had the guts to try.

But I can tear these muscle fibers apart and build them new. I can, I can. . . .

Seven.

Eight. Faster now. More burn. More shoulder pain but come on yes faster.

Lying on the floor while his shoulder wailed, listening to the sounds through the floor. The suck and squeal of the refrigerator.

189

Hum of the microwave. Its cheery ding. The murmur of voices from a television.

Nine.

Not long after the shoulder, Gabriel had brought the first cat. Oh no. The cat. He tried to avoid thinking about the cat.

It's just a stray, like you. And you need to feel strong again. Now, I'm going to hold its head down with this leather strap in its mouth, and I want you to put your hands right here, Jacob.

Ten . . .

I know it's squirming. Claws are nothing compared to the Purpose. Now push until you hear a crunch. Until you feel the power of taking a life. Exerting your will to the ultimate degree. Harder.

Ten . . .

I told you to push.

Ten . . .

Jacob, if you don't push, you know what I'll have to do—

"Hey."

Eli's eyes popped open. The bar was two-thirds up, his arms trembling. About to fall—

"Let me get that, pardner." Graham leaned over and grabbed the center of the bar. He lifted and Eli pushed, extending his arms with an explosive grunt.

"You had it," said Graham. He smiled, but only half of his face responded. His left eye was still mostly hidden beneath the puffy swelling. A deep, shiny purpleness that spread nearly to his chin, where a butterfly bandage covered a laceration.

"Thanks," said Eli. He blinked. The cat was still there. It always took a while to forget it, the soft feel of its fur, the crunch of its windpipe.

He sat up. "What are you doing here?"

Graham brushed his hair out of his eyes, careful of the bruise. "I had a cool idea. Something to make us feel a little better." He reached around and patted his black backpack. "Are you almost done?"

Eli checked the list of exercises on his phone that Lamar, his strength coach, had given him. He still had legs to do, but he couldn't even blink now without seeing those bright, desperate cat eyes. "I could be. Mom is picking me up in forty-five minutes."

"That's enough time," said Graham with a smile.

"How's your head?" Eli asked.

Graham's face fell. "No headaches today. Ribs still hurt, though. Doctor said they'll take a few weeks."

The police had ended up letting everyone go. Officer Dawes seemed to have orchestrated that. Pearson had called and filled in Eli's mom the next morning. Mom had been furious, shouting about pressing charges, but Pearson said the attention would be a problem. Mom wondered too if this Graham person was a good influence, whether Eli should be hanging out with him— but then she'd filled her wine again, and that topic, along with most other things, had been lost for the weekend.

"Aren't you supposed to be home resting or something?" said Eli.

"It's fine," said Graham. "My parents are going to a thing after work. Besides, the pain is a good reminder."

Of what?

But Graham was standing. "Let's get going."

"Where?"

"Outside." He patted his bag again. "Come on, it will be worth it."

"Lamar will want to know where I am. He's supposed to keep track of me."

"That bike trail is full of people. Just say we're going jogging."

"Okay."

Eli found Lamar across the room, holding a clipboard and standing beside a woman on a treadmill. They were chatting away. He seemed distracted when Eli asked, but he did look over Eli's shoulder at Graham, who was standing in the doorway. Graham delivered an innocent smile and waved.

"Yeah, that's probably fine. Just don't be long," said Lamar. "What happened to your buddy?"

"He fell off his bike," said Eli, the lie coming quickly, even easily.

Well, look at you.

"This place is pretty cool," said Graham as they left the weight room. "It feels like you're in black ops, training for the next mission."

"You should join," said Eli.

Graham sighed. "I don't think there's going to be time for that."

"Why not?"

"Oh." Graham had been sort of grinning, but it disappeared. "Just too much going on right now— Wait, I forgot." He stopped in a lounge area, sat on a couch, and tapped his phone. "Have you seen any of these yet?"

Eli sat beside him. The video was titled "Blindness," posted by Alpha_Ascendant. "No," said Eli. But maybe he'd heard kids talking about him now and then.

"Nobody knows who he is," said Graham, "but the rumor is that he goes to our school."

Graham handed Eli an earbud. The video began to play. It showed a blurry figure, mostly silhouette, the details of his face obscured by bright light and streaks, almost like they were watching through a dirty window.

"Greetings, losers, sinners, the meek and mundane," the figure said. "That's right, he's back, your judge, jury, and executioner, the one who sees you in all your wretched misery, who listens to your incessant whining and knows what you all really yearn for . . . the peace and wisdom of death."

"Intense, right?" said Graham.

Wow. Eli felt himself tensing up.

The Alpha chuckled. His voice was distorted by some kind of effect that made it low and menacing, with a rough, metallic edge. "Well, don't worry, sluts and gigolos, the Alpha hears your moans of despair and wants you to know that the time of judgment is getting closer. Do you feel it coming? You've all been asking when it will arrive, filling my comments with your"—there was a pause, like maybe he was reading from something—"desperate pleas. The Alpha hears your whining, sees the way you're all controlled, hooked up to the machines of sex and commerce and you don't even know it." He laughed harder. "No idea, really, it's sad."

"How long is this?" Eli asked.

"Just a couple minutes."

His head started to pound. Dr. Maria would tell him to remove himself from harmful stimuli. But was this harmful? *It's just a video.* "Shouldn't we get going?" he said.

"You gotta see this part."

"You know something's wrong, but you can't see it," the Alpha continued. "You lash out, so cruel and sadistic, hurting those who dare to question the privilege and status you think you own, but that's the great deception. None of this is really yours. You're just being used, prostituted, fucked again and again, tricked into liking it. Your cruelty is actually a subconscious wish, you are begging me to free you and I will, believe me, I will."

Eli blinked, and the Alpha's silhouette became Gabriel's. Maybe if he said he forgot something back in the weight room . . .

Graham was watching the video intently, holding his phone in both hands.

"How would you like to die?" the Alpha was asking. "A bullet? A bomb? My hands around your throat?"

"We really don't have long before my mom gets here," said Eli.

"Oh, right." Graham tapped pause and checked the time. "I just figured you might not have seen that. His videos have been really popular. Everybody's freaked out that he's, like, the next Columbine kid or something. But I mean, a lot of what he's saying is kinda true, you know?"

Maybe. "He sounds dangerous."

"Yeah, but . . . sometimes I wonder if maybe that's what we need. Someone to make the privileged and the bullies feel a little scared. Someone to shake things up."

Eli felt like his head was full of static. "Do the police know about him?"

"Probably. He's getting so much attention. I bet somebody's told the cops by now."

"If he's talking about killing people . . ."

Graham stood. "Yeah, but who knows if he's even serious

194

about that? I just think some of what he says makes sense. I thought you, of all people, would know what I meant."

"No, I mean, I get it. Being used. That stuff."

"Whatever." Graham turned away. "We should get going."

"Okay. Just a sec." Eli went to the locker room and changed by his corner locker, head down. He used to bring his clothes with him to the shower and change in the stall afterward. But he was getting better at the main room.

He found Graham and they headed downstairs, past the training rooms and the yoga studio, and out the back door.

"This is gonna be good," said Graham. He seemed happy again, so different from how he'd been at school the last couple days. He crossed the bike trail and charged into the woods that sloped steeply upward beyond it.

Where are we going? Eli stumbled through the brush behind him, swatting away damp branches. They emerged on a wide dirt path that traversed the hillside.

Graham started jogging up the forested trail. "When I remembered that your gym was next to Burke Park, I realized this was the perfect place."

To do what?

Cascading tangles of blackberry vines towered on either side of them. Eli hadn't been here very often, but it looked huge on the map. One of those weird Seattle parks that was mostly trails in the woods and eventually a beach somewhere down down down. This path seemed to keep to the upper section.

"How's your girlfriend?" Graham asked over his shoulder.

"What?" said Eli, adrenaline coursing through him.

"You were pretty worried about her the other night."

"I'm not allowed to talk to her anymore."

"That sucks. Probably for the best, though. You don't need her around reminding you about the past all the time."

"I guess."

"Plus, she didn't seem very stable. You never know who she'll go blabbing to."

"Yeah." But a wave of frustration surged inside Eli because it was actually sort of the opposite. During that week when he and Maya had been in touch, he'd actually felt better. Thought less about other things. Graham was like his mom and sister, saying it was better this way, and yet Eli was still thinking about her all the time.

"She was cute, though," said Graham. "I get why you decided to save her that day. Be the white knight, maybe get a shot at those tits."

That wasn't it. "That wasn't really it."

Graham stopped, winded, and slapped Eli's shoulder. "Sure it wasn't. You spared my life," he said, starting to shimmy and talk in a girl's voice. "How will I ever repay you?" He made a blow-job motion.

Eli sort of smiled, but only so maybe the conversation would end. *You should tell him to knock it off,* he thought. But he didn't really want to make Graham mad at him, especially over something that didn't matter anymore anyway.

"I just don't want you to get messed up over some dumb girl. And remember, you've still got me, though you'd better not try to suck my dick. Over here. This is it." Graham ducked onto a narrow dirt path that headed down the slope. They squeezed through a long tunnel of blackberry, the thorns nipping at their clothes, and emerged in a wide, bowl-shaped space with mostly open ground, a high canopy of trees overhead. Hazy amber sun filtered through the drying leaves.

"How did you know about this place?" Eli asked.

"I scouted it over the weekend. A good soldier always plans ahead before a sortie." Graham knelt and rummaged in his pack. Looked back at Eli. "Okay, you stand right there."

He moved to a nearby fallen tree and placed a square speaker there. Fiddled on his phone. Sideshow Fantasy burst into the silent woods.

"All you bitches better watch your backs.
You fucked with Freaks and now we're on the attack."

Graham darted across the clearing and knelt about twenty feet away. Arranged something, stood, and jogged back. Eli saw a cardboard cutout stuck in the ground facing them, shaped like the head and shoulders of a person.

"Cereal box," said Graham, "taped to a ruler. I think it will actually work pretty well."

For what?

"Check it out." Graham reached into the backpack again.

Pulled out the gun.

Compact. Sleek. Black.

Eli's stomach dropped. *Where did you get that?* He looked around, but there were only trees. Cedar and elm. Nothing moving.

"So cool, right?" said Graham. He slipped it from the holster, flexed his fingers on the grip. "It's a Ruger P Ninety-five. Marketed for self-defense, but it's equally good for"—he flicked off the safety, straightened his arm, lined up the target—"payback. What's up, Mateo? Oh, wait . . ."

He rolled his eyes and dug his phone from his pocket. Tapped at it, the gun dangling from his index finger. "Here, make a video, okay?" He handed Eli the phone and aimed the gun again. "Get me shooting, then zoom in on the target."

"Okay." Eli stepped back, heart hammering. Centered on Graham and pressed record.

"Now get on your knees; I'll make you say please."

Graham spoke in a deep, reedy voice. "Act like an animal and you'll be held to the laws of the animals. I'm predator. You're prey."

BLAM!

The sound detonated in Eli's ears, a breakwater of ringing tones echoing around the hillside, through the trees.

"Ow." Graham rubbed his forehead. His fingers came away with blood. A thin gash there. "That thing has a kick." He blinked, shook his head. "No, not at me, at the target!"

Eli forgot he'd even been recording. He swung the phone around and zoomed in.

Graham was already running over. He yanked the target from the ground and held it up. Pointed to a hole on the right side of the forehead. "Oh yeah, kill shot, baby! Would have been even better if I didn't have this fucking swollen eye." He stuck it back in the ground and returned to Eli, then aimed again, this time with both hands. "Suck on this, bitch!"

BLAM!

The target jumped, the ground exploding in a cloud of leaves and dust.

Eli staggered. It felt like someone was screaming right inside his ears, the rest of the world miles away.

"Woo!" Graham fired again.

The sound ballooned away from them. Eli scanned the forest. They couldn't be that alone. There were neighborhoods. People would hear.

"Come on." Graham jogged toward the target.

Eli followed a few steps behind, holding out the phone, hand shaking.

The target was lying flat on the leaves. Graham stood over it and aimed. "Say you're sorry, bitch. I want to hear you beg." He switched to a girly voice. " 'I'm sorry, Graham, I didn't mean to, I—' Tell it to Jesus."

BLAM!

A splintering crack, a hiss of air. "Ahhh, fuck!" Graham flinched, then kicked the target aside. Beneath it was a black rock with a fresh white streak. "Bullet ricocheted. I think it missed me by like an inch! Fuuuck." He shook his head and inspected the target. "Right between the eyes, though." Blew over the point of the gun. Grinned at Eli. "Pretty cool, right?"

Right.

He propped the target back up. Started walking back to where he'd first fired from. "Coming?"

Eli stared at the ground. His insides clenched. *We shouldn't be here.* He stopped the video and caught up.

"It's my brother's," said Graham. "He and his buddies went through a phase where they were training to be survivalists. They would go up to the pass and try to live off the land for the weekend. I think he was scared about terrorists. Jules is kind of highstrung. But he didn't take it to college, 'cause if you got caught with a weapon in the dorms they'd kick you out."

He gave it to you?

"He thinks he's got it so well hidden—Mom and Dad have no

199

clue he even has it, surprise surprise—but I found it. In his closet, in the box of letters from his old high school girlfriend. That's fitting symbolism, right?"

"What is?"

"Never mind." Graham spun the gun on his finger. Switched it to his other hand and held it toward Eli, butt-first. "Wanna try?"

I am not a weapon.

"Come on," said Graham. He pushed it closer. "You can pretend the target is Gabriel. No more *talking* about your feelings with some therapist. Time to deliver some righteous justice."

Eli gave Graham the phone and took the gun. Felt the weight in his hand, something so solid about it. He held it up and pointed it at the target.

"Okay, I'm recording," said Graham.

"Freaks are gonna rule the world, muthafucka.

I say, I say, Freaks are gonna put you under."

Breath held. Body a stone. His stomach lurched, like he might vomit. He blinked, aimed the gun with shaking arms. *You shouldn't have this, you're not a weapon— Yes you are, this is what you're meant for— NO.* He didn't want to. He did. Fingers flexing, pressing the trigger, then not, then harder—

You were made to deliver the Purpose. Crushing the little neck, the fur like air, the cat shrieking. Gabriel's hands on Eli's shoulders, chest pinned against the floor, held down—

BLAM!

The sound blistering, his arms crying out in pain as they lurched with the recoil, the explosion . . . the power. *DIE—*

BLAMBLAMBLAM!

"Whoa, shit!" Graham laughed incredulously.

His legs buckled, a storm of pain up and down his spine.

200

Acrid smell of gun smoke. A balloon of silence, the aftershock of the thunderous sound.

"Dude." Graham punched his shoulder. His hand fell over Eli's, still outstretched. His other hand still holding his phone out, recording.

Eli blinked. Lowered the gun. Fingers trembling. He felt emptied out, like there were acres of space inside him, but also an ocean of potential energy.

"I'm just going to take that, cowboy."

Graham slid the gun from his fingers. The metal, the weight . . . he didn't want to let go. Tore his gaze away and squinted at the target. "Did I hit it?"

"You had four chances."

"I shot it four times?" Eli's memory was a blur, like the gun had bypassed his mind, connected to some deep dark part of him. *You see? It's what you are.* "Sorry."

"It's okay, man," said Graham. "I *want* you to go ballistic. You deserve it. Jules's got a box of bullets back at the house, I just didn't bring that many with me. Next time, though. Let's see how you did."

They returned to the target. One bullet had torn the top curve off the head, left it dangling. The other three had missed.

"One is all it takes," said Graham. He bounced the gun in his hand. "It's awesome, isn't it? Judgment. The power to silence life. To shut them all up. Someone talks too much? Bang! Someone bullies you or takes your girl? Bang! We call the shots!"

He thrust his arm and fired again, this time off into the trees. A thwacking sound as bullet found branch.

Eli swam in his head. Wound up so tight. What would a bullet do to a lung? To Gabriel? If he'd had one in the red dark, on the mall escalator, in the trunk of the car . . . *BLAM!* A red hole in Gabriel's forehead.

A siren wailed in the distance.

"Shit!" Graham grabbed the target and ran back for his speaker, shoving everything in his bag. "Go, go, go!"

They hurtled through the blackberry, thorns raking their arms, and onto the wide trail. Eli's lungs burned. He scanned the trees in all directions, expecting police to appear at any moment.

"Come on," said Graham.

They sprinted down the trail and crashed through the woods, stopping just before they reached the bike path. Stood in the shadows, bent and huffing, as bikers and joggers passed in either direction, unaware.

The sirens, still out there, but they didn't seem any closer.

"We'll wait until the coast is clear. You head inside. Text me when you're home."

"Wait." Mom's car was by the front door. "You have to come in with me. I said I was with you, and if my mom talks to Lamar—"

"Oh, she's here already?" Graham brushed his hair and straightened his shirt. "Well, this is perfect. I need to meet her, right?"

"Well—" Eli hadn't thought it through that far. "She still doesn't know that you *know.* Also she's— Never mind."

"What? Tell me."

"She's not sure you're a good influence."

"Me?" Graham sounded shocked. "All the more reason, then. Come on, I got this."

He stepped out and crossed the bike trail, Eli trailing behind him. They went inside and up the stairs. Mom was standing in the lounge area, on her phone. As if on cue, Eli felt his phone buzz.

"Hey," he said as they neared her.

Mom looked up. In that instant, her face looked ashen, like it did at night when she was on the computer. Then she smiled, but it was the Eli-sized one—never quite as big as for Melissa. "Lamar told me you went to the trail with someone. Is this—"

"Hi, I'm Graham." Graham smiled and stuck out his hand. Mom eyed it and then shook it.

"Hello, Graham. I—"

"I know what you're thinking," Graham said in this friendly, almost adultlike tone, "and don't worry. Eli didn't tell me anything; I figured it out on my own because I had to write a report on the—you know—*incident*, last year."

"Oh." Mom looked at Graham uncertainly. Then at Eli.

"It was dumb luck," Graham went on, his eyes bright. "A shot in the dark. Eli denied it, but I swore to him, and I swear to you, that his situation is absolutely safe with me."

"That's good to hear," Mom said quietly. "Eli didn't mention that you—"

"He's been scared you won't want us to hang out," said Graham. "Which, frankly, would be a huge disappointment."

Frankly? Was this the same Graham he'd known?

"Eli is one of the nicest kids I've met at EHS. Sometimes it's a challenge for me to make friends, but Eli's one of the good ones." He held out his fist for Eli to bump.

Eli returned it, his fingers still tingling from the gun, and also tried to give him a look like *Okay! That's enough!*

Mom nodded. "Well, I'm glad Eli's been a good friend. I think, Graham, it might be good if I talked to your parents. Do they know about this, about Eli?"

Graham shrugged and made a teeth-sucking sound. "You know, I have to be honest, they don't. But Darren and Heidi would love to hear from you. That would be good too, because Eli and I have been talking about having a sleepover at my place."

We have?

"Okay, well, then maybe Eli can get their number from you later." Mom sounded worn out from the conversation. "We should get home. Do you need a ride somewhere or—"

"Nope, I'm good. The bus goes right to my house. It was nice to meet you."

"You too," said Mom.

Graham slapped Eli's shoulder. "Catch you later," he said, still with that professional smile, and turned and walked briskly out to the road.

Mom and Eli got in the car. As they buckled up, Mom cocked her head at the sound of a siren. Eli tensed, but it was even more distant than before.

"Wonder what that was all about." She scrolled on her phone. "Nothing on the police or fire feeds yet."

You could maybe not be always checking those, Eli thought. "Can we go?"

Mom scrolled for another moment, almost like she hadn't heard him, then popped back up. "Yeah." She pulled out onto the main road. "Your friend seems nice. He's more . . . outgoing than I imagined."

"He's not always like that. But he wanted to meet you."

Mom pursed her lips. "You didn't tell me that he knew—"

"Because you'd freak out." Eli's heart pounded. He hadn't meant for those words to just come right out.

"I wouldn't freak out, I just . . ." She paused while turning a corner. "I would have wanted to meet him sooner if I'd known. I guess I should have either way."

"I know how to hang out with another kid," said Eli. He wondered too, now that the truth was out, how Mom could really have thought he'd made a friend without being *himself.* How any one of these adults really thought that was possible.

"I want you to keep me informed, Elián—" She caught herself. "Sorry."

Exactly my point.

She sighed. "But I know this is all confusing. He *does* seem nice, and I'll talk to his parents, and hopefully they'll understand and be sensitive."

Tired of everyone being sensitive. Tired of everyone having to understand. "Okay."

They drove the rest of the way listening to NPR. Some long story about Congress.

Eli stared out the window. The gun kept going off in his mind. A high-pitched ringing still in his ears, soreness in his arm.

The holes in the cardboard, the way the bullets had made the air smoke, could damage rocks, cut through trees.

I am not a weapon.

But the power. The control. You just pointed and shot.

Before they could touch you.

See? You were a natural.

Shut up, I'd kill you.

Nobody stayed locked in a room if they had a gun. Nobody got touched when they didn't want to be touched. Nobody had nightmares where they were attacked. . . .

"Graham mentioned how we were talking about a sleepover?" he said a minute later.

"Is that something you'd want to do?"

"Yeah. A lot." There would be a whole night. Maybe another chance to feel that energy exploding out of him.

CHAPTER 16

MAYA

October 3

She stopped when she saw the splatter of blood on the milky-white snare drum head. The safe cocoon of sound died away around her. She'd asked to stay after rehearsal and play for a bit. Ms. Reid would be coming back from the office soon to lock up, but for a half hour it had just been Maya and the drums.

She'd been playing a tom-tom beat using paradiddles, fluid and alternating. Inspired by a show at the Vera Project on Saturday night. Dad took her, so lame to be there with your dad and yet also pretty cool of him. When was the last time they'd done anything like that?

Both her parents could tell she was down after the dance, and not just the hangover, which Mom went light on her about. They didn't know she'd found Eli in the first place, never mind lost him again, but they did both notice how her phone kept buzzing.

How she kept not looking at it. She knew who the messages were from.

Janice had started out apologetic:

Sorry we drank too much.

Didn't like seeing those boys messing with you.

Lucas and Mateo were kind of boring. Maybe just bc you weren't there.

To annoyed:

So this is how it's going to be?

Are you with your tech friends?

You like that better than me?

They've helped you through the hardest time of your life?

To pissed:

What the fuck?

To frigid:

Whatever. I get it.

So when Dad had picked her up for dinner on Saturday and asked her what she felt like doing, she'd told him to just drop her off at the Vera Project. He and Kendall could go to dinner or whatever. But he'd surprised her: *Can I come?* And Kendall had been like, *I'll meet my friend.* And then there they were, first watching a band called Powder Lips and then the Rusty Soles. Their excellent girl drummer had done this tom-tom beat that Maya had memorized. Dad tapping his foot, nodding. Maya now and then getting lost in the music.

Here in the band room, she'd turned off two of the three banks of lights and worked on that beat in the shadows. Sound and sweat, the Slinky-like compressing from polyrhythms to unisons, roar to growl, ferocious cymbal crashes. Eyes closed, humming melodies to herself that resonated through her skull and inside her earplugs.

She had an extra energy driving her today. Something in her back pocket. First, though, this bloody business on her knuckle.

She sucked the drop and dug into her bag for a tissue and a Band-Aid (four total today). She folded up the tissue, licked it, and wiped at the drum head. The blood mostly came off its rough surface, enough that you might mistake it for a coffee or soda spill.

She put on the Band-Aid and had just picked up her sticks again when she heard her phone buzz.

She gave her bag the side-eye, but instead reached into her back pocket. Her fingers tingled as she unfolded the blue paper. A piece of half-sized stationery with red lines. The edges were decorated with the characters from *Sentinels of the Neoverse*, the summer's hit movie.

She'd found the note inside her locker yesterday. Slipped through the vents. The page had a torn edge, like it had been ripped from a journal, the lines filled with careful, rounded hand-writing. Maya read it again, running her finger down the page:

Dear Maya,

Hi. How are you? Dr. Maria said that since I can't see you, I could try writing you a letter to keep in touch (I'm at her office now). She wants me to write more of my feelings down and I usually don't like to but this sounded okay. How was your weekend? I'm really sorry about Friday. I know those kids are your friends. We should have stayed away. ~~Or I don't know~~ Well, I hope you felt better, later. I'm okay. I have some bruises on my side. Graham got hurt pretty bad but he's fine. Sometimes it feels like things will never get better but then I'm supposed to

remember that good things happen. Like meeting you.
~~Okay let me know how you're doing. Your friend, Eli~~

Okay I'll write more (Dr. Maria told me to). There's
something I wanted to tell you on Friday but I didn't
have a chance. ~~Do you remember when~~ When we were
in the mall, when the bomb squad was working on us, I
started to feel like I couldn't hold on to the trigger
anymore, and then you said, "I got you." Do you remember
that? You probably didn't think that was a big deal but I
think about it all the time. So I'm glad I get to see you
around, and we got to talk that time, and just so you
know, I'm still sorry for last year and for everything
you've had to go through since then. I'm so ashamed.
How are you? Eli

P.S. Very cool that you play the drums. I've always wanted
to learn.

Maya wiped her eyes.

I got you.

She didn't remember saying that at all. How could she have
forgotten? All those hours surrounded by the bomb squad . . .

She was so glad to hear from him. That he was doing okay.

"It's not unusual to feel a connection to someone you've
shared a traumatic experience with," Renee had said at their session yesterday. "You both share it in a way that no one else does.
That can be a supportive relationship."

But then why was it making her sad? Except she wasn't sad,
exactly. It was more a feeling about the way things were so fragile. This thin paper, these little scratches of ink that made words,

those brief moments at Bauhaus and at the dance when she'd hung out with Eli, already days ago, and who knew what came next? For a minute their little dots had been together making a picture, but now they were drifting apart and it sucked. And yet a smile still crept to her face as she ran her fingers over the letter and then carefully folded it up. She'd write back to him tonight. Couldn't wait.

Her phone buzzed again. *Okay, fine.* She returned the letter to her pocket and got her phone from her bag. There was the small chance that it was her mom. Maya had texted that she was staying late, and maybe they could meet somewhere for dinner on her way home?

She had two alerts. An email from school titled ONLINE VIDEOS—URGENT, and a message from Janice:

Are u still here?

Maya swiped the text away, opened the email:

Dear Elliott students, parents, and staff:

A series of YouTube posts have been brought to our attention by both parents and students that contain threats of mass violence and specific mention of Elliott High School. The videos are credited to the user name Alpha_Ascendant. First, I would like to assure all of you that we are in close contact with law enforcement about these videos, and we are taking a number of additional measures to assure that our school environment is safe and secure. While we caution that these videos may be upsetting to view, we encourage all parents to watch them and, unless you feel they contain potential triggers, to also watch them with your child to see if there is anything that might point to the identity of the perpetrator.

To our students, if you know the individual behind these videos, this is not a time for withholding information. These videos represent someone in our community who needs help, not protection, and we strongly urge you to get in touch with the school. We have set up a hotline for your concerns and/or any tips you might have, listed below. And as always our guidance counselors are available to speak with students or families. We appreciate your help and welcome your questions.

—David Neyer, Principal

Maya closed the email, a chill running through her. So far, she'd avoided actually watching any of those Alpha videos. Like things weren't crazy enough right now.

Another message arrived from Janice:

I so need your help. On the stage.

Janice must have had one-acts rehearsal. Probably heard the drumming. Maya's heart spiked. They'd sat apart in bio lecture all week so far. Ate lunch at different tables.

"You're allowed to feel like the relationship isn't healthy," Renee had said. "Based on what you're telling me, I'm inclined to agree. And it's good to see you recognizing that, and taking steps to protect yourself."

A wave of adrenaline . . . There was probably no more avoiding it.

Maya put her sticks away and packed up the drums. Out in the back hall, a few students were still milling around the costume and prop closets. Maya headed through the backstage doors, walked between the curtains in the wings. Most of the lights were off, the main curtain open. Her footfalls creaked on the worn boards.

Janice was sitting on the front of the stage in a spotlight, dressed in a gray wool skirt and jacket, a pink shirt underneath, her hair up in a bun, speckled gray to make her look older. She gazed at the floor and sniffled, the sound echoing in the empty auditorium.

It's like a scene in a play. Maya paused at the edge of the cone of light, still in the shadow. *I should leave*—but she walked out. "Hey."

"Hey."

"I got your messages. What's up?"

"Rehearsal was a disaster. Ms. Mays was so harsh." She shook her head. "I'm not good enough."

Maya crossed her arms. "Of course you are, you're Janice. You're great at this."

She shook her head. "The show's in a week. The recording will be part of my applications, but whatever. So stupid to think I could go to Juilliard or whatever."

"No, it's—"

"And on top of that, my girlfriend's been icing me out. I've got nothing. I might as well disappear."

"Don't say that."

"Why not? What's the fucking point? If I'm gone, everyone will be better off and no one will miss me."

"Janice, that's not true." Janice only shrugged. "I—I think you need to talk to someone," Maya said. "I know my therapist would see you, or there's a hotline—"

"Jesus, Maya, I don't want to talk to *them*! I want you!"

I should go to her, she thought. *She needs me.* Just to give her a supportive hug. There couldn't be anything wrong with that. A good friend would be there, no matter what problems they had— *No, DON'T! Whatever you do!*

"Did you hear me?" said Janice.

I got you, she'd said to Eli.

Maya stayed where she was, heart hammering. She crossed her arms. "I'm sorry. But it can't be me."

Janice looked up at her, incredulous.

Say it, before you can't! "I'm sorry you're hurting, and I wish I could help, but I need some time." The words left her like fireworks, lighting up her sky. She felt light-headed, upended.

Janice laughed to herself. "Really."

Keep going! "Things haven't been great between us, and I need some space to sort it out."

"And you're saying that's *my* fault?" Janice rolled her eyes. "Maybe things haven't been great because of *you.* Did you ever think of that? Lately, you've either been totally avoiding me, or ruining my night at the dance, or my surprise costume party."

"I haven't been avoiding you. I—"

"What, Maya?" Janice stood up. "You need more space to be sad? To make life suck for everyone around you? To make me beg for your affection, shower you with compliments, all so you could do *this*?"

"I don't—"

Janice stepped toward her. The spotlight cast ominous shadows down over her face.

She knows it's doing that. Even if she doesn't. It's a stage effect and this is a Janice production and I'm the villain, or maybe just a prop.

"You know what?" she said. "It doesn't matter how much I try to help you, or care about you. It's like you *want* to be suffering like this, but only if the rest of us are suffering with you. You don't really care how we feel."

"I—" Words got jumbled. "I do care, I just—"

A step closer. "It's always *Don't touch me right now,* and *Maybe later,* and *I'm not really feeling up for it,* like you're the only one who matters."

If Janice got much closer she'd reach out and they'd touch—

Say it.

Her hands would be on Maya's arms again. The fingertips that left reminders—

SAY IT—

"I don't think you're good for me."

Janice stopped cold. "What?"

Tears fell. Maya breathed deep. "I think we should break up."

Janice laughed. "Oh my God, you bitch. You are so incredibly selfish! After I've totally been there for you, like, nonstop!" Icicle eyes stabbing into her. "Do you know how hard it's been to deal with you? When you just keep taking more and more?"

"I'm not the one who does that." Maya shaking. *Keep going!* "It's you. Everything always has to be how Janice wants it. It—"

"It's what?" Janice closer. Looming. Maya saw her hands twitch.

This is it. She'll hit me now. Finally. Stomach clenched. "It makes me worse," said Maya.

Janice wobbled on her feet and stopped. Looked at the ceiling.

215

Sighed. "You know what? Forget it. You're honestly not worth it. Go try and get fucked by those tech nerds." Janice pointed and twirled her finger. "No one else is going to want this." She strode past Maya—

Bracing—

Didn't touch her, just a whoosh of costume.

Maya turned. "Hey."

Janice paused in the shadows of the wings.

"Are you going to be all right?"

Janice wiped her eyes. Maya couldn't tell if there were really tears or not. "What do you care?"

"Just . . . you've said some things about hurting yourself, and I think—"

Janice cut her in half with a saber-like laugh. "Please. I'm fine. Unlike you." She smiled, glacial. "Delete my number."

Strode out.

And scene.

Tears . . . but then a little smile of her own. Maya's hand drifted to her pocket. To the letter there.

I got you.

She stood in the spotlight, watching the particles of dust float around her like they were swimming in a sea. A constricting squeeze—Janice might be right. No one might ever want her.

She nodded.

"I do."

She stepped into the dark—

But before her eyes could even adjust, light flashed around her. Maya paused. She was standing in another spotlight. The one she'd just been in had turned off.

She peered out into the seats, but there didn't seem to be anyone at the control boards.

She shook her head and walked—

The spotlight she'd been in clicked off. A new one burst
around her, this time a red light.

Maya halted again, her heart tripping on itself. She squinted
up toward the ceiling. Eli? But she'd seen him heading to his
bench when she was on her way to practice.

"Graham?" Her voice echoed in the empty auditorium.

Silence. The red spotlight gazed at her. So quiet she could
hear its slight humming.

"Okay, whatever," she said aloud, and started walking again.

Red light off. Dark . . . Just as she reached the wings, another
white light illuminated her.

She sped up, safely into the shadows. Kept walking fast, back
to the band room, through and outside into a damp, bracing
wind. As she hurried up the sidewalk, she glanced behind her,
but of course there was no one there.

What the hell had that been? Had Graham been watching
them again? That kid . . . What did Eli see in him? He did know
Eli's secret. Had gotten him on Tech Squad. And unlike Maya,
he was a friend Eli could actually be seen with in the world. Still,
though . . .

Her phone buzzed, making her nerves ring—*This will be Janice, the start of the retaliation*—and so she waited until she was
at the bus stop before checking.

But it was just Mom, running late at work, probably couldn't
meet up for dinner: Can you just go home and make something? Hopefully
I'll be there by ten.

Great. Frozen mozzarella sticks and ranch dressing it was.

Maya slumped back on the bus stop bench, and all at once it hit her: more alone than ever. No relationship, no fucking parents, no friends—

Maybe one. She wished she could text him right now. Maya fished Eli's letter from her pocket, got out her notebook, and started writing him back.

CHAPTER 17

ELI

October 5

"Have things been okay at school since the fight?" Detective Pearson asked as they drove to Graham's house.

"Fine," said Eli. "Nothing else happened." He tapped his pencil against a notebook, his binder half-open in his lap.

"How's the math homework going?"

"I'm almost done."

He hadn't even started. Pressed against the inside of the notebook was the letter he'd found in his locker today.

> *Dear Eli,*
>
> *Sorry it took me a couple days to write back. I've had tests in like every class. Also I broke up with Janice, although I think she's telling everyone she dumped me.*

Don't worry, I'm fine about it. Better, actually! I think your letter helped me do it. So thanks!

Right now I'm sitting on the floor in my little room, on my pink rug that's way too girly. It's raining but I noticed when I got home that the breeze smelled like the ocean, so I opened my window, and I swear outside I can hear the bells of the old lighthouses and the creaks of the sailing ships from two hundred years ago. Oars thudding. Spooky whale calls. Sorry, maybe that sounds weird. But do you ever think you can feel the history of a place? I read that smells are really strongly associated with memories and emotions, which can be bad and good. Maybe it means I was a ship's captain in a past life!

So what are you doing this weekend? My mom and I are going up to see my grandma in Bellingham. (It's actually my dad's mom, but he and Grandma don't really talk, so my mom still takes me. News flash: divorce sucks!) Have you ever been up there? There's not much to do, but you can walk on the beach beneath these tall bluffs, which are pretty beautiful. Also my favorite coffee shop in the world is there. They make these oatmeal cookies with chocolate chips that are the best-tasting healthy thing ever. Wow, can't believe I'm writing about cookies. Yawn! :)

Thank you for telling me about what I said at the DOL. I didn't remember, but there are weird gaps in that day for me. And it might have seemed like I was being really brave, but here's the thing: I was totally terrified. And ever since, I've been pretty messed up. But I guess I did know that I wasn't going to let go of your hand.

I wasn't going to die. (Though funny story: while we were standing there I also had to pee so bad that at one point I was considering asking the officers to, like, get a bucket and pull down my pants and how insane is it that I was thinking about that while we were stuck to a bomb and why wouldn't my body just know that and shut up? Was pee really more important than survival?) Okay, I kind of wish I could erase those last sentences. Curse you and your ancient ink-and-paper technology! (That's a joke. No curses. And paper is cool! It smells nice. Ah! More deleting!)

Anyway I know what you mean about it feeling like it will never get better. I've kinda felt like that my whole life. Even the sun is going to die someday, and Earth will be gone, and all the stars will go out. I don't know what to do about the fact that each moment will leave us and never come back. Sometimes it feels like what's the point if everything is just loss? Ah, sorry, morbid! Also, maybe that sounds stupid. You've been through a lot more than I have.

Okay, I am rambling! Hey, so I like being pen pals. I've never had one! Wish we could hang out, though. I saw you at Bauhaus again the other night and was trying to figure out how to get a message to you. Tucked in someone's panini? Flung with some kind of slingshot? Mouse courier? I saw one in there once. Just a mouse. Can't confirm its courier status. Okay, write back soon!—M

P.S. Don't be sorry about last year. I mean, if we were dead and in heaven together I'd definitely be giving you a serious guilt trip, but since we survived, no hard feelings. It's not your fault I don't have a thicker skin.

P.P.S. Kinda want to delete that P.S.

P.P.P.S. But then do you ever think about how many tiny things had to line up to put us in that exact moment that afternoon? Every single minute that had to go the way it did? For like hours and days and years? Sometimes on Doctor Who they talk about certain events being TIME-LOCKED, like you can't change them, and on the show it's really just a plot device so that you can't fix everything, but what I'm saying is, quantum theory would state that there were infinite variables and infinite possible ways that afternoon could have gone, and I bet most of them would have ended up with us dying, but the way it went, no matter how hard it's been, it got us out of there alive, therefore I hereby deem it TIME-LOCKED. (Did I mention I'm a Time Lord?) So no more apologies, okay?

P.P.P.P.S. Jeez now you must think I'm the biggest nerd.

P.P.P.P.P.S. Sorry this letter is so long!

P.P.P.P.P.P.S. Bye!

Eli had already read the note at least five times since he'd found it after lunch—though not right when he found it, because he'd been with Graham.

Graham didn't know about the letters. It had seemed better not to tell him.

Eli folded it carefully and tucked it into the pencil pocket of his binder. Then he looked out the window and felt a rush. They were heading north and west and weaving through steep, sloping roads. Earlier, they'd passed a sign carved in a large rock welcoming them to the Blue Ridge neighborhood. The houses were massive, full of giant windows looking north, where the land fell away to the silver expanse of Puget Sound. High gray and lavender clouds mirrored the water, just touching the tips of the Olympic Mountains in the distance. He thought of Maya on a beach somewhere out there, looking at this same body of water. She would probably be able to describe it in some really cool way. Could they message by orca courier? She would like that joke.

"I think this is it," said Pearson. They pulled up to a light blue two-story house, large compared to Eli's, but that wasn't saying much. Smaller than the other houses on this street.

"We'll have an officer keeping watch," Pearson said. "You have my number, right?"

"Yeah." Eli's nerves buzzed. He hadn't expected any of them to agree to the sleepover. But after Graham's performance at the gym, Mom had actually made the call to his parents, glass of wine in hand. They'd gotten along fine, and after that it was just about assigning an officer to watch the house.

Pearson reached over and rubbed his shoulder. "This will be fun." She pointed behind them. "Officer Warren is right there."

Eli saw a white car parked a few houses up.

"Have a good time, okay?"

"Thanks." Eli got out. Graham appeared at the door and waved as Pearson drove away. The swelling around his eye had mostly gone down. Only a slight purpleness with yellowed edges. The bandage was off his chin, just a scab there.

"I was afraid she was going to come in," Graham said as Eli came up the steps. "That would have been awkward."

"Why?"

"Oh, I don't know. Just, police are always looking at you weird, you know? Like they're always on the job."

Eli cocked his head. "She's not like that."

"Come on," said Graham. "You don't think every time she's with you, every word you say, she's not listening for a sign that you might be about to go bomber again? Hell, she's probably taping your conversations."

Eli shrugged. That had never occurred to him.

"Either that or they're waiting for their bait to finally work." Graham motioned to the car up the street.

"Bait?"

"Yeah, it's obvious, isn't it? The real reason they're watching you all the time is because they're hoping that Gabriel will come after you and they can get him."

Eli's head swam. "They don't think I'm bait."

Graham patted his shoulder. "Sorry, man, but they do. They don't care about you. They care about *him*. Keeping you safe doesn't get them promotions or news interviews. Catching *Gabriel*? That gets you played by Brad Pitt in a movie."

Eli's heart sped up. It made perfect sense. How had he never thought of it? Had his mom? Melissa? Did they all know and they'd just never told him?

"Think about it this way," Graham said. "Did anyone really try that hard to find out your identity last year? No. All the news reports were about who *Gabriel* was. How *he* could do what he did. Criminal profilers, psychologists, and on and on. We're obsessed with the criminal mind, because we all wonder if we're capable of the same thing. If we've got a monster inside us somewhere. But of course we do. Because what we really like is thinking about how we'd do the crime better. How we *wouldn't* get caught. Anyway, you were just the tool. And now you're the bait."

"They cared about Maya."

"A little bit," said Graham. "That's another thing we like: heroes, especially ones that are a little sexy and vulnerable. Did you hear that rumor that she hooked up with Bob Borkner from King Five News?"

"No."

"But even then, Maya's like a feel-good sidenote. Gabriel is the headline story."

Bait.

"Shit. I didn't mean to upset you. God, I'm an idiot. Hey, screw them, right? I don't think of you that way. So they hope Gabriel will come back. Maybe they're even hoping he'll show up here tonight. Course he'd better be ready if he tries to mess with us, right?"

Eli pushed a smile to his lips. Hands in fists to keep from shaking. "Do you still have the gun?"

"Of course. I put it back in my brother's room. But it's there if we need it."

Eli remembered the weight. The kick. "Can we shoot it again?"

"Nah," said Graham. "My parents are going to be around all night. Speaking of which, they're standing around like dumbasses in the kitchen waiting to meet you." He tugged Eli's sleeve. "Come on."

Eli glanced up the street again at the waiting car. Not watching. Waiting. He wanted to go over there and tell them to leave. Not going to be someone's bait.

We could take care of them together, Gabriel said. *When I come back. We'll show them.*

Shut up.

"Hey, man, come on!" Graham called from inside.

Eli entered and walked down the hall. There was a set of photos of Graham and his brother and parents on one side, Graham a little younger. Professional, taken at some bridge in the woods somewhere. Everyone smiling. On the opposite wall were framed pieces of artwork by Graham and Jules when they were little. The kitchen beyond was wide and bright, skylights, an open bar into a living room and dining room area. A bay window with a view of the sound. Everything clean.

"Mom, Dad," said Graham, "this is Eli."

They stood by the counter waiting to greet him. Graham's dad in khakis and a black sweater, his mom in jeans and a nice plaid shirt. Both introduced themselves by their first names, Darren and Heidi, shook his hand in a weirdly formal way. Maybe just like he was an adult. Or like they were being careful not to make him blow up.

"Graham said you guys have been having a great time on Tech Squad," said Heidi.

"Yeah," said Eli.

A pause.

"I'm glad you two found each other," said Darren. "We're always encouraging Graham to be more social."

"Aw shucks, Dad," said Graham. "I can't be Mr. Straight As *and* Mr. Popular."

A half smile from Darren. "When was the last time we saw straight As, again?"

"Eighth grade, third quarter," said Graham.

"The good ol' days," added Heidi.

"Back before I realized that school was just a tool of the plutocracy!"

"Okay, that's enough." Darren's smile had dimmed.

"Anyway, I told you," Graham went on. "Eli's just . . . different. It's a relief from all the other kids."

"There's my sensitive sweetie." Heidi reached over and ruffled Graham's head.

"Yup, that's me." Graham made a sheepish grin that reminded Eli of when Graham met his mom.

"Well, we don't want to keep you guys," said Darren. "I know Graham is anxious to show you the new Xbox prerelease I brought home from the office. We'll do dinner in two hours or so, okay? I'm grilling salmon. Do you eat that, Eli?"

"Yeah."

"Perfect," said Heidi. "Well, have fun!"

They headed downstairs to a carpeted basement room, with an L-shaped couch and a huge TV.

"We can blow up some alien hordes"—Graham lowered his voice and reached behind the couch—"while we hit this." He held up a slim rectangular bottle of Captain Morgan spiced rum. "I'll go get Cokes. You up for that?"

Eli nodded. *Sure.*

Graham hurried out, and Eli sat on the couch. Looked at the small window high on the wall.

Bait.

"Here we go." Graham returned with two cans and put one

on the table. He popped the other open, drank a few gulps, then poured the rum in. He handed the can to Eli and prepared the other one.

"Cheers," he said, "to pulling off this sleepover right under their noses."

They clinked cans and drank. The rum had a spicy-sweet smell. Eli winced at the burning sensation.

"Have you drank before?" asked Graham.

"Not really." There was one time, sort of: when his dad made a rare appearance on his birthday. He'd already been drinking—as usual—and at one point handed his half-finished beer to Eli. *Might make you feel better,* he'd said, opening another. Eli had only taken a few sips before pouring it out. It had tasted terrible. And stressed him out. His mother's wineglass did the same. He couldn't help feeling like they were all drinking *because* of him.

This was different, though. What normal kids did.

"We'll take it slow and steady," said Graham.

They started the new game called *Colony 17.* You were part of a squad of Metrotroopers that got ambushed by these cyborg alien creatures while investigating a destroyed colony on another planet. They ducked and soared and fired their way through exploding rooms, gore, screams, and now and then, beautiful space vistas.

Eli could feel the alcohol seeping into him. By the end of the second spiked Coke, his vision had streaks. His thoughts became surprisingly uncluttered and floaty. As they torched a nest of aliens with an upgraded flamethrower, he thought, *Fuck bait, fuck Gabriel,* and it brought a smile to his lips.

"Here," Graham said sometime after that, handing him an

unopened can. "Seltzer water. Gotta sober up a bit before we eat. You good?"

"Good," said Eli.

He was nearly silent through dinner, a slight headache setting in. No, he wasn't doing any clubs yet. Yes, he liked the Seahawks. What his mom did, where his sister went to school . . .

Darren and Heidi talked a lot about this family trip they'd recently taken to Thailand. Heidi was a history professor at UW, and so they'd toured ancient Buddhist sites.

"So boring," said Graham. "Buddhists just sit around trying not to feel anything."

"They're not trying *not* to feel; they're trying to observe their feelings without being controlled by them."

"To stay neutral," said Eli.

"Yes," said Heidi. "That's exactly right. Have you studied Buddhism, Eli?"

"I've just talked about it with my doctor."

"Mmm." Heidi and Darren both took big bites of food.

"I don't know," Graham blurted into the silence. "The Buddhists would rather die in peaceful protests than fight back. They light themselves on fire for no reason."

For the Purpose. You will be light.

"It's symbolic," said Heidi.

"Lot of good it's doing them."

Darren opened his mouth to reply, but Heidi touched his arm. "You thought the temple ruins were cool."

"Well, duh, yeah," said Graham. "Except we weren't allowed to explore on our own."

"Silly safety rules," said Heidi with a smile. "Well, it's our job to get you some culture, whether you like it or not."

"Not," said Graham, but again he flashed that smile.

"Okay, be that way," said Heidi. She took their plates. "Brownie sundaes for dessert?"

* * *

"Sorry about them," Graham muttered as they stumbled downstairs.

It was nice. "Thailand sounded pretty cool," said Eli. So did having two parents at the table.

"I guess. My parents are at that awkward point in life where they haven't realized yet that they're totally boring. And my mom with the Buddhist stuff . . . she's like a zealot. I mean, there we are in Thailand with all these cool beaches and snorkeling and super-hot chicks in, like, the tiniest bathing suits and she had us going off to look at dead people's things almost every day."

"My family would never go on a trip like that."

Graham shrugged. "Yeah. It's just that they're so clueless. So bought into the system, like this world is perfectly fine. They could never understand how we feel, you know?"

I guess. "You're good with parents," said Eli.

"The key is just to give them what they want, and they stay out of your way."

"What do you mean?"

"Haven't you ever noticed that when something's bad in your life, your parents always get stressed out and mad?"

Yeah.

"That's because they all wish they were still young and free and mattered like us. What they really want is for you to be fine so they can go back to thinking about their own dumb lives."

"Your parents seem interested in your life. Like it's important."

230

"Yeah, but they're only interested in the good stuff. So that's all I give them. That way, they stay out of my business. Be right back."

Eli sat on the couch again. He wondered if his mom wished she was free of him, and he felt certain that she did, like he'd already known this somewhere inside.

"Round two." Graham returned with two more Cokes and a small glass jar of bright red cherries. He prepared the cans, then dropped a cherry in each. "Classy now, like mobsters."

They watched a movie called *House of Slaughter,* where these teens take a dare to stay overnight in an abandoned mansion, and then get killed off one by one. Graham paused at a point just as one of the girls was having her head sawed off. She was on her knees, topless in just her underwear, back arched. Neck sliced open beneath wide glassy eyes.

Screaming in Eli's head.

"You've gotta see this porn she's in," Graham said, scrolling on his tablet.

"That's okay. Can we just keep watching?" *Melissa was never in that room.* Except Dr. Maria had pointed out that thinking of her when he saw these sorts of images was unfair to her, or something. Besides, he had to be tough. Normal kids watched stuff like this all the time and it was no big deal.

"In a sec. It's this one where she's a cop and pulls these three guys over but then bangs them all at once. Crap, looks like it's been taken down. Oh well." Graham unpaused the movie, and the girl's final scream choked away in a spasm of blood.

Eli's next thought surprised him: Maya would probably hate this movie. Although who really knew? He nearly texted her—why not?—but remembered that it would show up on his phone record, and Melissa had said she'd be watching.

Near the end of the movie, the killer had the last girl chained up in a barn and said, "The only point of this life is to get to death, to the other side."

Eli thought that sounded familiar. Where had he heard that?

Then the boyfriend everyone thought was dead burst in and shot the killer in the back, but when the credits rolled, the killer's body was gone.

After the movie they played *Colony 17* again. Long, rum-drenched stretches where Eli didn't think about Gabriel, didn't picture the red dark, but then others where he found the red dark clinging all around, imagined Gabriel coming for him, the footsteps up the stairs, the light as the door creaked open. The silhouette. Imagined shooting Gabriel in the head, in the crotch, then ten more times, his body tearing apart in chunks like the aliens they blasted in the game.

Other times he thought about Maya. What was she up to? Dark outside now. Too late for a beach walk.

"Take that, bitch!" Graham shouted at the screen. "Come on, Eli, get in there!"

A few more levels, another rum and Coke, an entire bag of Cool Ranch Doritos.

Around two a.m., they crept up through the dark house to Graham's room. Graham flopped onto the bed. Eli sat on an air mattress, arranged with some blankets and a pillow on the floor. He pulled his knees to his chest. His vision swam.

"Look." Graham rolled over and swiped open his tablet. "It's Mateo's profile page."

"You guys are still friends?" said Eli.

Graham laughed to himself. "I set up a dummy account. Mike Ballsakovich. Good, right? And dumbass took my friend request. So did a couple hotties, although I think they might be fake accounts. You know, like with the Russian girls. But check this out."

He opened a search window and typed *tiny penis*. The screen filled with results. "This one is perfect." He clicked on an image of a blond girl holding her fingers an inch apart and making a shocked face, while two friends laughed. He posted it on Mateo's wall. "What should we write?"

"I don't know."

"Oh, I got it." He typed and showed it to Eli.

It read: **Guess we know why Janice likes you.**

"Awesome," said Graham. He belched and hit post.

"He'll definitely unfriend you now," said Eli.

"Yeah, but I can just make another profile. Whatever, it's boring. Hey"—he sat up—"wanna go to his house? He lives like a mile from here. We could take a sortie and, like, throw rocks at his windows, or toilet-paper his trees."

Why? "I'm pretty tired."

Graham leaned back on his elbows and yawned. "Ah, me too. Little shit would probably call the cops anyway." He swigged off the rum bottle, spilling some on his chest. Offered it to Eli.

"Nah," said Eli. His stomach was listing sideways, his head starting to pound.

"I should go put this back, just in case," said Graham, swirling the rum. "Not like my parents would ever notice. They're so oblivious."

They seem nice.

Graham was gone—Eli watched the ceiling spin—then he dove over Eli and flopped onto the bed.

"Shit, I think I'm gonna pass out."

Eli lay back. When he closed his eyes, the darkness looped.

"Don't wet my sheets thinking about Maya."

I don't—

"Just kidding. I get why you like her. All homely and damaged. A real fixer-upper."

"She's nice."

"No, I know. Sorry, I shouldn't talk shit. I wonder what she'd say if you ever talked about blowing up the school. Like, would she be into it."

"About what?"

"Nah, I'm just kidding. Jokes."

Eli felt like he was swimming around in thoughts. "Sorry about Janice," he ended up saying.

"What? Nah, it's cool. She doesn't like dick anyway. It's her loss. I got other girls . . . online . . . a few . . ." It sounded like he was dozing off.

"Good night," said Eli. He swallowed, a sour taste. His tongue felt swollen. Still weird tremors in his stomach.

"You okay on the floor?" Graham asked a minute later.

Yeah. Then: "I'm kinda used to it."

Graham popped up on his elbow. "Oh man, you mean like when you were—"

"In captivity." That was one of the phrases Dr. Maria had suggested he try to use. He never had before, but it wasn't so bad to say it, he found now. Maybe a relief.

"Fuck," said Graham. "What, um . . . what was it like? I guess people probably ask you that all the time."

"Nobody ever asks me."

"Did he hurt you?"

"Yeah."

"Did he, like . . . rape you?"

"Yeah."

"Dude."

Taps against the window. It had started to rain.

Eli swallowed. Felt the ache in his ribs. "He had this piece of garden hose he would hit me with. Other stuff too, but that hurt the worst."

"Holy shit, man."

Eli closed his eyes. Saw the blur of the hose through the air. *Smack!* The welts after. He was glad for the rum. It made the impact distant, like watching it on a screen.

"So you were like a child soldier," said Graham. "Like one of those kids in the Congo that have to kill their own parents."

The rain beat harder, sheets across the window.

"He called it the Purpose." As soon as the words were out, Eli wanted them back.

"The Purpose? What's that, like, his manifesto or something?"

It . . . um . . .

"You totally don't have to talk about this."

"No, it's okay. He said that we had to follow the Lord's purpose. That America had been corrupted by money and power. The bankers and the politicians were Barons who controlled us. Like royalty. But they were really devils. He said we were going to start a revolution. That I'd reveal what the Barons were doing to the oppressed."

"Riiight," said Graham, "so, like, the mall was a symbol of capitalism, and the DOL was the state being in league with these Barons. I get it, I get it."

Eli wasn't used to people getting it. They usually called Gabriel a lunatic and a psycho. "He was crazy," he said.

"Well, maybe, but also kinda right. I mean, it's true, what he said. Don't you think?"

Yes. Eli saw things on the news, around the city, that reminded him of Gabriel's teachings. *Don't call them that,* Dr. Maria had said. *It wasn't teaching. It was coercion, manipulation. It was a crime.* But wasn't some of it true? The way he and his family had less than other families. The way some people seemed to have all the money. And how some commentators said Eli's disappearance would have been a bigger deal if he'd been white.

But the message was wrong. Killing innocent people.

Sheep. All are complicit.

Shut up.

They were quiet for a while. Graham belched. Eli's mouth was stale and dry.

"Did you ever want to kill yourself?" Graham asked. "You know, when you were in there?"

Eli listened to the rain for a moment. "Yeah."

"Did you try?"

"I don't think he would have let me die, and I didn't want him to hurt me if I tried."

"But you were going to die at the end."

"To escape."

"It seemed like the only way," said Graham.

Yeah.

"To stop all the pain."

Eli rolled on his side. "Have you ever thought about it?"

"Sometimes. When the world just seems so pointless, I've imagined taking Jules's gun and shooting myself, or slicing my wrists. Watching the blood slide out. Knowing all the noise and bullshit would be over."

Oh. "I've thought about how if I had blown up, at least everything bad would have stopped."

"That's what I'm talking about."

"But you don't really . . ."

"No," said Graham, "totally not. Because then I think, why should I be the one to go? Why should I have to die just to escape, when it's not the world that's stupid, it's all the people? It's like, if everyone else was gone, and it was just me, and you, and the natural world. . . ."

"No one hurting," said Eli. He thought of his mom and her wineglass, and wondered what online den she was in now.

"What this world needs is a good apocalypse," said Graham. "I'd be ready. You know, like, a nuclear war, or plague or zombies, and then we'd be out there, on our own, like with a posse, except eventually they'd turn on you and you'd have to put them down too."

"What if it was lonely?" said Eli.

"It wouldn't be. We'd have each other." Graham yawned and lay back, lacing his fingers behind his head.

They were both silent in the thrumming rain.

"We'd keep some hot ladies around too, obviously." Graham's words slurred toward sleep. "We'd be kings."

His breathing settled to a slow, steady rhythm.

Eli watched the ceiling spin. Watched the rain hit the window, refracting the streetlight.

He tried to imagine a world without people. Not the red dark. One with mountains and trees. And Graham. And his mother and sister. It had to be okay to bring their families along, right?

And Maya. Would she be allowed?

He pictured being high up in the alpine, like where they'd gone hiking one time when he was in fourth grade. Peaks all around, the silence, the peace, maybe a deer trotting across a meadow. A campsite where they sat around a fire and played games, and ate the berries they'd foraged.

His eyes fluttered shut.

*   *   *

Slippery hours. He wasn't sure when he'd been awake or asleep. Slid in and out of the red dark, heard Gabriel thumping upstairs, but then it was the Metrotroopers from *Colony 17*, storming in and taking him, except when they left the room they were on a spaceship. The ship hurtled toward a crimson planet, where they were to be left to die. Maya was in chains beside him, her clothes tattered, wearing that lavender bra. "Stop it, perv," she said to him, fiddling with her chains, her eyes like daggers. "We'll get out of this."

He woke and saw the rain streaking the window and wondered where he was. Back in his old bedroom? How old was he? Had the red dark ever even happened? But there was the sickly tangy taste in his mouth, the rum and the Coke gone sour. All of it welling up. Surging—

He stumbled to the bathroom, closed the door, hit the light—blinding—collapsed, and retched into the toilet. Searing pain behind his eyes. Three more times, then he flushed and sat against the wall, sweating and shivering.

Maybe passed out there for a while.

Then wobbled to his feet. Opened the door and flicked off the light. Echoes of rain. Graham's room to the left.

Eli turned right.

Gently opened the door. Streetlight in dancing streaks from the tree outside Jules's window. Eli moved to the closet. He pulled the sliding door open slowly, its runners making a squealing sound. His heart pounded. Had to stay quiet. But also be quick.

He pulled the chain to turn on the light. Neatly hung shirts, a hanging shelf of sweaters. Pairs of sneakers on the floor and some high black boots. Stacks of boxes on the shelf above the clothes: clear bins of comic books, letter-sized file boxes. Eli reached for the box that looked most like it was from a girl: a teal blue shoe box. He slid it from between a stack of comics and a brown cardboard box. On his toes, everything tipping . . . it slipped free. Pulled off the lid: a pair of cleats inside.

He put the shoe box back, looking for any clue. On the floor behind the shoes was a large black box with a lock, one of those trunks like you took to camp. The lock hung open, the key welded into it by rust. Eli knelt, flipped the latches, lifted the cover, and pushed it behind the hanging shirts.

There were clothes inside, notebooks, magazines, and a gift box that had been carefully wrapped in crimson paper so that the lid would still open.

Inside: a dried peach-colored rose, a skinny champagne glass with ELLIOTT HIGH SCHOOL SENIOR PROM etched in blue letters, handwritten notes of all shapes, a can of mint-flavored whipped cream.

And the gun.

Eli sat cross-legged on the floor. Slipped it from its holster and wrapped his fingers around the cool, quiet metal. Tested the weight in his palm. Ran his thumb over the safety, careful not to move it. Aimed at the window.

I've come to finish the Purpose.

Not today.

Not bait.

BANG.

He'd been hurt, scarred. He'd been tricked and used. But he'd survived. He'd healed and he could keep healing.

But this could do more. End a threat. Keep them safe. For real.

Energy surged through him, a strange memory of walking toward the DOL, the wobbling view through the wolf's mask. Fear, but also power. Power to destroy.

He switched the gun to the other hand. Aimed again.

Nearly a smile. *Happy anniversary.*

His heart raced. He wondered what Maya would think of it. The power. The control over fear. Maybe the three of them could shoot it sometime.

Graham probably wouldn't like that.

Eli's arm started to ache.

Yawned. Fresh throbbing in his skull.

He holstered the gun and put it back in the box, in the trunk. Latches, light off, doors closed. Tiptoed to his bed and huddled under the blanket. Graham was snoring. The rain falling harder. He closed his eyes, still flexing his fingers, feeling the metal there, imagining the bullet finding its target.

* * *

Sometime later: a sound.

He may have been sleeping. Blurry dreams, but the sound dug through the spaceship hull and the red dark and the Burke

240

Park trees and the bedroom walls. Something vibrating the floor-boards, the small area he had managed to warm with his body. A grinding, humming sound, followed by a squeal, like of forced air. The whir of something beginning to move, then a banging. It sounded like . . .

Eli's eyes flashed open.

Graham's room. A trapezoid of rain-streaked window light on the ceiling.

Now, not then.

But outside—

A sound he knew.

Another whine and hiss of air. Eli sat up. He leaned over Graham, palms on the window, forehead against the cool glass. Rain sheeting against it. His breath making a disk of fog.

Yellow lights flashed and whirled. Up the street, a green-and-white garbage truck had backed into the driveway of a pool club they'd passed on the way here, its motor rattling the window-pane, the bones of the house.

Late at night.

This. He knew this.

"What is it?" Graham looked up groggily.

"Nothing," said Eli. He watched the truck. Hydraulics hiss-ing as it lifted a trash bin, the banging as it emptied. Whir of its compactor. Revving of its heavy engine as it pulled out of the driveway and rumbled away.

He'd heard it so many times before.

And he knew from where.

* * *

"So," said Mom as Eli got in the car the next morning. "How did it—"

"We need to call Detective Pearson," said Eli, his guts trembling from more than just his hangover.

"What is it? What happened?"

"I remembered something. About where Gabriel kept me."

CHAPTER 18

MAYA

October 13

"Everything all right?" said Dad.

He'd been in the long Saturday-morning line ordering their coffees and muffins when the alert had popped up on her phone. **You have 23 new updates! See what your friends are talking about.**

She'd clicked over and found that her mentions were full of comments. She scrolled to find their source, but her glimpses of what they said already had her heart racing.

At the bottom:

Jcs_moon47 tagged you in a post.

Janice.

Maya's stomach clenched, adrenaline spiking.

Don't click on it.

No. She could do this. Because who cared? There was a

thousand percent chance that this was some sexy shot of Janice and that girl Marni she'd been hanging out with all week, or her and Mateo and Marni, meant to taunt her, show her what she was missing.

She tapped it.

It wasn't that.

Oh God.

The photo was through a partially opened door. The view of a bathroom. Of a girl standing there considering herself in the mirror, her head turned so you could see the mangled, deranged, sickening sections of her scalp. Bald and scabbed with the occasional tuft still dangling there. The girl looking at herself forlornly, almost fearfully. A damaged girl. A sick girl.

When Maya had been getting ready for the dance. When Janice had gone to get the schnapps and makeup. Maya had been alone, she'd thought, but she'd been drinking and the music had been on loud. . . .

There was a caption beneath the photo:

TFW you realize you've been wasting your time. #cantfixcrazy #havesomeselfrespect

"You said skinny latte, right?"

Maya did her best to keep her cool, to rip her eyes away, but she'd already seen the first comment.

Ewww get out of that mess, girl!

It had twenty-three likes.

And the second:

I've seen her around school. Such a lost cause! You can do so much better. (Nineteen likes.)

Her eyes swam up to her dad. He'd put her drink and her

blueberry scone in front of her. "Yeah," she managed to say, fighting tears. "Thanks."

Sipped the latte. Put it down and pulled her hat lower on her head.

She'd been doing better all week. Competent during extra rehearsals for the upcoming jazz concert. Shockingly aced a math test. Wrote notes to Eli, and had only two serious flashbacks that she could remember. It had been over a week since the breakup, and it had really seemed like all Maya would be getting from Janice were the leering gazes in the hallway, the way she was all over Mateo and also Marni, the childish whispering to one another whenever Maya passed by. Janice had also skipped bio lab, but Maya had done the assignment better without her anyway.

So that was that.

In the clear.

Such a stupid thought.

GROSS! I'm so sorry for you! (Twenty-one likes.)

"Mom says the jazz band is going good," said Dad. "I'm looking forward to the concert. Next Friday, right?"

Maya nodded. Lips pursed. Willing her eyes to stay dry. "I don't really want to talk right now."

"Oh, what's up?"

"Nothing," she snapped.

She looks like a badly shaved dog. (Thirty-eight likes.)

From behind with a wig, though. (Fourteen likes.)

Each comment froze her deeper, shrank her, pushed her farther down. Starting to feel that tingling in her neck and the white spots in her vision. Tight. Hard to breathe. She needed a

Serenitab, but whenever she took one around either of her parents they'd inevitably ask some searching, mistrusting, belittling fucking question. The bathroom. But there was a line.

"Sorry," said Dad. "I wasn't trying to pry. Things seemed fine a minute ago."

"I know."

Dammit, they'd been having a good time! Like a real, uncomplicated good time. Just the two of them; Kendall was at an aromatic Pilates retreat up at Whistler. Last night they'd ordered pizza and Dad had given Maya a beer and they'd watched the new Marvel show on Netflix, his laptop on the couch between them, their shoulders warm against each other. Sure, Dad had been texting with Kendall almost the whole time, but even that had been fine.

Fleas! Put her back in the kennel! (Twenty-two likes.)

She couldn't go to school Monday. Everyone would have seen this. Couldn't possibly face all the knowing, the laughing, the comments, the judgment.

Renee would probably tell her to close her phone immediately, but she kept scrolling. Her own destruction happening right in front of her. Had already happened. It was almost surreal.

A GIF of some movie star making a grossed-out face. (Fifty-one likes.)

J you're a saint for trying. (Twenty-five likes.)

7/10 for the ass though. (Eight likes.)

"Hey." Dad reached for her hand. "Is this about that breakup you had?"

She pulled her hand away. "Can we just go?"

"But what about reading?" He held up the *GQ* he'd bought at the 7-Eleven next door. Maya had gotten an *Entertainment*

Weekly. It was supposed to be a thing. An actual good idea of her dad's. Now the tears came.

Isn't she the bomber chick? My bff at Garfield said she's a slut. (Forty-eight likes.)

"Okay, let's read," she said before she started leaking too badly. She could feel her dad watching her still. She wanted to be invisible, to disappear completely.

Janice you're the most beautiful girl in school smh why someone would treat you like this. (Twenty-six likes.)

Damn straight, beautiful, you can do SO. MUCH. BETTER. Guys and girls will be lining up. (Thirty-seven likes.)

Maya moved her hands under the table and started digging into the callus at the base of her middle finger. One of the solid drumming ones. It had been needing work for a while.

This was it. How everyone at Elliott would see her for the rest of the year. Damaged, *that girl,* and anything inside her that was good? That was hopeful, that healed?

UM NO THANKS. (Forty-nine likes.)

Even if her hair grew back, even if she was playing flawlessly onstage, even if she was dressed her best—

Have some self-respect! (Fifty-seven likes.)

Maya closed her eyes.

Three . . . two . . . one . . .

Shut off her screen and pushed it away from her. Sipped her latte, looked out the window at the cars streaming by in the misty air. Instead of opening her new magazine, she fished a small, battered blue journal from her bag.

Tucked inside the front cover was the most recent note that Eli had left for her. She reread the middle section, which had been sticking in her head.

When you wrote the other day that it smelled like
the sea and you could hear the old ships and whales,
I could picture that. I always think it's amazing how
you see stuff. Is every moment like that for you?
I want to notice more. Dr. Maria told me to write
down the details around me sometimes so I can feel
more connected to the world. I bet you could do
that really good.

The words coaxed the briefest smile to the surface. What a nice, un-shitty thing to say. And not something she'd ever really thought about.

She ran her finger down a list she'd started making last night in her journal, the first words she'd written in it since before the DOL:

Amazing Stuff

Drums
A ride cymbal: vibrating time, like an earthquake
    clock
Bass-drum beats: moving air
Unison saxophone melodies: weary, knowing
The view when you look up from beneath the
    surface of a pool
The veins on the undersides of leaves
The underside of almost anything

She looked around her now.

Steam from a coffee cup

Woman shaking sugar packets to death before

she opens them. (What's on her mind? Her

annoying kid? Her annoying boyfriend?)

Dragon hiss of the espresso machine

Dandelions in a sidewalk crack: pioneers, the Zen

of wind travel

Her phone buzzed. Her stomach flared.

You have 19 new notifications!

"You want to tell me?" Dad said, flipping a page.

"No. It's just dumb." For a minute there, she'd felt good. Her brain calm. Just focusing on details.

Maya eyed the phone. Fucking thing. Every time you went in you had to catch up to the past and present and future and they were all twisted together. Old posts with new comments, old friends and possible futures and what you did three years ago and what you'd never done and what your friends were doing right this second and what you should be doing. What had people said? What would they say? What if you missed something being said right then? It was a time machine and an alternate-reality machine. It took away your skin. Gave your three-dimensional brain four-dimensional paranoia.

She should throw the damn thing in the trash can, into the middle of the street. Take it to the beach and hold a funeral for it, Eli holding a candle. They'd share a knowing look, and then she'd hurl it into the waves. Freedom!

And yet still, she wanted to reply to Janice so badly. Tell her to delete the post. Tell her it was a horrible thing to do.

But Janice wouldn't care. In fact, that was probably what she wanted.

Come on. Beg me to take it down.

Her phone buzzed again. She grabbed it. Thought about deleting her account entirely, but all those years of pictures and memories . . . Did she really want to erase herself?

It's not erasing yourself. You're right here. With the coffee steam and the hard wooden chair and the mist outside.

Deleting her account would be a win for Janice too.

But she did delete the app. For now. Slid the phone into airplane mode and shoved it in her bag.

Deep breath. More latte.

Latte froth clinging gently to your upper lip

"What are you reading about?" she asked Dad. As he talked, she almost listened.

*   *   *

They were halfway home when Dad's phone buzzed. "Mom says she can't reach you."

"Oh, yeah, had my phone off."

She could feel Dad weighing different responses. Finally, he said, "She wants to be sure you're coming home now. Wants me to come in too, for some reason."

"That's never good."

They shared a brief smile. Dad tapped his phone. "We'll be there in five minutes."

"I'll let her know we're on the way."

Dad parked in the street near Mom's apartment. It was the second floor of a cream-colored triplex. There was a blue car parked behind Mom's in one of the spaces out front. Maya tensed. Was this why Mom had texted? She always thought it was incredibly important to introduce Maya to all her friends and colleagues and pretty much anyone, which was the last thing she needed right now. Although normally that would not have included Dad. Had she done something wrong? Oh God, had Mom seen Janice's post?

The photo still behind her eyelids, the comments worming deeper into her brain.

"In here," Mom called as soon as Maya pushed open the apartment door.

Maya and Dad found them in the kitchen. Her mom, as well as a tall woman in a black pantsuit—

And Eli.

Her heart flipped, spun around. Hammering. Ringing in her ears. Metal taste in her mouth.

He sat at their kitchen table, hunched over in his baggy Seahawks hoodie, hands in the pocket. He only looked at her for a moment, then at the table.

Mom put an arm around her. "I know, just sit." She guided Maya to a chair. Eli was right across from her, and yet he seemed miles away. What the hell was going on?

"Maya, I don't know if you remember me," said the woman in the suit. "I'm Detective Pearson. We—"

"We met at the hospital last year." Maya kept her hands in her lap. Resumed work on that callus.

"I'm sorry to surprise you like this," said Pearson. She brushed her black hair behind her ears. Nails painted blue. Small silver rings on a few fingers. "But we've had a break in the Cedar Gate case and we'd like your help."

"Me?"

"Yes. It took some luck," said Pearson. "But Eli remembered that he often heard a truck in the late-night hours where he was held, and saw flashing lights. We theorized that this was most likely a garbage truck, and so we pulled the pickup schedules for the general area where we believe Eli was held. There are only a handful of sites that receive nighttime pickup, and then only a few houses on each route from which he could have seen the lights, and . . . yesterday we found it."

Maya slid her foot under the table, searching for Eli's. Maybe with a tap she could say, *Oh my God! How are you doing with this?*

"We're taking Eli over this morning to confirm the location," said Pearson, "and to get his account of the space and evidence. There's a preliminary forensics team there now, and we want to bring Eli through before we move in the full team. That's going to attract the media."

"What does this have to do with me?" Maya asked.

"Eli asked for you to accompany us."

"Why do you need her?" Dad asked.

"I think it might help me remember," said Eli.

"We know you two have been in touch," said Detective Pearson.

Maya looked at her mom.

"It's all right," she said. And yet her eyes said it wasn't.

"Eli's had a difficult time accessing his memories from that period," said Pearson. "And challenges with communication. He says talking with you is helpful, and his psychiatrist confirms the progress since you two started communicating. It was his idea, but everyone's been briefed.

"Not her father," said Dad.

"That's why we're here. And this is totally up to you," Pearson replied.

"What about the danger?" Mom snapped. "What about this Gabriel?"

"There's no danger," said Pearson. "We've already been through the house, and we've had surveillance on the neighborhood. Maya will be completely safe. But I understand if—"

"I want to go."

"Maya—"

Dad touched Mom's arm. They shared a glance, some kind of telepathic communication that caused a lump in Maya's throat.

Mom bit her lip, looked at Maya. "Are you sure?"

"I'm sure."

"Thank you," Eli said to her parents.

Mom nodded, tears rimming her eyes. Dad shrugged, arms crossed.

"As soon as you're ready," said Pearson, "we should go."

*   *   *

They rode in Pearson's car. Maya and Eli sat in the back. Eli stared out the window.

"You know," said Pearson, "you guys really took a risk by writing those letters to each other. If anyone had found them . . ."

Maya frowned but didn't reply. Probably wouldn't be wise to start mouthing off to a detective.

"Dr. Maria said it was a good idea," said Eli.

"I get that," said Pearson, "from her point of view." Her phone started to buzz. "I gotta take this."

Maya found her hand twisting at her hair and pulled it away. "When did this happen?" she asked Eli.

"I was sleeping over at Graham's."

"Did you tell him?"

"Not yet. I mean, we're not supposed to tell anyone yet."

Maya lowered her voice. "Hey . . ." She thought of the other afternoon, on the stage. "Is he cool?"

"Graham?"

"Yeah, I mean like, I don't know, he seems a little . . ." She didn't know what word to use. Weird? Creepy? Off somehow? Not much different from the words she'd been called just now. She settled on "different."

"He takes things hard," said Eli. "And everyone bullies him. He's been a really good friend."

"No, I know, I just—"

"Nobody else has. . . . I mean, except for you." Eli turned toward the window.

"Sorry." Shit, that was stupid. "Forget I asked." Like Eli didn't have enough to worry about. "Hey." She reached across the seat and ran her fingers over his hand. As she did, more voices scolded her—*Slut! Eww! Lost Cause!*—but she was just trying to be supportive. Touch didn't have to mean anything more than that. Didn't have to be weird or suggestive or go anywhere. And she wanted him to know she was here. He could pull his hand away if he wanted, and he didn't. "How are you holding up?"

His jaw moved. No words.

"Maybe this is the beginning of the end," she said.

Eli sort of chuckled.

"Sorry, I didn't mean that in, like, an ominous way."

"It's okay. How are you doing?"

Maya shook her head. "It's been a crappy morning."

"What happened?"

Maya felt a surge of nerves, but she took out her phone and reinstalled the app. Logged in and pulled up the photo. Held it out to Eli. "Janice."

Eli peered at it. "She posted that?"

"Yeah. It's been super-fun."

"It looks bad."

Maya yanked her phone away. "Thanks. That's what everyone's saying."

"No, I mean, it looks like it hurts." He touched his own scalp behind his ear.

"Oh. Yeah, it really does. But it also kinda helps. Maybe less than it hurts."

They merged onto the highway.

"Hey." Maya got her journal from her bag. "I was writing back to you this morning." She held it out for him to see. "I started making this list."

Eli looked at it. "Those are cool."

"Your doctor lady is right, by the way. It does help you kind of calm down."

Outside they were passing Cedar Gate Mall. Exiting.

Maya wrote another line in her letter. Showed it to Eli and pointed toward the floor of the seat.

Energy-bar-wrapper graveyard

Eli kind of smiled.

They wove through a neighborhood of small houses and past a large brick school. "We're going in the back," said Pearson. She turned down an alley between two streets of houses.

They rolled slowly, gravel crunching. On either side were tall fences overgrown with vegetation, clusters of recycling bins, and odd discarded items: a stack of tires, an aquarium, a soggy mattress. They stopped beside a metal garage door built into a high wooden fence. The door was open, revealing a carport with an old white Ford Focus.

"Is that his car?" said Pearson.

"I think so," said Eli. The color had drained from his face.

They got out, stepped around the car, and stood facing the house: two stories, its yellow paint chipped and faded. A brick path crossed a small, overgrown backyard to a short set of slanted wooden steps that led to a door. The door was white, but it and the windows hadn't been cleaned in so long that they were caked in a layer of brown grime. The windows all had heavy black curtains drawn across them.

"No phones while we're in there," said Pearson. "We'd have to confiscate them if you tried to take any pictures or video."

Maya shivered. Her mouth was dry, white edges to her vision. She could feel it, the secrets behind those curtains, the darkness lurking. The yard was surrounded by the high fence, but there were gaps, boards askew. Maya saw toys scattered in the yard to the left, impeccable greenery and a fountain in the yard to the right. Nice houses. In between: a lair.

"Jennings, this is Pearson," she said into her phone. "We're coming in the back door, over."

"Copy that, Detective."

Pearson started slipping on rubber gloves. "The house is owned by Ellen Carter, but Ms. Carter has been in a nursing home up in Shoreline for nearly eight years. She has one son, Stephen Carter, age forty-four. We believe that's Gabriel." She started across the lawn. "His father, Archie, died in 1981, when Gabriel was eight.

Suicide. He'd worked for Boeing, fought in Vietnam. Records about Stephen are harder to find. He finished high school here in Seattle near the top of his class. Was National Guard, and his unit got called up for two tours in Afghanistan. After that things get pretty spotty. No recent credit history. We've requested his military records and are looking for any additional employment records. The only thing we know is that he has a post office box up in Lynnwood. House and car are in his mother's name, and based on their condition, we think he left quite some time ago. We're checking the visitor logs at the nursing home, as well as car rentals, bus and train tickets, airlines, all the way back to the day of the attempted attack. But that's all we have to go on. Maybe you'll see something that will help. Ready?"

Eli's shoulders were slumped. His face like ash, his eyes huge. He nodded.

Maya reached for his wrist. His hand slipped out of his sweatshirt pocket, fingers lacing into hers. Clammy with sweat.

"It's probably obvious, but don't touch anything," Pearson added, starting up the steps. "We'll be dusting for prints."

They entered a small kitchen: salmon-pink linoleum floor that matched the counter tiles, a white oven with those old electric burner coils, pearl-white table edged in chrome, a tiny plastic microwave, avocado-colored refrigerator, a picture of a religious woman—Mary, maybe?—over the stove.

"Just like Grandma left it," said Pearson. She ran a gloved finger over the table, making a streak in the thick layer of dust. "Does this look familiar?"

Eli shook his head. "He always brought me straight to my room."

They moved to the living room. Two detectives were

photographing everything. Another room right out of a time warp, with white-and-gold couches, a glass coffee table, and beige carpeting. There were all these glossy statues of Dalmatians cluttering the side tables. You could imagine a friendly old lady sitting there watching her soap operas.

Pearson put a hand on Eli's shoulder and led him over to the mantel. "Is this him?"

Amid a cluttered line of framed photos, mostly of younger parents and a child—the petite mother, the father with a mustache and tinted sunglasses, the boy all limbs and bones and never smiling—one that seemed to be a high school graduation photo. A skinny teen in a suit with a hairstyle like a rectangle on top of his head, and a somber smile.

Eli nodded stiffly. "That's him."

A chill ran through Maya. She tried to imagine that kid, her age, and what he would become. Could you tell? Knowing what they did now, she felt certain she detected a darkness in those blue eyes, something false in that smile, but could anyone have known back then? His friends, classmates?

Pearson turned to the other detectives. "Let's get this picture aged up and circulated wide." She motioned for Eli and Maya to follow her down a hallway.

"Aren't we going upstairs?" said Eli, glancing at the staircase that climbed the far wall.

"You should see this first."

They passed a bathroom decorated in cheery pinks and frills. A door on the right led into a bedroom with pastel colors and a bed with a white lace blanket.

No light beyond the door to the left. A large padlock hung open on a steel latch.

Pearson pushed the door wide. "We think he kept you in here."

Maya felt Eli trembling. "You don't have to go in," she said.

"Yeah, I do."

He went first, and Maya followed. The room was bare except for a sagging mattress on a metal bed frame against the wall. A dirty pillow on the bare wood floor. Thick plywood over the window, and the tiniest sliver of light through a gap in the base. A metal bowl, overturned. A twist of light blue blanket snaking across the floor.

Clipped to the bed frame, a gooseneck lamp with a red bulb.

A dried rotten smell, like something long dead. A green plastic pail on its side in a corner.

Eli gripped Maya's hand tighter. She squeezed back, trying to imagine . . . but she couldn't, not even close. Her own room, her world, all of it was so big and so assumed. She just wanted to cry, to hug Eli, and yet this other voice inside her was screaming to get the hell out of here, as if this room could somehow swallow her up. Its purpose, its very existence, that you could be grabbed from a street and locked in a place like this. How could you believe your life had meaning, or a plan, if this could happen? This room didn't care about your jazz concert, your dreams. She wanted to unsee it, to be as far from it as she could.

But she kept holding his hand.

"I went back over your statements," said Pearson. "There were some confusing details. You said this room was at the top of a staircase, but also that you heard your sister from upstairs. You also mentioned hearing sounds from the kitchen. But this is the room, isn't it?"

"This is it," Eli nearly whispered. He released Maya's hand

259

and took small steps across the room. Crouched by the wall, by the sliver of light beneath the window. Ran his fingers over rows of scrapes in the floorboards.

"I tried to keep count," he said. "I've always wondered how close I came to being right."

"There's more we want you to see," said Pearson. "Upstairs. When you're ready." She walked out, footfalls echoing in the empty room.

Eli and Maya stood in the silence. "I slept there." He pointed to the spot where the blanket lay on the floor. "Not in the bed. I don't know why. The floor seemed safer."

"I'm so sorry," said Maya.

He shook his head. "It's just a room."

"I would never have made it out of here."

"Yes, you would have."

Maya tugged his hand. "We should go with the detective."

"Okay."

They returned to the living room. Pearson was waiting at the bottom of the staircase.

Eli paused in the middle of the room. He looked into the kitchen. Looked back down the hallway.

"What is it?" said Maya.

Shrugged. "Nothing."

"You never have to be here again," said Maya.

"I know. It's just different, seeing it now. Not as bad. But . . ." Eli whispered something, barely moving his lips, but Maya couldn't hear what it was, and didn't think she should ask.

They followed Pearson up carpeted stairs, the walls angling with the roof. At the top, a small landing and then a single door. They entered another bedroom, this one bright and fully decorated for a boy. A twin bed with a *Star Wars* bedspread. A Mariners 1984 team poster on the wall, a couple player posters too. Daylight pouring through two skylights. A desk with neatly arranged art supplies. A toy chest.

A room frozen in time, like a ten-year-old might come in from playing in the backyard and flop on the bed.

Pearson stood by the desk. There was a small television there, the old kind with the curved glass and the thick body. She looked at Eli. "This is disturbing, but I think it will make sense of some of your more difficult memories."

Pearson switched on the TV. The screen a blank blue. She pressed buttons on the clunky black appliance beneath it. There was a sound of clicking gears and spinning.

The screen flashed: grainy images. And screaming. A woman on her back, naked, her hands tied, and a guy all over her. She was shrieking and gasping, writhing against the ties on her wrists, her neck twisting. The man forcing himself onto her, grunting words and striking her. The TV was wired to big speakers on the floor, making the sound much louder than it normally would have been. Making the furniture rattle.

Maya nearly couldn't watch.

Pearson turned it off after a few seconds. "Is that what you heard?"

Eli nodded, his face pale.

She picked up a worn cardboard jacket from beside the TV. "It's called *Stolen Property.*" She dropped the case on a stack of others. "Six volumes, apparently."

"I'm so stupid," Eli said quietly.

"No," said Pearson, "absolutely not. With what he put you through . . . there's no way you could have known."

261

Maya rubbed his shoulder. "She's right."

Eli nodded. Didn't seem convinced.

"Any details up here that might match things you remember him saying?"

Eli shook his head. "No."

"Okay. Then we should go down," said Pearson. "Time to call in the full team."

They returned to the living room and entered the kitchen. As Pearson opened the door, Maya felt a flood of relief at the sight of daylight outside—

But Eli paused again. This time in the doorway between the kitchen and the living room. Peered down the hallway.

"Eli," said Maya. "What is it?"

He gazed at the floor. Closed his eyes, like he was concentrating. "Something isn't right."

CHAPTER 19

ELI

October 13

The red dark closed in around him.

The details of the room fresh in his mind. Lying on the floor, curled up, arms around his knees. The rough boards against his hip and aching shoulder. The sounds of Gabriel in the kitchen coming through his pillow. Clanging of pots and pans. Scrape of fork against plate. The whistle of a kettle. The murmur of a TV . . .

Then the footsteps: the ones that made his heart bolt. Thudding up creaking stairs. The locks clicking, Gabriel's looming silhouette in the light from a single naked bulb.

Eli opened his eyes. Looked around the sunny kitchen, its frosting and floral colors, its layer of dust. Back to the hallway with its cream carpet.

The footsteps did not come down that hallway.

The kitchen sounds did not come from here.

"Eli, what?" said Maya.

"Everything okay?" Detective Pearson said.

"Something's missing," said Eli. Adrenaline surged through him. The word barely whispered from his lips. "Basement?"

Pearson looked at him quizzically. "There isn't one."

"Are you sure?" Maya asked.

Pearson looked at the two officers in the living room, but they just shrugged. "We pulled the property records from the city and there was no mention of a basement." She scrolled on her phone. "Yeah, no. The house is on a cinder block foundation. Just a crawl space beneath the floors, not uncommon in these older places. Why?"

Eli closed his eyes again. Did he have it wrong? He tried to see the room, not in the red dark, but like moments ago. Just a room. Tried to remove the shadows, the pain aching from so many parts of his body. Tried to lie back down on the floor in his mind and see the doorway. Where had Gabriel come from?

The creaking steps, the click of the heavy lock, a zipping sound, like something being pulled aside or rolled up, the groaning of hinges, Gabriel appearing—

And then one other sound. As Gabriel approached, he would bend and grab on to something, and there would be a squeal like metal twisting.

"The closet," said Eli. "I think there's a door."

Pearson just looked at him for a second. Then her eyes tracked down to the kitchen floor. "Everybody out. Now."

Eli and Maya followed her down the steps into the backyard. Pearson motioned to the other two officers. "Secure the perimeter. I want all vantages covered." She tapped her phone. "This is Pearson. Move the SWAT unit in immediately. No sirens. Approach by the alley, over."

"You think he's here?" Maya whispered, gazing at the house and hugging herself.

Pearson spoke quietly. "We can't take any chances." Her phone buzzed. "ETA five minutes." She slid her phone into her pocket. Pulled out her gun.

Eli looked at it. Wished his fingers were flexing around it, solid in his hands.

They stood in the yard and waited. Frozen. No one spoke. A breeze rustled the leaves overhead.

In Eli's head: the clinking of dishes from below. Remembered when Gabriel would come into the red dark and put the hood over his head. Being marched downstairs, arms held tight behind his back, then along for a while . . . "We climbed up to get out. Like a ladder?"

Pearson looked around the yard. "Okay . . ." Into her phone: "Eyes peeled on the yard as well. It's possible there's another exit point."

Eli wished they could just leave, that he could erase this place from his head, erase himself just to keep from having to think about it.

Maya stared vacantly at the house.

"Sorry."

"No, just . . . this is crazy."

You put her in danger. Again.

Pearson worked busily on her phone, gun still in her hand.

Finally, a deep engine rumble from the alley. The opening and closing of heavy doors. The sound of gear slapping and jangling.

The first SWAT officer appeared: thick vest, helmet with the plastic visor pushed up above his head, rifle in his hands.

Pearson pointed to the back door. Spoke quietly: "We think there's some kind of basement. Access through a door hidden in the closet of that room." She indicated the curtained window to the left of the kitchen. "Possibly another exit point somewhere in the yard." Turned to Eli. "Is there anything else you can tell us about the door?"

Eli shook his head. "I never went near it."

The SWAT commander nodded and motioned to the four officers behind him. They filed past him and moved up the stairs, rifles raised to their shoulders, boots clicking lightly on the boards. As they disappeared into the kitchen, the commander opened a tablet and watched their progress on the screen, which was split four ways to show their body cameras.

Eli and Maya moved closer to watch.

"Maybe this will be it," said Maya, managing a weak smile.

Eli nodded but couldn't quite return it.

The cameras bobbed as the officers filed down the hallway, pushing into the dark bedroom. Two officers stood aside as the other two slid into the closet and studied the back wall. Fingers found a seam. "Here's the door," the first officer said quietly, his breathing heavy into the mic. "Opens from the other side."

"Run a camera," the commander said into his headset. "Everyone stay frosty on the perimeter, in case we flush him out."

The lead officer produced a drill. It whined, boring into the wood. They made a single hole and fed a fiber-optic camera through, the second officer watching the camera on a tablet of his own. The feed popped up on the commander's screen.

"Okay, looks clean. Single deadbolt lock. Staircase on the other side. Torch it."

The officers exchanged the drill for a blowtorch. Its ignition momentarily whited out all the feeds.

Eli looked away from the screen, back to the still house. He pictured the door, the sounds of it opening.

You can't catch me this easily. I'm too smart. You know it.

"Lock is disabled," said the officer. "We're about to breach—"

Wait! Eli thought. "Wait!" he whispered.

"Hold up," said the commander. "What is it?"

"There's something else. A weird sound when the door opens."

"What do you mean?"

"Like something winding up."

The commander frowned. "Feed that camera in farther. Let's take another look."

"Copy," said the officer. The view of the camera wobbled and then panned around the narrow alcove behind the door, back on the door itself—

"Wait, freeze it," said the commander. "Holy shit." He zoomed in on the screen and pointed. "Looks like a trip wire flush with the base of the door. Pan up and left."

A green canister duct-taped to the wall.

The commander exhaled hard. "Flash grenade. Thanks, kid."

Pearson patted Eli's shoulder. Eli didn't react, couldn't, his body locked in place.

"Okay, you're going to need to drill in just above the base of the door to clip that thing." The commander turned toward the alley. "Everybody behind the truck."

They filed into the alley, past another officer who was kneeling with his rifle trained on the yard, to the other side of the giant truck. Eli heard the distant sound of the drill. . . .

"Okay, all clear," the lead officer said. "Opening the door."

They watched it yawn open.

"Tight formation," said the commander.

"Here we go." The first officer's camera swung to reveal a narrow wooden staircase. His gun out in front of him, a light on its end spearing into the dark. The other officers following.

Eli looked away, bracing himself.

They won't take me without a fight.

The cameras swept into a narrow room. Hard to make out what they were seeing in the dipping and darting lights. The sound of boots, some clattering noises.

"Room is secure, sir."

"Copy that," said the commander. "We're on our way in."

Pearson turned to Eli. "Would be good to get your observations, if you're up for it."

No, Eli almost said, but Maya gripped his hand and they followed Pearson back into the house. Down the hall, into the room. Eli tensed as they neared the closet. *He's not here. It's just a door.*

They ducked into the little space and through the doorway. Beyond, a naked bulb illuminated the plain wooden walls. The grenade, the trip wire, clamped to a wall beam. There was that photo Eli remembered catching glimpses of: an old woman, frowning at them. Gabriel's mother? Grandmother? What would she have thought of her son's work? Did it run in the family? Movies like *House of Slaughter* always gave their psychos brutal backstories.

The stairs leaned to the right. Another lightbulb stuck out of the ceiling at the bottom.

They found themselves in a cramped, rectangular space, barely big enough for the five SWAT officers, Pearson, Eli, and Maya. The floor and walls were dirt; the ceiling was the cobwebbed floorboards of the house. The air cool and damp. Pearson, Maya, and the officers had to duck slightly, though Eli could just stand straight. There was a trench around the floor with metal pipe half-concealed by gravel. On one side of the space was a cot, with a white sheet and a green wool blanket folded neatly beside a pillow. A lamp on a child's bedside table. Nearby, a folding card table with a small old-style TV and a single blue plate, a single cup, a fork and a knife, all clean and neatly arranged. Against the wall, a camp stove on a portable table with a small sink, a green hose running from its faucet up to one of the pipes along the ceiling, and another hose leading from the drain to the crushed gravel border of the space. Orange extension cords ran to outlets hanging from the ceiling rafters.

The officers were opening a pair of metal cabinets beneath the stairs. One filled with chemicals and electronics. Another filled with canned food.

"Over here," said the commander, by the back wall. A squat tunnel led into the earth. Clanging and thumping from in there, and then daylight. Eli peered in and saw two officers crouched beside a small stepladder, looking up. "Comes up right beside the car."

"Do you remember being down here?" Pearson asked Eli as she surveyed the room.

"I think he took me in and out this way, but I never saw it." Eli looked at the single plate. At the little stove. Over in the corner, he spied a green plastic bucket sitting beneath a fold-up toilet seat on metal legs. "How long since he's been here?"

"We'll have to do a detailed analysis." Pearson moved to the metal closet and picked up a bottle of habanero sauce, a can of beans. "Dated next year. But these things have long shelf lives."

"Detective." One of the officers was running his fingers up and down four cables that hung from the ceiling. "USB," he said.

Pearson dug into her bag and pulled out a tablet. "Here." She connected the cable, tapped through settings, and a window popped open. It showed a distorted view of the street in front of the house, partially blocked by leaves. "He had a camera system." She unplugged the first and tried a second. This time, a view of the alley.

"Is that important?" Maya asked.

"It means it's possible that he saw our initial surveillance."

"Like he might have been here?" Eli asked. "Three days ago?"

Pearson shook her head. "It doesn't prove anything." She continued plugging the cables into her tablet to check their feeds.

Something caught Eli's eye, and he moved to the sink. Spotless inside. Everything put away, except for a small glinting object: an inch-tall plastic robot with orange feet and a clear domed head through which you could see its inner gears. It had a key on its side like you could wind it up. Eli checked over his shoulder. Everyone still preoccupied with other parts of the room—

He slipped the tiny robot into the pocket of his hoodie and returned to Maya, who was staring at the cot, or maybe just into space, hugging herself.

"Why would he live like this?" she wondered quietly.

The Purpose demands sacrifice. "Maybe so no one could tell he was here."

"It's so weird," said Maya, "and, like, lonely."

Had Gabriel been lonely? *Was that why he took me?*

I loved you.

STOP. These thoughts felt like a trap. But he turned the little robot over between his fingers, picturing Gabriel as a kid in that room upstairs.

"All right," said Pearson. "Let's clear out and let the full forensics team get in here."

They headed up the narrow staircase. As they crossed through the red dark room, Eli paused. Took a long slow look. The blue blanket on the floor, the bowl, the plywood-covered window and its sliver of light.

You miss it. You miss the Purpose. No one cared about you like I did.

NO. But he'd been here for so long . . .

Maya took his hand again. "Hey. Let's go."

Eli nodded. Strode through the door.

CHAPTER 20

MAYA

October 13

They crossed the backyard, past the now-open trapdoor, which was in the shadow between the car and the fence.

Maya looked back at the house. Its worn paint. The way that, in the window of Eli's room, you could sort of tell that the curtains were pressed against the glass by the plywood behind them. The lawn tangled with weeds. Little details, and yet otherwise there was no real sign that this house could possibly contain such evil.

No one spoke until they had gotten into the car and started down the alley.

"Doesn't look like the press has been tipped off yet," said Pearson, scrolling through her phone with one hand, "but still, why don't you both duck for a minute while we pull onto the street?"

Maya slouched down, her insides knotted, one hand inside her hat. "How are you doing?" she asked Eli.

"Fine." He stared straight ahead.

"Come on," said Maya, elbowing him. "I'm not fine. That was a lot."

"Yeah."

"Okay, we're clear," said Pearson. "Maya, I'll take you home first."

Maya sat up and gazed out the window. She watched the little houses slide by, all normal-seeming. Why would you think otherwise? And yet what secrets, what closed-off rooms and hidden basements lurked in each of these little dwellings? There was no way to know.

Her fingers came away with a few strands of hair and she pushed them into her jacket pocket. Felt herself listing, the waves around her getting bigger. A Serenitab would be good, but she didn't have many left, and the nights before the jazz concert would be minefields of nervous energy. She imagined being home in a few minutes, her mom's questions, not to mention the mushroom cloud she'd been ignoring on her phone, of Eli having to go home . . .

"Hey," she said. "Do you want to get food or something?"

"Like what?"

"I don't know. We could go to Red Mill."

Eli looked at her and blinked. Like he was returning from far away. "Yeah."

"Would that be all right?" Maya asked Pearson. "Just for like an hour?"

She looked at them in the rearview mirror. "I can see if the detail that was going to be at your house can reposition," she said to Eli. "You both need to clear it with your parents."

"What about him?" said Eli.

"Gabriel?" Pearson said. "Sorry—Stephen. We should use his name. We'll see what the forensics sweep uncovers, but for the moment, I don't think there's any more reason to believe that he is in the vicinity than before. Even less, now that we found his house." Pearson's phone buzzed. "And . . . okay, the press has caught wind of our activities."

Maya fished her phone from her pocket. Just the sight of it made her heart somersault. She turned off airplane mode, blurred her eyes as alerts started flashing—

Take the dog to the vet! (Eighty-six likes.)

—and messaged her mom. We're going to stop for Red Mill. Eli is kind of shaken up. For about an hour. Okay?

"Am I bait?" Eli asked Pearson.

"What? No, absolutely not."

"You mean like for Gabriel?" said Maya.

Eli nodded.

"Guys, no," said Pearson. "We would like to catch him, of course. But we're not using you, Eli. Your safety will always be our top concern."

Eli didn't react, just returned to his phone.

Maya's mom replied: Is it all right with the police? Will they be there? They'll be watching.

Her response seemed to take forever. Is it helpful for Eli to have you there?

Yes, Mom. Maya rolled her eyes. Sure, it was nice that Mom was being understanding, and she was probably worried, but you could also practically hear her saying: *See how you're a hero?*

274

Okay.

"My mom's cool with it," Maya reported, sliding her phone back into airplane mode. "What about yours?"

"She says it's okay. Melissa will come get me." Eli looked at Pearson. "My mom wants you to call and fill her in."

"Tell her I definitely will, but"—Pearson's phone buzzed again—"I need to get back to my desk and keep things moving. Calls are starting to flood in and I have to update all the different departments and agencies."

"She's not going to like that," Eli said to himself.

"What do you mean?" said Pearson.

"Nothing."

"What?" Maya asked.

Eli frowned. "Sometimes it's like she cares more about the case than how I'm doing. If she'd been there today, she would have been asking about every detail."

Pearson sighed. "We're aware of your mom's online activities regarding Gabriel. She's actually crossed paths with our agents, without knowing it."

"Has she done anything wrong?"

"No, but . . . I have to admit that she's one of the reasons we still have a detail watching you. We don't want her pursuing any leads that could put her in danger. There are some pretty sketchy characters lurking online."

"Is that why you said you couldn't bring her along today?"

"Essentially."

"It was just so hard for her."

"It's probably hard for you now," said Maya.

Eli shrugged and looked out the window.

Pearson dropped them off in front of Red Mill. "The detail

is en route," she said. "I'll wait in the lot until they arrive." She pulled around to the side of the building, leaving them standing in front of the restaurant.

Maya looked up and down the street, couldn't shake a feeling that they weren't safe. That there were eyes, agendas, lurking behind every closed window of every house.

"How do you do it?" she asked Eli.

"Do what?" he said, his gaze lost in the pavement.

"Not be afraid."

"I'm always afraid."

"Well then, how do you handle it?"

"I think I'm just used to it."

"I don't want to get used to it." And besides, that was no way to live. Maya took his hand. "Come on, let's go bravely eat some greasy burgers."

The line began just inside the door, the restaurant packed with families, clusters of teens and twenty-somethings. Shouts and sizzle from behind the counter. Only after they'd stepped into line did Maya consider that there might be kids from school here, that they might be seen. Also surprised Pearson hadn't thought of that, though she'd had a lot on her plate. But then, maybe everyone would actually be safer if they knew each other's pasts and secrets. Maybe then they wouldn't be so fractured and lonely, and people like Gabriel wouldn't be able to do the things they did, might not even get to the point of doing them in the first place.

"Hey," the pink-haired girl behind the register said. "You gonna tell me what you want?"

"Oh," said Maya. "Sorry, um . . ." She looked at the menu and laughed.

"What?" Eli asked.

"I was about to order a garden burger, but then I remembered how Janice always gave me shit for ordering them. She told me I should get a cheeseburger, since I liked them best." For an hour or so, she'd nearly put the whole photo situation out of her mind. Now it roared back.

"Do you like cheeseburgers best?"

"I think so? It was just weird. She tried to control everything I ever did. So now a part of me kind of hates cheeseburgers, even though I love them. Everything got flipped around."

"She seemed scary."

Maya laughed. "Yeah, maybe."

"Should I take the next order?" said the pink-haired girl.

"No, sorry. I'll have the chicken sandwich. Never tried that," she said to Eli. "Want to split onion rings? Janice hated those."

"Are they good?"

"They're why you come."

They got their trays and sat on stools at the narrow counter along the front window.

A slapping sound echoed from around the corner. Eli flinched, glancing around quickly.

"It's just the bathroom door," said Maya.

"Sorry."

"You don't have to apologize. How often does that happen?"

"A lot. It's probably going to be worse now." He sipped his soda.

"You don't believe Pearson that Gabriel's far away?"

"I think I do, but the fear is still there. He also— Never mind."

"What?"

"The anniversary is coming up."

"Thirteen days away," said Maya, adrenaline shooting through her, "but who's counting?"

"Sometimes I worry that maybe he's not done with me."

"Well," said Maya, "now he's gotta deal with *us*." She made fists like a boxer, coaxing a quick smile from Eli. "How are you holding up? That must have been hard, in there."

"It was, but I feel a little better now. How about you?"

"I don't know. I mean, fine. The thing that freaked me out was that it looked so normal from the outside." Maya nodded out the window. "Now I look around and every single house is a Schrödinger's cat of psycho abductors."

"A what?"

"Have you heard of Schrödinger's cat?"

"Nope. But you know a lot of really smart stuff, so I'm sure it's true."

"Well—okay, first of all, thank you." She smiled. "It's this idea that if you put a cat in a box with some poison—"

Eli's face paled. "Why would you do that?"

"No, I mean, *I* wouldn't. I don't think anybody actually did. It's just a thought experiment, but it uses a cat."

"Gabriel made me kill cats."

Maya's mouth fell open. "Are you serious? Oh man, I had no idea. I didn't mean to bring that up."

He shook his head. "If you worried about everything that might connect to my past, there'd be nothing to talk about."

"I'm still sorry."

Eli bit into an onion ring. "Don't even get me started about the bunnies."

"Oh God, really? Bunnies?"

A smile tugged at the corner of his mouth.

Maya gaped. "You're kidding! You jerk!" She play-punched his shoulder.

His smile grew. Maya's laugh burbled out of her and the next thing she knew they were both cracking up, covering their mouths to stifle their laughter as nearby customers looked over.

"We should absolutely *not* be laughing," said Maya.

"I know," said Eli. They cracked up again. But then his face darkened. He looked at her seriously. "Thank you for not treating me like I'm broken."

"Well . . . right back at you."

"So what is the cat thing?"

Maya waved her hand. "Oh, it's just the idea that until you look in the box, you don't know if the cat is dead or alive, so both realities kind of exist. Except they don't actually. In the box, the cat is definitely one or the other. But in your experience, it could be either. It has to do with probability and quantum mechanics. I was just saying that, until you know there's no psycho in each house, there is some probability of one being there."

"But thinking that way makes the world terrifying."

Maya shrugged. "Tell me about it. Science is cold, man. I mean, I guess there's also a probability that each of those houses has an entire room full of chocolate, but I only ever think about that bad stuff."

"What bad stuff?"

"Well . . ." Maya collapsed an entire onion ring into her mouth. Felt her chest constricting as she chewed. This was usually the part where she shut up. "Sometimes I just freak out and feel like, what's the point? Why love something, or try at something, or care about something, when nothing is safe? It feels too dangerous. And I can see myself being too afraid to say what I want to say, or feel what I feel, and I know I shouldn't drift, but I can't stop it. And some of that is the trauma—I'm supposed to call it that—of the DOL, but some of it was there already. Maybe it always will be."

"I'm sorry."

"But that's not even all. And for the record, no more apologies, okay? I feel even worse because all these people are trying to help me, and I'm not loving them back, or not showing it at least, and it's like, how can I be so selfish? Except then I also think: why don't they feel it too? That close proximity to death, the probability of the dead cat, right there, all the time. Are they blind? Ignorant? Or am I the dumb one for not being able to ignore it? But then it seems more like maybe everyone is messed up and suffering, but we're all hiding it, trying to be something we're not. God, it all sounds so ridiculous when I say it out loud."

"No, it doesn't," said Eli. "Gabriel called people sheep. He said everyone was complicit in the world being unfair."

"Oh man, I don't want to be looking at the world like a psycho." Maya shook her head. "Maybe it's not that they're complicit, but more like we're all too afraid to tell each other the truth. Like we're all part of this universal costume party. I mean, I wear this hat, but it's a costume. The real me is that photo, but I can't show it. Today proves that."

"People suck."

"Yeah, but it's like, why? Even Gabriel looked normal when he was a little kid, but what happened? And how come nobody knew? I've had this reporter hounding me to do a one-year-later

280

story and I feel like this is the stuff I'd start saying, but then that seems like a bad idea."

"Why?" said Eli. "People will listen if it's coming from a hero."

Maya rolled her eyes. "Come on. You and I both know I wasn't a hero. It was just dumb luck."

"I believed in you."

A warm little sunburst inside. "Well, okay, but if your bomb had worked . . ."

"I thought you said it was time-locked."

"Oh, well, yeah. But—"

"Besides," said Eli, "sometimes I think about how if I'd been one minute later walking home from school, maybe Gabriel never gets me. It goes both ways."

"True, except that kind of goes back to my point about how we're not in control. Except you're making it sound less terrible. So why does this all do such a number on me?" Maya picked up her soda and saw that her thumb was bleeding.

Eli made a strange, short sound, almost like a frog croaking, but then coughed.

"Are you okay?"

He cleared his throat, and then spoke in a gravelly voice: "Never her mind on where she was." He started poking Maya's arm with each word. "What. She. Was doing."

"Is that Yoda?"

Eli nodded. *Empire Strikes Back.*"

"He's got a point. Oh, that reminds me." She got out her notebook. "Let's do a list here. Everything we can write down."

"Like a list of right now?"

281

"Yeah. I'll be the scribe. Ready?"

Eli surveyed the street. Pointed at a woman walking by. "Crazy striped socks."

"Nice," said Maya, her pen scribbling:

> *Vines of flowers on a white fence*
> *Rainbow-painted crosswalk*
> *Cloud shaped like a hippo*
> *Weird pink splatter in the road like a dried-up spill*
> *Old car with its engine ticking*
> *Guy taking apart his burger and eating it one part*
>   *at a time*
> *Squirrel with a french fry*
> *Skinny older lady, fast tiny steps, yellow pants,*
>   *green hair, a captain's hat*

They filled the page, and then Maya read the list back to Eli. "There's like a story behind each one," said Eli.

"Here." She wrote a title at the top and underlined it:

> *The Beautiful Now*

Maya tapped her pen against the paper. Her throat suddenly constricted and a tear slipped down her cheek.

Eli put his hand gently on hers. "What's up?"

"It's like, every moment is so much, but then you have to lose it. I hate that."

"You don't have to lose it. You could let it go. Like a flock of birds."

Maya smiled through more tears. She'd thought of drumbeats that way, but it had seemed sad then. "That's a pretty great way to look at it."

Eli shrugged. "I just thought of it."

Maya reread the list. "Should we post this?"

"We can't. It might blow our cover."

Maya laughed. "That's right." She immediately hated that she'd even had the thought. Besides, it wasn't just that they couldn't let anyone know their connection; maybe she didn't *want* anyone to know. "Hey," she said, her heart starting to sprint before she quite knew what she was saying, "I have a concert next Friday. If you wanted to come, I could save you one of the reserved seats?"

"I'd like that."

"Good," said Maya, feeling a little flush. She smiled at Eli, but his expression had turned stony.

"My sister's here."

Melissa was waiting to turn into the parking lot. She saw them through the window, and Maya felt sure that her gaze was disapproving.

They shoved down their last few bites and headed out. Melissa met them by the door.

"Thanks for coming," Eli said to her.

"No problem," Melissa said. "Hello," she said to Maya.

"Hi." The bus stop was down the street. "I'm just gonna—"

"Eli," said Melissa. "Go to the car, okay?"

"Why?"

"I want to talk to Maya. It's girl stuff."

Eli's brow furrowed. "See you later." He shoved his hands in his hoodie and started toward the parking lot.

"Listen," Melissa began.

"I'm sorry," Maya said immediately. "It wasn't my idea to hang out with him, but—"

"I know it wasn't. Look, I get that you guys have this connection, with that day." Melissa glanced at the restaurant window. "And it's cool seeing you two sitting there chatting, like Eli's normal, I mean . . . It's just, I know you feel like you guys get each other, and don't take this the wrong way, but you really don't have any idea how much he's been through, how damaged he is."

"Oh. Okay. But he seems good when—"

"I know he does," Melissa almost snapped. "I'm not saying you're not good for him. I think you are. I was probably wrong to tell you to stay away. It's hard not to be overprotective. . . . I'm saying be careful. If you ever catch yourself thinking that he's normal, or that what's going on in his head is the same as in yours or anybody else's, just remember that it's not, or even if it is, it's really fragile. Nobody's really sure how he's dealing with stuff, not even his doctor. You might mean something one way, but he might take it totally differently."

"I'm not— I didn't—"

"Just keep it in mind, okay?"

"Okay." But Maya wasn't sure. Eli seemed fine when they hung out. Maybe he was actually more himself around her than around his family. But it didn't seem like a good idea to say that.

"We're all lucky you were there," Melissa said. "And I do think he's lucky to have you now. Sometimes we think he's getting better. Other times . . ."

They both looked at Eli, leaning against the car with his headphones on, staring at the ground.

"I, um, invited him to my jazz concert next week. Is that still okay?"

"Yeah," said Melissa. "He could use some better taste in music. That Sideshow Fantasy shit is repulsive."

"Totally." That reminded Maya. "Hey . . ."

Melissa's phone buzzed. "Shit," she said, checking it. "I'm totally going to be late for my study group. We gotta run. What were you going to say?"

"Oh." Maya had been about to ask about Graham. What did Melissa think of him? Did *he* seem good for Eli? But she also thought of how Eli had shut down in the car when she'd mentioned him, and maybe he'd be mad if it seemed like she was going behind his back. "It's nothing. You should go."

"Okay. Thanks for listening." Melissa hurried toward the parking lot.

Maya waved to Eli, but he didn't look up as he got in the car.

CHAPTER 21

ELI

October 15

He found a note in his locker after lunch on Monday. But it wasn't from Maya:

> *Meet me at Olympus. After school.*

He'd expected to hear from Graham over the weekend, but he hadn't. And Eli hadn't contacted him. The thought of talking about Saturday would just make it real; but of course, it already was. He'd heard the whispers around him in the halls and in class, all day:

"Did you hear they found the house where the kidnapper guy lived?"

"I heard his room had no windows and he had to shit in a pail."

"And the kidnapper had this bunker under the house."

"My mom says the guy is still in Seattle and is going to snatch another kid."

He wanted to tell them all to shut up. They talked about it like it was so interesting. Like the latest episode of a TV show. And yet for them, it was. Gabriel's house and the investigation were plastered all over every station and site.

They didn't know what it was like to have that room fresh in your mind, no matter how much he told himself it was just a room. Didn't know that he could barely focus on anything since then. Could barely sleep. Lying on the floor, drenched in sweat, telling himself he'd never be there again.

"Nothing has changed," Dr. Maria said at their emergency meeting this morning before school. "There is the past, and the present, and they inform each other, but they are different."

"From what I've studied, he's more likely to run," Melissa had said last night.

Opinions coming at him from all sides.

Lying awake near dawn, Eli had stared at the little robot he'd taken. It reminded him that Gabriel wasn't just a monstrous shadow looming in a doorway. He was a screwed-up guy who'd been hiding out in his mother's basement, who was a person, who'd been a kid, who'd had a normal thought about liking this tiny robot at some point. But that barely helped. He'd still done what he'd done to Eli. Nothing changed that.

And I'll do it again.

Classes had been a lost cause today. He'd had a quiz in social studies and literally forgot to answer the questions on the back of the paper. Like his grade needed that. Hadn't remembered to do his math homework either.

Every time he walked through the halls, his eyes flashed to each doorway alcove. To the shadow space beneath the bottom flight of stairs. Out windows to parking lots. He used the faculty bathrooms, even though he'd gone a solid two weeks using the normal ones.

The Purpose must be finished.

One good thing: all day, he'd had a strip of blue paper coiled around his finger. A note from Maya that had been in his locker when he'd gotten to school:

YOU GOT THIS!! :)

He hoped so.

After school, Eli made his way to the auditorium. When he arrived he found the main stage lights on, the first few rows of seats filled with the drama club. Ms. Mays stood onstage with Janice, blocking out the movements for a scene.

Eli slipped through the shadows and climbed the back stairs. The trapdoor was open, Graham's backpack lying there. Eli left his beside it and crawled out onto the catwalk. Ms. Mays's voice echoed up from below. He moved slowly, trying to keep the squeaking of the supports to a minimum.

Graham sat near the end of the catwalk that led toward the stage, legs dangling off the side. "Hey," he whispered as Eli sat beside him. Just beyond their feet was a gap in the ceiling and a bank of stage lights. Through it, you could see half the drama kids. "You got the memo."

Eli nodded.

"What's wrong— Oh, right, damn, how are you doing? The house was all over the news! I didn't hear about it until this morning. Was busy working on something top secret over the weekend, but, dude, that's huge! Did they tell you about it ahead of time, or did you have to hear about it like the rest of us?"

"They took me there Saturday morning."

"No way!" said Graham. "You should have texted me! And sent pictures."

"They said no pictures."

"Oh yeah, of course. What they showed on TV . . . the room you were in, the sicko porn setup, and that spider hole hideout . . . insane. So do they have anything on Gabriel now? Do they think he's still in Seattle? He might get desperate, now that they're closing in. You must be freaking out."

"I'm trying not to think about it."

"Well, here, this will take your mind off it." Graham handed Eli a torn scrap of notebook paper from a pile in his lap.

Graham balled one up and popped it into his mouth. He made a sucking motion and then removed the tiny spitball. "Wanna play?" he said. "First one to hit a sheep wins." He leaned against the catwalk railing and flicked the spitball down through the gap in the ceiling. It bounced off the lights and fell toward the seats, landing two rows behind the kids. "Crap. It's actually really hard."

Eli held the scrap for a second. What were they doing? His brain felt like mush.

"You make a ball with your tongue," said Graham, working on another one. "Come on, try it."

Eli scrunched up the paper and put it in his mouth. Took it out and flicked it. It soared toward the kids below, narrowly missing a girl and landing in the aisle.

Graham flicked another. It flew wildly off course. "I should have brought a straw." He handed Eli another, but before either of them could ready their next one, Ms. Mays said something and clapped her hands, and the whole group stood and started filing up onto the stage.

"Oh well," said Graham.

"I thought we were going to your house," said Eli. It had been almost the only thing on his mind all day. "Pearson is probably outside by now."

"Yeah, we are," said Graham. "I just wanted to meet up here for a second to show you what I was working on all weekend. I even cut gym today to finish it."

Eli swung his feet back and forth in the empty space beneath them. The air felt somehow heavy on his ankles, like it wanted to pull him over. "I thought you said you liked floor hockey?"

"Nah, it's stupid." Graham picked up a notebook from beside him. Eli saw him wince and rub his shoulder.

"What happened?"

"Nothing . . . Mateo and I got into it in the locker room."

So you did go to gym, at least the beginning. Eli decided to let that go. And yet it pricked him a little: a feeling like he had to keep tabs on whether Graham was being honest with him. "Was it because of the thing you posted on his wall?"

"What? Oh, at the sleepover? Nah, this was different. And I didn't really fight back. Can't afford to get suspended right now." Graham ran his fingernail along the little slats in the catwalk.

"Sorry about Mateo."

"Nah, fuck him. Anyway, it was good because it gave me an excuse to finish this." He opened the notebook to a page full of writing. "Remember the other night when we were talking at

290

my sleepover? About how awesome it would be if there was an apocalypse?"

"Yeah . . ." Had they? He sort of remembered that, but there had been a lot of rum.

"I wrote something about it. Want to hear it?"

"Okay, but do we have time?" *Be cool!* he shouted at himself. Couldn't sound too anxious to get to Graham's or it might arouse suspicion.

"It's only going to take like a minute. Is Pearson really going to freak out if we're *one minute* late?"

"No, but I should text her." He got out his phone and sent a message: Running a little late. Be right out.

"Okay," said Graham. "I don't have a title yet, but here goes: *'Chapter 1: Another Day at the Office. They call me the Exterminator. My mother named me Jacob—'"* His eyes flashed at Eli.

Eli tried to smile, but his body clenched at the same time.

"But my mother is dead. They're all dead. Well, almost all of them. When humanity first saw the spaceships arrive three years ago, they greeted them with open arms. But the Trax from Centauri X weren't interested in making friends. They hit the planet from orbit with de-atomizing bombs, instantly vaporizing the population. Seven billion gone, just like that. Only a few hundred thousand survived, through dumb luck.

"That's where I come in.

"The Trax began mining the planet for precious minerals. But the surviving humans resorted to guerrilla warfare. So the Trax put out a call: any human willing to hunt down the others would be given dominion over Earth once the Trax were done with it. But first you had to pass a test of worthiness. Five hundred

contestants lined up outside the great Trax governing ship. All of them were deemed unworthy and vaporized where they stood.

"All, that is, except for me. Let's just say the Trax didn't only want to see that you could kill; they wanted to see that you had a flair for 'entertainment,' and so they outfitted me with a robot horse, a handheld de-atomizing cannon, a quiver of exploding rocket arrows, and if all else failed, a machete made of pure quartz. I named the horse Lucyfer.

"It was time to get things done.

"Now, the sun is setting on another fine day, the buildings covered in vines, the sky clear of human filth, and I'm galloping through the silent streets of Los Angeles. Well, soon to be silent, that is. Because about a hundred feet ahead of me, there's a woman screaming her head off, dragging her little daughter behind her. She's running straight up the middle of the street just like the dumb sheep that she is. She's lost one of her shoes, and her shirt is half-ripped off. I gallop behind her, closing in but also taking my time. The rest of her clan is behind us, their bodies maimed and draped on the overturned cars and crumbled walls.

"The woman trips and falls. I stop Lucyfer, who snorts with annoyance. She can smell the blood and she's programmed to home in. The mom looks back at me, sees me just standing here. Waiting. It's no fun if she's not trying.

"The kid tugs at her and she gets up and starts running and I kick Lucyfer and we're off again. As we go, I thread an arrow and pull back the string. I could have taken them both out with the cannon by now, but this seems more sporting. And like I said, the Trax like a good show, and they're always watching. So I let them run a little more, let her turn and see me one more time, then I send the arrow soaring through the evening sky. It *catches the mom in the back and blows the top half of her body clean off. Another direct hit.*

"The daughter is thrown sideways and lands against a burned-out bus. She's covered in blood and brains, and when she sees the bloody stump of her mom, she just starts screaming. What an annoying sound.

"As my shadow falls over her, she quiets down. Her wide eyes look up at me in awe. She's still whimpering.

"'Stop crying and I'll let you live,' I say.

"She stops crying.

"'Good girl.' I lunge forward and get her with the machete, right across the neck.

"I ride out of town and up into the hills where Lucyfer can feed on the car batteries in the driveways of the formerly rich and famous. As she sucks down acid, I look back on the dead city. The only sound is a huge Trax ship humming high overhead, and the wind through the grass. Planet Earth the way it was always meant to be, free of the human plague. Peaceful and beautiful and finally in the hands of the worthy.

"I take a swig from my canteen. This morning I filled it with the finest scotch from some dead executive's office in Beverly Hills.

"A smile comes to my lips.

"Just then, the alert goes off on my scanner. There's an enclave of humans nearby. My smile grows bigger. Time to get back to work."

"What do you think?" said Graham. "In the next chapter, he's going to meet up with another hunter, and they become partners."

"It's good," said Eli, drumming softly on his legs. He couldn't quite look at Graham as he said it. "I could really picture it." The images lingered, and his pulse had quickened.

"Yeah. Wouldn't that be awesome? Riding across the land, making it ours?"

"It would be sad, though, right?"

"Why?"

Eli hesitated. "Just having everybody be dead."

"Oh." Graham closed the notebook. "I don't know. That's not really the point. I mean, I wrote it for *us,* but if you think it's stupid . . ."

"No, I just said I liked it. You're a good writer."

Graham shrugged. "Whatever."

"No, really. It was cool." Eli checked his phone. "We should go."

"Right." Graham perked up, balling the paper scraps and shoving them into his pocket. "We need to get there before my mom gets home. I have something even better to show you!"

They crawled to the trapdoor, got their backpacks, and headed down. The drama club was spread out onstage, rehearsing a scene. They left the auditorium and pushed through the double glass doors that led outside. The sky was heavy with clouds. Eli couldn't help scanning the area: that triangular corner where kids often smoked, the bushes by the stairs to the front entrance, that nearly vacant parking lot.

Don't be foolish. When I come, I won't be this obvious.

His phone buzzed. It was Maya: Are you around for Tech Squad? I have rehearsal. Meet up after?

No sorry. I'm going to Graham's.

Boo.

"Who you texting?" Graham asked.

"Just my sister."

"You're quiet today, even for you."

Sorry. "I don't like people knowing what the house looked like." He'd actually been thinking about Graham's story, but for some reason it had also made him picture Gabriel's house.

"Why not?"

It makes me feel weak. "It makes me feel weak."

"Oh, no way," said Graham. "I think it's the opposite. Do you know how many other people would have died in that place, or blown themselves up in that mall? That's why I called the character in my story Jacob. If the Trax ever came to Earth, you'd definitely be one of the worthy. You're, like, the strongest kid I know."

Eli looked up.

Graham smiled and brushed his hair out of his eyes. "It's true. You proved it. Most of us never get that chance. Well, not that you wanted *that* kind of chance, but you are. Strong."

Thanks. Could he really see himself that way? Graham wasn't the first to tell him he'd been strong to survive, but coming from adults, it had always sounded like something out of a book.

They reached Pearson's car, idling by the bench, and got in.

"Sorry we're late," said Eli as he took his afternoon pills.

"Good to see you, Detective," said Graham. He flashed that smile he always put on for adults.

"Nice to see you too, Graham." Pearson pulled away from the curb, glanced at Eli in the rearview mirror. "So . . . how did it go today?"

"Okay. It, um . . ."

"Detective," said Graham, "I saw the reports about you

finding Gabriel's house. Are there any clues yet about his where-abouts?"

"Well, first off, his name is Stephen, and even if there were, I couldn't share them with you. We're still analyzing the house, and we're getting the suspect's picture and information out there, so we hope it will only be a matter of time now."

"Is there going to be, like, a nationwide manhunt?" Graham asked.

"Essentially there already is," said Pearson, "and has been, this last year. But these things don't work quite like you see on TV. It's a slow, thorough process."

"I heard this guy on the news saying that now that you knew his identity, it might make him desperate and he might try to blow himself up or kidnap another kid or something. Or he might even come after Eli."

Eli's insides burned.

Pearson eyed Graham in the mirror. "People on the news are entitled to their wild speculation, but I can assure you that's not the case."

Eli lowered his window, his face in the breeze. *Cool damp air, my hair blowing around, the whoosh as other cars pass . . .* Good things for a list with Maya.

"What's your policy on the suspect?" Graham asked. "Is it, like, shoot on sight?"

"That would never be our policy. We are still in the business of building a case, making an arrest, and having a trial."

"Hmm," said Graham. "Suit yourself, I guess."

Eli saw Pearson frown.

"How was Maya doing today?" she asked.

"Fine, I think." *Don't bring her up!*

"You guys keep tabs on her too?" Graham asked.

"I was just referring to Saturday," said Pearson. "It was hard on everyone. I thought I might check in on her tonight."

Eli felt Graham looking at him and couldn't quite meet his gaze. "She came with us," he admitted.

"You brought *her* to the house? Like, to look at evidence?"

"Kinda."

"It was nice of her to come," said Pearson. "Very supportive."

"Huh." Graham shifted and looked out the window.

It's not a big deal. Except Eli had known it would be.

When they arrived, Graham got out of the car and headed straight for the door without saying goodbye.

"What are you guys up to this afternoon?" Pearson asked.

"Just hanging out, I think," said Eli. A wave of adrenaline crested inside him. *Just stay calm. She has no idea.* He was so close, couldn't blow it now.

Pearson looked at the house. Graham had already gone inside and left the door open. "Sorry if I made things awkward by mentioning Maya," she said. "Graham seems like he's pretty sensitive."

"Yeah," said Eli.

"And it's all right? Spending time with him?"

Eli wondered why she was asking. "Yeah. He's a good friend."

Pearson watched the door for another moment. Eli wanted to shout at her: *Go!* Finally, she pointed up the street. "Jennings and Hart are here. They'll take you home at five. Have fun."

"Okay, bye." Eli walked up to the house. Checked the high hedge at the corner of the yard, the sidewalk in both directions, the car up the street, watching him. Their bait, hoping he'd attract a fish from the deep.

Still too obvious. When you least expect it.

No. I'll be ready.

The front door was open, the kitchen silent. He heard a thumping sound and went downstairs to the basement. Found Graham coming out of the guest bedroom, struggling to carry a large, circular mirror.

"What's that for?"

Graham knelt on the couch and thrust the mirror up against the wall behind it, balancing it on the back of the couch. It slipped a little, catching his finger.

"Fuck!"

Do you want some help?

"I got it." Graham adjusted the mirror and stepped back, breathing hard and checking himself out in it, then brushed by Eli out of the room again. When he came back, he was attaching his phone to the end of a selfie stick.

"Is this what you were going to show me?"

Graham shoved the coffee table toward the TV, then stood in the middle of the room facing the mirror, holding the stick toward it. "Yeah," he said. "I mean, if you don't want to see it, you can leave. I don't care. I have a lot to do."

"No, I do."

"Fine."

Graham grabbed the standing lamp beside the couch. He positioned it at a triangle with himself and the mirror, then twisted the lampshade to angle the light toward the mirror. The reflected glare hit him in the face. He pulled a pair of black sunglasses from his back pocket and slipped them on.

"You know," he said, "I'm not sure I believe your detective."

Why not?

"If Gabriel spent all that time working on you, training you, it seems weird that he'd just give up on you and run away."

Stephen, not Gabriel. He's just a man. "What do you mean?"

"Well, isn't it obvious? That he's waiting for your anniversary?"

Yes. "I don't know." But the very same thought had been on his mind. One of the reasons he was so anxious to get here this afternoon, why his heart was hammering now.

Graham shrugged. "That date was probably important to him. And the anniversary makes it double significant. If I were him, that's when I'd come after you and Maya the hero, but who knows? Maybe he won't. Or maybe he grabbed another kid and is gonna blow them up."

The red dark when he blinked. Eli looked at his finger, the roll of paper there. Rubbed his other finger against it. *You got this.*

Graham's hand fell on his shoulder. "Sorry, man. I didn't mean to freak you out."

"It's okay."

"And don't worry, I don't care that you brought Maya to the house on Saturday. I get it. But you did see the picture of her that's been going around, right?"

"What about it?"

"Just . . . yikes." He shrugged. "Then again, give a mutt like that any attention at this point, and she'll do whatever you want. That's actually not a bad angle."

Angle? What was he talking about?

"Here. The show's almost ready. Have a seat." Graham put the selfie stick down, motioned to the couch, and then jogged up the stairs.

Eli sat. His heart racing. His lungs felt thick and heavy, made of metal. *Anniversary.* The mask against his face, the weight of the bottles strapped to him, the warm, sweat-slicked metal of the bomb trigger in his hand. Gabriel's fingers on his neck . . . He blinked and saw the hidden room, the cot, the pail.

Of course I'm coming back. We belong together.

"Okay." Graham returned holding a large blue-and-silver plastic microphone. "Check this out." He held up the mic. "Welcome to your destruction." It made his voice low and distorted and monsterlike. "You want some now, you—" The electronic voice cut out. Graham frowned and shook the microphone. "I got it at Value Village. Only problem is the batteries run out super-fast. But I have more." He disappeared again and came back with a small screwdriver and a handful of AAs. He knelt and started unscrewing the panel on the side of the microphone. "Has one of those stupid childproof covers. This will just take a sec."

Now! Go now! Eli dragged himself to his feet. His lead arms. His steel lungs. His red thoughts. "I'm gonna use the bathroom. Should I get us Cokes?"

"Yeah, totally. I put the rum behind the couch, as is tradition."

Eli headed upstairs. Reached the bathroom door and swallowed hard.

Stay focused! Can't mess this up.

He closed the door without going in. Slid off his sneakers. Crossed the hall and started up the wooden stairs on his tiptoes.

The blinds were down in Jules's room, the shadows deep. Eli opened the closet, carefully undid the latches on the trunk . . .

The cool steel of the gun. The weight of its potential. It immediately calmed him, and yet he could still feel his heart racing.

We'll be safe now.

He checked the safety, left the holster behind—too thick—then stood and slipped the gun into his pants. Pulled his hoodie down as far as it would go.

"Did you bomb out my bathroom or what?" Graham asked when Eli returned to the basement.

"Sorry." Eli tossed a Coke can to Graham, but with his anxious energy he threw it too hard.

"Whoa!" Graham fumbled the catch and dropped it. "Sheesh, settle down, killer." He picked it up. "Fire in the hole!" Popped it open and it sprayed onto his shirt and the floor. Held the bottom of the can to his mouth, the foam dribbling in.

Eli sat back down on the couch. Slowly, feeling the unyielding press of the gun inside his belt. The point digging into his abdomen. One hand in his hoodie pocket to make sure it was covered.

Graham unleashed a long burp, rolling his head in a circle. "Allll righty then, I think we're good." He put down the can and unfolded a piece of paper from his back pocket. Laid it on the floor just in front of him. Eli saw that it was full of writing.

Graham stood and slipped on the sunglasses. He faced the mirror, bathed in the glare of the lamp, selfie stick in one hand, kids' microphone in the other. "I can't wait for you to see this, at long last. Ready?"

Eli nodded. *For what?*

"Greetings!" he boomed into the mic. "Oh . . . recording didn't start." He tapped the phone and held it back out. "Greetings, losers, sinners, the meek and mundane." Graham grinned as he spoke, his voice warbled and twisted by the microphone. "That's right, he's back, your judge, jury, and executioner, the one who sees you in all your wretched misery, who listens to your incessant whining and knows what you all really yearn for . . . the peace and wisdom of death. And also my cock."

He laughed: a low chuckle. "Well, don't worry, jocks and bitches, the Alpha has a promise for you."

Eli stiffened. Glanced worriedly at the window, as if someone might be watching.

"You've all been wondering when I'll have my say," Graham continued. "You've lit up my account with your horny eyes. You're all desperate for me to reveal my big plan. When I'm going to decree silence upon your miserable lives. When I'm going to enroll you all in STFU University. Get it?" He sighed. "Probably not. Well, you're not worth it, but what the hell, I'm going to tell you anyway. Here's the big announcement. Ahem! I've decided on a date for your salvation, for my retribution, and it couldn't be more perfect. Because this world needs saving from the Barons"—his eyes flashed at Eli—"from their greedy and corrupt system. You're all sad little sheep, and that's why I'm going to free you, because it's not even your fault. You didn't ask to be born as whining little consumers, swimming around in fashion and popularity and hate and jealousy, unable to admit your despair, to understand the true purpose.

"So, Elliott High, I declare that the date is close at hand. We're going to shut you up and set you free, so very soon, on the same day that you were almost saved last time. Have you figured it out yet? I hope not. That would spoil the big surprise. Then again, I don't expect you to be the thinking types. If you are, maybe you'll be one of the chosen who survive the fall. Who help me rebuild on the other side. See you soon, sheep. Oh so very soon. Until then, remember: I'm in the corner of your eye, I'm the shiver in your spine. That fear you feel? It's real. It's me."

Graham chuckled again, a thin smile on his lips. Then he stopped recording. Sighed and took off the sunglasses. He was breathing hard, his face red. Dropped the mic and grabbed his Coke. After a big swig: "What did you think?"

Eli's heart hammered. His hand was pressing the gun into his abdomen so hard that it hurt. "You're the Alpha."

Graham bowed. "In the flesh. I've been waiting to share that with you forever! I think that was my best one yet. We'll see if it gets any more views. My first post got over five thousand, but the last few have been going down." His face fell. "But now that I've got a date, that should get people's attention."

"You talked about the Barons," said Eli. "And the Purpose."

Graham shrugged. "Was that cool? I thought it was such good material. I mean, just the parts that are true. Your Gabriel was a sick fuck, but you have to admit some of that stuff is right on the mark. Visionaries are usually pretty tortured. But if you think about it, on principle, blowing some shit up definitely seems like a reasonable solution these days. How else can you change anyone's minds? It's cool too, because if people Google that stuff, it will connect back to the mall case and that will freak them out, you know?"

I know. There was a metallic taste in his mouth. A wide expanse in his head, like he was floating in space, up and down getting confused. *You should say something.* But what? And why? Graham wasn't really serious. *He sounds serious.* But this was important to him. *He sounds like Gabriel.* But he wasn't. They were just videos. They weren't real.

Graham was busy tapping his phone.

"You're really going to post that?" Eli asked.

"Not from here, are you crazy? Didn't you see that email the school sent home?"

"My mom mentioned it. She didn't think it was a good idea for me to watch the videos. I've only seen the one you showed me . . . and today."

"That's okay," said Graham. "I had to watch one with my parents! Talk about awkward. Anyway, the Feds could trace the IP address, so I need to post from somewhere anonymous. I'm going to take this over to the Broadview library. Someone always forgets to log out of a computer. Then I'll upload it from there so it's clean. I do a different library each time. You want to come with me?"

"I don't know. . . ." *Say something!* Eli thought, except at the same time: *Keep quiet! Questioning the plan is weakness!* No. He struggled on. "I mean, I've heard kids at school. They think the Alpha might be real."

"I am real," said Graham.

"No, I know, but I mean, like, serious. Like seriously going to attack the school or something."

"Well, that's what people are supposed to think." He gulped down the last of his soda and held out the camera, the video playing. "See, it looks cool, doesn't it? Totally stealth."

The shot was mostly washed out in the lamp, but then there was this silhouette of Graham, distorted by light and glass.

"What's the date of salvation?" Eli asked.

Graham stopped the playback and smiled. "I didn't want it to be too obvious, but I figured at least *you* would put it together."

"The anniversary."

"Uh-huh. October twenty-sixth. There's even some assembly

that morning for the whole junior class, I think. Sheep in a pen. Speaking of which, that got me thinking."

Eli swam in his head, the outside world beyond thick glass. "Gabriel was wrong."

"Oh, dude, I know." Graham sat down beside him, searching on his phone. Eli moved his forearm across his lap, over the gun. "What he did to you was vile. But he's not the only person who knows something needs to be done. All those people watching the Alpha videos online too. The only way to stop being power-less is to *use* power. I mean, that part makes sense, right?"

"Yeah." A shadow by the window. Just a cat, sliding by. "But . . . what would you do?"

Graham's eyes got wide. "I don't know, I mean . . ." He held out his phone. "Check this out."

Eli saw a diagram on the screen. *How to Make a Pipe Bomb.* "Did Gabriel teach you how to make those?"

"He never taught me anything."

Except the Purpose. I taught you that so well that you've re-cruited another.

"Well, that is the beauty of the modern age," said Graham, tapping more. "You can literally get a bomb-making book on fucking Amazon. And the supplies are totally easy to find. I mean, my dad just so happens to have some of the right-sized pipes out in the shed. And I've gotten a couple other supplies too. We could make one of these like it was nothing."

Not nothing. "It's not . . ."

"Not that easy, I know. But we could practice in my garage."

"No, I mean"—Eli hesitated—"you can't just . . . kill people."

Graham frowned. "You were going to."

"I . . . I was trying to escape."

305

"By killing a bunch of people."

"You'd go to jail for like the rest of your life."

"But see, that's the same old bullshit." Graham stood up and pointed at Eli. "Those rules only apply if you're *not* the one in charge. Our leaders kill thousands a day and go unpunished. They drop bombs and poison water and enslave workers. It's all a scam, and there's no bigger symbol of it than school. Honestly, the world would be better off if it were more like my story, but since there's no alien race coming, we have to take charge ourselves. Besides, you only go to jail if they catch you."

"I don't know," said Eli. What could he say? "There are problems. But also the world is kinda—"

"What?"

"Nothing."

"Tell me!"

"It's beautiful," Eli mumbled. "Sort of."

"Pffw." Graham rolled his eyes. "Says the one who got raped in a red room for three years. Who told you that, your *girlfriend?*"

I—

"This world is cruel, and lonely, and toxic." Graham's face darkened. "Some part of you must have wanted to do it. When you were walking into that mall, with all those soulless zombies around you. You must have felt powerful."

Had he? "I think I was scared." But the gun was power. He felt that now.

"Well, of course you were scared. Fear is a sign that you're doing something brave. And you were about to sacrifice yourself. But that's the thing: what if you didn't have to die, or even get caught? Can you just imagine it? One well-placed explosion and we wouldn't have to go to school. We'd have our days to ourselves. And if we did it right, others would be emboldened, like copycat attacks. It could change everything. Revolutions always start with a single act. The shot heard round the world."

The sheep are begging for it.

Eli shifted. "I can't tell if you're serious or not."

Graham looked straight at him. "Do you want me to be?"

Yes, you do. Life has sucked this last year. You're broken. The only thing you've ever been good at is the Purpose. Look how you followed it without even knowing it, and it led you right here. Now is your chance to finish what we started. Before I come back and make you.

Shut up. No.

The outline of the gun.

Graham slapped Eli's shoulder, making him flinch. "Okay, I get it, sorry. I fried your brain. Look, relax. Let's just call it wishful thinking for now. Just an idea randomly shared between two friends on a Monday afternoon, one of whom happens to be an infamous online revolutionary and the other a former soldier."

It was MY fault that trigger didn't work. You were perfect and you can be again.

SHUT UP. FUCK YOU.

Graham chugged the rest of his Coke. "Want to play *Colony 17*?"

"Sure." Eli could barely breathe.

Graham ducked out and returned with a second Coke. Got the rum bottle. "Want some Captain for courage?"

"Yeah."

"You didn't even open your soda." He grabbed it from the couch beside Eli and spiked it.

They played with the volume at max, shrouded in explosions

and screams and gunfire. Eli managed to sink into the game now and then—the rum helped—and two hours passed and it was time to go.

"Gotta use the bathroom again," Eli said as they walked upstairs. He brought his backpack with him and transferred the gun, sliding it between his books.

"I totally forgot something I had to tell you," said Graham as Eli reached the front door. "Sideshow Fantasy is playing Friday night down at the Crocodile! It's all ages. My dad said he would take us. Can you go? It would be amazing and also kinda perfect, because the music is like the soundtrack to what we talked about."

Eli stared at the ground. Friday night. *Don't tell him*. . . . "I can't. I already told Maya I'd go to her jazz concert."

Graham looked at him for a second, then turned away and shoved his hands into his pockets. "Oh, sure. Forget it."

"Will they come around again?"

Graham shrugged. "I don't know. They're not on tour all the time. This is like a once-in-a-lifetime chance and it was supposed to be our thing, but I guess I was wrong about that."

"No, I like them. It sounds fun, I—"

"It's cool. I just showed you, like, this huge, special thing, but, hey, blows before bros, I get it." Graham started down the hallway, head hung.

"I'm sorry," said Eli. "I didn't think—"

"Whatever, man."

"Hey, are you really going to post that video?"

Graham paused. "Why? You gonna rat on me if I do?"

"What? No. I wouldn't. . . ."

"See you later." He disappeared down the stairs without looking back.

Eli stood there, his mind blank. He felt blindsided by everything. What had he just done? Why didn't he ever know what to expect?

The officers' car idled at the curb. Eli walked stiffly toward it. He slid into the backseat, his backpack in his lap, breath held until they pulled away.

On the way home, he found a message from Maya: Heading out to dinner with Dad. I'll write later!

Eli messaged Graham: I'm sorry about the concert.

No response.

A mile later, he realized the tiny roll of paper from Maya was missing from his finger. He checked his pockets, the seat around him, the floor. Gone. If Graham found it, he'd be even more pissed.

Everything felt like too much! But maybe now a little less. Eli rubbed his hand over the backpack, feeling the faint outline of the gun. Better than a good-luck note. Now he could keep them both safe, for real.

CHAPTER 22

MAYA

October 19

A polished wooden floor. An edge of burgundy curtain.

The brushstrokes of red and blue and green lights fanned across the gleaming cymbals and pearlescent finish. The architecture of drums arranged on a frayed oriental rug. Two rows of black folding chairs. Music stands with papers clipped.

The river babble of a crowd, the red seats filling up.

Maya stood just behind the open curtain. Sticks in one hand. The other—

Get back here! Her hand skittered away from her French braid, which hung from beneath her black hat. Ms. Reid had frowned at the hat but allowed it. Maya pressed her hand against her black wool skirt, itchy even through white stockings. Tucked-in white shirt also uncomfortable, the seams digging into her armpits. Black tie too tight at her collar.

Her stomach tingled with adrenaline. Head ballooning. *This isn't exploding. This is just nerves.* More than a year since she'd been on a stage. She studied the drum set. Everything was set up just like she liked it. She slipped a coiled scrap of paper from her index finger. Eli had left it today:

YOU GOT THIS!! :)

Made her smile. But there were a lot of people out there. A lot of people who would see her, hear her, no hiding, no excuses. A lot of people who knew what her hat was hiding. She'd managed to never respond to Janice's post. Managed to survive a week of smirks and snickers in hallways. This was her chance to reply.

Dad was ten rows back with Kendall, who wore a low-cut shirt like they were at a Belltown club. Mom was in the third row with an empty seat beside her.

Maybe Eli had trouble getting here. Maybe something had gone wrong.

"Ready?" Trevor appeared beside her.

"I think so. You?"

Trevor swallowed hard. "Uh-huh." He wore a similar white and black outfit, his hair slicked back, making him look like his own younger brother. He'd shaved but left a mustache so questionable it almost crossed over to rebellious. "You'll be awesome," he said. "You've been so good in practice."

"Thanks. You'll do great too."

Trevor peered around the curtain and sighed. "Lot of people came."

Maya leaned into him and looked too. Didn't mind how Trevor sort of stiffened as her shoulder brushed against his. Nor

311

his millisecond glance at her chest—*Settle down, Trevor*—and yet it wasn't terrible, knowing there was interest.

But still no Eli. She should text him—

"Showtime." Trevor gave her shoulder the world's most desperately tentative pat.

She tried to muster a smile as the rest of the band filed past them onto the stage.

Maya waited until Jory passed, carrying his bass. Followed him out, Trevor behind her. Applause crescendoed, then died away as they sat down. She placed her feet on the pedals, double-checked her seat height and distance. Her stomach knotted. All those eyes. How many of them knew who she was, for good reasons, bad reasons, both?

The seat beside Mom was still empty.

Three . . . two . . . one . . .

She uncurled Eli's note, read it again, and slipped it into her stick bag, which hung from the floor tom. Put her sticks under her arm, checked to make sure the snares were on. Reached around and twisted the knobs on the hi-hat, the ride cymbal stand, the legs of the floor tom. Took the shiny drum key from its perch on the music stand and tapped lightly around the edges of the snare. Tightened two lugs. Everything ready.

Sweat on her neck . . . that braid had to go. A chain saw, a steak knife. Her skin revolting at wool, at stockings, at the constricting pull of her shirt. She should have taken Serenitab, found some vodka—but no. All week she'd been taking less, and not drinking at all.

She was going to be here. Be this. No distractions.

Metallic tapping. Ms. Reid hitting her music stand with her baton. She started to swing her arms. Maya moved her head to the tempo, muscles tensing, checked the audience one more time as the houselights dimmed—

Eli coming down the aisle, sliding into the seat by her mom. Maya smiled at him. Could he see it?

He held a hand up just in front of him, a little wave.

Ms. Reid was counting: "Five-six-seven-eight—"

Maya gathered the bugs and the white energy in one deep breath—

Bap-BAM!

She lashed out and tagged the eighth-note hits at the top of the tune so loud, so hard, so THERE that she rushed the beat and Jory flinched and Ms. Reid's eyes darted back to her.

It's okay, I got it—Maya closed her eyes, reining it in and relaxing against the quarter note, her arm swinging and tapping the cymbal, her foot bounding bass-drum beats like carefree hops across a meadow. The song flowed, and she dipped and dived, slapped accents that echoed to the rafters, sneaked through quiet sections, rumbled crescendos that shook the whole stage, and she was sweating all over and she could she could she could.

To be the moment. That's what music was. To feel something that was just now, like sitting in a waterfall as it poured over you, or maybe more like being a fish in that flow.

The list she could make for Eli right now: bass thud, snare head sizzle, slap of horn stabs, ache of calf muscle, the daring tumble of a drum fill over the bar. But she had to concentrate: bobbing her head, the count a quiet whisper at her lips. And for moments, and then minutes, she was an explosion carefully released, like a star. She played and smiled at the applause and no one blew up and she nailed it.

"You sounded really good," said Eli after. He met her in the aisle after she'd gotten hugs from her dad and Kendall. They'd brought her flowers—she'd noticed Mom noticing—and had already left. Her plan with Eli was to talk in the parking lot, but Maya paused anyway. Everyone was either filing out or grouping around the other players, taking pictures.

"Thanks," she said. "It went pretty well. Can you still hang out?"

Eli nodded, secret-agent-style. "Where should we go?"

"I was thinking—" Maya flinched. Had something just tapped her on the head? She looked up, but there was only the distant ceiling. Nobody nearby either. Down at the floor . . . lots of feet busying around and she didn't see anything.

"Did something just hit you?" Eli asked.

"It felt like it."

Eli peered up at the ceiling. "We should go outside. Do you want to go to Molly Moon's?"

"That's where the band kids are going."

"Oh. Sorry."

"No, it's fine. I had another idea anyway. Let me finish packing the drums and then meet me by our car, okay? Just follow my mom."

"Okay." Eli looked at the ceiling again, his brow wrinkling.

"What is it?"

"Nothing. I'll be outside."

*　*　*

"So what did you think of the concert?" Maya asked as they drove across the city.

"It was pretty interesting," said Eli. "I've never listened to that kind of music before."

"But did you like it?"

"It didn't really have a beat, but it was cool."

"Of course it had a beat, just not, like, a *beat*." She made a little dance motion. "Here: go like this." She tapped her fingers against the seat between them. "This is the basic swing pattern. Ding ding-da-ding ding-da-ding. Try it, just with one hand." Maya took his hand and moved it with hers. "Like this. Got it?"

"I think so."

"Now stomp your foot on each quarter note. Like this." Eli copied her. "That's basically it. Keep doing that." Maya started improvising snare beats on her leg. Eli kept the beat going for twenty seconds before it fell apart. "Yeah, like that! Not bad."

Eli slid his hands back into his sweatshirt. "I'll work on it."

"Come on, try again now." Maya reached for his wrist, just inside his sweatshirt pocket—

Eli jerked his hand out, brushing her away. "Let's try it another time."

Maya recoiled. "Everything okay?"

"It's been a weird week."

"Weird like you want to tell me?"

Eli stared at the back of the seat in front of him, his lips moving like he was going to say something. "It's your night," he said. "It's stuff I can tell you another time."

"You sure?"

Eli nodded.

"Okay, well, I think you're going to like where we're going." Maya grinned at him, but he just looked out the window.

Why had he brushed her hand away like that? *Maybe he thinks you're trying to make it a date.* Was she? She didn't think so. At least not in a romantic way. But maybe more than a friend date?

315

He might not be able to be what you want him to be.

She tore a thin strip of cuticle from her index finger. *Ugh, just chill!* But also Eli was still looking away, so she popped it in her mouth.

Her mom pulled to the curb a few quiet minutes later. "When should I pick you up?" she asked.

"It lasts like an hour," said Maya. "But I thought maybe we'd get gelato after? It's right around the corner."

"How about if I go to Elliott Bay and get you at ten, right back here?"

"Thanks, Mom." She should probably remember this moment of Mom coolness the next time she was annoyed.

They got out of the car on a street lined with gnarled old trees, their giant yellow leaves papering the sidewalks. Capitol Hill was one of the older parts of Seattle, big houses with sagging roofs. The night air was cool, blue-tasting, with that dry smell of decay. The highway hummed from down the hill.

Before them was a giant old cathedral unlike any other in town: no spires, ornate carvings, or gargoyles, just a great stone square, broad and heavy, illuminated in yellow lights.

"Cool, right?" said Maya.

"What is it?"

"St. Mark's Cathedral. They do this monk singing every week. Renee has been telling me to come for a while. Have you ever heard them?"

Eli just shook his head. Was he still mad, or whatever that had been in the car? She had a feeling like she had no idea where he was. Maybe this was what Melissa had been talking about.

"We don't have to go if you don't want to."

Eli finally looked at her. "No, sorry. I do."

"Okay, good."

They joined the stream of people arriving, passing through the big wooden front doors and sliding into one of the straight wooden pews near the back. The room was high and square, great white pillars reaching up to a carved wooden ceiling. Chandeliers filled with candle-shaped lights cast a golden glow over the crowd. Tall, clear glass windows stretched up the walls, the lavender evening beyond. Straight ahead, a huge circular window like an eye on the western sky, the faintest light still frosting the clouds out there, a sliver of moon above them.

At the front of the room, a group of men in white robes were gathered in a semicircle. One of them was speaking, a short reading, but the crowd was still settling and it was hard to make out the words. Something about God and stuff.

A pause: and now the choir began to sing in unison, slipping through melancholy intervals. *It's a good place to connect with yourself,* Renee had said. Maya focused on her breathing, listened to her heart thumping slowly. The voices rose and split into three-part harmony, spreading to high and low registers that filled in gaps Maya hadn't even known were there, as if the music were somehow expanding the space around them.

A pause for another spoken phrase: something about prayer and love. Maya felt a little guilty, like she should have known what it meant or where it was from, and yet this place didn't seem to expect it of her.

The singing began again, this time in Latin. The melody more dramatic, the notes resonating in a perfect reverb through the room.

Maya got out her notebook and opened it to a new page. She laid it between her and Eli and started jotting details:

Falsetto = bird tornado

Baritone = dark wooded library

Basses = catacombs, the bones of the lost and
    forgotten

Sliver moon out the giant eye window

Heads bowed

Hard straight backs of the pews

The melody soared, a new dramatic turn, and Maya put her pen down. As the singing continued, she felt herself spreading out, losing the pew, losing her legs; her fingers even forgot her scalp. Had no scalp. This was different from playing music, when you were part of a flow, attached to it with each note you struck. More like she was joining a great space, no longer just in this cathedral, no longer just in Seattle on a Friday night. Also out among the evening clouds, part of dawn on the far side of the world, part of galaxies in all directions, but also in some kind of embrace. *The beautiful now,* she'd written somewhere, somewhen, the kind of thought that could make you tear your skin off with its possibility and its tragedy, because there was only so much you could experience in your firefly life, a blinking trail across a dark meadow, a few moonrises and we are gone. And if we are open to the melody of the universe, then when one person blows up, when one person slips and falls, when one person is threaded by bullets, we are all blown up, dropped, gutted. A thought so tragic, and yet it also meant that everyone was connected. There were no walls, no borders, everything was intertwined, all the little dots making a single great picture from clouds to cells and oh God, oh God that she didn't necessarily believe in unless this was what God was all along, not a thing but a feeling, a sensation, of all the possibility,

why, why did she not wake every day with wide eyes and a smile
and run like a fucking cheetah across the brilliant world hugging
all of it? What other purpose could there possibly be?

They were alive, invincible, and yet already dead. They were
everything and nothing.

Maya picked up her pen and wrote:

Church of Now
The bomb is not today.
The bomb is not tomorrow.
The bomb never was.
The bomb will always be.
Behind us.
We are.
Getting better.

She looked at the words and the first thing that popped into
her head was that she should post it. A picture of the singers, and
these words. Her triumphant return to the feeds.

She left her phone in her pocket.

Instead, she put down the pen and leaned to Eli's ear:

"Do you feel it?" she whispered.

Eli's eyes were closed. "Yes."

It occurred to her that she didn't know what *it* was for him.
No matter how connected she felt, there were limits, skulls and
skin, his chemicals and hers. Different pasts.

Nobody's sure exactly how he's thinking.

But whatever was going on inside him, it was a *yes.* That had
to be a good thing, right?

She found his hand on the pew, wrapped her fingers around

his. Closed her eyes. Her arm a string, the rest of her a balloon, rising.

Sometime later, the song ended. The choir's final notes echoed up into the shadows and alcoves. Dissolving into a perfect silence.

Maya opened her eyes, returning to herself. "Like a flock of birds," she said to Eli.

He smiled.

The whole point, she thought, was to set them free.

*   *   *

Afterward, they went for gelato, ate it while walking up and down Broadway. Capitol Hill was electric on a Friday night, so many people and voices, music and lights. Maya felt light, so different from a night out with Janice, with Todd. There was no extra layer of doubt. Just herself. Was that Eli? Or just her? Or both?

"What did you think of that music?" she asked. "Pretty amazing, right?"

"It didn't have a beat either."

Maya frowned at him.

His half smile. "I'm kidding."

"Jerk." She play-punched his shoulder.

"For a while I didn't think about really anything," he said. "It felt safe. And really big. I liked that list you made."

"Thanks."

They talked about teachers and classes and kids, about the Seahawks and the Sounders, and every now and then Maya glanced at Eli and considered again that he might be kind of cute, that she wanted to walk with her arm a few inches closer to his—

Be careful.

But wasn't she? Hadn't she been so goddamn careful? Couldn't she have a normal thought for once? Here, now, in this moment? They were having a great time, and Maya liked being with him!

Should I tell him that?

But they were nearing the cathedral and there was her mom's car, waiting on the street.

Mom asked a lot of questions on the ride home, about the choir, about Eli's mom and sister, each one seeming to further break the spell of the evening. By the time they'd reached Eli's, Maya was on edge, could barely contain herself.

"I'll be just a sec," she said as they pulled up to the curb.

"Okay," Mom replied. Once Eli had stepped away from the car, she added: "Good job, honey."

Maya paused, holding the door. "What's that supposed to mean?"

Mom glanced at Eli walking up the path to his front porch. "It's just good, how you're spending this time with him."

"Mom, he's not a charity case. He's my friend."

"No, I know, I just mean—"

"You know what? I don't want to know. I'm not doing this so you can be proud of me." She shut the door and hurried after Eli. Unbelievable! Apparently that earlier moment of coolness was an aberration. Leave it to Mom to totally miss the point.

"Hey." She caught Eli by the arm just before he started up the steps. "I have an idea for our anniversary."

He turned to her. "What?"

"Our anniversary. The twenty-sixth. It's next Friday."

His gaze fell. "I know."

"Well, I was thinking we could make it a good thing. Do you like mini golf?"

"Oh. Um, I guess."

"Go-karts?"

"I've never done them."

"Okay, it's settled. We'll ask our parents if we can go down to the Family Fun Center for the day."

"Isn't it on a Friday?"

"Yeah, but who cares? We need something to take our minds off the whole thing. If we tell them we're freaking out, and the idea of being in school is unbearable, they'll definitely let us go. I know my *mom* will."

"What do you mean?"

"Nothing, she just thinks I'm hanging out with you to, like, help you. Which I'm not."

"Oh."

"I mean, of course I want to help you. That's just not the only reason I hang out with you."

"Okay."

"Wow, I am flailing here. Listen, no pressure about the Fun Center. Think it over. Though did I mention they have this skydiving ride where you're like free-falling and big fans keep you floating? Sounds cool, right?"

"What if someone recognizes us?"

"Well, all the other kids will be in school. And also lately I'm starting to feel like maybe who cares? Like, bring it on."

Eli nodded. "It sounds fun. I'll have to ask."

He didn't sound like it sounded fun. *Slow down!* Didn't want to push him. Put too much pressure on him. She knew what that felt like.

Maya took a step back down the path. "Just let me know. Thanks again for coming to my show. And to the cathedral."

Eli's lips moved for a moment, like he was talking to himself. Finally, he looked up, his eyes meeting hers fully. "I had a good time."

Maya glanced at her mom's car. They were standing in the shade of an umbrella-shaped Japanese maple. Red leaves on the sidewalk beneath their feet. Shadows deep enough that their specific movements likely couldn't be seen. *You should go.* But she didn't. Felt her heart speeding up. Stepped closer.

"Can I tell you something?" she said.

"What."

"Tonight is the safest I've felt in like a year. Isn't that strange?"

Eli shook his head. "No."

"Can I give you a hug? I swear it won't get weird."

"Okay."

Maya wrapped her arms around him. Her chin brushed against the top of his ear and when she pressed against him and closed her eyes she did not explode. For a second, Eli didn't react, but then he hugged her with one arm, the other still in his hoodie.

"You make me better," she said quietly.

"You too."

She felt him breathing fast. Maybe even felt something hard in his pants, but it might have just been his other hand, and she knew those things had a mind of their own sometimes. Also maybe she didn't mind if he did feel like that.

Okay, psycho! Don't come on too strong.

Maya pulled away, left a hand on his arm. "I should go."

"Thanks for showing me the singing." Eli met her eyes for a second, then looked at the ground and shuffled his feet. "Thanks for being my b—my friend."

"Ooh!" said Maya. "Were you going to say *best* friend?"

"Maybe. I don't know."

"That's okay, I get it," said Maya. "You have Graham. Don't want him to feel like I'm muscling in."

"It's complicated."

"Dude, what could be more complicated than us?" And yet the mention of Graham . . . "Hey, is he the 'weird' that you were going to tell me about?"

Eli shrugged. "I don't really know. He'd be mad if he knew I was talking about him behind his back."

"That's fair. Maybe text me about it tomorrow or something, if you want?"

"I should go in. See you Monday." Eli turned toward the porch.

"Ask your mom and Pearson about the anniversary."

"Okay."

Maya watched him go, bouncing a little on her feet. "Good night, Eli!"

He'd just started up the steps when he paused. Maya felt a twinge of nerves. Was he going to turn around? If he came back down here, was she going to kiss him? Was that what he was thinking too?

But Eli didn't turn. His head cocked to the side.

"What's up?" Maya asked.

He moved slowly up the steps onto the porch and stopped again. Bent over. Picked up something from the doormat.

Just stood there, shoulders slumped.

"Hey, what is it?"

Eli turned around and held out the wolf's mask.

CHAPTER 23

ELI

October 19

You knew I never left.

Detective Pearson and her officers stayed late. Checked the mask and the porch for fingerprints. Checked the yard for any other evidence. Set up what they called an invisible perimeter around the house, the neighborhood. His whole life: walls closing back in.

"We can't jump to conclusions," Pearson said as they sat at the dining table. Maya and her mom were there, Melissa and his mom. "If this really is Stephen, it's very bold behavior for the subject of an FBI manhunt. Even desperate."

Eli kept his eyes on the table. The blinds were drawn and yet he still expected to see Gabriel in a window.

He'd hidden the gun under his mattress before the police arrived. Had it with him all night, at the concert, at the cathedral, and every time he slipped his hands into his hoodie and felt the impression of it there, a certainty: they were safe. He could protect himself. Maya too. Would never have to picture her screaming upstairs— *There was no one in that room!*

By the end of the night, he'd started to feel like maybe the gun itself was keeping danger away—

And then the mask.

He should have shown Maya the gun. She looked so freaked out now, across the table. Then she would have known he could keep them safe. But he'd frozen up, stupid and useless, and then Maya had called to her mom and knocked on Eli's front door.

"He was right there," his mom said, staring at the door. The footage from their front porch camera only showed a shadow getting close to the steps and tossing the mask up.

"The mask has a few partial fingerprints," said Pearson, "but we haven't turned up any matches in our database so far. We'll be doubling your detail round the clock, briefing the school, and adding a second plainclothes officer. Publicly, we're saying the police activity here tonight was because of a prowler. That should keep the media off the scent."

She looked at Maya and her mom. "We'll be posting officers at your house and wherever you'll be as well."

Maya's mom just nodded, her mouth pursed.

"Do you think it's because of the anniversary?" Eli's mom asked. She held Melissa's hand. A mile of table between them and Eli.

Afraid. You've put them in danger again.

"Maybe," said Pearson.

"Could it be someone else?" Melissa asked. "Someone who knows Eli's identity?"

"I don't think we can rule anything out," said Pearson. "Obviously Stephen might have done this, but it's also possible that someone has figured out who you are and did this as a prank or as an act of harassment. The anniversary certainly could be motivating them. But there's been no other sign of people knowing Eli's identity that we're aware of, right?"

Melissa and his mom shook their heads. Eli too. *Right.*

"What about Graham?" Maya asked.

"What about him?" said Pearson.

She glanced at Eli but then quickly away. "I don't know. I don't think he likes that Eli and I hang out. Or maybe just doesn't like me. I've caught him spying on me a couple times."

Eli burned. *Come on, Maya!*

"Spying?" Maya's mom asked.

Maya shook her head. "It's no big deal," she said quickly. "I don't know."

Pearson turned to Eli. "Do you think we should ask Graham about this?"

No! Graham would be so pissed if he knew about this conversation. They'd barely spoken outside of school all week, and during their Tech Squad times Graham had been tight-lipped, easily annoyed by almost anything Eli did. Also, Eli was pretty sure he'd been in the rafters tonight, except why would he skip his favorite band to watch the jazz concert? *Because he's hurt. Because I'm his best friend, maybe his only friend, and I picked Maya over him.*

But still. He wouldn't do something like this.

And if Pearson questioned Graham, it might somehow lead to them finding out about the Alpha videos, and Graham would get in huge trouble. *Maybe he should get in trouble for those?* But what if Graham got arrested? Or even expelled? And it would be all Eli's fault, and Graham would never forgive him.

I'll talk to him myself.

"Eli?" his mom said.

Eli shook his head. "This wasn't Graham. It's Gabriel."

"His name is Stephen," said Pearson. "Gabriel was a story he told you."

"Whatever. He's back because it's the anniversary and I let him down."

"Elián," said his mom, sniffling. "That's not what you did."

"That's how he thinks," said Eli.

"Do you have any other leads?" Maya's mom asked.

"Not a whole lot," said Pearson. "The wolf's mask sold big online right after the incident. The manufacturer pulled it from as many retailers as they could, but you can still find them on places like eBay. We're requesting sales records to see if there's someone in the area who purchased one. And we're continuing to look for any leads on Stephen's whereabouts."

"What are we going to do in the meantime?" said Eli's mom. "Should we go somewhere, or—"

"I think the best thing would be to go about your normal lives. The FBI is increasing its team and we'll be moving major resources to this investigation and your protection."

"But the anniversary—"

"There is no way Gabriel is going to be able to get near you on the anniversary," said Pearson. "You have my word. We're doing everything we can."

It won't be enough. I've outsmarted them before. If it hadn't been for that girl, everything would have gone according to plan.

Eli pushed his leg against Maya's under the table. *I got you.* He flexed his fingers, wishing he had the gun right now.

He looked at the mask on the table. It stared back at him with its hollow eyes. The style was slightly different from the one he'd worn—a thicker elastic band, black instead of red—but he still felt it, wet from his breath, pressed against his face. The weight of the bottles, the pinch of the trigger making a red imprint on his thumb . . .

Eli drummed lightly on his legs, gritted his teeth.

It was all coming back.

It had never left.

It did, he told himself. *I was getting better. But only because I was stupid.*

"If you're ready to go, we have a detail to follow you home," Pearson said to Maya and her mom.

"Can Eli and I keep being in touch?" Maya asked.

"It's all right with us," said Pearson. The moms agreed, but for a moment as they were turning to leave, Eli caught a look from Maya's mom: maybe fear, maybe hate, maybe both.

You are a weapon.

*　　*　　*

The police left just before midnight.

Eli huddled on the floor against the side of his bed. The hours ticking by. The gun in his hand.

There would be no trips to play miniature golf, to ride go-karts and skydive. No more sleeping over at friends' houses or someday getting to go to a Seahawks game. There would only be this: more darkness and locked spaces. Swallowing him up.

Not fair, not fair, not fair.

He lay on his side, staring at the wall as time and space collapsed around him. The solid ground of these last few weeks gone. His life was a bottomless pit; he'd tried to escape but it was sucking him back in.

Walking home, eleven years old, looking at his cards when he should have been looking out. His life ended then. He'd been stupid to think he would ever be free again.

You should have blown up. Now everyone you know is in danger.

He held the gun up in the light from the window.

Only one way to keep them safe.

If you take away the bomb, no one can get hurt.

At the very least, all the noise will stop.

Maya would never forgive him. But at least she'd be safe. . . .

Something thudded from downstairs.

Now a crash.

Eli sat up. A window? The door?

I'm here.

He stood, shaking, flexing his fingers around the cold metal.

A voice from downstairs. "Mom?" It was Melissa.

Eli opened the door. "Are you okay?"

Melissa looked up the stairs at him. "Yeah. It was from the basement. I think Mom's down there. I'm going to look."

"Hold on. . . ." Eli shoved the gun back under the mattress and hurried down the stairs as Melissa opened the basement door.

"Mom?" No answer. Only a faint light. Melissa started down.

Eli followed her, past pantry shelves stocked with food and household supplies on either side, the rickety wooden stairs creaking with their footsteps. The stairs turned at the bottom and they had to duck under a large floor beam. The basement was long and low, unfinished concrete walls, cluttered with stacks of boxes and metal shelving packed with more boxes and bags. Washer and dryer and water heater at the far end. There was an old dining table along the near wall for projects or ironing. A lamp on it with a dim bulb. Shards of a wineglass there. A puddle like blood.

Mom was kneeling on the old frayed rug beside the table, head in her hands. Sobbing.

"Mom . . ." Melissa stepped carefully toward her. Paused to point out a curved shard of glass on the carpet.

There was a notebook in front of her, lying open, one of those graph paper composition books like Eli had been given in science lab. Pages were torn out and crumpled around her.

Melissa knelt and put her arms around Mom's shoulders.

Eli just watched from a few feet away. Melissa looked up and motioned him over. He stepped closer, heart pounding, and knelt in front of them.

"I'm so stupid," Mom said into her arms.

Melissa flipped through the notebook with her free hand. Eli saw page after page of clippings and printouts: articles, photos, excerpts from online forums, each one surrounded by small, careful writing with arrows pointing to this or that underlined phrase or circled detail. Some pages were x-ed out, while giant stars and exclamation points marked others. Hours of work. Years.

One page with a single photo: Eli's class picture, grade five. A smile he never remembered having. That boy had no idea what was coming.

Eli looked around the basement, another dark lonely space, where Mom had been doing this secret work.

"It's okay," Melissa was saying. "We're here. Eli's here."

Mom lifted her head, her eyes bloodshot and full of tears, her eyeliner streaked, cheeks puffy. She grabbed the notebook and hurled it across the room. It slapped against boxes. "It's all such a waste!" She sobbed more. "There was never anything I could do, and there's still nothing! He comes right to our door. . . ."

Eli sat there, frozen. His mother was broken and it was his fault. Another life he'd ruined.

"But he didn't come inside," said Melissa. "We're safe, if we stick together. We need you, Mama." She tugged Eli's arm. He nearly fell over, then shuffled closer. She wrapped them both into a hug, Eli's face in his mom's hair.

I'm sorry, Eli thought, holding them tight.

Melissa crying too now. All of them breathing, together.

＊　＊　＊

He finally fell asleep, and woke up near noon. Melissa made pancakes and they watched *Planet Rangers*. It was the new version of a show from when they were little. The remake wasn't quite as good, but okay. They did the whole thirteen-episode season, until October twilight shrouded the windows again.

Mom threw herself into working in their little garden out back. Clearing weeds and raking leaves.

Eli messaged with Maya a couple times. She was okay but said it was weird at home. Her parents had been fighting, but she thought it was because they were both worried.

His one message to Graham went unanswered. How was Sideshow Fantasy last night?

An hour later, he added:

I'm still sorry I couldn't go. Also things have gotten dangerous with Gabriel. I'm kinda freaking out.

Graham didn't reply.

*   *   *

Until Sunday:

The concert was amazing. But don't worry. You don't need to pretend like you care.

I do care, Eli replied. I said I was sorry.

She doesn't even like boys. You know that, right? Also you tried to kill her. She probably likes you because of some messed-up Stockholm syndrome. Maybe you can put that to use.

Eli sat still on his bed, the phone lying on the bedspread as more texts rolled in. Another night lying awake until nearly dawn. At least this afternoon there would be a football game to watch.

Don't even bother coming to Tech Squad this week. I can handle everything. You can spend all your time trying to get into Maya's pants.

If she's not too busy pulling the rest of her hair out.

Just FYI, I've heard she's kind of a slut. She was fucking two guys last year. They probably did her from both ends.

Again just FYI.

More, two minutes later, Eli's pulse quickening each time the phone vibrated.

Because I have BIG THINGS to do this week and I don't need your help.

IMPORTANT plans to make. No more time to waste on bullshit friendships.

There's only one righteous path for the worthy and we must walk it ALONE.

It's true, I guess: a lone wolf really is better after all. No one to let you down.

What plans? Eli replied.

Oh, and one last thing: I'd appreciate it if you wouldn't betray me any

333

further. I shared my most personal and important ideas with you, back when I thought I could trust you. Everyone's talking about my work, and the least you could do is not take that away from me by snitching.

We are friends, Eli replied. You can trust me.

REMEMBER I have this:

A moment later, a video file appeared. Eli clicked it and his heart pounded. Saw himself, holding the gun, shooting at the target in the woods.

Please delete that, Eli wrote.

No response.

Please don't do anything dangerous.

Still nothing.

*　*　*

Sunday night barely sleeping. Monday a held breath.

Saw the police car out in the parking lot, its lights off. Kids eyeing it on their way in. Eli found himself peering at the trees along the edge of the lot, at the gaps between nearby houses. Gabriel could be lurking anywhere, watching.

Saw Officer Dawes talking to another woman by the entryway. They paused as he walked by. He gave them a slight smile. Walked straight. *Keep it together.* There was no way they'd be able to tell that he had a gun in his backpack.

Saw Graham, a couple times in the hall. He acted like Eli was invisible.

Saw Maya twice. The first time she was at her locker, staring into space with her hand rooting around in her hat. The second time standing by the stairwell doors in the science hall, scanning the passersby. When she saw him, she raised her eyebrows ever so slightly and tilted her head toward the stairs. *Let's talk.*

But stairwells were isolated and exit doors led to car trunks and Eli lowered his eyes and gripped his backpack straps and passed her by.

*　*　*

Graham wasn't at lunch. Wasn't in study hall last period, and there was no pass waiting for Eli from Mr. McNaulty. He asked Ms. Walsh, who ran the study hall, if he could go to Mr. Caletti's office. Ms. Walsh wrote him a pass and handed it to him like he might explode.

He sat in Mr. Caletti's office and wrote to Maya:

> How are you doing? Did you see the extra police this morning? I'm sorry I didn't talk to you in the hall. I don't want to put you in danger. You're a special person and you don't deserve it. It's probably best if I stay away from you until after Friday. After that hopefully things will be better. I miss you but I want you to be safe. -Eli

After Friday . . . Eli closed his eyes, but he couldn't picture it. Like his life didn't go that far.

*　*　*

Pearson had nothing to report on the drive to Dr. Maria's after school. Everyone still working hard, but no new leads yet. When she asked about Eli's day, he felt like he couldn't even remember it, like it hadn't happened.

"Did Stephen ever say anything to you about why October twenty-sixth was significant?" she asked.

335

"He only ever said it was the best day for the crowds and stuff."

And a good day to die, don't forget that.

"But nothing about anything symbolic, or meaningful in his past?"

"He never talked about any of that. Why?"

Pearson shrugged. "It's the anniversary of the Moscow Theater hostage crisis in 2002. Often people planning mass attacks will align them with prior events, as part of their statement, but we have no idea what connection Stephen might have to that event. He was in one prolonged combat mission in Kandahar Province over that date in 2006, and his unit took significant casualties, so one guess is that it relates to that, but otherwise we can't find anything. Maybe it's something personal, from his childhood."

Like I'd be that obvious.

Eli could only shrug. He stared out the window and thought about Graham. He had used the twenty-sixth, just like Pearson was describing. Maybe he should mention it, but the thought made his stomach burn. *Snitch.* Besides, it was Eli's fault that Graham even had those ideas about the Purpose, and the Barons, and the anniversary. Just another life he'd messed up. Telling Pearson would only mess it up further.

In their session, Dr. Maria coached him through breathing exercises to help him stay present. To remind him that he was safe. She asked him about his family: *Fine.* About his friends: *Fine.* None of them were fine, but everything felt like noise in his head and it was all his fault.

"I'd love for you to share some of it with me," Dr. Maria said. But the words weren't there.

He spent the evening playing Xbox with Melissa, but his eyes kept straying to the windows, to the dark doorway to the kitchen.

Mom sat beside them, reading something on her tablet. Drinking wine. But she wasn't on her computer. Not in the basement. Now and then she stood and peered through the blinds, at the car parked out front. She'd nod to Eli on her way back to the couch.

Eli tried to smile back but couldn't quite do it.

There were messages on his phone from Maya since just after school:

Thought of you on the bus today because two different people were dozed off and snoring in stereo and it was the funniest sound but nobody noticed because they were all wearing headphones. It would have been a good start to a list!

And later: Hello?

Good night, Eli wrote. He put his phone on Do Not Disturb and lay down on the floor, the gun close by. He thought about getting it out, but instead tried the breathing exercise Dr. Maria had given him. Picturing a calm place and counting. The cathedral, Maya holding his hand.

Three . . . two . . . one . . .

* * *

Graham wasn't at lunch again Tuesday. Eli looked for him in the halls, even stopped by the auditorium. He didn't seem to be in school at all.

Eli heard kids talking before class about the Alpha videos. Apparently, there was a new one, and some people were freaked out. Others had heard that the videos were actually a theater project. Someone else said there was now a mash-up where the videos were remixed to some weird dance song.

Are you sick? he texted Graham.

No reply.

After lunch he found a note from Maya:

Eli—I know you're avoiding me because you think that is protecting me but I don't want to be protected! I want to be with you during this. My week's been hard. Everything is starting to feel like it did before, and it doesn't feel safe when we're not communicating. Let me know how you're doing!

Eli flipped over the paper. He tapped his pen against it. Wanted to write everything down, tell her about how he couldn't see past Friday, his dark thoughts with the gun, how he was starting to worry about Graham, how everything felt like his fault, and yet it all felt like noise. Finally, he wrote:

Just a couple more days.

*   *   *

"We've had some developments," said Pearson when she picked him up that afternoon.

Eli swallowed his afternoon pill, held his headphones in his lap.

"We've been talking to Stephen's mother. She has late-stage dementia. Some days she insists that she's seen Stephen that very day, other times that she hasn't seen him for years. We can't get a straight answer. But we did find an alias in the visitor logs, Arnold Wallace. Turned out to be a fake driver's license, but the nursing home had scanned it and the photo is a match to Stephen."

Eli went cold. "Has he been there recently?"

Pearson exhaled slowly. "Turns out he's been visiting like clockwork every two weeks. His last visit was two weeks ago tomorrow, just before we found his house."

Eli held his breath. A wave of adrenaline rising.

"We also got the lab work back from the basement hideout. Stephen was very neat, but we did find some food particles. Analysis confirms that they'd been decaying for less than a week."

"He was still there."

The whole time.

Pearson shook her head. "We don't know whether it was our discovery of the house that flushed him out, or whether he just so happened to be away when we arrived. Either way, it looks like we just missed him."

If I'd remembered a week earlier.

"We're staking out the nursing home in the hope that he makes an appearance. Though I don't think the odds are very good."

Eli could barely hold the thought in his head. This whole year, every day, Gabriel had really still been right here. "What was he doing?"

"You mean while hiding out?" said Pearson. "At the moment, we have no idea."

Eli pressed his feet against the sides of his backpack, the gun in there. "So now what?"

"We increase our protections around you all. And we keep looking. You let us worry about it."

Yeah, right.

Alone with the thoughts, late into the night: *He's still here. He'll come.* The gun beckoning as Eli lay shivering on the floor. After the last sounds from downstairs, he crept to the kitchen, found his mom's wine bottle, and filled a plastic cup. He buttered a piece of bread, and took both to his room. The wine blurred the hours, kept his darker thoughts away, but it also muddled when he was awake and asleep. Confusing bedrooms, confusing shadows.

He was on the cold wooden floorboards again, with the thin blanket, the lumpy pillow. Heard the footsteps coming. The door creaking. He shot Gabriel in the crotch, found Maya in the bed upstairs, showed Graham where to hide in the walls of the red dark room. In the dream there were gaps in the boards, spaces you could slip into, to watch through the cracks when Gabriel came in and kicked at the blanket. There had been no real cracks. No one in that bed upstairs. No gun to stop Gabriel.

Sometime around four, the wine having worn off, he was lying on his back watching a light rain fall against the window when it occurred to him:

They'd all been wrong the whole time.

For a year everyone had been telling him that Gabriel was most likely gone, that he'd fled, and they were wrong. How could he trust anything they said?

Why would I stay here, if it wasn't to finish the Purpose?

He texted Maya, even though he knew she'd be asleep:

You have to stay away from me.

Added: I'm so scared. But deleted it.

He was on his way to lunch Wednesday, dizzy and cotton-mouthed and nerve-dead exhausted, when people started brushing by him. Eli hunched, trying to keep his backpack from being jostled.

A whisper, passing through the crowd: *fight, fight, fight . . .*

Eli let the tide flow around him as he headed for the lunch line entrance. Out of the corner of his eye—commotion over by his usual table. People swarming. He caught a glimpse of Mateo at the center, his long black locks whipping, his face red, his arm punching downward.

"Yeah!"

"Get him!"

"I know it was you!" he heard Mateo shout.

Eli slid along the windows and found a gap. There was Graham, hunched over the table, arms curled around his head to block Mateo's blows.

"Hey!" A teacher was shouting, wading in. "Break it up!"

"Stay away from my house!" said Mateo, slapping his hair out of his eyes. "You got that?" He pushed away through the crowd in the opposite direction from the teacher.

He'd taken a few steps before Graham was up, lunging, slashing at the back of his head.

"Ah!" Mateo stumbled forward.

The weapon splintered on impact, a white plastic spork, pieces sailing in all directions, Graham—face beet red, blood around his nose, his eyes like sparkling dynamite wicks—still wielding the broken white handle.

Mateo grabbed at his neck, his fingers bloody. He spun around. "You're a lunatic!"

"Stop it!" the teacher yelled, pushing closer.

341

"I'll kill you!" said Graham, breathing through his nose in furious bellows. He lunged—

The teacher wrapped her arms around him. "That's enough—"

Graham thrust his elbow backward. Smashed her chin. She staggered and clutched at her mouth. Graham lurched free but bounced off the side of a table and slammed into a girl who shouted and shoved him. Other kids scattered. Graham whirled, like a concussed fighter.

Eyes found Eli.

Please stop, Eli thought.

Graham paused—Lucas slammed into him, his forearms clubbing Graham in the cheek and whipping his head back. They both went down, Graham's head whacking against the built-in seats on the side of the table.

"Who the fuck throws dog shit on someone's house?" said Mateo, running over and kicking Graham in the ribs. Another one of their buddies grabbed Mateo and pulled him away.

The teacher was back up, blood around her mouth. "That's ENOUGH!"

Eli saw Janice watching, eyes wide. Didn't see Maya anywhere.

Graham pushed up from the floor, wobbling on his feet. "Don't look at me!" he spat at the crowd.

A nearby girl snickered with her friends. Other kids started cracking up too.

"Shut up!" Graham shouted.

The school security officer pushed in. Eli saw Officer Dawes and his new colleague watching from the entrance.

"Get them to the office," the teacher said, dabbing at her mouth with a fistful of napkins.

The security guard yanked Graham up, twisted his arm behind his back, pushed him out.

Graham grinned, making eye contact with as many people as he could. "You're all smiling now!" Blood-laced spit flew with his words. "Just you wait!"

"I'll go, it's cool," said Mateo as the teacher motioned to him.

Eli faded toward the wall as the crowd dispersed. He looked at the lunch line, at his table, at the rest of the busy cafeteria. Got a pass to the library instead.

Did you see that? Maya messaged. Is everything all right with him?

We haven't talked, he wrote to her.

He texted Graham:

Are you okay? Want to meet up after school?

No reply.

He heard kids talking in math class about the swimmer kid and the Tech Squad nerd, how they'd both been suspended for fighting. That one was going to press charges against the other for assault and vandalism.

Halfway through class, his phone buzzed. Finally, a reply from Graham.

I'm better than ever. Things are perfectly clear to me now.

What do you mean? Eli asked. Graham didn't respond.

Graham?

* * *

His house was nearly silent that night. Melissa had skipped her evening lecture, all of them sitting on the couch watching the baseball playoffs even though none of them cared about baseball. Mom on her tablet, Melissa and Eli sharing a bowl of popcorn.

343

During a commercial break, the local news station previewed their top story:

"Cedar Gate, one year later. Interviews with eyewitnesses, the killer still at large. Tonight at eleven."

Mom turned off the TV.

"Xbox?" said Melissa.

Eli got out the controllers. At one point while he was waiting to respawn, he found a message from Maya on his phone:

Two days to go. We're going to make it. :)

He almost smiled. Almost believed her.

Later, an alert sounded on Mom's phone, and Eli noticed that her eyes stayed on the text for a long time.

What is it? Eli breathed deep. "What is it?"

She wiped her eyes. "Pearson says they traced that fake ID and found a storage unit up in Lynnwood. It had a cache of guns. Rifles, handguns, some kind of assault weapon. None of them have permits, no identification. They also found a hard drive full of photos of street corners and crosswalks. All near schools. Most from the past year. But also from before: there is a set of locations from the time when"—her voice quavered—"when he took you."

A set of locations. Not just one.

"So he was scouting places?" said Melissa. "Maybe he wants to grab another victim. Like on the anniversary."

"Maybe," said Mom. "They're posting officers at all the locations. But why would he have all those guns? Unless he was planning something else?"

To protect himself, Eli thought to say. In case they came for him.

We're so alike.

We're nothing alike. Eli realized Mom and Melissa were looking at him.

"Did you hear me?" said Mom. Eli shook his head. "Did he . . . ?" She looked away as she spoke. "Did he ever say anything about a shooting attack?"

"No." *I was his weapon.* But not anymore. He hadn't been special. Could have been another kid at another spot.

You were my son.

I was just an instrument. A tool.

"Maybe it's good news," said Melissa. "At least they know where he might be now."

"I knew it," said Mom. She smiled through tears. "He was still looking for his next victim. I knew it."

Eli watched her nodding to herself. "What were you going to do?" he asked.

"Hmm?"

"If you'd found him yourself."

Mom sipped her wine. "I thought I'd try to get him to show up somewhere . . . and . . . I have a crowbar in the back of the car. I thought about buying a gun, but then your uncle Julio told me he would come along. He has a rifle with a good scope."

"Jesus, Mom . . . ," said Melissa. "What if Gabriel had a gun too? You never thought of that, did you?"

Mom sniffled. "I had to do something. For what he did to Eli, what he took from us. The thought that he might do that to someone else . . ."

Eli stood. "I'm going to bed."

Mom touched his arm as he walked by. "They're going to catch him with this. Hopefully we can all sleep a little better."

But he lay awake again, the clock blinking past one, two—

when he heard Mom go to her room, he crept down to get more wine—past three. In the dark, the ceiling a blur.

I hope you're hanging in there tonight, Maya wrote.

You're still special, Gabriel said, breath hot in his ear. *You know what the mask meant. I wanted those photos to be found. Let them spread out far and wide, looking for me. You know where I'll really be.*

Eli pictured Gabriel's silhouette, in the red dark, in the auditorium entrance, in the school halls, this time holding a rifle. Maybe he wasn't coming back to get Eli, maybe he was coming back to finish the job Eli couldn't, only this time it would be bullets, not a bomb, his classmates, people he knew, someone he cared about. . . .

Eli gripped the gun, aimed it at the trapezoids of streetlight on the wall. *Come on,* he thought. *I'll be ready.*

*   *   *

Early Thursday he saw Dr. Maria. Tried to answer her questions—how it felt, what he worried about—but there was so little he could say, and her suggestions just slipped by, his brain like a glass ball full of fog. "I know this is difficult," said Dr. Maria, "but try to stay connected to other people. They keep us grounded. They keep our fantasies in line."

"But I'm a danger to them."

"That's not true. *You've* never been the danger, Eli."

You don't know.

He tried texting Graham again, on the way to school. I want to be your friend again.

No response until he was sitting at lunch:

Don't come to school tomorrow.

Eli wrote back: Why not?

Graham didn't reply.

Because I'm coming.

Shut up. Graham. Not Gabriel. A warning. But why?

Because he's serious, Eli thought. What if he really, really was serious about everything he said as the Alpha?

Graham wouldn't— But was that really true? Or just what he wanted to be true?

Eli slid his phone beneath the table. Got out his headphones. He searched and found the Alpha_Ascendant videos. The newest one from yesterday, titled: Your Time Has Come. Eli checked to make sure no one was watching him. All week he'd been alone at this table, worried that it would make him a target, but it seemed like everyone's radar had turned off. They were all wrapped up in the relationships and dramas that had begun in the last month.

Eli hit play. The video was like the prior ones. There was the blurry silhouette Graham created with the mirror and the lights, the distorted voice through the toy microphone:

"Greetings, jocks and sluts, the meek and mundane. It's your judge, jury, and executioner again. I know you want it more than ever: not just my cock, but the great relief of death. Life is loneliness, isn't it? Every smile a lie. Deceit is the law, disappointment the norm, betrayal the currency. We only ever have ourselves. No one else can be trusted. You see, the Alpha knows. The Alpha has always known. I feel all your pain. I hear you crying out in your silence, in your low-cut shirts, in your laughter. You are all begging me, Please, Alpha, make it stop. I hear you even though you turn away. A thousand less views on my last post? That just tells

me that your grief is getting deeper. And so the time has come: this will be my final word. It's all been said. All that's left now is to DO. I will decree a peaceful everlasting silence upon your miserable lives. Congratulations, graduates! You'll all be getting your acceptance letters to STFU University.

"Like I said before, the date of salvation has been chosen. This is it. The final preparations are being made. You'll see the Purpose behind it in the end. I've watched you from above for so long, lorded over you without you even knowing it. My judgment will rain down upon you, very soon now. Very soon . . .

A pause. The camera jiggling for a second.

"Don't be sad, Elliott friends. I'm just easing your burden. You see, I used to have a friend. Someone I thought really understood me. Just when I thought there was no one left. One more try at opening my mouth, one more try at fitting into the lie. But it was just another trick. There is no one. And there never will be. Goodbye."

The video ended.

Eli's heart raced. *Look what you did.* But he could hear Dr. Maria: *It's not you.* Graham had started making videos before they'd even met. Just like Gabriel had started scoping out places to abduct kids before he took Eli.

But it *was* him. He'd hung out with Graham, told him about things like the Purpose, listened to his stories, even watched him make his videos, never speaking up. Thought he'd been acting like a friend . . .

I have to stop him.

Graham wouldn't answer his texts, and Eli had heard he'd been suspended for the fight. But he knew what Graham was planning, didn't he? Graham had told him; Eli had just been too stupid, too distracted, to realize it.

He threw out his food and got a pass to the library.

Headed to the auditorium instead.

The stage was dark. He ducked beneath the control boards, using his phone's light to find the spare tech keys that Graham kept hidden there. Climbed the back stairs, to the catwalks. He crawled through the door, all the way out to Olympus.

As he swung his legs over the edge, Eli noticed an X scribbled with a black marker on the catwalk, just beside one of the support beams that was bolted into a thick steel girder that ran across the ceiling.

Can you imagine that? This whole roof? Like BAM. That would shut them up.

Eli dug into his backpack, past the gun. Pulled out a composition notebook. Stared at the blank page for a moment, then wrote:

> Dear Graham,
>
>   I'm still sorry about missing the show on Friday. I wish you weren't so mad about it. I think it's okay that Maya is my friend, but I want you to know you were my FIRST friend, the first real one I've had. It means a lot to me that you wanted to be my friend even when I'm so messed up. It shows how kind a person you are. But I don't think I've been a good friend back to you. I think that you have been going through some hard feelings, and I should have asked you about them. Also, I don't think I've told you enough that I'm sorry things are hard for you,

and that I care about you and I don't want to see you or anyone else get hurt.

You are:

Really creative

Funny

Super-smart

Awesome at tech stuff

But I don't think you are really the Alpha. People are scared of him, and if you're serious about doing something that would hurt people, I think you should talk to someone. I mean, someone who can really help.

It's not me. I can't help anyone. I think I only made things worse for you with all the Gabriel stuff. I don't know.

But I do know that nobody needs to die. You don't need to die. I think you feel a lot of sadness and loneliness and I know I don't totally understand it but I do know that you are strong and good. And you are not alone.

Text me after you read this. Or come over. Just be in touch. Please.

Your friend,

Eli

He read it to himself and thought Maya would say that it was good. Would it be enough? Graham had to listen. He couldn't be a hundred percent serious.

Eli got out his phone and snapped a picture of the letter. He put it in an email and sent it to Graham, then folded up the paper and left it on the catwalk.

He started to crawl out. Noticed a second *X* up closer to the end of the catwalk, also by a support beam.

Please don't.

Eli reached the trapdoor and climbed out.

"Hey."

Maya was standing at the top of the steps. "We need to talk."

CHAPTER 24

MAYA

October 24

She ran a finger over the smooth black finish of the bass drum, a black scale of dust forming on her fingertip. Wiped it on her jeans, picked up her sticks. Ready to play—

Winced at a stinging pain from her finger. Ate the slice of skin and sucked the welling bead of blood. Checked the clock: five minutes had passed. All week had been like this. One frozen pause after another, one drift to the next.

All week: the officers parked outside her house.

All week: a man out there somewhere and she was maybe a target.

All week: a friend out there feeling more and more lost to her. *You have to stay away from me.* She didn't want to push him. Kept reaching out. The distance growing.

It had gotten to the point where Maya had asked her mom

just to take her to Eli's, but of course she'd said no. Mom had been mental all week. Focusing all of her crazy on Maya's safety. Kept suggesting Maya just play sick Friday, to the point that Maya wanted nothing more than to go to school, even while the idea terrified her. How much worse could Gabriel be than this? Okay, a lot worse. But still . . .

Renee had reminded her on Monday that she had all the skills she needed to make it through this week. Reminded her that compared to two months ago, she'd made tremendous progress. But now it was Wednesday and that was starting to ring hollow. Yesterday, she'd had her biggest flashback episode in a while— the clicking of a Bunsen burner lighter in bio lab; Janice and Marni quietly snickering at her when she came out of it. The blood-dotted hair wrapped around fingertips-turned-white. All the old thoughts returning:

You are never going to get better.

TFW you realize you've been wasting your time.

She looked at her drumsticks. Looked at the drums. Thought about a beat to play . . .

Another sting, another spot of blood, another five minutes lost.

How was Eli? She'd seen him at Graham and Mateo's fight. Graham with the psycho move with the spork. That kid . . . Of course, he was probably suspended after today.

The door opened and Ms. Reid walked in. "Oh, hey, Maya. Didn't you get the message that there's no practice today?"

"Oh, right." Maybe there had been an email about that or something.

Ms. Reid crossed the room. "I'm sure you've been hearing what a great job you did last week."

What? *The concert*. Another life. "Thanks."

"Did you want to stay and jam out a little?"

"Nah, that's all right." Maya stood and slid her sticks into her bag. Slouched down the levels. Headed for the door.

"Maya." Ms. Reid smiled kindly at her. "I know it hurts."

"I don't—"

She held up a hand. "I know about what happened last year, but that's not even it. What I mean is: the world hurts, and you feel it. I see it on your face. The same sensitivity that lets you feel music so well, that lets you express yourself through it—that's the same thing that leaves you open to the hurt and suffering. And sometimes it's overwhelming."

Maya brushed away tears. "Yeah. How did you know that?"

"Takes one to know one. And I can tell you from experience that it will get better, but it also won't. Being open to the world is a gift, but the pain is part of it."

"It doesn't feel like a gift."

"Some gifts come with responsibilities," said Ms. Reid. "Like a puppy. I'm not trying to make light of it. Your creativity comes with the duty to protect yourself, to train yourself, but also to accept yourself. To take the beauty and the pain you experience . . . and make its music. I'm not saying that will always make it go away. But it will always help."

Maya nodded. "It doesn't feel that easy."

"No, I know. And everybody's different. But you've been through a lot, and you're the kind of soul that feels a lot. I think just being aware of that is a good way to start. Make sense?"

"Okay." She turned toward the door—

Ms. Reid tapped her shoulder. Maya turned and they hugged. "I've seen you do it," Ms. Reid said quietly. Maya felt herself welling up as Ms. Reid let go. "Now, where do you think you're going?"

"Just home."

Ms. Reid shook her head and gave her a gentle push toward the drums. "Get back up there. I want to feel my office walls shake."

Maya smiled. "Okay."

She played until the cities were built and smashed and built again. Until her elbows and wrists were sore and she was covered in sweat, and the walls didn't exactly shake, but a trombone case did fall over.

On her bus ride home through sheeting rain, lighter: the feelings not gone, but asleep in their cages.

She texted Eli. Two days to go. We're going to make it. :)

It was okay that he didn't reply. The houses and street corners and the rumble of the bus were beats and she could feel every one. She got out her purple notebook and made a list to leave in his locker.

*   *   *

Her worries stayed at a whisper through the evening. Mom was working late, so Maya made her specialty three-course frozen dinner courtesy of Trader Joe's: mac and cheese, turkey meatballs, and peas. Did her homework while eating, and was settling into the international home-buying show when Mom arrived.

She was barely through the door when she said: "Detective Pearson called." She explained about the cache of guns, the hard drive, the locations Gabriel had been scouting.

Maya felt it seeping in, rattling the cages of the adrenaline-soaked sewer creatures that had been sleeping so soundly. Not just this shadow man, out there, but guns, bullets spraying into crowds, the way they did in so many places, but she'd never pictured her neighborhood.

Don't let it get to you.

Maybe this news made her and Eli safer. Other places he was scouting. Other victims. But that wolf's mask . . .

She tried to focus on the show, but it wasn't enough. Needed to scroll through her feeds too. Even a week later, there were still alerts from Janice's post. Maya glazed her eyes and pushed past them and read other people's updates: soccer games and swim meets, impromptu karaoke outside Cupcake Royale, new outfits, new tattoos, new romances. Some now, some yesterday, some about to happen. That familiar awareness that she was a weirdo for not posting, that not being part of this conversation meant she didn't fully exist.

Maya dug the Serenitab bottle out of her bag and tapped out a pill. She rolled her tongue around, gathering a shot of saliva, then popped the pill in and swallowed.

Came upon an angry post by Janice and froze. Maya had unfollowed her, but sometimes she still showed up through mutual friends.

This sick misogynistic shit needs to STOP.

Janice had linked to a new video by Alpha_Ascendant called "Your Time Has Come."

Maya clicked it. Couldn't resist.

The video was like the prior ones she'd seen pieces of. This weird, washed-out figure with a wannabe video-game-villain voice:

"Greetings, jocks and sluts . . ."

Blah blah something about his cock. But as he went on, Maya found herself paying closer attention.

"Life is loneliness, isn't it? Every smile a lie. Deceit is the law, disappointment the norm, betrayal the currency. We only ever have ourselves."

She rescued her fingers from her hair. This pervert was gross, but as fucked up as he was, she *knew* those feelings he described. Had watched their fearsome shadow theater in her mind, torn herself apart to avoid them. Not all that twisted stuff about judgment days and whatever. But the sadness, the loneliness: she'd been there.

And yet . . . maybe she wasn't there anymore. This week felt harder, more uncertain than ever, but not as bad as last month, or any other time this year. Was she actually getting better? Renee had said that at some point, her brain would heal, her chemicals would balance, she would at least reach a manageable state. It might not be possible to tell exactly when you got there—you couldn't watch your brain heal like a cut on your finger—but one day you'd realize that it had happened.

Maybe, just maybe, she was improving.

But also: was anything more being done to find this Alpha? The school had sent that email. Said they'd notified the police, but they were so busy with Gabriel.

Most kids seemed to treat the videos as a prank, but Maya wasn't sure. The hurt in them felt real. And deep, even deeper than she'd been. Who knew what you would really do, if you were hurting badly enough?

Maybe she was making too much of it. Maybe she was just on edge about Friday . . .

A few minutes slipped. *Hush,* said Serenitab, arriving with the deck chairs and blankets and a steaming mug, the fog thickening beyond the ship railings.

I hope you're hanging in there tonight, she texted Eli.

Mom slumped onto the couch beside her with a microwave burrito in one hand and a plastic shopping bag in the other. "How are you holding up?"

"Fine. How about you?"

"Work was insane. One of those days when you think about moving to Fiji."

"Can it be Bora Bora?" Maya nodded at the home-buying show. "Really cute fish."

"Some days it sounds pretty nice to run away from everything." Mom put the plastic bag on the coffee table. "Will you settle for one pint of Ben and Jerry's each? There was a sale. I got hot fudge too."

Maya smiled. "I'll get spoons."

* * *

She got to school Thursday with a plan: connect with Eli, no matter what. He thought he was keeping her safe by keeping his distance, and she'd decided that was bullshit. She wasn't going through these next two days without him.

The plan began at lunch: sitting a couple tables over from him. She'd follow him out at the end. Find a moment. Make a moment, dammit.

Except ten minutes after lunch began, he packed up and left. Maya got a pass to the library and followed him at a distance. But he didn't go to the library. Instead, he took an odd route through school: downstairs to the math wing and then back up by the gym, avoiding the office, walking quickly with his head down, tugging his backpack straps, high-top sneakers scuffing.

What was he up to? She nearly called out to him, but there was always an open door, a straggler or two.

When he entered the auditorium she peered inside and saw him going up to that door in the back. Remembered what he'd told her, about the catwalks that you got to climb around on for Tech Squad—or use to spy on girls—how he and Graham liked to hang out up there. Although wasn't Graham suspended?

She sat down in a red seat in the first row of the rear section, waiting for Eli to come down. It squealed as it reclined, echoing in the giant, empty space. She leaned back, resting her head on the cool metal rim of the chair. Stretched her legs out. In the silence, she could almost hear her body humming, processors spinning at full speed. She closed her eyes and tried to play through one of her new charts by memory, her thighs the snare and ride.

Then she heard the faintest creaking sound and gazed up at the ceiling. Hundreds of angled white tiles. Eli, up there somewhere.

You can look down on the seats, he'd said. She wondered if he could see her.

But her mind wrote another measure to this song, ideas with similar melodies linking together:

I've watched you from above for so long. . . .

Maya sat up.

My judgment will rain down. . . .

She stood and hurried up the stairs, her heart galloping. Pulled the door open and climbed the steep staircase, hands on the walls to either side. At the top: a short hall and then the trapdoor in the wall. Open. She stopped and stared at the door. Removed the cuticle on her left ring finger—*Ugh, why now?*—and wondered if she should climb in there or not.

Then the metal creaked and Eli's sneakers and legs appeared. He slid out and saw her and froze.

"Hey," he said.

"We need to talk." Maya eyed the trapdoor. "Graham's not here, right?"

Eli shook his head.

"Listen, I have to tell you something. I'm not a hundred per-cent sure about it, but I think—"

Eli's face drained. "Is it Gabriel?"

"No, this is about Graham. I think he might be . . ." She saw Eli's eyes widen. "You already know, don't you? That he's the Alpha."

Eli's head dropped. "Yeah."

"Oh my God. Have you told anyone?"

"Like who?"

"Like the police? Detective Pearson?"

He sort of shrugged. "He'd get in big trouble. And I don't— I don't think he's really a danger—"

"Have you seen his latest video? He's talking about a date of retribution. That it's coming up. About this friend who aban-doned him. That's you, isn't it? Do you think the date he's talk-ing about is tomorrow?"

"Yeah. But I don't—"

"Eli! We *have* to tell someone."

"They're just stupid videos," said Eli. "Graham gets big ideas, but he's also sad about the world. And he doesn't have any other friends."

"I get that, but he's talking about killing people, and I've seen how violent he can get. What has he said to you lately?"

"We haven't talked. He's mad because I chose you over him."

"How exactly did you do that?"

"Because I came to your concert instead of going to a show with him."

"Okay—not sure he should be upset about that, but whatever. Look, do you really think he's not a danger?"

"I . . ." Eli sighed, a lonely, defeated sound. "He talked one time about making the roof collapse. There's a junior class assembly tomorrow morning."

"Eli . . ."

His shoulders slumped. "It's my fault. He got all those ideas from me. I'm too dangerous. I just sent him a letter. . . ."

Maya stepped over and hugged him. "You are not the one who's dangerous. You never have been. Gabriel is dangerous. Graham is dangerous."

"I was dangerous to you. I messed your life up."

"Okay, I mean, sorta, but my life was already messed up. And you're definitely not messing up Graham's life, you're *saving* it." Maya put a hand on his head. "We're going to fix this. Together."

Eli sobbed into her shoulder. "I can't go back."

"Where?"

"The dark."

"You mean Gabriel."

"I know he's coming."

"He's not—" Maya stopped. "You're not going back. I won't let you. We're going to make it."

"Okay," Eli said quietly.

"What else has Graham said?"

"He showed me pipe bomb designs online. He said his dad had the right kinds of pipes."

"Does he know how to build them?"

"I don't know. He asked me if I wanted to help him. With his plan." He touched his head. "He said that it was the only way to make all the noise in here stop. Don't you ever feel like he's right? That the noise will never stop?" He reached around and patted his backpack. "Sometimes I think . . ."

"What?"

"Never mind."

Maya hugged him tighter. "All I know is, it stops when I'm with you." She gripped his shoulders and held him out in front of her. "Come on. We're calling Pearson. Okay?"

"Will they put him in jail?"

"I have no idea. But whatever they do, it will be the safest thing for him. Now let's go."

"You go first."

"Right. Meet by the back doors. Behind the auditorium, okay?" Maya started down the stairs. Looked at him. Smiled. "We got this."

Eli just nodded.

Maya returned to the auditorium. When she reached the doors leading to the hallway, she stopped and watched the top of the steps.

Waiting . . .

Eli emerged, head down, holding his backpack straps. And a minute later he joined her outside the back door.

Stood there silently as Maya made the call.

Going to class was nearly worthless after that. Sitting there, simmering, not absorbing a thing. But Maya also didn't go anywhere else in her head. Not back to the mall. Not beneath her skin. Didn't explode. She floated on the surface. Pinned to now. Counting the minutes until the end of the day when she could text Eli. Check on him. Math, bio . . . finally, she was on the bus.

How you holding up?

Fine. Dawes is driving me home. Do you think Pearson is already at Graham's?

No. She said they needed to get a warrant. Everything's crazy with the hunt for Gabriel, but they should have it first thing in the morning. They're watching him now, though.

Okay.

It was the right thing to do.

I know.

Maya sat on the crowded bus home. Wondered if there were officers on board, watching her too. Around her: people with lives, busy in their heads. People who had no idea what was out there. Graham's house probably looked just like Gabriel's from the outside. You just didn't know.

*   *   *

Her phone buzzed just after nine.

Hey.

How was the rest of your day?

Fine. Bad. I feel guilty.

It's not your fault. We did the right thing.

I should have talked him out of it. I don't know why I didn't.

Hey, I just said it's not your fault. :)

I know. But still.

Look at us. We get to be heroes again.

Eli didn't respond. Maya looked over the texts and realized she'd just referred to herself as a hero. If her mom only knew . . .

A minute later she wrote:

You there?

Yeah.

I'm going to say something weird, so don't think I'm weird.

Okay.

Maya paused. *You have to be careful, you don't know what he's—*

Typed anyway.

I love you, friend.

She added: I told you it was weird, but I don't mean it weird. Maybe love is a weird word to use. But I care about you. I know you feel lonely but I'm never going to leave you alone, you got that?

I care about you too. I want you to be safe.

I am safe. Safer now than I was before, I think.

We're not safe.

No, but we have each other.

Dots appeared as if Eli was responding, then vanished.

Hello?

I have to go. Melissa just got home. Late dinner.

Roger. See you tomorrow! A good ol' normal Friday. Completely unimportant.

Thanks for being such a good friend.

You are very welcome. 'Kay, good night. Love you in the not-weird way. xo (Not weird either!)

Eli replied with a thumbs-up.

CHAPTER 25

ELI

October 26

"Time to wake up," Eli's mom said, cracking open his door.

Eli stared at the ceiling.

Today is the day, my son.

"How'd you sleep?"

Had he slept? It seemed like he'd watched each hour tick by.

One year ago, this very moment: the razor sliding down his torso in smooth strokes so the duct tape would stick best.

Today I will return.

All you have to do is let go.

When was when? A year or a moment ago? Like he'd come so far and nowhere at all.

"I got a message from Pearson," said Mom. "They're on their way to Graham's."

Eli eyed the clock. Six-forty-five. Graham always slept in as late as possible. He might not even be up.

"It was the right thing to do," Mom added. She stared at the floor. "You were strong to resist him. I know it was confusing." She sniffled.

"It's okay, Mom. I should have said something sooner."

She shook her head. "I can't believe none of us saw it. It was more than you should ever have had to deal with."

Because you're broken.

And yet he had dealt with it.

"Want me to make you eggs?"

"Sure." Eli sat up, his heart already beating fast. He checked his phone and found a message from Maya:

Happy insignificant Friday! The sun is out! (There are also two police cars on my street, but hey!) See you soon!

They're going to Graham's, he replied.

I heard. Are you worried about him?

Yes and no. More like feeling guilty. Knew he shouldn't be. But still.

He got dressed slowly.

One year ago: scalp still stinging from the bleach, cool gloved hands on his bare hips, the pull and stretch of the duct tape shrieking off its roll, the cold cylinder bottles pressing against his abdomen, restricting his breathing.

Before he left his room, he slipped the gun from beneath his mattress and tucked it into his backpack.

Downstairs, Mom had put out his pills with his juice. He sloshed them down and looked around online while he was eating. No mention of police raiding a kid's house.

"Pearson said they're watching all the sites from Gabriel's hard drive. And his mother's home. So far, nothing."

Melissa reached over from across the table. Squeezed his hand. "It's going to be okay. If he's smart, he won't try anything. And if he's dumb, they'll catch him."

Eli nodded. He started a text to Graham: I'm really sorry. I hope it's not too bad.

Didn't send it. Graham was probably so angry. . . .

Then he sent it.

"Finish up," said Mom. "We should go."

Eli scarfed down his eggs.

One year ago: his stomach quaking, hadn't eaten in days, shivering nearly constantly. The hood slipped over his head. Taken by the hand and led down the stairs, the bottles sloshing beneath his jacket. Laid in the backseat. The soft interior so different from the trunk. He had become a delicate instrument.

Outside, he noticed the extra police car up his street. A woman walking her dog. No one else around. *He's not coming.*

I am coming. You know it.

"I think this is the right decision," said Mom as they drove. She kept checking the rearview mirror, the officers behind them. "You'll make it through today and it will be normal and that's important."

One year ago: the sounds of cars and traffic so much quieter in the backseat, a sound like on the day he was taken, so many years before. All of it overlapping. Almost free of the nightmare, or was it just starting? Had all those years in the red dark even happened? Had it all been in his head?

Outside, the sun brilliant, the trees blazing with fall color, the air crisp and cool, then and now. Eli, eyes down, trying to focus on a recap of the Thursday football game, trying to stay calm.

*   *   *

"Are you ready?"

No.

Two more police cars parked in front of school. Lights off. Two officers standing beside them, watching the entry area.

Mom and Eli sat in the drop-off loop, cars pulling around them, kids getting out. Doors thunking closed.

He wondered if those police had checked the auditorium for evidence against Graham. Where was he now? In one of those windowless interrogation rooms somewhere?

Mom rubbed the back of his neck. "You're going to be safe."

One year ago: the two fingers rubbing up and down.

Tell me you believe, Jacob.

"Okay." Eli opened the door.

"I love you."

Go swiftly into the arms of the Lord.

Squeezed his eyes shut. *Stay here.*

Eli leaned over and wrapped his arms awkwardly around her. "Bye," he said into her hair.

Mom sniffled. "You'll be okay. We'll be okay."

Eli pulled away. Got out and ran a hand over his backpack, could just feel the impression of the gun in the front pocket. He slung the pack over his shoulders and started up the steps, body tense, cold sweat, head down. Dawes and the other undercover officer stood on either side of the entrance. More vigilant eyes today. Had to be cool.

Paused at the top of the steps. Mom was still watching, of

course. He waved. She blew him a kiss. He'd always assumed she waited to be sure he made it safely inside, that he wouldn't disappear. But maybe she also watched him for as long as she could, in case it was the last time she'd see him.

The first bell rang. Eli nodded to Dawes. Dawes gave him a quick thumbs-up.

On his way to English, he passed Mrs. Davina's Earth Science class. Graham's empty seat.

You did the right thing. But the wrong thing before that. Let his friend end up a criminal. There had to have been some way that things could have gone differently. Something he could have said.

So many things like that. His whole life.

Eli walked into English and sat and heard nothing.

The clock inched along. On to second period.

One down! Maya texted him.

Always a hand slipping beneath his desk, tracing the impression of the gun.

One year ago: the noise of the food court. The slick of sweat on the mask. The view through the eyeholes.

We'll find the Purpose once more.

Third period. Getting closer. Static in his head and the noise of class distant. A wildfire spreading through him. He should have stayed home. Or run away.

Blink.

The sunlight through the atrium roof.

Blink.

Pressing his thumb down. Gripping. Pain shooting up his hand and arm.

Blink.

Counting the steps. Forty-eight . . . forty-seven . . . forty-six . . .

All you have to do is let go.

He found himself at lunch. Barely remembered walking there. Sitting at his usual table alone. Wondered about Graham. Looked out the windows behind him. A police car in the front drive, gleaming in the midday sun. Another officer down by the road.

It's your light. You will make light. You will be free.

Stared at his lunch. A cheeseburger and some limp fries and a pudding. Why hadn't he brought the bowl? *Because you haven't in weeks.* How was he supposed to eat without it?

Opened his pudding and tasted it, put his spoon down. Picked up his cheeseburger—dropped it.

You fast before you detonate.

Checked out the windows again. Scanned the room from one table to another. Laughing kids, shouts of surprise, jokes and smiles and arguments and noise noise noise.

Sheep.

No.

You will never be one of them.

Eli squeezed his eyes shut. Opened them and noticed a few boys at a nearby table watching him. *Hold it together.*

He ran his hand over his backpack. Imagined seeing Gabriel across the room. Standing up and shooting.

Blink.

The lit sign for the DOL.

Blink.

Lungs aching, straining. Thumb muscle straining. Elastic around his head straining.

No no no.

Eli found himself tapping his hands against his legs. Heard an explosion of laughter. Those boys were still watching him, enjoying the show.

Had to get out of here. Finish eating, go to the library. He picked up his cheeseburger again—

"Hey!"

Just ignore them.

But the shout had come from somewhere else. And maybe he heard other raised voices, all of them making him look up—

And see the wolf.

Coming toward him.

The mask with its black eyes, its snarling snout, blood-coated fangs, marching right into the lunch room. Right at him.

Eli's heart spasmed. He was here—Gabriel! But no, too short and skinny.

It was himself, Jacob, the wolf coming to finish the job. *I'll blow this place up. I'll walk right to the middle. All I have to do is let go.*

WAIT, that's not you—

Storming in, shoulders stiff, an angel of death, a young boy in a wolf's mask mere days before Halloween. Holding out his hand, something long and silver in it, waving around.

"You!" the wolf shouted, voice muffled. "You called them! Didn't you?"

Eli lurched backward, his chair overturning.

The wolf marching toward him. The black elastic—*it was red*—around shaggy hair—*it was bleached-blond*—the mask off-kilter.

"You son of a bitch!"

371

The wolf, here. All along. Been Jacob. Always Jacob, never Eli. Here now to blow it all up, this cafeteria or this dream—had he ever left the red dark?

All around him voices were rising, people pointing.

"You ruined everything!" the wolf shouted.

Getting closer.

Twenty-five . . . twenty-four . . . twenty-three . . .

Shoved a girl out of the way, sending her stumbling, her lunch spilling.

"It's a mask like the mall kid!" Someone saying at the next table over.

"How could you do that to me?" Jacob stopping right on the other side of the table.

Just release your thumb, and your work on this Earth will be done and you will see your sister's smiling face. All you have to do is let go—

Blow himself up. Finally stop existing. Stop endangering everyone.

Pointing at him. "He's the one! Right there! That's the Cedar Gate bomber! He's here to kill you all!"

Everyone in the mall—no—the cafeteria—turning, urgent whispers . . .

Eli fell against the windows, raising his hands, had to act before it was too late—

"Oh my God, he's got a gun!"

Who did?

Gabriel— No, he did. The gun in his hands. Pulled it out of his pack before he'd stood . . . to stop the wolf, to stop himself. . . .

It's not you!

Screaming. Chairs flipping and trays scattering. People diving under tables. Crying, pleading, falling over one another as they ran.

"Do it!" the wolf shouted, waving the silver object in his hand.

You are a weapon.

"The kid from the mall!"

"Call the police!"

"Come on, do it!"

You won't blow up! I'll stop you!

Do not hesitate, not even for a second—

But Eli blinked, gulping breaths. His body a bolt of lightning. Saw his hands outstretched, gripping the gun. Pointed at the wolf, who was holding a length of thick metal pipe—

Not a trigger. A bomb—

"Do it!" the wolf shouted again.

DO IT! YOU WILL BE LIGHT—

NO!

He was here. He was Eli. Against the window. The wolf could not be him. Had to be . . .

"Graham?" Eli finally recognized the hair, the green jacket with the Sideshow shirt underneath, the jeans, their knees dirt-stained and torn.

All around him, kids under tables. The sudden, eerie silence in the cafeteria.

Graham waved the pipe around, eyes unseen behind the mask. "Do it or I'll kill us all, I swear!"

CHAPTER 26

MAYA

October 26

She realized it on the way to lunch. How she'd been feeling all morning. Different. Lighter. Stronger? Maybe.

Weird things like slipping on her shirt and being aware that she had nice shoulders. Shoulders that could do shit. Or like brushing her hair and thinking, from the right angle, that she had nice hair, where she had it. Hair that could grow back, that was already pretty. Things like drumming on the counter while eating frozen waffles, her fingers zipping along and thinking, hell yeah, drums. The rhythms a second language that she knew so well.

At school, not blowing up, but also aware: of her classmates and all their little oddities. How Gretchen, who sat in front of her in history, flicked at her own earring over and over. How Jeremy's head twitched while he was watching the lecture. How Lyla methodically chewed all her nails during calculus. Little blips all around her. They were all imperfect machines, wired well enough to survive, but every one of them flawed and yet grinding on.

And Maya wondered: maybe all their smiles online weren't actually taunts, but shows of bravery. *I am still here and I am well,* they said. All the moments weren't good, but maybe the good ones were worth sharing, worth celebrating. And they didn't have to mean that you weren't doing well by comparison. They weren't about you at all.

Sending Eli a text between each period. One down! Two down! Even though he wasn't replying.

Only one Band-Aid on one finger.

She sat alone at lunch, on the end of a table where some freshman boys were playing a card game. Not as close to Eli as she would have liked, but she could see him over there, had craned her neck a few times hoping to get his attention, but his head was down.

While she ate, she tapped her phone. Went to her feed and pushed back through time, until she came to the photo Janice had posted.

Lost cause! Gross!

The picture was as bleak as ever, but her gaze in that mirror: it was more than just disappointment at seeing herself. She'd also been fed up with Janice, knew it needed to change. Excited to see Eli later. Scared, but determined. There had been hope, despite how she looked. Despite what she'd been through. She might be the only one who could see it, but still.

Maya pressed her thumb against the photo and saved it to her phone. Clicked over to her profile picture, which had been a shot of her feet in the surf for most of the last year. Considered

Janice's photo again. She tapped the edit features, would put a filter on it, maybe blur the edges—

No. It should just be what it was. What she was. No more hiding.

I am still here and I am not well, but I am working on it.

Her heart tripped on itself. Her parents would see. Grandparents, cousins, summer camp friends, the wide wide world—

Maya hit post, held her breath, and watched the status bar load—

Just as the wave of screams and panic reached her.

Someone slammed into her table and everyone was scrambling to their feet, shoving one another and running for the doors, the corners, hiding behind the pillars, the soda machine. For a second Maya couldn't see what was happening, but then she noticed that every head that wasn't ducking or running was craning toward the windows.

Eli.

Maya leaped up. Jumped to see over people. A panicked girl sprinted by and bumped her shoulder hard. She caught one glimpse through a gap—

The gun in his outstretched hand.

ELI! Was it Gabriel was it—

Didn't matter. Needed to run. An emergency exit door behind her. The lunch line doors nearby. The main entrance not too far beyond that— *No!* To him.

Kids screamed and dived beneath tables, overturned others. Maya lunged into the chaos, heart pounding, white at the edges of her vision but NO, not blowing up, not here not now. She pushed through the terrified bodies, ricocheting off shoulders.

A guy grabbed her arm and tried to yank her away. "He's got a gun!"

"The kid from the mall!" someone else shouted.

"The bomber kid!" Phones were coming out everywhere.

"Let go!" Maya tore herself free and staggered on. Tripping—a girl lying on the floor with her hands over her head, terrified and trembling and weeping to herself. Another under a table, whispering a prayer. A slam as the doors to the lunch line were thrown shut. The main entrance doors too. A few stragglers pounding on them and screaming to be let out.

The fire alarm began to blare, a serrated tone on and off. Everyone by the doors getting down on the floor. Through the windows, streams of kids pouring out of the building, led by teachers.

In the cafeteria, no one moved.

Except Maya, closer now, almost to Eli. Where the *fuck* did he get a gun? He leaned against the windows, both arms outstretched, aiming at someone standing with his back to her. The hair, the clothes: Graham. Now she saw the wolf mask, the length of silver pipe in his hand: a bomb, oh God, another bomb.

"Do it already!" Graham shouted. "Or I'll set this off, I swear to fucking God!"

Maya moved at an angle. Someone grabbed at her ankle, but she shook it off. Still out of Graham's view. She waved her hands. Eli saw her, his eyes wide. He motioned with the gun as if to say, *Get away!*

Graham turned. "Of course you're here, you bitch," he snarled, his neck and ears beet red. His jacket and knees were filthy. He wore dirt-covered socks but no shoes.

Maya reached Eli's table and edged around it, her eyes darting from Graham to Eli and back.

"Actually, I'm glad," Graham spat. "This is your fault too. So let's all go together!" He shook the pipe at the two of them.

Maya heard sirens beyond the shrill blaring of the fire alarm. She felt the bugs with their swords in formation on her skin. Blinked against the blast at the edges of her vision, the sabotage in her head. *STAY HERE.*

"You need to get away from me," said Eli.

"No," said Maya. "Put the gun down."

"Shoot me or I'll do it!" Graham waved the pipe again. "A hundred dead bodies or one! Just finish the fucking job you started by ratting me out to the cops!"

Maya moved beside Eli.

"Please," he said, waving her away again. His eyes darting back and forth, his hands shaking. The gun shaking.

She stepped closer.

"Come on!" Graham shouted.

A glimpse of movement through the windows: police with rifles moving across the courtyard. Lights flashing as more cars arrived out front, more officers, the crowds of students streaming between them to safety. Maya reached for Eli's hands, for the gun, but he flinched away from her.

"Eli, you have to put it down," she said, her voice trembling. "The police will think you're the threat."

"I am, I—"

"No, you're not," she said.

"Do it!" Graham shouted. Maya saw him glance at the courtyard too.

"This isn't you. It's *him.* He's manipulating you and that sucks and it isn't fair and"—Maya raised her voice toward Graham—"he's an ASSHOLE and—"

"Shut up! I'll blow you up! Everyone! I—"

"Then go ahead!" Maya whirled at him. "Go ahead and do it, Graham, if that's what you want!" She motioned to Eli. "But he's not going to become a murderer just to fulfill your sick fantasy."

"It's not a fucking fantasy!"

Maya looked back at Eli. Finally, his eyes meeting hers . . .

He lowered the gun. "I'm not a weapon." He slid it onto the table and sank back against the windows, staring at the floor, shaking.

Outside, the police officers had overturned picnic tables. Training gun sights.

In the corner of her eye, a crying girl looking up at her from beneath a table, eyes pleading.

She turned to Graham. Had to move fast, and she thought about him, and looked at the pipe in his hand . . . and this part would forever be a blur, but she took a step around the table toward him. The cafeteria was the DOL and here she was once again, moving in the wrong direction, directly toward death.

"You're right," Maya said to Graham. "It's not a fantasy."

Graham's eyes somewhere behind those dark eyeholes.

A step closer: she could see him trembling too.

"But he's not going to shoot you, so you're actually going to have to deal with it."

"With what?"

"The pain," Maya said. "You're hurting, and that's what's real."

"I'm not—"

"It's lonely and it's hard, and you don't get chosen, and people let you down," she said, "but it's more than that. It's empty. The whole big universe and we barely mean a thing."

A step closer.

"You don't know," said Graham.

"You're right. I don't know about you. I'm talking about me. *I* feel alone. I feel like, what's the point? Like there's no meaning at all. When I was a kid my life felt so real and permanent and steady, like everything orbited around me, and then suddenly you realize that it doesn't, that you *so* don't matter. That maybe no one really gives a shit, and maybe they never really will. Maybe it's always going to be just you, and that feeling never goes away."

A red light flashed in the corner of Maya's eye. A laser sight, dipping and darting around, choosing its victim. Danced off her, danced off Graham, buzzed Eli.

"You have to put the bomb down," said Maya. "Before they make you."

"Let them," said Graham.

"Come on, Graham!" Maya shouted.

"It's never going to get any better. You just said it! It'll never change. And now there's going to be nothing! They'll arrest me and my life will be over."

"Maybe you're right, but you don't know." Maya pointed at Eli. "He almost killed me. And when people asked me how I had the courage to stop him, I felt so stupid because I didn't remember having any courage. I just remembered being scared and not wanting to die. But I remember something else now. Just before I grabbed his hands, I thought he sounded sad. Like whatever he was about to do, he didn't want to do it."

"So?"

Maya shrugged. "I don't think you want to do this."

"You don't . . ." The pipe shook. Graham shook.

"You're right, I don't. All I know is it's really hard. That we're all doing the best we can and sometimes it's still not enough. The universe doesn't care. It has no plan, or vision, or message. Everything in our lives, everything that feels so important, any second it can just be gone. I mean, you could do that, right now. End a hundred lives. The universe literally doesn't care if you do or not. And even if you don't, tomorrow it could be an earthquake or an asteroid. Everything is so close to happening all the time. It's all so fragile." Maya shivered, tears streaming down her cheeks. "And then there's all the good things that don't happen. The things we want most that just don't quite work out. Those things feel even worse, because what if they never happen?"

Graham made a sighing sound. "You don't know."

Maya took another small step. She could almost reach him now. Grab that pipe. Graham seemed to sense it and took a small step back.

The red light danced over them again. Settled on Graham for a moment. His arm, his shoulder, his cheek.

Shit. Running out of time. "Okay, here's the thing: the universe may not care, but maybe we can. If we really are this close to the edge all the time, then we have to be the ones to see each other and forgive each other and accept each other like there is literally no tomorrow, and believe me, that sounds really scary, and I bet people haven't done that for you, not nearly enough. Sometimes I feel like it would be easier to just die, because it's a huge risk, opening our hearts up. Those are the real bombs, and

381

mine feels like it's going to explode, like it already has, so many times."

"What the hell are you talking about?"

"I've got the scars to prove it." Maya reached up and pulled off her hat. "I've been tearing myself apart. Can barely stand to look at myself. But I'm not going to give up. On me. Or on you. Or anyone."

The mask twitched as Graham looked at her. Then down at his own chest, where the red light was buzzing like a curious bee.

His shoulders hitched. "I didn't even have anything," he said in a choked whisper. "They came to search my house. . . . I wouldn't even have been awake yet if you didn't text me," he said to Eli. "Then I heard them at the door and ran out the back. I never even . . ." He turned the pipe over in his hand. "Now my life is over and I'm going to go to jail because of you!" He wagged the pipe at Eli.

Maya exhaled hard. *Focus!* The pipe didn't seem to have any wires or electronics. Just a length of metal. Nothing else in his hand. She could have been wrong—could have been a cloud of atoms by now, smeared across torn walls.

But she wasn't. She was alive. Again.

The red dot still dancing over Graham. "You have to put it down," said Maya. "They think it's real. What you're feeling definitely is, but not that bomb, right? Graham, don't die for something fake. Live for something real."

"Like what?" he said quietly.

"For me, it's giving myself to the world, to the moment. I don't know what it is for you. But there's only one way to find out. Please?"

"Fuck." Graham slumped. The pipe dropped. It clanged to

the floor and rolled, coming to rest against a table leg. He leaned against the table. "What am I going to do now?"

Maya took one more step. Touched his hand for just a moment. "Try to get better. It's possible. There are people who can help."

She turned to Eli. He locked eyes with her, then faced the window and put his hands up.

Maya got out her phone. "We should all text," she said to anyone around her. "To let them know it's safe to come in." She sent a message to her mom:

Tell the police it's safe to come in.

Put her phone away before she could see a reply. The sound of messages being sent all around the cafeteria. Then she moved to the windows and started waving her arms. The officers stood cautiously, motioning to one another. One of them seemed to be getting a call.

She heard soft thudding—Graham running for the lunch line doors. He reached them and started tugging on the handles.

The doors to the main entrance burst open and a line of helmeted officers rushed in, guns up. The barrels found Eli, his hands still high . . . swung around to the rest of the room.

"He's over there!" a kid shouted.

The first officer rounded the corner, gun raised. "Freeze! Down on the ground!"

Graham kept rattling the door.

"Graham, stop!" Maya shouted. She turned toward the officer. "He doesn't have anything!"

"Hands up! Now!"

Graham slowly turned around and put up his hands. Dropped to his knees.

More officers coming in, radios squawking.

Maya stepped toward Eli, her whole body hitching, shaking, releasing.

Eli wrapped his arms around her. She felt his heart hammering, hers too, drums sending code to each other:

I got you.

NOVEMBER

"It's not much farther," Maya said, looking back over her shoulder.

"Cool," said Eli, red-faced, hair plastered to his forehead despite the brisk breeze.

"You okay?"

"Great."

They climbed through the sweet-smelling spruce, stepping carefully on the slick rocks, breathing hard, legs burning. Both in shorts, sweatshirts, and knit hats, Maya's with rainbow stripes and a pom-pom, Eli's with a Seahawks logo. Another minute, and they crested the ridge. The land beyond fell away in sweeps of red-leafed meadows, down into branching valleys of pine. In all directions, rocky peaks, sugarcoated with the first snow, shimmering in angled sun.

An unlikely November day, sure to be the last before the sheeting storms and the piling drifts.

"Okay, now we just follow this for a bit." Maya led the way along a narrow trail through tufted grass, loping up and down over the gradually ascending spine. They climbed around a mud hole. Scrambled up a scree slope. The wind increased, at times nudging them. The shadows damp and frosty, but the sun warm on their faces as they climbed up and up, and you could see it getting closer, the moment where the ridge met sky and there seemed to be nothing beyond it but puffy clouds.

Maya dropped to her knees and crawled the last twenty feet across the bare rock, her hands tingling, and then lay flat. Eli crawled beside her and did the same. They inched forward until they could just see over the edge.

"Whoa," Eli said.

The cliff face dropped away, a sheer, dizzying free fall hundreds of feet, the scree slopes so far below that the air gathered a haze between here and there. In the distance, the gray snake of highway droning. Beyond that, more mountains, and even farther, the crown of Rainier, its glaciers sparkling.

"Rampart Ridge," said Maya. "I told you."

"Cool," said Eli.

Melissa had agreed to drive them to the pass but had opted for a walk on the low trail around an alpine marsh.

They'd talked nonstop on the hour hike to the ridge:

About how Graham had been suspended for a few weeks, pending an evaluation. About the upcoming school board hearing on whether he should be expelled. Parents were up in arms about it, up in arms about Eli too, now that his identity had been revealed.

About how, so far, Eli was staying where he was. It wasn't exactly comfortable at school. He still spent his days mostly alone, but at least now he had Maya to talk to at lunch and in the halls.

About how Maya had declined the renewed calls for interviews after word got out, after the narrative was shaped that she'd single-handedly thwarted a second would-be bomber. About the perception that she was some sort of trouble-smelling sleuth, and the predictable blowback that somehow she was responsible for both events.

About how she had agreed to do an interview with Tamara at Chalk, who actually wanted to know about the year in between, not just the beginning and the end. Tamara wanted to use Maya's new profile picture, the one with the savaged hair, as the cover image for the story. She'd called the photo "Brave." Maya had said okay.

About how Eli was trying out for basketball.

About how Maya had decided it wasn't too late to look into a few colleges, especially ones with good music departments. Or maybe a program abroad next year. She was starting to imagine futures, more and more all the time.

About how this past week they'd both still had nightmares, flashbacks, lost moments.

But maybe fewer.

A gust of wind so strong that it shifted them on the rock. Then a calm eddy.

"Ready for your lesson?" said Maya. She pushed back from the edge, sat cross-legged, and pulled two pairs of drumsticks from her backpack.

Eli sat across from her. He clicked the sticks against the rocks. Little echoes flying free.

"Today we're going to do paradiddles," said Maya. "Do what

I do." She tapped her sticks slowly, waiting for Eli to learn the pattern and lock in. After a minute, they were synced up, and Maya started to throw in accents, tap other parts of the rocks, getting different tones. She let herself go, playing further and further off the beat, until Eli's rhythm started to fall apart. She rejoined him, locked it in, and then went exploring again.

After that, they put away the sticks and demolished a sleeve of Pringles.

"Want to stand?" said Maya, licking her fingers.

"Okay."

Maya reached over and took his hand. They locked eyes, and she nodded. Got to their knees, slowly to their feet, a balloon-headed feeling as the precipice yawned away beside them, beckoning.

They turned to face it, holding each other's hand so tight.

Eli leaned and peered down the impossible face.

"Doesn't it feel like we'd definitely be able to fly?" said Maya, the urge strumming her nerves like guitar strings. What sense did it make, your body urging you to do something that would kill you? Was that a memory from some flying ancestor? A genetic wish for her great-great-grandchildren?

"Definitely," Eli agreed. "All the way back to the city."

"Around the world."

They were quiet. A vulture floated past them at eye height, rocking on the wind.

"Not today," Maya called to it.

"Whisper of the pine trees," Eli said.

"Slickness of the rocks."

"Sweet smell of the dirt and trees."

"The sense of geologic time turning right beneath our feet. Ages and epochs and here we are."

"The silence," said Eli. "Like we're the only people on the planet."

"The hum of the highway letting us know there will still be fast food on the way home."

Eli smiled. "We should write this down."

"Maybe later."

Another chilly breeze curled around them.

"Have there been any leads?" Maya finally asked.

"No."

There had been no sign of Gabriel on the anniversary. No sign of him at the nursing home. No missing kids. No bullets, no bombs. "What happened with that tip from Oklahoma?"

"Nothing. It was a dead end."

"Are you worried he's still around?" Maya hated asking it. Knew it triggered memories she could never quite fathom.

Eli dug into his pocket and produced the small wind-up robot. Turned it over in his fingers. "Today is a good day to live," he said.

"What's that?" Maya asked.

Eli's jaw moved, like he might reply. Instead, he flung the robot out into space. It sailed, arced, fell and fell, out of their view. There was no sound of its landing.

"Fuck Gabriel," he said.

Maya cracked up. "Definitely fuck him." She pulled on his hand and the move made them stumble, and the breeze gusted, and for a spine-freezing moment they teetered on the edge.

Breaths held.

Stepped back.

Eli exhaled slowly. "Let's go check out those little lakes we saw."

"One more minute." Maya put her arm around him and gazed out over the bright world. The billions of trees, the million-year-old mountains. She watched the glints of cars on the highway far below and wondered if anyone looked up and saw the two of them, standing here, perched on the edge.

Two dots, moving closer.

ACKNOWLEDGMENTS

This was a difficult book to write, not just because of the subject matter and the research it required, but also because really digging into Maya's and Eli's heads meant digging into my own, though I put them through far worse than anything I've experienced. Still, my biggest thanks go to my wonderful family: Annie, Willow, and Elliott, who had to live with me while I inhabited this story, and who were endlessly patient, understanding, and supportive. Thanks also to my brilliant first readers: Annie (again), Amanda Maciel, Liz Gallagher, Sara Zarr, Mel Barnes, and Erica Silverman. Their insights and encouragement always seemed to come right when I needed them most. Thank you to my excellent editor, Phoebe Yeh, who believed in this story when it was just a few raw chapters and who pushed me to make it far better than I'd thought it could be, and to Elizabeth Stranahan and the rest of the team at Crown Books and Random House for bringing this book to the world. Thanks as always to my agent, Robert Guinsler, and everyone at Sterling Lord, Literistic, who have believed in me and my career through many chapters. Thank you to the teachers, librarians, and independent booksellers I've been lucky to meet and who do such great work. And to my readers, who inspire me always.

ABOUT THE AUTHOR

Kevin Emerson is the author of numerous novels for young adults and children, including *Breakout, Last Day on Mars,* and the Exile series. His books have been published in ten countries. A former science teacher, Kevin is also a singer and drummer. He lives in Seattle with his wife and two children. He has won a spelling bee and lost a beauty pageant, and he once appeared in a Swedish television commercial. Visit Kevin on Twitter and Instagram at @kcemerson or on his website kevinemerson.net.